BY THE
VAMPIRE KINGS

Bundle: Part 1 - 6

CHARLENE HARTNADY

Copyright and Disclaimer

Copyright © June 2015, Charlene Hartnady
Cover Art by Melody Simmons
Copy Edited by Kimberly Reichmann
Produced in South Africa

Published by Charlene Hartnady
PO BOX 456, Melrose Arch,
Johannesburg, South Africa, 2176
charlene.hartnady@gmail.com

Chosen by the Vampire Kings is a work of fiction and characters, events and dialogue found within are of the author's imagination and are not to be construed as real. Any resemblance to actual events or persons, either living or deceased, is purely coincidental.

With the exception of quotes used in reviews no part of this book may be reproduced or shared in any form or by any means, electronic or mechanical, including but not limited to digital copying, file sharing, audio recording, email and printing without prior consent in writing from the author

First Paperback Edition 2016

Dedication

*To my dearest Mommy.
I will always be grateful that heaven
didn't need another angel that day.
I hope your eyeballs don't pop out
when you read this serial.
This one is for you . . .*

Part 1

Mate's Lore

Chapter ONE

IT HAD BEEN MANY years since he had been in such close proximity of his birth enemy. Zane looked as arrogant and as full of shit as ever. Barking orders at his royal guard like they were his servants instead of trusted subjects. In some cases, those receiving the harsh treatment were probably his best buddies. Then again, the bastard probably didn't have any friends. Shaking his head, Brant turned and surveyed the crowd. He felt sorry for the female that would soon be chosen to become queen to the likes of that ruthless king.

It wasn't his concern though. His own queen was out there. Brant shuddered, praying that the events of one hundred years ago would not repeat themselves. A bloody war between their fathers had been the result of the last choosing. It couldn't happen again, the vampire species would not survive another war at this point.

As his mind returned to thoughts of his own female, he knew that he would not be able to remain sensible where she was concerned. His focus was on protecting his coven, and he would dispatch the other male without hesitation if he so much as looked at what was his. No matter the odds, and the knowledge of Zane's ruthlessness, Brant would allow nothing to harm her. She was too valuable, too precious of a gift to him.

Turning, he surveyed the crowd again. Feeling the electric pulse of her closeness. According to the lores, he would be able to sense her and to tell of their compatibility almost instantly even in a crowd full of females. From the noise projecting from outside, he could tell there were many females present. He hoped his chosen would be willing from the start. The last thing he wanted was to force her, to have to go caveman on her and throw her over his shoulder. The thought did not appeal to him, but the choosing was not something that could be ignored. She would feel it as well, whether she wanted to or not.

"Ready?" his head guard Xavier asked as he moved in next to him. His brother's eyes never faltered as they stared straight into his. Brant knew the reason for the intenseness. Xavier harbored similar feelings of distaste and distrust for their neighboring king. In order to maintain their strenuous hold on the truce between them, it had always been necessary to keep interactions between the two covens to a minimum. This event was no exception.

"Yeah, as ready as I'll ever be," Brant replied while taking a moment to scan the room.

"Your eyes are glowing my lord, maybe you should stop looking in that direction."

Brant looked into Xavier's clear grey eyes. *Always the cool one in a situation.* "My eyes have nothing to do with that bastard at the moment, and everything to do with my female. I can sense her, and the urge to mate is strong. I just hope that she'll be agreeable to a speedy union."

"I told you to take a female, ease your need. Humans are . . .

easily broken. We don't want any accidents." Xavier spoke softly, ensuring that no one else would be privy to their conversation.

"I have a plan."

"Please, tell me you at least drank recently," Xavier's eyes narrowed. When Brant didn't reply, his brother's eyes narrowed even more. He made a sound of disbelief and continued, "Brother, should you harm our future—"

"Enough," Brant growled.

Xavier lowered his eyes.

"I said I have a plan. My future queen will come to no harm."

Xavier nodded. "Yes, my lord. It is time."

Brant took a deep breath. He had been raised for this moment. His decision and the events of the next few minutes would determine the future of his coven.

No pressure.

Tanya had seen tabloid pictures of the vampire kings and they really weren't all that attractive, unless you were into the ultra-big, ultra-built and ridiculously bad non-human types.

She so wasn't.

The whole choosing ceremony was so outdated to the point of being down right sexist. Yet, every hundred years, all of the eligible women would assemble to be chosen. A queen for each of the kings. The worst part was that vampires and humans never mixed so there was very little known about them. Their traditions, their ways, their expectations, she shuddered.

For at least the twentieth time, she wished that her best friend Becky was there with her. The whole thing was a real circus. Tanya hadn't realized how many women there were in

Sweetwater between the ages of twenty one and thirty. Aside from age, there had been a long list of requirements. Everything from weight and height to a clean medical exam.

Tanya sighed as a group of giggling women squeezed past her trying to find a spot closer to the podium. Becky was divorced, a complete no-no. It had automatically disqualified her from being allowed to attend the choosing ceremony. Attend, hah, not hardly, the right term would be forced. If all aspects of the criteria were met, it was mandatory to be here. For whatever reason, the human justice system went along with this whole farce once a century. Only those wanting a fast track to jail failed to show up. What scared her the most though was the thought of how many of these women were actually hoping to be chosen today.

Vampire queen.

Tanya cringed at the thought. For once she was thankful for being a little curvy. Most men were into wafer thin model types, so she would be safe.

The whole courtyard vibrated with an excited hum.

The two kings were royalty but they were also vampires. They drank blood for heaven's sake. Had these women lost their freaking minds?

It was early afternoon yet you wouldn't guess it by how some of them were dressed. Little back numbers, low cut tops, sequins and jewelry were the order of the day. The amount of skin on display was obscene. Tanya did a double take as one of the ladies walked by, she was wearing a sheer dress without underwear. Her lady bits on display for all and sundry. With all that exposed skin, she hoped that the woman had used sunblock. The highest possible factor.

Tanya looked down at her jeans and t-shirt. Maybe she should've tried a little harder but then again, she wasn't planning on getting noticed. She had a life to get back to. It wasn't much but she had her little book store. Some might consider it to be boring, but she liked it just fine.

She'd owned The Book Corner for two years now. Reading had always been a major passion, that and coffee. It had been her ultimate dream to own a little coffee shop on the side. That way potential customers could browse through purchases while enjoying a cappuccino and maybe a little pastry. So far she was way behind on those goals. She was supposed to have had half the money she needed already saved in order to do the required renovations. As it stood though, she may not even have a store soon, let alone an additional coffee shop. She couldn't afford to hire someone to fill in for her today. Just the thought of the closed sign on the door, of losing potential customers, had her looking at her watch. Hopefully this would be over soon. The last thing she needed in her life was a man . . . let alone a vampire who would not only uproot her from her goals but from her friends and family as well. She only had one BFF and her aunt, but she loved them both a ton.

It had been a while since she'd dated and her last relationship had ended . . . badly. Sex was overrated anyway. She could just imagine how much worse it would be with a blood sucking vamp. Wishing she was back at the store, she glanced at her watch a second time.

It wasn't like one of the kings would ever think of choosing a plain Jane like her anyways. What a waste of her precious time.

There was silence followed by gasps as two of the biggest, meanest looking men she'd ever seen walked onto the platform. Tanya had expected fanfare. A trumpet call. An announcement at the very least. What she hadn't expected was to be shocked stupid. Pictures she'd seen of the men didn't do them justice.

Tall, *check*.

Built, *check*.

Mean, *check*.

Ridiculously hunkalious, *double check*.

Several women swooned. One woman, closer to the front, fainted. Medics pushed their way through the thick crowd and placed the young women on stretchers.

The king on the left was slightly shorter, from tabloid pictures she'd seen, he had to be Zane. Although short was the wrong description, the big vampire must be at least around six and a half feet. He was meaner looking, with close cropped hair. From this distance she could tell that he had dark, hard eyes. A nervous chill radiated through her body.

King Brant was taller and even though he had a massive chest and bulging arms, he wasn't quite as broad as the scary one. Neither was classically good-looking. Though both radiated raw energy and sex appeal like nothing she'd ever seen before.

"Pick me!" One of the women closer to the platform shouted waving her arms.

The kings ignored her.

A group to the side hoisted a '*Look over here'* sign. *What was it with these freaking women?* For some reason it bothered her that they were so desperate to become one of the next vampire queens that they would do anything to get noticed? And the question of the hour was, *why?*

Turning back to the platform, she noticed that the taller one, Brant, had medium length dark hair, his eyes were dark and his mouth generous. Tanya was certain he would be even more attractive if he smiled.

Both men were tense. They just stood there, hands fisted at

their sides. The crowd grew restless. Some women tried to push to the front while others tried to catch the attention of one or both of the men on the elevated platform.

Eventually, Zane stepped forward, his hard eyes were fixed on her. *What the hell?* Adrenaline surged through her blood, but her mind immediately rejected the idea that he was actually looking at her. It had to be some sort of mistake. His eyes seemed to stay on her for a few more seconds. Just as she began to feel the need to look around her for the true object of his fascination, his gaze moved to the back of the crowd. She breathed out in a gush.

"You," his gruff, smoky voice was a low vibration. He pointed somewhere behind Tanya.

An equally big, equally mean looking man came onto the platform from the side. King Zane didn't take his eyes off the female he had set his sights on the entire time he spoke to what had to be his head guard. All of the surrounding men were dressed in full leather. Though, this one wore a silver family crest on his chest.

Tanya shivered, thankful she hadn't been chosen by the likes of him.

Zane continued to shout orders. The head guard, flanked by two vampires, stepped off the platform and stalked through the crowd. Tanya shifted to the side as they approached. They were big bastards. The women surged forward. One dared to touch. The king's head guard paused, without turning to face the culprit, he growled. His top lip curled revealing sharp fangs. The air caught in her lungs. Her pulse quickened.

They were so close, Tanya could smell a musky male scent, could almost feel heat radiate off their huge bodies as they passed.

"You," a deep growl sounded through the crowd.

"No," a feminine wail responded. "Let go of me!"

Tanya was too afraid to turn. So close to the action, she was fearful of being noticed.

Another wail, louder this time.

"Put me down!" the woman shrieked. It seemed Tanya was not the only one there that didn't want to be chosen.

Tanya moved with the crowd as the guards passed, the woman was slung over the shoulder of the head guard. She kicked and screamed. The big vampire didn't seem to notice though. Tanya caught the look of sheer terror on the young woman's face.

This wasn't right.

How could this be allowed to happen? Tanya looked around her at the multitude of willing ladies. Women that were practically throwing themselves at the vampire kings. *Why did the SOB have to go and pick one of the few that wasn't interested?*

Tanya took a few steps in the direction of the platform. *Not happening.* She stopped. She didn't want to get involved. Couldn't afford to. She didn't even know the girl. It wasn't like she could change the situation even if she tried. This ritual had been going on for hundreds, possibly thousands, of years.

A large group of women at the front screamed to Zane that he pick them instead. One of the young ladies even lifted her top.

The king didn't take his eyes off his chosen woman the entire time that his guard maneuvered through the crowd. They narrowed though as they got closer. The girl screamed louder.

"Please don't do this. Please, I beg you." The screams had turned to sobs at this point.

Tanya couldn't bear to hear them. Each word struck a nerve.

Zane nodded in the direction of the waiting SUVs.

"Oh God, please no," she was sobbing in earnest.

The nerve quickly rubbed raw until Tanya couldn't take it anymore. "Stop!" She marched in the direction of the vampire king. "Stop that at once. Let her go."

Neither king took any notice. Maybe some of the others in the crowd were feeling the same way as she did because the women parted to let her through. "What you are doing is nothing short of barbaric."

The crowd hushed.

"She doesn't want to go with you. Let her go right now." Tanya projected, sounding more confident than she felt.

Zane glanced her way before turning in the direction of the waiting vehicles.

"This is a sexist, disgusting tradition that needs to be put to an end. Why can't you choose someone that's actually interested in going with you? Why does it have to be her?"

He turned back, his dark eyes zoning in on her. Her breathing hitched. Her heart rate increased, a whole damn lot. *I just had to get involved. Couldn't leave it alone.*

"This woman has been chosen as my mate. What is done cannot be undone." He turned and made for the waiting vehicles. Like that was a reasonable explanation. *So not.*

"Bastard! Leave her alone!" She must have completely lost her mind because she walked after him and straight into the massive chest of one of the guards. There was only one thing to do in a situation like this, she beat against the chest in her way while screaming obscenities at the retreating back of the bastard king.

"Easy," a low rumble that had her insides vibrating.

Tanya looked up into a set of dark, penetrating eyes. She froze. It was Brant. The second vampire king.

"What would you like me to do with her?" asked a voice to the right of the king.

His eyes stayed on hers. His nostrils flared and his body tightened. It was then that she realized that her hands were flattened on his chest. She snatched them away.

"Lord Brant?" the voice enquired.

"She's coming with me." He took her hand and strode towards the remaining vehicles. She wanted to pull away, to dig her heels in the ground, but her traitorous feet kept on moving in time with his. It was only when they reached the waiting SUV and Brant opened the door and gestured for her to enter, that she finally snapped out of it. Part of her didn't want to believe this was happening. As ridiculous as it seemed, King Brant had chosen her.

No. Surely not.

"Wait."

His eyes snapped to hers. Dark, fathomless, deadly.

"This isn't happening," she whispered. Maybe she'd tripped, knocked her head and was stuck in the middle of a really confusing nightmare.

His mouth hitched at the side. Damn, but he was good to look at. His dress shirt clung to him in all the right places. Dark jeans hugged legs of steel. For a second she was tempted to get into the car, to forget about her life. To focus solely on the delicious man in front of her, but who was she kidding? He was a monster. He drank blood for effort's sake. It wasn't going to happen.

He lifted his brows.

"I think you may've made a mistake," she somehow managed to croak out.

Compared to the mob of screaming ladies, she was greatly under dressed. She loved cupcakes far too much, especially vanilla ones with strawberry icing. As a result, she had plenty of feminine curves. Her ex had complained on many occasions, he'd even gone so far as to set up an appointment with a dietician for her.

"No mistake," his deep voice did strange things to her insides. Those dark eyes slid down the length of her body and a furnace switched on at her core.

Tanya climbed into the SUV. How could she not? Once they were somewhere private, they could talk this out and he would soon realize that he'd made a huge mistake and take her back.

Somewhere private.

On second thought, maybe they should discuss this now. Brant slid in next to her, his scent engulfed her. All man. So delicious she bit down on her lip to stop herself from whimpering.

Using every last ounce of resolve she had, she turned to face the big vampire. "So you drink blood?" Damn, that's not what she meant to say.

His lips twitched in anger? . . . amusement?

"Sorry. Forget it. I don't know what I was thinking. Do I call you Lord or Your Majesty?"

"You may call me Brant." This time he did smile and her heart did a flip flop. The cutest dimples appeared on either side of his sinful lips. When he swept his tongue across the expanse of those generous folds, she had to suppress a sigh.

"As to the blood . . ." Something flared in his eyes as they dropped to the pulse at her neck. "I only partake from other vampires, so you have nothing to fear."

She nodded feeling oddly disappointed. It was like she'd actually felt excitement at the prospect of him biting her. *No freaking way.*

"What is your name?" He stretched out on the soft leather seat, his thigh brushed hers. Heat seared at the area where their bodies touched.

It took a few seconds for her to register that he had spoken. "Oh, um . . . Tanya Milan." *What an idiot,* she extended her hand out.

His eyes crinkled at the edges, he leaned forward and clasped her hand in his much bigger one. The air must have thinned because she struggled to draw a breath.

"It is good to meet you Tanya Milan."

Man oh man, she was so screwed. She loved the way he said her name. Loved it far too much for a woman trying to escape.

Chapter TWO

DELICATE, DELECTABLE SO UNDENIABLY beautiful he couldn't help but take her in. Dark hair that cascaded halfway down her back. Tall for a human. Tanya's curvaceous body had him drooling. She wore a shapeless t-shirt that did nothing to hide lush breasts. Her hips were flared and her ass was shapely enough to take a firm hold of . . . if the need arose. His cock twitched at the thought of all that warm softness underneath him. Brant tried to adjust his seat, needing to relieve the pressure building behind his unforgiving zipper.

Another thing he liked was her fierceness with more than enough determination to match.

"Why did Zane . . . I mean King Zane choose that woman? She didn't want him. It's nothing short of rape." The moment the words were out, she bit down on her plump bottom lip. *Twitchy as a deer down a hunter's scope.*

It was with great effort that he managed to lift his gaze. Her large hazel eyes were beautifully framed by long, black lashes.

"It's understandable that she is afraid, yet you must know that her fear is unjustified. Zane might be a bastard but he would never force himself on a female."

"She doesn't know him and she didn't look like she wanted anything to do with him."

He found himself smiling at her . . . again . . . how bizarre. "Are you afraid?"

"Should I be?"

Her heart rate remained even. The only time she'd shown any major physical emotion was when he'd shook her hand.

"Come here," he patted his lap.

"I don't think so." Her eyes were wide. They gleamed with defiance.

"I won't bite. Not much anyway."

Her heart sped up. Tanya made a noise of refusal. Brant leaned forward and clasped her by the waist and carefully slid her onto his thighs.

"No. Hey stop! I really don't think that this—" she ended the sentence on a sound of frustration. The female squirmed but didn't try to move away. "I'm too heavy to be—"

"Bullshit, you weigh no more than a delicate flower." He left his hands encased around her waist.

She blushed. The pink complemented her wine stained lips perfectly.

"I realize that humans don't have great senses, so it would help if you put your nose into my neck."

"No way."

"If you were to scent me, you would understand what it is I need to explain to you." He moved his head to the side and gestured to his neck.

"I really . . ." She stammered.

"Do it."

She obeyed. Her hot breath fanned against his skin. A lesser man would've reacted by pressing her to him, by having Xavier stop the vehicle so that he could take her. Against a tree, on the soft earth. It wouldn't matter just as long as he was inside her.

He may be a vampire, but that didn't make him an animal. She squirmed some more but his hands held her firmly in place. If she moved just a little bit higher she'd know exactly how she was affecting him.

"And?" he raised his eyebrows as he spoke.

Her pulse raced. Her breathing was uneven. The scent of arousal filled the confines of the vehicle.

"And what?" her voice was shaky.

"Do you like the way I smell?"

"You smell... fine." The scent of arousal kicked up another notch. His driver turned up the fan on the air conditioner.

Brant chuckled. "My turn." He buried his face into the soft skin at the base of her neck and inhaled deeply. Tanya moaned. His cock hardened up a whole lot more. He ached with the need to bury himself in her. "Fucking delicious."

She tensed. He hadn't meant to say that.

"Please don't eat me."

"I promise that when I . . . eat you, you'll love every minute." He pulled back catching her look of shock as her cheeks flushed.

Part of him wanted to apologize, but she was here as his soon to be mate. His chosen female. If he were to follow tradition, he would bed her immediately. Seal the deal as soon as they made it back to the manor house, but some traditions could be altered. Brant would give her a chance to come to terms with her circumstances first before making her his.

"Okay, if you can't admit what your senses are telling you, I'll be honest then for the *both* of us."

She tried to look away, so he took hold of her chin. "I love your scent, I will even begin to crave it once we are mated. Of all the other females at the ceremony today, I picked you because I could scent that we would be sexually compatible. On a baser, instinctual level, you will feel the same way about me. I will not have to force you to my bed just as Zane will not have to force his female." Brant had known the second he'd stepped onto the platform that this human was the one. He hadn't zoned in on her immediately for fear of Zane choosing her out of spite. He wouldn't put such a move past a bastard like him.

That lush ripe lip went back between her teeth.

"Stop that."

She gasped, "Stop what?"

"You keep biting on your lip. It's distracting me, makes me want to kiss you."

Tanya's eyes widened and she pursed her lips instead. This was going to be a very long few days. He wanted a relationship born out of mutual respect. If that meant taking it slow then so be it. Brant would not push her into anything she wasn't ready for.

"Oh my," she gasped.

They had driven through the main gates and were rounding the bend. The manor house had come into view in all of its magnificent glory.

"Is this where your people live?"

He tried to suppress a laugh, but failed. "No, I live here. The grounds are vast, no need to share."

"Just you?"

He nodded, "And my staff."

"Where does Zane live?"

Brant turned to stone beneath her. His hands tightened on

her waist almost to the point of pain.

"Why do you want to know so much about him?" His dark gaze held hers.

If she didn't know better she would think he was jealous. "I'm interested and I don't want to hear that girl's screams."

His eyes narrowed. "Any screams you would hear would be screams of pleasure. I assure you. Unless . . ." he paused. "Never mind. Zane does not live here. We are birth enemies. You will not see him again."

"Birth enemies? What does that mean?"

"Our fathers were enemies before we were born which makes us birth enemies."

"Sheesh, talk about holding a grudge."

He shook his head in what seemed like disbelief. A half smile graced his glorious mouth. "If it helps any, we are no longer at war. A truce has existed for the last twenty or so years."

"But you don't chat?"

The smile grew. "No, we very definitely do not chat."

"He's not your brother or anything is he?"

"No. Enough about Zane." A low growl.

Tanya had to work to keep herself from biting her lip. Having Brant kiss her would be bad. Oh so very bad considering she still had to convince him to let her go.

The vehicles ground to a halt directly in front of a set of stairs that led to immense double doors. Tanya had meant to ask him how old he was, but she couldn't help but stare at the beautiful house and surrounding grounds. Two wings of old school with a distinctly modern twist. Slanting slate roof tiles with wooden, roof trusses and enormous glass windows. Flat green lawns, a lake, even a sprawling forest. Acres of land as far as the eye could see.

Brant cleared his throat. Her eyes shot to his. He looked amused. His big hands squeezed her waist.

Oh heck. They'd been parked for several minutes and she still sat on his lap. She scrambled off, turning to face the opposite door. Brant took her hand. "This way." He grinned at her and out popped those dimples. She had the ridiculous urge to kiss them. *Not going there.*

The iron knocker was shaped like a bat. Someone's idea of a sick joke? Everybody knew that vampires did not turn into flipping flapping night creatures.

The interior of the house was somewhere beyond impressive, more into the realm of awe inspiring. Plush carpets, gleaming wooden floors and big crystal chandeliers. Real crystal no doubt. A nobody like her didn't belong in this world.

"So, you're seriously loaded?"

Brant chuckled, "Old money."

"And a fair amount of it is new . . ." A tall woman said as she rounded the corner.

She was regal in stature. Her short, bleach blond hair was slicked back to her scalp. Big blue eyes and a full mouth completed the picture. She was riveting.

"Tanya, meet Stephany. My assistant."

"Are you a vampire?"

Stephany winked. "A woman not afraid to speak her mind. I can tell I'm going to like you." She inclined her head. "Yes, I'm a vampire." They shook hands. "I'm sure you're tired from your . . . ordeal, can I show you to your quarters?"

Brant turned to face her. "Stephany will take care of your needs. I'll see you at dinner." He flashed her a half smile.

Tanya nodded and allowed herself to be led by the other woman, she could feel Brant's eyes on her as she followed

Stephany up the tall staircase.

Her quarters turned out to be bigger than her whole apartment.

"Jesus . . . I mean goodness. This place is stunning."

The tall vampire turned to face her. "I can tell why Brant chose you."

"Oh, you mean another reason other than I smell like I might be a good fuck . . ." She bit her bottom lip. "Apologies, I'm trying not to swear so much."

The other woman laughed. "Please don't hold back on my account. All relationships need to start somewhere and if you ask me, being good together in bed is a good foundation. You seem"—the vampire walked over to her and ran her hands firmly down her arms and hips—"sturdy enough."

Tanya choked. When she finally managed to get herself together she asked, "Is sturdy a nice way of saying overweight?"

"Hardly. It's just that humans are so soft and fragile, some more than others, our males can break you very easily. That is why it is forbidden for us to be with your kind."

"So why the whole every hundred year thing? Brant said that he wouldn't bite and he said that although he would eat me"—she felt her cheeks heat—"it wouldn't be in the way I was thinking. Now you're telling me that there's a chance he'll break me? I have to put an end to this. I'm sure he can choose someone else."

Stephany shook her head, and clasped her hands. "He cannot choose another as he has already chosen you. Once a king has chosen, he may not choose again." Stephany's blue eyes widened. "I've already said too much. This is not for me to divulge. You must speak with Brant."

"Please, Stephany. I don't want to die. I want to go home."

She squeezed the other woman's hand.

"This is your home. Just be thankful it was Brant that chose you and not Zane." She looked away and sighed before putting her glacier eyes back on her. "I shouldn't be telling you any of this. Brant is a good man. He will be careful. There is a risk of damage during mating. Not all humans survive."

Fuck, oh fuck.

Tanya had to try and get away. As soon as it was dark she'd escape.

"Damage," she choked out the word. "What do you mean by damage?"

"I've said too much already, I will draw a lavender bath." She turned and disappeared through a door. Tanya followed. It turned out to be a huge restroom complete with a jacuzzi bath. Stephany turned the faucets. "Relax. Freshen up. I'll send for Alexandra to massage and dress you."

"Relax?" *As if.* "I still don't understand. Why does he need to mate with a human in the first place? I'm sure they could have their pick of vampire females that could handle them."

Stephany shook her head, her face clouded. "Although on the rare occasion, it is possible for vampires to breed with one another, our wombs will not quicken with royal seed. The whole turn a human into a vampire myth is just that, a myth."

What the . . . heck? "Are you trying to tell me that they are taking mates to bear their children?"

"Their heirs. It is imperative that the bloodlines continue, this is for the safety of the covens. The shifters . . . or the elven-kind would exterminate our species in years to come otherwise. If the kings do not take human females then the royal lines would die out. With the lack of dominant royal blood to rule, our species would become extinct. The covens would eventually implode."

Her fate, it seemed, was sealed. If she somehow managed to survive the mating, she would end up barefoot and pregnant. Locked away in this beautiful prison.

No freaking way.

Chapter THREE

Tanya's heart pounded in her chest. "Where is he?" That vampire king needed a piece of her mind. She turned and strode out of the restroom, through the bedroom and into the hall.

"You need your rest. Brant is . . . busy. He wouldn't want to be disturbed."

"Well tough luck for him." She kept moving, glancing into each of the rooms as she passed them. Decadence personified, but she would not allow herself to get drawn in by all of this. She wasn't some kind of baby making machine and neither was she a pin cushion. If he thought that she would just agree then he was mad.

None of the rooms were occupied so she made for the stairs. The reception, living area and kitchen were all empty. *Maybe the second wing.* To the right was the twin, marble staircase.

"Please don't. He'll be mad."

Great. She was getting warmer. Tanya made quick work of the stairs and strode down the hall. There was a definite noise, just ahead, to the left.

Not just a noise, it had been a gasp. Distinctly female.

Tanya rounded the corner. There were two people on the bed. Tanya clasped the doorjamb when she realized that the man was Brant. His big stature, broad back, dark hair. *Definitely him.* His shirt was off. The woman beneath him was in jeans and a bra, her breasts heaved. His face was at her neck. The woman moaned.

Her first instinct was to creep back out. To walk away. But hell . . . he had brought her here. Had chosen her as his future mate, yet here he was . . . drinking from another woman. The woman in question moaned again. It sounded like she was halfway to an orgasm. Her slender fingers slid around his neck as her hand tightened on his bicep.

"No fucking way." Tanya was grateful that her voice sounded just as angry as she felt. His head spun. His dark eyes widened as they landed on her. In one graceful motion, he leapt, coming to a crouching halt in front of her. Blood on his lips, fangs extended. Brant pulled himself to his full height.

His massive chest had a smattering of hair. His biceps bulged as his hands pulled into fists. If it weren't for the half naked woman on the bed behind him, she'd have found him attractive. Much to her irritation her body reacted to him even though he was a grade A asshole.

"Leave," his voice sent fearful shivers rushing through her.

She took a tentative step back.

"Not you."

There was a distinct sound of rustling as the woman got up and gathered her top. Instead of leaving, she stepped in next to Brant. Blood dripped from the two holes on her neck. Leaving no room for error on what they had been doing, or more precisely what he had been doing to her. Although Tanya had no rights over this man, she burned with anger. Jealous over a stranger. Frustrated because he held all the cards.

The vampire female was tall. So far that seemed a prerequisite. She was slim with perky breasts. Perfectly straight shoulder length hair encased a startlingly attractive face. The woman slid her eyes down the length of Tanya's body. A smirk quickly took residence on her face.

"I see you chose a robust specimen."

Brant growled. Tanya seethed inside. Just her luck to be chosen by a species where all the women were toned and athletic. A few extra pounds was hardly something to be concerned with. Her doctor had assured her that she was perfectly within a healthy range.

"Leave now." His voice was a low rumble that brought goose bumps to her flesh. She took a small step back again even though she hadn't meant to.

"Robust, but timid."

"Out."

The leggy brunette made for the door, turning just before leaving. "Let me know when you need me again."

Tanya had to bite her lip to keep from telling the smug bitch what she could do with herself. By God, if Brant tried to kiss her, she'd kick the shit out of his family jewels. She didn't want to carry his heirs anyway so it would be no loss to her.

"Asshole."

"Fair enough."

"Is that all you have to say to me?" Why did she even care so much? It wasn't like she was staying or anything.

His eyes softened. "Please come with me."

"We need to talk. I'm not going anywhere with you."

He shrugged. "This is Alexandra's quarters. If you would prefer to stay . . ."

"Alexandra as in the . . . the woman that just left . . ."

Brant raised his brows and nodded once.

Tanya looked around the spacious suite. The fabrics were done in soft lavender and peach, the four post bed was a glaring reminder of what had just taken place. She narrowed her eyes at him in what she hoped was a dirty look. "Let's go."

Brant pulled on his shirt and moved to take her hand. "I don't think so." She put both arms behind her back and prayed that the look she was giving him had daggers attached.

He held her gaze for a few beats before striding from the room. Tanya had to work to keep up even though she got the distinct impression that he was moving slower than usual. They made their way through the house back to the opposite wing, entering the room directly after hers. Brant closed the door behind her. He removed the shirt and unsnapped his jeans.

"What are you doing?"

"I need to take a shower."

"Like hell, we need to talk. You're not showering while I'm in here," she sounded panicked.

"You are my female, I don't understand the problem." He pulled his jeans off. She thanked God that he left his boxers on. Brant turned and made for the bathroom. Her eyes lowered as he walked away. It happened without her permission. They refused to listen because *holy hell* he looked fantastic. The silk material accentuated glutes made of steel.

"I refuse to mate with you. Find another human if you're looking for a baby making factory." He tensed, then stopped and turned his head to the side.

Tanya recalled how the female vampire had moaned while he drank from her and her own blood turned to acid all over again. "Why don't you just use a surrogate? That way you and your . . . little friend can carry on with whatever the hell it was that you were doing."

"It wasn't sexual." He carried on walking.

Had Brant and that hussy been having sex, *maybe not,* but was there something sexual about him drinking from her, *hell yeah.*

There was a sound of water running and a door closed. Tanya inched her way to the bathroom entrance. *To hell with it.* She walked in. His back was turned. Lord, oh lord his ass had been sculpted by the gods. It almost physically hurt to turn away.

"I don't think that us mating is a good idea. Besides all the other impossible factors of the situations, I hadn't planned on having children any time soon. This just isn't going to work for me."

The water stopped and the door creaked open. She hardly dared to breathe.

"You can turn around."

"I'd rather not."

"I'm decent."

She turned. More like totally indecent even though everything was sort of covered. The big vampire had a white towel wrapped low around his hips. Moisture still dripped down his magnificent chest. He leaned back on the vanity and crossed his arms.

"We will mate. That is not negotiable."

"So you are going to force yourself on me?"

His eyes darkened, "I told you that force would not be necessary."

So freaking full of himself. "Not happening bucko, so it would be force."

He ground his teeth. "I do understand why you're so mad."

"Really? I highly doubt it."

"You think that there is something between Alexandra and

myself. Well let me assure you there isn't. I already told you it wasn't sexual."

"Whatever." It may not have been sexual for him, but it sure had been for the female vampire. Her moan had been in sheer pleasure.

"We will mate and that is final."

"Listen up asshole—"

His mouth twitched.

"—you chose me. It wasn't the other way round. There were a whole lot of willing ladies that I'm sure would've been thrilled to be your . . . um . . . queen. I didn't ask to be here." She wagged her finger at him. Tanya knew she was being a bit childish, but couldn't seem to help herself. "Then I find out that not only do I stand a very definite chance of not surviving the mating . . ." she paused and his eyes first widened then narrowed and his brow furrowed. "I'm also expected to give you heirs . . . as in yesterday? I don't want to be damaged during the mating. I kind of like living and I'm not ready to be a mother."

Brant shook his head in disgust. "Stephany. She normally would never betray me like this."

"Look . . ." Now she was worried about the lady vamp. "Please don't punish her for this." She'd never once stopped to consider how this would affect the other woman.

He raised his brows. "You must think I'm some sort of monster."

He said it.

"I made her tell me."

Brant smiled. Out popped those sexy dimples. As much as she hated to admit it, he looked edible, in a gourmet five star restaurant kind of a way. Good thing she was on a strict diet.

"*You* made her tell?" He shook his head in disbelief. His face turned serious. "The only reason I took blood from Alexandra was so I would be more in control with you." He pulled himself upright into his full magnificent glory. By human standards, Tanya was considered tall for a woman, yet she had to look up as he took a step towards her.

"Don't you dare come near me."

For a second his face clouded with . . . hurt. *No way.* The emotion was gone before she could be sure.

"I will be patient. We can take this slow. Let's get to know each other." His eyes became hooded as his gaze dropped to her lips.

"When you say get to know each other, you're referring to conversations and . . . I don't know . . . long walks through the forest or the beach maybe?"

His eyes glittered and he readjusted the towel at his hips. She looked down at the smattering of hairs that started at his navel and disappeared under the material. Her mouth went dry. Damn him, she didn't want to be this attracted to the big vampire.

Brant threw her a lazy smile. "Yes, I most definitely want to learn a lot more about you. We'll take long walks, but . . . we'll also do other things."

Tanya struggled to keep her breathing under control. "What other things?"

"I want to get to know your body better too."

"My"—she swallowed hard—"body?"

His eyes burned. Her pussy clenched. The thought of having sex with this man was not nearly as offensive as it should've been. Hell, according to her body it was all systems go.

"No," she whispered.

His eyes softened. "I told you we wouldn't do anything until you were ready. All I'm asking is that you give us a chance."

"Do I have a choice?"

"Yes. You have my word that nothing will happen without your permission."

Had he completely lost his mind?

The survival of his people depended on them mating successfully and, more importantly, of them raising potential heirs to the throne. It was his duty as king.

His race had been divided for one hundred years. A bloody war had already claimed so many, making them vulnerable to attack from other species.

Having no future heir would bring chaos and further division. This would lead to the desecration of his coven and potentially of Zane's as well. Although he cared nothing for his birth enemy, the knowledge still burned in his gut. The last thing he wanted was for his race to become extinct.

Yet, knowing all this, he still couldn't force this female to mate with him. Although 'force' was not the right word. With one kiss, one touch, he knew he could take her easily, but he didn't want to leave her with regrets.

Brant wanted a willing mate, he wanted more than a relationship. He wanted a partnership, a family. Deep down he knew he could have that with a female like Tanya. If that meant patience, he would deal.

"You have my word Tanya. No mating until we get to know each other and you get to decide how fast or slow we take this."

"Fine, but there will be no . . ." Her cheeks turned fiery hot. "Alexandra or any other women for that matter if we're going to get to know each other."

He should've seen this coming. It was the one thing he couldn't give her. "Cenwein, for your own good, I can't agree to that."

Her brow creased, "Why?"

"Blood lust would make me dangerous to you, especially during sex. I would never forgive myself if . . ." He stepped towards her and brushed a wayward strand from her face. She shivered. So sensitive. So pure. He could easily lose himself with her.

Her eyes narrowed and her mouth tensed. "No sex then which suits me fine since we don't know each other well enough anyway."

"We *will* have sex."

"You just gave me your word that I get to decide and I say no sex as long as you are drinking from that hussy. She has feelings for you. It may not be sexual to you, but it is to her." Her eyes blazed. "You can't deny that the act is intimate."

Brant couldn't deny it. He wanted to. The lie was on the tip of his tongue. He ground his teeth instead of releasing it.

"Drink from me or there will be no sex. The choice is yours." Her eyes widened like she was shocked at having offered her blood to him. He knew better though, neither of them would be able to deny the attraction. Even though he had offered her time, he knew it wouldn't take long. They had been made for one another.

Brant raked a frustrated hand through his hair and strode towards his dresser. Agreeing would place her in danger, there was no choice to be made. "I can't."

Brant turned to watch her enter the room after him. Tanya closed her eyes. The disappointment was easy to read on her face.

"Fine by me."

He cursed. "You would taste too good. I don't know if I would have enough willpower to hold back." Just the thought of tasting her blood made excitement rush through his veins.

"Excuses, excuses." She made a noise of exasperation and walked out of his quarters. Brant heard her door slam.

As tempted as he was, he couldn't do it. Her life meant everything to both him and his coven.

Chapter FOUR

TANYA PACED FROM ONE side of her spacious suite to the other. *What an asshole.*

Brant wanted to *get to know her better,* yet he expected her to turn a blind eye every time he sank his teeth into the sexy female vampire. The brunette clearly would do anything to get him into her bed if she hadn't already.

She paced faster. Chances were good that they had been lovers. Would he remain faithful once they were mated? This wasn't going to work for her. No freaking way. She so didn't want a mate, but if she had to have one then he would need to be completely monogamous. Fangs and all.

"There you are." Stephany entered her room, she smiled as she walked towards Tanya.

"Listen, I'm so sorry. I hope I didn't dump you in the shit . . ."

The other woman reached out and touched her arm. "No biggie. Brant will get over it. I shouldn't have said anything anyway."

"No, I'm so glad you did. I still know so little about the ways of your people, of what's expected of me." Tanya sank down onto the edge of the bed. "I don't know what to do. I never expected to be here. If it were up to me, I would leave." The vampire people were not her own, yet she couldn't just leave knowing that their future survival rested on her shoulders. It irritated her but she was also drawn to Brant in a way that scared her. It was as if their lack of knowledge of one another didn't matter. Like they were being brought together by unseen forces. It was weird and it freaked her out just a little.

"Brant is a good man. Please give him a chance. "

"Except he isn't a man is he?"

"No, he isn't but that doesn't mean you can't have a successful union." Stephany sat next to her.

"We can't have much of anything if he keeps seeing Alexandra. This is so messed up."

"I'm sorry you had to see that"—she tilted her head—"It wasn't . . . like that between them . . . you do know that don't you?"

Tanya sighed. "Yeah, right. If it was up to Alexandra it would so be like that." Her jealousy felt like bugs crawling over her skin. Tanya detested the feeling yet couldn't manage to shake it. No matter how many times she mentally swatted, there were plenty more vile bugs to take the place of the dead ones.

"Don't let her get to you. I shouldn't tell you this, but Brant hasn't had sex with anyone in months. That includes Alexandra."

Great. Confirmation. So the two of them had some sort of a thing in the past. The bugs crawled faster.

Stephany must have seen or sensed her reaction because she quickly added. "It wasn't like that. Vampires are highly sexual. Since males are not permitted to take humans it is accepted that all unattached males and females are free to fornicate at will."

"Alrighty. I understand." *Like hell.* Another thought entered her mind. "That means you . . ."

"I'm celibate. Brant and I have never . . ." She blushed. How strange. Even though Tanya was fully aware that most known facts about vampires were myths, she shouldn't be so surprised at normal bodily functions. Vampires were not the undead. *Far from it.* They were just another species. Like humans or shifters. They were very much alive. As far as she knew, they could age. It was said that they lived twice as long as humans though and were tough SOBs, they could be killed but it wasn't easy.

"What's with the whole blood drinking thing anyway?" So far, this seemed to be the only semblance the species had with the myths that surrounded them.

"We can and do partake in food and drink. The problem is that our metabolisms are too fast to be able to consume sufficient human nutrients to survive. For whatever reason, blood slows down our metabolic rate. We need to drink every few days. Also, animal blood doesn't work, it has to be vampire or human blood."

"Oh, so Brant will have no choice but to go back to her?" The thought of him with the full-of-it brunette stung still. It was just so unimaginable to her how she could so quickly feel attached to him, in a way that made her feel so much animosity towards the other woman. Confused, she tossed around the idea of leaving again. After all, there had to be another way to save the vampire race. She couldn't be the only answer for them. Maybe there was a way for Brant to choose again? The idea hurt so badly, that she knew it was pointless to continue these thoughts. Just thinking about it hurt like a paper cut to the eye ball.

"He won't drink from you?" Stephany sounded surprised.

"No, he says it's too risky, that I would be in danger."

The blonde remained silent for a time. She seemed to be contemplating something.

"What?" It stung that the Stephany didn't want to confide in her any more, although she couldn't blame her.

She pursed her lips, turning her sea blue eyes on Tanya. "I wouldn't worry too much about it. He will have to drink from you sooner or later. Be patient and do not let Alexandra get to you. She can be a bitch."

Tanya laughed, feeling a ton better.

"By the way, we're going out this evening," Stephany winked. "Brant wants his people to see the future queen. I'm sure he wants to show you off. I'll come back later to help you get ready."

Tanya smiled back. Even though she knew it was pointless, her mind turned back to thoughts of escape again. If they were going to town, then there might be an opportunity. The real problem was that if the time came, she wasn't sure she could really do it.

———⊂*⊃———

Stephany's dress glittered under the street light. "Please remember, our drinks are pretty much neat alcohol. Be sure to ask the bartender for something human."

She gasped, "Are you telling me that we're going to a vampire club?"

Stephany laughed, "Of course silly. Very few humans have been permitted to cross the threshold. It's Brant's club. Aorta does extremely well, even members of Zane's coven sneak in on a regular basis."

"Doesn't it cause trouble? Fights I mean."

"Nah. Nowadays the beef mainly exists between the kings.

They seem to think the hatred between each other is just as bad between the covens. In reality, we get along just fine with more than our fair share of cross matings." Tiny diamonds twinkled at the vampire's ears.

"Cross mating huh? I'll bet." She could just imagine. "What happened to cause the original feud?"

Stephany's eyes narrowed. "Oh no. Brant can tell you but make sure you catch him in a good mood. He hates to talk about Zane on the best of days."

Zane, an image of the ultra sexy, extra mean vampire came to mind. Dark, haunting eyes. Broad, muscled shoulders. Meaty thighs encased in soft leather. Her heart shouldn't beat faster, but it did. He scared her shitless. So it was a perfectly normal reaction. *Right?*

A long crimson rug stretched out from an abnormally high door. There was a queue halfway down the block. Mostly comprising of skimpily dressed women. Tanya looked down at her own attire. Stephany had been quite the busy bee. While Tanya had an afternoon nap, Stephany had gone shopping on her behalf.

She'd picked up many outfits, from sundresses to cocktail gowns and everything in-between. There had even been a few sets of sexy lingerie, and in all the right sizes.

This dress must have cost more than everything in her own closet combined. The black fabric fit her like it had been tailored to her frame. Normally she would never have had the guts to attempt to pull off something so daring, but Stephany had assured her that it looked perfect. The neckline dipped low in a scoop that accentuated her breasts. The figure hugging fabric topped mid-thigh. At least she had decent legs and the dress sufficiently hid her curvy hips and thighs. High stiletto heels completed the outfit. Due to her height, Tanya had never wore heels and had to grip Stephany's arm for support. She had to admit though that they looked really good on her. Making her legs look longer and leaner than they really were.

Large golden hoops hung from her ears. They were heavy. Tanya was beginning to suspect that they were real. She'd have to be extra careful with them. She wouldn't have worn them if they hadn't looked so darned good on her.

The nostrils flared on the big . . . vampire at the door as they approached.

He inclined his head, "Stephany."

"York." They kissed cheeks.

His gaze settled firmly on Tanya and he visibly sniffed. "I take it this is her. The chosen human."

"Yup," Stephany answered.

His nostrils flared again, "Sweet." He winked at Tanya and unclipped the rope. Complaints erupted from behind them. The big guy growled a warning and they quietened down.

They moved down a long dark corridor. "Please tell me that was slang and he thinks I'm a nice human."

Stephany laughed. "He was referring to the way you smell."

"Thought it was a bit strange, but I'm not wearing any perfume."

"No, silly. Your scent."

This whole scent thing was starting to get to her.

Stephany whispered in her ear, "Mates choose each other in many ways, scent being one of them."

Oh happy days, something she actually knew about. "Brant told me."

"Yeah, well humans smell . . . good to us vampires. Like I said earlier, it is normally forbidden to mingle with your kind. You'll be . . . attractive to our species."

"What?" Tanya stumbled and Stephany caught her by the

elbow. The blonde led her into a quiet corner.

"Relax. Scent is just one part of it. Granted it's a major part." She rolled her eyes. "It's not like everyone will want to mate you, but they might want to sample you."

"Sample as in . . ."

Stephany flashed her fangs.

Tanya felt her blood drain from her face. It was probably trying to run away, sensing the impending danger. "Well they can't."

Stephany laughed again, this time she threw her head back in an all-out sides heaving chuckle. The vampire finally managed to pull herself together. "They wouldn't dare. You are the chosen. Brant would skin them alive. You are his."

"Hardly."

"He considers you his even if you don't. Stay close, we still shouldn't take any chances."

The place was packed. Tall, lithe women and big, hard looking men being common place. There was a large glass vat behind the bar. It looked like it had been filled with tomato juice but Tanya knew better. Bloody Marys in a place like this took on a whole new meaning.

The tiles shone like polished crystal. Everything was stainless steel, glass. Big sparkling mirrors on all the walls. The whole club had been put together in clean, elegant lines. The music was a transient beat and not as loud as what would normally be expected in a club like this. Not that she'd ever been in a club quite like this one.

Tanya tried not to notice how people . . . vampires had started to stare, most in fascination but some in hostility. It was mostly the females whose eyes narrowed, whose fangs flashed in annoyance. *Ex bed mates of their king maybe?*

Tanya tried not to think about it. She scanned the crowd

seeing Brant on the far side of the room. He dominated a balcony area that overlooked the dance floor. Hordes of giant sized bugs crawled over her skin as she spotted the woman with him. Alexandra whispered something in his ear. Her hand clasped the bicep closest to her. She wore an impossibly small white dress that show cased her athletic body to perfection. The light stretchy fabric contrasting perfectly with her dark hair and eyes. Brant laughed and the bugs crawled faster. Damn it, she didn't want this to affect her. She didn't want to care. In a couple of days he would take blood from the sexy brunette again and she was helpless to stop it. She didn't know why she even cared, seeing how she was still toying with the idea of escaping and leaving him behind.

"Let's go get a drink."

"Brant will be looking for you," Stephany motioned in his direction.

"I don't think so. If he is, he can wait."

"Don't let her get to you. You also need to remember that Brant has several in his circle that he considers friends. Alexandra is one."

"Friends with benefits," Tanya mumbled.

Alexandra whispered something, she pushed her body firmly against the impressive king. As she did this, her eyes locked with Tanya's. They gleamed in a self-satisfied fashion, it felt like shards of glass were trying to push their way through her veins.

"Jealousy doesn't look good on you. Men regardless of species do not like clingy, whiny women."

"I don't want to even be here, but based on what you've told me I don't really have any choice. I'm supposed to mate and make babies soon, yet I'm also supposed to just accept that another woman is all over him like a bad rash. He can drink from her and I mustn't show my jealousy or react in any way?"

"Are you done?"

Tanya felt her cheeks heat.

"You need to fight fire with fire as the saying goes. You are a smart human. Use your brain." Stephany smiled deviously and linked her arm with Tanya's. "About that drink."

Tanya squeezed the other woman's arm. She was grateful for the advice even though she didn't really know what to do with it. As much as she knew she was being silly, she just couldn't help it.

Tanya gasped. As she got closer, she noticed that the bar looked like it had been sculpted out of ice. She touched its smooth surface realizing it was glass.

Stephany ordered. The bartender went to work and within minutes he placed a pink cocktail in front of her.

"Right. Drink that and make sure you keep your cool. I expect that Brant—"

A really good looking man stepped into their personal space and interrupted, "Who's the human?"

He spoke to Stephany but kept his crystalline, blue eyes on her. Dark hair, six o'clock shadow. Enough to have the most iron willed virgins clutching at their panties.

"Brant's chosen so I suggest you back off."

"Interesting," he turned his eyes on her, nostrils flaring.

"Hi," she croaked. Her hand going to the fluttering pulse at her neck. A normal reaction since his gaze had dropped there.

"What's your name?" he purred.

"Get lost." Stephany took a step towards them using her body to partially shield Tanya from him.

"It's a reasonable question. The human will soon mate with the king of this little coven."

"I would suggest—"

"I'm Tanya." She put her hand out and he took it. Stephany took a step to the side. His eyes flashed for a second as their hands touched. So quick she almost thought she'd imagined it. Her arm extended as he brought her palm to his lips, lingering longer than what was necessary.

A familiar, feminine laugh snared her attention. It was Alexandra. Somewhere between them arriving at the bar and ordering their drinks, Brant had approached with the annoying vampire in tow. They had stopped ten or so feet away, huddled together in animated conversation.

Alexandra's dress was even shorter up close. If she so much as sneezed then her girly bits would pop out. Although, with a tight body like that, they would more than likely gracefully slide into view.

The bitch.

Brant noticed her looking and threw her a half smile. He leaned back against the railing behind him and crossed his arms across his massive chest. Dressed in all black, he looked all the more dangerous, and so damned attractive.

Bastard. It irked her that he didn't come over to greet her.

"I'm Reece." The vampire in front of her had a deep voice, it made Tanya realize that her hand was still in his, so she snatched it away. He smiled in a way that should've had her legs turning to jello. Probably would've, if she'd never met Brant.

"Good to meet you, Tanya. I'm surprised you're still unmated." Reece cocked his head. "I happen to really enjoy strawberries."

"Healthy choice." Tanya risked a glance in Brant's direction. Alexandra had plastered herself to his side, but his eyes were still fixed on her. The brunette whispered something in his ear but he didn't react.

"... and cream."

She looked back at Reece. Tanya wasn't sure whether Brant minded her talking to another man or not. He didn't seem to, which irritated her even more. Either way though, she needed to take Stephany's advice and not react to Alexandra. The best way to do that would be to attempt to maintain at least the semblance of a normal conversation. "Cream is less healthy but quite delicious."

"Sumptuous. Oh so very tempting." He took another step towards her. So close that his body was mere inches from hers.

Tanya tried to step back but with the chunk of glass behind her there was nowhere to go.

"You are after all unmated."

"So you keep saying."

Stephany tried to step closer but Reece beat her to it by taking another half step which placed him almost against her. Her neck hurt as she craned to keep eye contact. This time there was no denying it, his eyes were glowing. Bright, glacier blue. They were electric, mesmerizing.

"I don't think..." Tanya wanted to ask him to move away.

"Nonsense," Reece said.

Was it her imagination or were his fangs way longer than they had been seconds ago? He clasped her hand.

"Please give me some space." She had a bad feeling about this, but she didn't want to cause a scene.

Reece pulled her hand up, his eyes landing on the blue veins on the inside of her wrist. He inhaled deeply. Tanya tried to remove her hand from his firm grasp but to no avail.

"Never had a human before. Just one little, itsy, bitsy..." his fangs flashed.

"No." She should be screaming. Fighting. Something. Yet

all she could manage to do was to whisper that one little word.

"It would be best if you crawled back to your side of the fence," Stephany whispered. "Stop now before this gets ugly."

Reece ignored Stephany, he pulled her hand closer turning her arm so that the underside of her wrist was more exposed.

"Let her go," soft spoken, yet with deadly intent. "Now," a growl.

Tanya could recognize his voice anywhere.

"She is not mated," Reece kept his eyes on her as he spoke.

Brant laughed. The sound sent shivers of icy fear up her spine. "Are you saying you wish to fight me for her?"

Reece turned to face Brant. Tanya let out a pent up sigh.

"I . . ." he paused to consider his answer. In a flash, Brant was at her side, there was a god awful scream together with a cracking sound. Reece flew back several feet landing on his back.

"You touch her again and you die. Am I clear?"

Tanya gasped. Reece's hand was at a right angle to his arm, broken below the wrist. He cradled the mangled extremity and nodded.

"I'm sure you're feeling proud of yourself," Alexandra hissed. "Feeling full of it." She spoke directly into her ear. Tanya felt too shell shocked to respond. "Two big vampires fighting over a little human."

Tanya did her best to ignore her. Even though a feeling of uneasiness weighed like a rock in the pit of her stomach.

"Well . . . let me bring you down a wrung or two. You interrupted us earlier." A pause. "Brant had only just started to feed. He'll need me again before the night is out."

"Get out of my face." Using one hand, Tanya shoved the brunette away.

Alexandra laughed, the sound twisted Tanya's gut.

Brant spoke with York. He gestured at the downed vampire and then at the door when he turned to her, his eyes were blazing. Two quick strides and he was at her side. "What were you thinking?"

"It happened so quickly."

"Until we are mated, anyone can challenge me to drink from you. To fuck you."

The air lodged in her throat. Maybe because an icy fist had surrounded her air pipe. "What?" She managed to choke out.

"You heard me."

"No one would, right? I mean surely . . . you're the king." She was shaking.

"You're such a temptation." As he spoke, his nostrils flared. Her heart rate picked up and his eyes dropped to the fluttering at the base of her neck. She so needed to buy herself a turtle neck or a scarf maybe.

"Stop that," Brant growled.

"What?"

"Calm down. You smell fantastic and this is heightened when your heart beat speeds up. In case you didn't notice, we're in a room full of vampires." His voice a low vibration.

Shit. Shit. Surprisingly, Tanya still held a mostly full cocktail. She downed the liquid in one quick motion, placing the glass on the bar. "How do we fix this?"

"The only way to fix this would be for me to mate with you."

"Oh," Tanya fought to keep her breathing even. "No way."

"Look, even if you were, by some miracle, to agree I still wouldn't mate you." His eyes had narrowed. His dark lashes touched.

"Why not?" The words were out before she could stop them and she mentally kicked herself. Had the whole Reece thing put him off her? Surely not. It wasn't like it was her fault or anything.

"Do you know how vampires . . . mate?" He ran a hand through his hair.

"Sex."

Brant ground his teeth. Every muscle hardened. "Not just sex," he paused. "I would need to drink from you at the same time."

"I thought that was a myth."

Brant shook his head. "You saw how that vampire reacted to you?"

Tanya nodded.

"He had to have known I was watching."

"You never know, you were over there"—she gestured to where he had been standing—"and it's busy, maybe . . ."

"He's a vampire, he knew yet he came after you anyway."

"Which means what exactly?"

He sighed. "Two things and neither are particularly pretty. Firstly, you're too appealing to go anywhere without me. At least until we're mated."

"Wait just a—"

"Look, it's up to you. Would you like to become an all you can eat buffet? If so, then be my guest." His eyes had turned an impenetrable black.

Not trusting her voice, she shook her head.

"Good choice."

Not really much of a choice. What Tanya really wanted was to go home, but since she knew there was no chance of that happening she kept the thought to herself.

"I also can't mate you right now because I don't trust myself. I'm . . ."

Stephany arrived with another little pink cocktail. "I

thought you could use this." She handed the drink to Tanya and a glass of the red stuff to Brant. Keeping a glass of the stuff for herself.

"Is that . . . ?" Tanya gestured to Stephany's glass.

Stephany nodded, "With vodka, my favorite." She winked and took a long drink.

Tanya's stomach lurched and she must've made a face.

"Just wait until you're a mated woman. Then you'll sing a different tune."

"Excuse me?" She shook her head.

Stephany swayed to the beat. "Some humans develop a taste for blood after they're mated and I'm willing to bet big money that you're one of them."

"Not happening." *No way in hell.*

"Want to take a little bet?" She raised her eyebrows.

Tanya shrugged. She had nothing to lose since there was no way in heaven or hell she would ever drink someone's blood. Just the thought had her feeling faint.

"Sure thing."

Stephany held her gaze for a few moments. "I don't know you well enough yet to discuss terms. You agree that terms are to be decided and agreed at a later stage?"

"Don't do it," Brant looked amused. "She always wins."

"She won't win this."

He shrugged as if to say *do this at your own peril.*

"Fine, but we both have to agree to the terms."

"Not so sure of yourself then? Sip?" Stephany raised her brows and held out the frosted glass to Tanya. The ice chinked.

Tanya looked down at the beverage for a few moments. "Fine. You get to decide the terms. I'm never drinking that stuff."

Brant chuckled. "Pregnancy doesn't count."

"You love spoiling my fun." Stephany mock punched Brant on the arm. "Fine," she sighed. "Pregnancy doesn't count. I'll let you know the terms."

"I feel sorry for you." Brant looked Tanya's way. His eyes lingered on her lips. He put his hand on the side of her arm and stroked her. "Stephany is never kind when it comes to bets."

Her flesh heated at the contact. Shivers raced up her spine. She had to work not to lean into the touch. Her mind fogged over, yet something nagged at her. "What's that about drinking blood during pregnancy?"

Stephany's eyes sparkled. "All humans drink blood while they are with child. The thirst will begin even before we will be able to scent the changes to your body."

"About that," Tanya whispered.

Brant slid his arm around her waist and onto the small of her back. He stepped towards her, his heat and scent engulfed her. Almost making her forget what it was that she wanted to say. *Almost.*

"This whole mating thing, as well as the whole making babies thing. It's not going to work for me. I need to get home."

"Do you need to see your family?" Brant kept his arm firmly around her, his voice was filled with concern. "I would never keep you from your loved ones."

That familiar feeling of emptiness returned like a slap across the face. "No," she said sounding a little too sharp so she added, "Well, I would need to visit my aunt at some point but there's no rush. There's also my best friend, but also no rush on that one either."

"Are you mated to another?" he asked in a low growl that had her panties turning wet and her heart pounding with fear all at once.

"No."

"What is it then?"

"Tell Brant, I'm sure he can help you." She'd totally forgotten that the female vampire was still with them. In some ways it felt weird that she was listening to their private conversation, yet it also felt somehow natural.

"My parents died when I was sixteen."

Brant made a growling noise. His eyes were angry. "I'm sorry you had such a thing happen to you." His hand stroked her arm. His eyes urged her to continue.

"I lived with my aunt until I was eighteen and have made it on my own ever since. At twenty one I received a small inheritance. I used the money to buy a book store. Every minute the store is closed I risk losing it. It hasn't been doing so well lately."

"Leave it with me. Don't let it worry you." His voice had the ability to calm her, yet she pushed away at its comforting effect.

"You don't understand . . . the store is all I have—"

"Listen to Brant. He will take care of it." Stephany's eyebrows were raised, her beautiful blue eyes earnest.

"It's not just that. I didn't ask for this. I'm still not sure about this whole mating thing. I'm not ready to be a mother and I definitely don't want to die." It all came gushing out. This was so the wrong place, but she couldn't help it. "Now you tell me I'm some sort of forbidden fruit to other vampires until we seal the deal. It's damned if I do and damned if I don't."

"Is the thought of mating me so bad to you?"

Tanya hated that sad look that clouded his face.

"It's not that."

"Brant would rather die than hurt you. The coven would

prefer that you start having heirs immediately, but it can wait . . . not too long, but it can wait." Stephany clasped her wrist.

"I don't think I can do it. Please just let me go home."

"We will mate, Tanya." His voice was soft but the words were delivered with determination. "I have given you a choice as to when it will happen, but there is no choice as to whether or not it will happen. Am I clear?" He probably didn't realize that he had pulled her flush against his body. Her breasts flattened against his chest. Her hands were on his broad shoulders.

She nodded, not trusting her voice.

"I will have you." His eyes burned. Hungry. Hooded with desire.

"You don't have a choice." Stephany's voice seemed to make him snap out of it and he released her, turning her so that her back was against him. "Your desire to mate will grow with each passing day. You need Brant just as he needs you. Trust that you are meant to be together. Don't think on human terms. Humans need time to court before they find their mates. It is unnecessary with vampires. Brant would've known the moment he laid his senses on you."

"So I really don't have a choice?" The silly thing was, if Brant had approached her in a club she would've been all over him like white on rice. Not like she was a slut or anything, but heck Brant was just so utterly male . . . so yummy he had her mouth watering for a taste.

"No choice," he whispered in her ear. His hot breath doing strange things to her insides. Part of her hated the fact that he had that effect on her, while the other part reveled in it.

"I need you to take Tanya home safely. Xavier will accompany you," Brant said to Stephany.

Her eyes narrowed. "You have such little faith in yourself.

You were just a boy dammit. When are you going to forgive yourself?"

"Leave it alone. I know what I'm doing."

Tanya twisted her head to catch a look of Brant's face. His eyes were narrowed at Stephany. Whatever had gotten the female vamp so upset could not be good.

"I highly doubt that. I don't blame the human for her lack of faith in you." Stephany ran a hand through her hair.

Brant released his hold on her. "I need to have a quick chat with Stephany." He spoke through clenched teeth, his eyes never leaving the vampire.

Before she could argue or even pull in a breath, they were on the other side of the bar in a heated argument. Stephany gestured wildly.

Another much less welcome voice whispered into her ear. "He's staying so that he can drink from me."

So not letting her get to me.

"I orgasm every time he sinks those perfect fangs into me," Alexandra purred. "I just can't help it."

"What the hell is wrong with you?"

"Brant was mine before you came along. He'll always be mine." Her eyes blazed. "You're nothing more than a pet to him. One he can fill with his young. A baby making pet. Once he's had you enough times, filled you with his seed, he'll come running back to this." She cocked her hip and pushed out her perfect bite sized breasts.

"I'm about to become his mate which is more than you'll ever be." Tanya knew she shouldn't sink to this female's level, but she couldn't help herself.

Alexandra put manicured nails onto her waist. Her eyes narrowed to hard slits. "Listen up *human.*" She spat the word like it tasted bad. "Have you looked in the mirror lately?" She pulled a face and wriggled her pert nose in disgust. "You were chosen because of your . . . build. Perfect for incubating heirs. Just look at those wide hips and overly large mammary glands."

Tanya felt like sucking in her tummy even more than she already was, and unfortunately she couldn't help but to wrap her arms across her chest. Alexandra's eyes gleamed and a wide self-satisfied smile slowly took residence on her face.

"He will drink from me and there is nothing you can do to stop it."

Tanya willed herself to drop her arms, to square her shoulders and to take a step towards the vampire. "I will be his mate and bear his heirs, which is better than being a blinged up sippy cup. All you are to Brant is a quick fast food meal."

Alexandra made an incredulous sound and quick as a flash had closed the space between them, hand raised.

"Touch her and die." Brant's voice had ice filling her veins even though she knew the animosity wasn't directed at her. "You no longer work for me and have until the end of the week to move out."

"Brant, I wouldn't have struck her. She—"

"Was simply stating the facts. You seem to have forgotten your place."

"It won't happen again." Her eyes were wide . . . pleading.

"You're right it won't." His warm hand clasped Tanya's and they made for the exit. Xavier and York flanked them. It wasn't easy keeping up with his long strides. She wobbled a few times on her stilettos. Brant wrapped his arm around her waist and tucked her into the crook of his arm, practically carrying her.

The moment they were in the back of his vehicle he turned his full attention on her.

Chapter FIVE

THE SUV PULLED AWAY. Though Brant, who at first had seemed to have had a lot to say to her, now looked out the opposite window. His body was a tense silhouette against the back drop. Even with minimal light, she could see that his jaw was locked. Ten minutes later, nothing had changed. She was beginning to get seriously irritated at his continued silence. Especially since the whole Alexandra thing had been his fault. Just as she was about to give mister tall, dark and irritating a piece of her mind, he turned to face her.

"What were you thinking provoking her like that?"

"She provoked me first."

"She's a vampire. Could've snapped you like a twig." His jaw worked. "If I had lost you." He turned blazing eyes on her for a few seconds before looking out the side window again. His back was set, every muscle tense.

"You were going to drink from her again. That's why you and Stephany were arguing."

"I don't want to hurt you."

"You would've hurt me if you'd taken from her again. Don't you see that?" She bit on her lip for a few beats. "You won't injure me." Her voice came out sounding timid. How would he ever believe her if she didn't believe herself? "Did something happen in your past to make you think that you would?"

"I almost killed someone once."

"A human?"

"I was young, stupid. I wanted to taste of—as you humans would call it—the forbidden fruit. Surely the prince would be capable of maintaining control. I was so arrogant, damned stupid." He laughed without any humor. "Well . . . I almost killed her. It took three of my friends to pull me off." He ran a hand through his hair.

"Look . . . you . . . me . . . this . . ." She gestured between them. "It's happening. Whether I like it or not. I didn't ask to be here. It would be best if you remembered that." It was so difficult to talk about this stuff. "If this is to work." She shook her head not believing what she was saying. "You really need to know that I don't like sharing. It's really as simple as that. I refuse to share you." She found that she didn't feel in the least bit guilty about that now that she had started to accept the situation. Going forward though, it would be on her terms.

Brant's mouth pulled into a half smile before becoming serious. "Are you saying you want me?" His voice had dropped a gazillion octaves. The vibration washed over her like mulled wine.

Tanya folded her arms. Brant dropped his gaze to her cleavage. His body tightened, those long dark lashes practically fused as his lids hooded.

"Yes," she squirmed in her seat. "I do, but not while you're drinking from Alexandra or any other female for that matter. You drink from me and you will be having sex with nobody but me. I refuse to continue on this crazy path otherwise."

Tanya hoped that he would agree. Aside from her store, there was nothing to go back to. Becky could come and visit. She could think of worse things than becoming the sexy vampire's mate. She may have been a little off balance for a bit there, who could blame her? But things were going to change. She was going to have a big say in her own future. Brant would need to deal or she was gone. It was as simple as that.

Brant swallowed hard, lifting his dark eyes to meet hers. He was secretly thrilled that she had staked her claim on him. At the same time, doing this her way could end in her death. "We need to do this in stages. Alternating sex and drinking frequently until I feel strong enough to handle both." He had to work to keep his voice even. Especially when his cock sprang to life at the thought of tasting her, of sinking deep inside her, with both cock and fang. "Too much too fast and—"

"Yeah, yeah . . . I die. You had your friends help out before with the human, so why not have them around again?"

A low growl resonated from inside his chest. "I don't share well either."

"No, silly. Your guards can be prepared to intervene. They don't have to be in the room with us."

Xavier coughed into his hand. His way of letting Brant know that he wasn't game. "Xavier is my brother. He would be honored to stand guard and assist if necessary. It's a great idea." His brother eyeballed him in the rear view mirror.

"Which are we going to do first?" She pulled her lush bottom lip between her teeth.

"I need to drink first. Being inside you would drive me crazy without the need for blood to complicate things."

"Oh." She took back her full bottom lip. Brant was sure she had no idea she was doing it. It drove him wild. He pulled her onto his lap. Tanya gasped as she slid into place.

"I told you what would happen if you kept biting that lip." Brant slanted his lips over hers. Bursts of berries with a splash of vanilla accosted him. She tasted better than she smelled and her scent was utter heaven. He knew that her blood would be rapture. They both moaned as his tongue clashed with hers. He slid his hands up the sides of her body dipping down until he clasped the globes of her spectacular ass. He squeezed. Tanya whimpered. He ate up the sound as he deepened the kiss. Brant would definitely need to drink before he took her. Otherwise, all her lush feminine curves would make him lose his mind completely. Particularly when coupled with her delicious scent.

The vehicle came to a stop. Brant secured his arm around her and stepped out. Gravel crunched under his boots as he stood. "Put your legs around me."

Without hesitating, she obliged locking her ankles behind his back.

"Hold on." Her fingers bit into him as he sped up. It didn't take long to reach his suite. Every second felt like an eternity though. Once there, he put her onto wobbly legs and shut the door. Her hair was tousled, her lips plump from his kisses. The dress she was wearing accentuated each and every lush curve.

Brant ran his hand through his hair. Damn, now that he had her in his space, the scent of her arousal thick and heavy, he wasn't sure he could keep a rein on his bloodlust. The thought of Xavier just outside the door eased his fear somewhat.

"Are you having second thoughts?"

Brant nodded. "It's not because I don't want you. You need to know that the opposite is true."

Tanya narrowed her eyes at him. Her small human hands going to the swell of her hips. "This happens or I'm leaving. When I say leaving I mean gone. Not just out the door, but out of your life."

He believed her. The thought of her leaving disturbed him.

Even with this knowledge, the thought of hurting her, even worse, of killing her, kept him from moving. Tanya pulled her dress over her head.

Heaven help him.

Her skin was milk with the barest hint of honey. Her breasts were much larger than any vampire he had ever been with. So sexy, he licked his lips. Plump globes strained against soft black, filmy material. The fabric wasn't translucent enough for him to be able to make out the contrast of her areola, but thin enough to be able to see the outline of her nipples. Her thighs were made for wrapping around a male's hips. Her waist narrow in comparison. A tiny slip of the same tantalizing fabric covered her sex.

His cock swelled. His mouth watered. His fangs extended.

"Your eyes are glowing."

"Don't be afraid, it happens sometimes, like when we're turned on or extra aggressive." He had to work to keep the growl from his voice.

"When you say aggressive are you referring to a frenzied bloodlust?"

He choked out a laugh, "In this case more like just plain lust."

"Oh."

"We shouldn't do this." It was his last ditch effort to talk some sense into her. Into both of them.

"We are doing this, so suck it up." She laughed at her own joke and his need for her grew.

"Lie on the bed." He had to work to keep his cool. To keep from going at her and taking her in every way possible. He fisted his hands at his sides. He would retain control, even if it killed him.

"Okay." *Timid. Unsure.*

"You don't have to do this."

Her eyes turned defiant. "If I don't, you'll drink from . . ." She left the sentence hanging.

"Another female."

"Yes." Her mouth thinned and her little hands clasped into fists.

Brant had to suppress a smile. It felt good to know that she felt so strongly about this. She already regarded him as hers. Once the mating took hold, she would be much stronger and he would be able to take from her freely. Until then, they would have to be very careful.

Tanya spread herself out on his bed. She was the first female he had ever allowed in his space. Her long dark hair cascaded over his pillow. Her skin even more translucent on his black, silk sheets. Brant removed his shirt. It had nothing to do with getting blood on his clothes, he wanted to feel her skin. He moved to the first button on his jeans. *No, best he left those on. More of a barrier.* He didn't want to accidentally claim her in the heat of the moment.

It had been months since he'd last had sex, and the need to bury himself inside this female, *his female,* hit him hard.

Brant slid in next to her, the front of his body against the side of hers.

Tanya was tense, her eyes wide. "Will it hurt?"

"No."

"Are you sure?" a breathy whisper. She was afraid but he could also scent her excitement. Tanya had been a good choice. Not all humans could tolerate blood drinking. His father had only been permitted to take blood from female vampires. His mother did not allow him to drink from her vein.

Blood drinking could be a sexual act enjoyed greatly by both parties. All vampires drank during sex, it heightened the experience. His father had to have suffered greatly to have been denied drinking from his mate.

"It won't hurt Cenwein. I promise." He positioned his hand above her head and slid the other across her stomach. Her breathing hitched.

Brant leaned in, partially covering her body with his. Her nipples hardened against his chest and her breathing turned choppy. He hovered over her neck savouring her delicious scent. Strawberries with cream and a hint of vanilla. Brant didn't normally have much of a sweet tooth.

Yet sweet had never smelled so damned good.

His fangs extended further, almost beyond their normal reach and his gums burned. *Careful. Easy.* Oh so gently, he kissed her soft skin. Felt her pulse against his lips. She moaned. An exhilarating sound. She would make many more of such noises if he had anything to do with it.

Brant opened his mouth and almost on autopilot, his fangs extended piercing her delicate skin.

Her rich, sweet blood slowly trickled into his mouth. Drop by delicious drop. Brant closed his eyes in pure ecstasy. It was his turn to moan.

Tasting her was thrilling, it was also pure torture but only because he wanted so much more. How in the hell was he supposed to stay in control when both his fangs and his dick were inside her? As it was, he had a strenuous hold on his restraint. Sweat beaded on his brow as he took a tentative pull.

The tiny trickle became a steady flow and her delicious blood filled his mouth. He moaned as he swallowed.

———⸺☙⸺———

At first she'd meant to ask him what Cenwein meant. He had called her twice by the name. Probably the vampire word for human.

All reason left her as his mouth made contact with her neck though. His touch scorched her. The heat moved through her body causing her nipples to tighten to the point of pain. Moisture pooled at the juncture of her thighs.

There was a small sting as his teeth broke her skin and then blinding pleasure as he sucked. The pull tugged on her aching nipples. It caused her clit to throb. She moaned. A strangled, animalistic sound. He eased the pull and she whimpered. When Brant sucked again, she cried out. This time her hips bucked.

Every nerve ending awoke. Every cell screamed for release. Next thing she knew, his hand moved to the elastic at the top of her panties. He paused. She wriggled needing his touch more than she'd ever needed anything before. Another cry was torn from her as he sucked again. His hand didn't move. He was waiting for her permission. "Yes," a strangled cry.

His hand cupped her pussy and her hips jerked. Two fingers breached her opening while a third stroked her throbbing clit. Brant took another pull at her neck, simultaneously thrusting his fingers deep inside. Tanya screamed as an orgasm took her. Waves of pleasure crashed through her. Her back bowed off the mattress and she screamed again.

A loud crash.

"What the . . ." Brant covered her with his body. Every hard muscle was taut.

"Fuck, Brant! I heard the scream. I thought." It was Xavier who had been positioned at the door. Tanya recognized his voice. Knew it had to be him even though she couldn't see a thing crushed under Brant's huge body.

"You heard wrong. If you had been any other male I would have had your eyes."

"Your female is . . . delectable."

Brant growled, "Get out." Tanya swore he sounded like he was smiling.

She caught Xavier's chuckle as the door banged shut. Brant eased his weight off her by bracketing his arms on either side of her but he stayed on top. Her body covered by his.

"That felt very sexual to me."

Brant laughed, his chest vibrated against her. Her hands were on his biceps. Her fingers only managed to circle half way.

The man was freaking huge.

His very large very hard erection strained against her belly. His eyes still glowed and his face was taut. "It doesn't have to be sexual for vampires, but it's always sexual for humans. I guess I should've warned you." A mischievous glint appeared in his eyes.

She smiled, unable to get upset with him. She'd just had the best orgasm of her life and they hadn't even had sex yet. "Yes, you should've."

"I take it I didn't hurt you?"

Tanya couldn't help but to laugh again. "Oh, like those were screams of pain."

He smiled. "Are you feeling okay?" His face took on a concerned edge.

She stretched, "Fantastic."

"I would like it very much if I could get to know you now."

He dipped down raking her nipple with his teeth. The fabric of her bra only served to heighten the experience. His erection seemed to throb between them. "I need to be inside you."

"Inside?"

"As deep as your body will permit me."

Her clit throbbed like her recent orgasm had never happened.

"Um . . ." He must think she was a serious slut. There was no way she could turn him down. The need to feel him inside her body almost overwhelmed her. "Just for the record I normally don't fuck on the first date."

"Well it's okay then." He clasped her thighs and pulled them around his hips settling his straining erection at her core. "I will take you hard the first time but make no mistake, Tanya. We will be making love."

Fantastic to look at and romantic. Could a girl ask for more? Just one little problem. "What about protection?" She moaned as he rocked against her.

"You're not fertile at the moment."

"Oh."

Brant nuzzled into her neck lapping at the spot he had just drank from. Shots of pleasure had her pussy clenching and her clit throbbing. She moaned.

"First, I need to get a good look at you." Brant flipped her around putting himself on his back and her on top.

Tanya felt her cheeks heat and had to work not to cover up even though she was still wearing her bra and panties. She licked her lips. "I'm kind of a lights off girl."

"Well that's about to change. Firstly, I see just as well in the dark and secondly, you have to be one of the sexiest creatures I have ever had the extreme pleasure of looking at." He placed his large hands on her waist. His eyes glowed. His gaze dropped to her chest as his hands moved up to cup her breasts. "I never knew it, but I think I might be a breast man." He tested their weight before running his fingers over her already tight nipples. Brant was good with his hands, she found herself arching into his caresses.

Cool air on her skin was the only indication that he had removed her bra. He growled in approval. "Definitely a breasts man. So pink." His hand circled around her back and he pulled her closer closing his hot mouth over an oversensitive nipple. His teeth raked her flesh, his tongue twirled around her sensitive nub. The ache in her core became almost too much to bear.

"Please," she gasped. Tanya reached for his pants, she released the snap and pulled down the zipper. The biggest cock she'd ever seen jutted forward. Before she could think on it, her hand circled his impressive girth. Velvet covered steel. Tanya licked her lips. "Um . . . I don't think it will fit."

He chuckled. "Want to bet?"

"What is it with vampires and betting?"

Instead of answering, Brant flipped her over onto her back, he caged her with his massive body. Nudging his cock at her very wet, panty covered opening. He made a sound of frustration. She gasped as he rubbed against her swollen clit. Brant rocked against her again. There was a pulling and a ripping sound.

Skin to skin.

Tanya cried out as his swollen tip breached her tight sex.

His jaw locked and his eyes glowed. Sweat beaded on his brow as he slid in another inch. Brant moved agonizingly slowly. Tanya had never felt so full. So stretched there was a light sting intermingled with the pleasure. He pushed his hand between their bodies, his thumb finding her clit. Tanya panted with each lazy circle of his finger. She pulled her thighs higher up onto his body, wrapping her legs around him.

Brant pulled back and pushed in, just the tip of his manhood inside her yet already he was hitting all the right nerve endings. Out and in. Deeper this time. He rocked and thrust stopping only when he was balls deep.

"You okay?" Brant spoke through clenched teeth.

Not trusting her voice, she nodded wriggling beneath him. Needing more.

He brushed his lips over hers. "Never felt so good before." He squeezed his eyes shut. "I need to take you hard."

"Yes," a whispered plea. Tanya raked her nails down his back, clasping his meaty ass. The action deepened his penetration and they both gasped.

He choked out a laugh. "Woman, you are going to kill me." His eyes turned hard. "You can't touch me. I'm barely holding on. You're just so tight. So perfect . . ." Brant took hold of her wrists and lifted her hands above her head. He held her in place with one hand and used the other to keep the majority of his weight off her. His cock throbbed in her pussy.

She couldn't move. Couldn't think. Could only feel as he took her hard. His hips pistoned back and forth, his balls slapping against her. He changed position slightly, hitting every spot. Most she hadn't even known existed. She struggled to breathe. Threw her head back as the first flutter of her orgasm hit her deep inside her core. The feeling growing and spreading like, thick warm molasses. Brant jerked against her, deepening the connection. Heat filled her belly, increasing her pleasure. He roared, continuing to thrust into her over and over again. Her orgasm kept on coming, just when she thought she would come back down another wave hit. Brant finally slowed. He eased in and out extending their pleasure before stopping. He stayed inside her. They both panted. Brant released her hands and wiped a wayward strand from her face.

"I'm still alive." She grinned at him and he rolled his eyes "I almost killed you a couple of times."

Tanya searched for any sign of humor and found none. "I doubt that," her tone was questioning even as she sought to reassure him.

Brant grinned and out popped those sexy dimples. "I think we're going to be just fine, Tanya Milan." Still semi erect, he eased himself out of her. Brant moved to lie on the bed pulling Tanya into his arms. For the first time in her life, she felt content. Like maybe she belonged.

Chapter SIX

BRANT STIFFENED BENEATH HER. The first light stole its way through the bedroom drapes. Tanya's leg was between his and her arm was casually slung over his chest. She snuck a peek at his face. Beneath his five o'clock shadow, his jaw was tense, his eyes wide.

"Something is wrong," he whispered sitting upright. "Stay here, I'll go and check."

"Should I be worried?" She stretched. The sheet dropped to her waist.

His eyes glazed over, heating as they followed the contours of her body.

He growled. "Too much activity for this time of the morning. I'll make it quick. Don't you dare move." He pulled the sheet further down exposing the thin strip of hair between her thighs. "I know what I'm having for breakfast."

Her insides turned to jello at the thought of what his hot, expert mouth could do to her. He slid from under the covers and retrieved his pants, which were in a pile on the floor. His body was muscled. His cock, hard. It took some repositioning before he could zip himself up. She felt herself grow warm in anticipation of what was to come.

"Stay right there. Just like that."

She looked down at all of her exposed naked flesh feeling a little shy all of a sudden. "Maybe on my tummy." She moved to lie on her front. His eyes dropped to her ass. He groaned. In that moment, she had never felt more desired, never more beautiful. "I'll lick you until you come and then I'll take you from behind." His face dropped, " . . . but then I won't get to see your breasts. Maybe you can sit on top of me. I'll get mirrors installed."

"You're nuts, but I like the sound of everything you just said. I guess that makes me nuts too." A door slammed. The sound of footfalls in the hall. His eyes flashed in the direction of the noises.

"Go already," she said.

He pulled on a shirt.

"Just make it quick." She arched her back enjoying the choked groan as he moved towards the door.

Her ex had left her feeling inadequate. Images out there in today's world were always of wafer thin models. Although Tanya was far from overweight, she had a few more pounds than what was considered acceptable. Most of those extra pounds were on her chest with the other few on her hips and thighs. She'd always been blessed with a narrow waist and flat tummy. Dieting didn't help much, she'd come to the conclusion that this was how she was meant to look.

In such a short time, Brant had managed to make her feel like the most valued treasure. There was a delicious ache that resonated from between her thighs reminding her of how he had made love to her last night.

Brant had said not to move, but she doubted he would mind if she poured them a bubble bath. Her whole body felt a little sore as she stood. Tanya padded to the bathroom and turned the faucets on in his enormous tub. There was no bubble bath in sight. After a thorough search, she decided he didn't have any. Big, burly vampire types did not soak in tubs evidently. Well that was about to change. Her room was just next door, she exited Brant's suite leaving his door open. Xavier was still outside. She wondered if he had been there all night.

"Go back in. Brant will be here shortly." Xavier was just as tall as Brant but not as built. This still put him in the bigger than most human males category. He was movie star good looking. Tattoos flirted at the bottoms of his shirt sleeves. She noticed he had beautiful silver grey eyes with the same dark hair as Brant.

"What's going on?"

"Something happened at Zane's coven. Some disturbing rumors are flying around."

"What kinds of rumors?" Her heart sped up. For whatever reason, she knew that whatever was going on would affect her somehow. Although she hadn't seen it immediately, for the first time in her life things were going her way. Something in her gut told her that everything was about to come crashing down.

Brant rounded the corner. His strides ate up the floor. His face was a contorted mask of anger. His hands were tight fists at his sides. Every muscle bunched and ready. Her heart landed in her throat. Just seeing him confirmed her worst suspicions. This was bad.

His eyes softened as he neared her.

"Is it true?" Xavier asked.

"Yes, only worse." He slid his arm around her, pulling her close. Holding her so tight that his embrace almost hurt.

"How could it possibly be worse?" Xavier fisted his hands into his pockets.

"The bastard has invoked the Mate's Lore," Brant's voice had dropped low, deadly. Xavier openly gaped, flashing those silver eyes in her direction.

She swallowed hard. "Could someone tell me what the hell is going on?"

Brant's chest heaved as he inhaled deeply letting the air out on a sigh. He released his hold on her somewhat. "Let's go inside."

"It's bad isn't it?"

His jaw tensed. "Yeah, Cenwein. I'm afraid it is." He put a hand to the small of her back and ushered her into his suite but turned back to address Xavier. "Have the vehicles ready in an hour."

"So soon?"

Brant nodded stiffly and closed the door. He inclined his head towards the wood for a few seconds. What was so bad that he needed to compose himself first before telling her?

Brant turned, his face was pale. "Zane killed his chosen during the mating. It happened last night."

Tanya gasped. She wobbled on her legs, thankful that the bed was only a step away. She sank down onto the soft mattress putting her head in her hands. "That poor girl. Oh my God. I should've tried harder to save her."

Brant knelt in front of her. "Trust you to blame yourself. I know I haven't known you very long, but I have never been more certain than in this moment that you were the best choice to be my queen." He brushed a tear from her cheek. She didn't even realize that she'd let it fall. "It's not your fault.

"There was nothing you could've done to stop this. Zane is a brutal bastard." Brant paused. He ground his teeth and shook his head.

"Wait just a minute." Dread welled up inside her. "This gets worse how?"

"He's invoked Mate's Lore." Brant was looking at the floor.

"Which means what exactly?"

"In the history of our people, no one has ever invoked this lore." He put his dark eyes on her. "I need you to know that I will try and stop this. I'll try and talk some sense into him and failing that, I will fight for you." The last came out in a growl.

"Wait just a second. Tell me what Mate's Lore means."

"He's giving you the opportunity to choose."

"Choose what?"

"To choose between the kings. If one of the kings loses his mate before the other has claimed theirs, then he can invoke Mate's Lore," his voice cracked. "I should've mated you when I still had the chance."

Panic rose up in her. Xavier was getting the vehicle ready. Was he to take her to the murdering king? Zane's eyes were as hard and as cold as a block of black ice. She twisted her head to the side. Her neck was still tender. There would be two small healing holes on her neck. "Take me now then."

He shook his head. "I wish I could. I am bound by the lores. It wouldn't work. We will be forced to share you until the new moon. Once the mating ceremony has been conducted, you will need to decide who you want as your mate."

"I choose you."

"It doesn't work like that, Cenwein." He clasped her chin in his hand. "I will try and talk some sense into him."

Deep down, Tanya knew it wouldn't help. "No. He won't listen. I'm strong I can do this."

His eyes roved over her face, as they turned deadly. "No. I'll fight—"

"No, the covens won't last another war. Don't do this. You said yourself that the other species are a potential threat. You have to let me go for the good of your people." She couldn't believe she'd just said that.

"Spoken like a true queen." He gave her a tight smile. "You will need to spend equal time with the two of us for the next ten days. Whatever you do, don't let him drink from you. He may end up killing you if you do." His brow was furrowed. His eyes burned. "If nothing else, promise me that one thing. I need you to come back to me in one piece."

"How long do I need to stay with him?"

"We'll share you equally in twenty four hour periods."

Twenty four hours. It may as well have been an eternity.

Part 2

Torn Desires

Chapter ONE

THE FEMALE WASN'T MUCH to look at but her scent still intrigued him, as it had from the first time he had seen her. It was carried to him on the early morning breeze. Ripe berries mingled with the fresh scents of nature that surrounded her. Pine needles, sunshine and succulent female. Surely he had never scented anything as good.

Zane recalled how much she had affected him on the day of the choosing. How her hands had become little fists. How angry she had looked when she had tried to save his chosen female. How with her high emotion, her scent had blossomed into something much more intoxicating. His cock had twitched then just as it did now.

She sat on a bench on his front porch, the one that overlooked the lake. A small overnight bag at her side. The female wore jeans and a sweater. Why she had chosen to cover herself from neck to ankle was beyond him. They didn't have much time before he was expected to deliver her back to Brant.

Zane sighed. He wasn't sure how to proceed, had never had to court a female before. They had always just been there, willing. Most pursued him. Somehow he doubted she would be like any vampire female he had ever encountered.

It was long overdue to find out though. Zane moved from the cover of the trees and strode towards his cabin. The female's eyes widened as soon as she spotted him. She stood, her hands closing around herself as a form of . . . protection. Her scent changed. The bitter smell of fear permeated.

She was right to fear him. Many had died at his hands. He proceeded, hoping she was stronger than what she looked.

He stopped in the space directly in front of her. Her large, hazel eyes widened even further reminding him of a timid deer. Her chest heaved. The bitter scent becoming so intense that he could taste it on his tongue, and he had to fight not to grimace.

He wanted to tell her that she was safe but knew the words would be a lie, so he clenched his jaw instead. A tiny whimper left her throat which brought his attention to the area. Two tiny red holes had blood rushing to his ears.

Brant had drunk from her. Possessiveness like nothing he had ever felt before took a hold of him. Now that he was up close, he could also smell the other vampire's scent on her. They had rutted recently. The feeling of possessiveness increased. It was an unusual feeling. Not one he had felt before. He didn't like it. The need to mark her with his own scent almost overpowered him. He leaned in to sniff at her throat so that he could hone in on her own unique scent. He needed a second to ground himself.

The female whimpered, "Please don't hurt me."

Zane ignored her plea and instead he shoved his leg between her thighs, pushing himself against her. Her breasts were generous, soft mounds that flattened against him. He put a hand under her top, flattening his fingers against her belly. She had warm, satiny skin.

"Please." The scent of fear went up another notch. Her chest no longer heaved which meant she was holding her breath.

"Be still. I don't plan on harming you. I only wish to explore what is mine."

A shuddering breath. "I thought I could choose. I'm not yours."

"For the next twenty four hours you are under my roof. I can do with you as I please and touching you pleases me."

Her eyes hardened. "Brant was a complete gentleman. He allowed things to progress at a pace that I was comfortable with."

"Then Brant was a fool." Zane slid his hand up her smooth stomach wrapping his fingers around her breast.

She made a sound of protest, which he ignored. Zane squeezed lightly watching as her pupils dilated before him. He growled in approval at the soft flesh beneath his palm. Her nipple hardened beneath his caress. The heady aroma of her arousal had his dick hardening between them.

"Take off your clothes."

She gasped and shook her head.

"You might say no, but your body says yes." He used his free hand to clasp her jean covered mound. "If I were to dip my finger inside you, I would find you wet and ready."

"Please, I don't want to die."

Zane had to work to keep his hold on her relaxed. "What kind of bullshit have they been feeding you?"

"Did you kill that girl?"

"I am a ruthless killer and in answer to your question, yes I did but not in the way you think."

Her eyes threw daggers at him. Zane found that he didn't like how readily she believed the worst of him. Especially when he shouldn't give a shit either way. He reminded himself that he needed her. Make that, his coven needed her. "Come inside I'll show you around."

Her shoulders slumped in relief as he moved away from her. Females had always clambered for his attention. Had been honored when chosen to warm his bed. They had always enjoyed his touch. This was all new. In short, he didn't like it. Not one bit.

It was important that they test their compatibility before continuing on this path. To rut with her in various positions. To test their fit. The urge to take her hit him hard. Somehow, he found the strength to ignore it.

"I'm afraid it's not the mansion you've grown accustomed to, and unlike Brant I don't have a servant at every turn waiting to wipe my ass."

"Hey," her eyes narrowed as she spoke. "It's not very nice to talk badly about someone when they're not even here to defend themselves."

He fought a smile as he walked ahead of her, holding the door open so that she could enter first. He tried to view the cabin as she would. It was spacious with large windows and a high ceiling. The views of the lake and surrounding forest were spectacular. Otherwise there was nothing opulent about it. Sparsely furnished with a large rug in front of the fireplace. One sofa, a small table and chairs. The upstairs loft housed his king-sized bed. The only modern touches were in his kitchen. He liked it just fine. He came here as often as his vast responsibilities would allow. Sometimes he wished he could run away from it all. Being a king had its major privileges, but they always came at a price. Lately he was beginning to think that the price might be a little too steep.

"Which is my room?"

This time, he couldn't stop a smile from forming. The little human wouldn't like his answer one bit. Zane bound up the steep stairs to the loft, dropping her bag on his bed. "Two choices. On the left or"—he let his hands slide down his chest—"right here on top of me."

Her mouth gaped for a half a second before she snapped it shut. "Is that the bed where you killed the girl?" Her eyes welled with tears.

Zane couldn't help it when his hands curled into fists and white hot rage filled him. He leapt from the top of the stairs, landing in a crouch in front of her.

―――・⊂*⊃・―――

Tanya watched as the impossibly big man leapt from the loft landing in a predatory stance just a few feet in front of her. His muscled body was coiled as if to strike. A feral gleam in his eyes.

Her aunty had always told her that her sassy mouth would get her in trouble one day. By the look of Zane, she found herself wondering if that day had come.

The vampire pulled himself to his full height. Tanya craned her neck to maintain eye contact. If she was to die, she would maintain dignity doing it.

"I made a mistake with that female," he growled.

Anger burned holes in her gut. "A mistake." So mad she couldn't think straight anymore. "Is that what you call it? What? You mistakenly tore her throat out? Or maybe you mistakenly snapped her fragile body like a twig? Mistake? Really?" She closed the small distance between them. It was over for her anyway so she may as well let him have a piece of her mind before he killed her. "Are you at least sorry you did it?"

Tanya must have completely lost what was left of her anger

riddled brain because before she knew it she was beating her fists against his chest. The action probably hurt her more than it did him, but she couldn't seem to stop.

Zane took hold of her wrists so she kicked him in the shin. Pain vibrated up her leg.

"Stop." His voice was low, evenly delivered, for some strange reason it calmed her. "You're going to hurt yourself."

Tanya sniffed and realized that she was crying. His eyes had softened. Zane released her wrist and used the pad of his thumb to wipe away a hot tear as it tracked down her cheek.

"The only mistake I made was to give her space . . . time to come to terms with her situation. I left her with the females— "

Zane shoved her hard and she crashed into the wooden floor. Her shoulder took most of the impact. Tanya kept her eyes firmly locked on Zane as she fell, fully expecting him to come at her. An arrow lodged into his shoulder.

She blinked hard. Sure enough, an arrow complete with feathered end jutted from his flesh. Zane dropped down next to her. There was a cracking sound and a grunt as Zane broke off the end of the arrow.

"Stay down."

She knew from experience that vampires could be fast, but the way Zane moved was insane. A smudge of lightening flew across the room and out the door. Almost too quick for her mind to register. Tanya crawled behind the safety of the sofa. Once there, she was too afraid to breathe let alone move.

From outside she made out a man's scream, a grunt and a meaty thud. Zane was out there fighting for his life. Make that for both their lives. It was clear that whoever had shot that arrow had meant to kill her, so it wasn't Brant. She sure as nuts didn't want to be here with Zane, but whoever was out there didn't harbor any good intentions towards her. That was clear.

So she could only pray that Zane managed to fight them off. She scrunched her eyes shut for a few seconds trying to ward off the panic. Why the hell would someone want her dead? Another scream punctured the cabin. She couldn't tell if it had been Zane or another man making the god awful noise. Tanya clasped a hand over her mouth to smother a scream. If they managed to kill Zane then she was next, of that she was certain.

"What have we here?"

She yelped in surprise as she snapped her head in the direction of the voice. The man that stood in front of her was freaking huge, almost as big as the vampires. He wore a pastel blue robe complete with silk sash and pixie boots.

Who the hell in their right mind wears pixie boots?

Maybe he was wearing a costume. He smiled revealing a single row of sharp teeth. Not human. Okay so maybe he wasn't wearing a costume after all.

"It's a little rabbit." His thin eyebrows arched, his golden hair fell in a sheet across half his broad back.

He advanced.

Tanya knew she should be petrified but there was no time for such luxuries. She whimpered and made a show of pulling herself into a tight ball. Pixie boy was so arrogant that he kept advancing. He strode up to her and bent to pick her up. Using her position to her advantage, she kicked out nailing him with both her boots straight in the face. There was a crunching sound and he was knocked back. The bastard managed to stay on his feet though. She leapt up while he righted himself.

Using the back of his hand, he rubbed away the blood that dripped from both nostrils. He looked at his bloodied hand with a shocked expression. "I'm to take you in dead or alive. Which is it to be little rabbit?"

"Screw you."

He chuckled and regardless of the satin robe and cute pixie shoes, shivers ran up her spine. He lunged at her. Somehow she managed to twist away just in time. Tanya sprinted for the kitchen, more precisely, she made for the big butcher's block where she'd spied a set of steak knives when she'd first come in.

Pixie boy grabbed hold of her waist as she reached the block, he yanked her back. Tanya kicked down hard on his foot and elbowed him using every ounce of strength she had. Air was forced out of his lungs and he released his hold enough for her to pull away. Ignoring the butcher knives, she grabbed one of the smaller blades instead and turned to face him.

His eyes were stern. His mouth a thin white line.

"I will use this." Tanya waved the knife praying that she would have enough guts to do as she threatened.

"I'm losing patience. Surrender or die."

His hard eyes told her that he meant every word. She widened her stance and gripped the knife with both hands.

Big arms banded pixie-boy's neck, followed by a sickening crunch. He dropped, eyes open, mouth gaping. Tanya was certain by the vacant look in his eyes that he was dead. She shuddered. Tanya had never seen a dead person before.

Zane's chest heaved, he was covered in blood and gore. He rocked for a second or two before falling to one knee. "I think you had him, Ysnaar."

Tanya gasped. "Best you keep that in mind," she paused. "Aside from the arrow wound, are you hurt anywhere else?"

"Why? Would you kiss it better for me?"

She choked out a laugh trying to sound braver than she actually was. "This is no time for silly jokes."

"Do I look like I'm joking?" Using all his strength, he rose to his feet with a grunt. His face a mask of pain. Zane had a washed out pale coloring that scared her. Dark circles were forming under his eyes.

"Help me to the sofa." He leaned on her, sinking himself into the soft cushion. His jaw was locked and his brow furrowed. Drips of sweat beaded on his forehead. "You need to get it out."

"Don't joke."

"Still not joking, sweetness." His head rolled back. His breathing coming in short pants. "The arrow tip is poisoned. I'll die if you don't remove it soon."

"Fuck. Tell me what to do." Panic seized her.

"There is a shed outback. In it you'll find"—he paused and grimaced for a few beats—"tools. Bring pliers, a hammer. . . . that knife you had a second ago . . . I need you to push the arrow out."

"As in . . ." She shook her head instead of finishing.

"You can do it, Ysnaar. The arrow tip is already at the other side." He reached up and ripped his shirt at the shoulder, groaning as he tore it from his enormous body. She leaned forward examining the wound.

"God that must hurt like a bitch."

He started to chuckle and moaned between gritted teeth instead. "Not so bad, I've had worse. It's the poison. You need to get it out."

Tanya jumped to her feet and made for the back door. She ran for the wooden shed and worked the bolt. The door sprang open as the bolt slid free. There was a whole array of tools. She grabbed two sets of pliers, a sturdy looking hammer and some screw drivers for good measure before running back the way she came.

Zane lay perfectly still on the sofa. If not for the rise and fall of his chest, she may've thought him dead. She sat next to him.

His eyes opened slowly. "Hit the arrow out enough to be able to use the pliers to pull it free from the other side. Do it now."

Tanya picked up the hammer. An eye for an eye, Zane had rescued her so like it or not she felt it was only right if she helped him. She straddled the big man keeping her eye on the wound which was crusted in blood. His hands found her hips and he squeezed lightly. "Do it."

She took the hammer in both hands and hit the arrow straight on.

"Harder," he spoke through clenched teeth.

She pulled back and swung again hitting as hard as she dared. It would be too easy to miss or break the stem.

"Again," he growled. She did as he instructed.

Zane dug his fingers into her hips. "One more time should do it." Another hard hit and he groaned leaning forward. He rested his head on her chest for a few seconds.

"I think that did it." He was breathing hard. Sweat beads had formed on his brow.

Blood oozed from the wound. Tanya moved back to the side staying on her knees. Zane remained forward so that she would have easy access to his back. She tried not to react. Half of the arrow head protruded from a mean looking gash.

She picked up a pair of pliers, moving towards the arrow head. The thought of pulling the thing out made her feel queasy.

"Do it."

She clamped the pliers on to the piece of metal and took a deep breath. Tanya pulled and he made a pained noise through clenched teeth.

"I'm so sorry."

"Don't worry about me, just get it out."

"Scoot forward. I need to get in behind you."

He did as she said and Tanya slid in. She kept her knees bent at her chest using them as leverage against his back. Tanya used both her hands to clasp the pliers and pulled as if her life depended on it. She tried not to think too much about what she was doing, just focussed on the mechanics. She pulled and then she pulled some more. Just when she felt almost ready to give up, the arrow head tore free.

Zane grunted letting his head fall into his hands. His elbows rested on his thighs. "Thank you."

"You're bleeding quite a bit."

She tried to staunch the flow with his ripped shirt.

"Leave it. I want the poison to bleed out. I'll heal quicker in the long run." His low voice was uneven and weak. "Give me a minute and then get me to the shower."

She felt useless. Not sure of what to do. "Do you have a first aid kit? Maybe . . ." She tried to move out from behind him.

"Stay there. I find your touch oddly soothing."

His biceps filled her hands, her legs had fallen open and her chest rested against his back. Her breath caught in her throat. Even amongst this blood and gore, their position seemed oddly intimate.

"You didn't kill that girl did you?"

Zane sighed. "She didn't die by my hand but I feel responsible," he paused. "I thought that giving her space would be the best thing. That she could do with time to adjust. I was wrong." His voice broke and she wasn't sure if it was because of the physical pain or the emotional kind.

"Those guys were after me weren't they?"

He nodded. "You are the only female capable of bearing vampire heirs now that my chosen is . . ." he shifted wincing as his wound pulled. "With you out of the way, vampires would become extinct." Before his words had a chance to sink in, he turned his head slightly. "I need to get to a hot shower. The wound needs to bleed some more and hell . . ." He looked down at himself. "I could use a wash. You need to help me." He still looked like shit but at least his voice was a little stronger.

Getting him off the sofa took a few attempts. Using his good arm, he leaned on her and they made slow but steady progress.

The shower was all glass with a stunning view of the forest. There was no shower door or curtain. Come to think of it, there wasn't even a door on the restroom itself. "Not so big on privacy?"

"I prefer open spaces."

Chapter TWO

IT OCCURRED TO HER that if she tried to leave right now, he might end up falling. The guy might be all muscle but he was seriously weak. "How are we going to do this?"

Using his good hand, he ripped what little remained of the shirt from his body and unbuttoned his jeans. "Help me get them off."

Her first instinct was to tell him to go to hell but when she glanced at his ashen face she swallowed her words. She took her lip between her teeth, took hold of the lapels on his jeans and tugged the denim down. Clearly Zane enjoyed the freedom of commando. His thick cock rested, what seemed like, halfway down his left thigh. Even covered in congealing blood and dripping with sweat, he was a sight to behold. A warrior in every sense of the word. He cleared his throat. "I'll let you explore me thoroughly some other time."

Heat scorched her cheeks when she realized that she clung white knuckled to his pants, which were still half way down his thighs. Avoiding his gaze, as well as other parts of his anatomy, she dropped to her haunches and took his jeans down to his ankles. He stepped out of the fabric. Zane rocked and took a shuffling step backwards. She sprang up, just managing to catch hold of him before he fell.

"Damned poison has done a job on me." His eyes were scrunched shut.

"I'll help you."

He nodded once, clearly not used to being at the mercy of another. Zane put his arm around her. Tanya glanced down at her cashmere sweater. His eyes were still closed. Damn it, she wasn't going to ruin the garment. They shuffled to the vast cubicle and he leaned against one of the glass windows for support. Tanya took the opportunity to peel off the sweater, throwing it a safe distance away. Her jeans could handle the water, there was no way in hell she was taking those off. She turned the faucets on, squealing as freezing water hit her square in the chest. With a quick adjustment of the showerhead, she breathed a sigh of relief. Cold showers were so not her thing. When she turned to face Zane, his eyes were focused on her chest in untethered . . . hunger. So feral she had to stop herself from taking a step back. His cock jutted from his body. Heavy, seeking, it had her blood heating.

"Um . . . I thought you were on death's door."

"Sweetness, you're like the water of life to a dying man. If I was just a little bit stronger I'd take you right now." Zane swayed, having to use his hands on the glass to keep from falling. "I need you to get the water as hot as possible."

◆———·C✷✦·———◆

Zane tried hard not to focus on her lush breasts. He'd never seen cleavage so deep. Had never wanted to bury himself into a female more than in this minute. Her nipples were tight buds against the sheer white fabric of her bra. Pink smudges on deep curves had his mouth filling with drool. His focus blurred reminding him that he was in no condition to be thinking along these lines. Pain throbbed across his shoulder shooting down his limbs like scorching heat through a flame thrower.

When the water steamed, he angled himself under the steady stream. "I need you to reopen the wound."

She stepped into him, those hard little nipples abrading his chest. A wave of vertigo had him clutching her shoulder for support.

"How?"

"Use your fingers."

"Oh my God. You are so going to owe me for this one."

Zane had closed his eyes but could hear that she meant every word. He felt his lips pull into a smile. "Do not worry sweetness, I will repay you the favor tenfold." He circled his thumb on her satiny skin.

Not for the first time since meeting her, he smelled the intoxicating scent of her arousal.

"Whatever," she mumbled. "What should I use, how— "

"Stick your fingers into the wound . . . both sides."

The female made an incredulous noise but moved to his side. A better angle to do as he had instructed. Her chest heaved against him. The smell of arousal was replaced with . . . fear.

"I don't want to hurt you, Zane."

He forced his eyes open and turned his head to face her. Large eyes that seemed to be made of melted chocolate stared back at him. For the barest second he forgot what he wanted to say. His need to fuck her was obviously affecting him.

"Do it," he bit out harsher then he intended.

Her eyes darted from the wound on the one side of his shoulder to the one on the other. Her hands held a slight tremor. "Here goes."

Zane bit down hard. Any more of this and he'd surely crack

his molars. She pushed her little fingers deep into both wounds. White, hot pain seared through him. Just when he thought she must be done, she scissored her fingers further tearing the wound. He greatly admired her bravery. The human females that he had encountered were usually weak, timid creatures. Based on experience, she had to be flawed in some way. It was just a matter of time before this became apparent.

Feeling his hot blood pump from the gashes, he angled his shoulder so that the spray from the shower would help prevent the wounds from sealing too quickly. He could already feel some of his strength returning. Vampires healed quickly and it wasn't long before he felt his flesh begin to knit. There was only one thing that would help him more at this point.

Blood.

Zane needed to drink. His fangs extended at the thought. The female's delicious scent wasn't helping things.

"Wash me."

"No freaking way. Just who do you think I am?" Her voice came out in an angry rush, but another intoxicating burst of arousal filled the small space. His fangs throbbed and he felt his dick begin to fill. Damned if he could stop it. He didn't like the lack of control though.

"You are my female and I need you to wash me."

"Listen buster. I'm not your female." Her beautiful eyes blazed as she dragged them down his body ending on a harsh gasp. She pointed at his manhood. "Stop that right now."

"I can't. It seems the thought of your hands on me is appealing."

"I refuse." She folded her arms over her chest and her eyes narrowed. His eyes dropped as her breasts were forced further together. Zane itched to touch her soft flesh. To run his hands up and down her body.

"Hey buster, my eyes are up here."

With extreme reluctance, he lifted his gaze. Her auburn hair was plastered to her scalp, her cheeks were flushed from the heat, a look of defiance firmly in place. How had he ever thought her plain? Using his good arm, he reached behind him grabbing the soap. Her eyes stayed on his. Truth was, at this point, he could probably manage on his own but where was the fun in that. Zane had a burning need to feel her hands on him. To have her do as he requested.

The overly large vampire was even more attractive wet. Then again, maybe it was the fact that he was naked. Rivulets of water caressed every contour of his magnificent body. With roped muscle on every single solitary inch, ridges and valleys were plentiful. Tanya suddenly felt thirsty. She also felt like a dirty slut perving over a man just hours after she'd had amazing sex with another.

She shook her head. "I can't. I'm sorry." Was her voice really tinged with regret?

His eyes hardened. He reached forward and slipped a bar of soap into her hand. "I am not offering you the choice. Do it now female." He had a deep voice. The lowest baritone she had ever heard on a man. Tanya always assumed that she would hate it if a man told her what to do. In this setting, in this moment, the command sent shivers down her spine. She had to work to keep her breathing even as her nipples hardened. Hopefully he didn't notice. There was something she liked about it, yet she had the feeling if he used it too often it might just irritate her. Right now it titillated.

"Fine, but only because I don't want to spend the rest of the day with a dirty, grumpy vampire."

Something in his eyes flared and his lips twitched. She moved her hands under the spray and worked the soap into a healthy lather. The thought of touching him excited her. Tanya tried to keep her hands from shaking.

Where to start?

There was so much of him. She'd start at his back. It was safest. Tanya swallowed hard as she took in his broad back and beefy ass. Avoiding his bad shoulder, she placed her hands on his skin. He jerked at the first tentative touch. She followed the natural contours and was soon finished so she moved to his arms which were relaxed at his sides. So freaking big. So gorgeous to touch. After a deep breath, she slid her hands over his ass. Sheesh he was all hard muscle. Oh so good to squeeze. His legs were long thick steel. His chest was hair free yet so manly that her breath caught in her throat as she rubbed her hands across his pecs. Feeling his nipples harden beneath her touch. The light smattering of hairs led down from his belly button to . . . she avoided even looking at his very hard cock, concentrating rather on the firm ridge of muscle that led down from his hips. The ones that spoke of how well built a man was. Next she slid her hands up and down his legs, keeping her eyes away from a certain area. When she finally finished, she dropped her hands at her sides and looked up at his face. His eyes were darker than she'd ever seen, his jaw was locked in a tight line.

"You're not done." He glanced down at . . .

No freaking way in hell. Excitement coursed through her veins.

Tanya shook her head. "I couldn't possibly," her voice was shaky.

"You can and you will." Deep, commanding. Everything in her tightened.

"Fine, but you had better not enjoy it."

Instead of answering, Zane ground his teeth.

More soap. Extra lather. Tanya used one hand to palm his balls while the other wrapped around his wide girth. His cock jerked and he hissed. His cock throbbed beneath her finger as she slid up and down his length. She moved to his other ball, lightly squeezing the sensitive flesh.

"Your touch . . ." His voice was filled with surprise. "I have never felt such a thing before. So soft, so good." A low growl that had her insides turning to mush.

He rocked his hips forward as she slipped back down his long length. His eyes closed and his head fell back. Tanya had planned on tugging on him a few times, on getting him horny and then leaving him, but suddenly she wanted to see him find completion. Needed it.

"Move back."

His wild gaze landed on her.

"I said to move back." She tugged on his cock. His mouth parted and he groaned taking a step back as she commanded. Spray hit them both. Within seconds the soap was removed from his body.

"Take a step towards me." Another tug this time as she zoned in on his head.

Zane growled as he stepped forward, his mouth opened exposing long, scary looking fangs. Damned if they didn't make him look sexier. Deadlier. Who was she kidding, he was a killing machine. For some ridiculous reason though, this heightened her excitement.

Here went nothing. Tanya knew she shouldn't be doing this but dropped to her knees anyway.

"What are you . . . ?" His words turned into a snarl as her lips closed over his head. She swirled her tongue over the tip before sucking lightly. Another snarl erupted from above her.

"Whatever it is . . . do not stop." His hips rocked. His hands were fisted at his sides. She took him deeper, as far as he would go, his head hit against the back of her throat. He made the cutest little grunting noises as she pulled back. A drop of precum hit her tongue. *So yummy.* She swirled her tongue over his tip then circled his rim. She glanced up, dark, dangerous eyes stared back. Every muscle on his hard body was corded and ready.

It was time to kick it up a notch.

Tanya found she was enjoying this. It was a heady feeling to know that she was in full control of this warrior. In this moment he would probably agree to anything she demanded just so long as she kept sucking him off. She took one of his heavy sacs in her hand while taking his cock deep. Zane snarled. If he liked the feeling of that, then he would enjoy this even more, using a finger, she massaged the sensitive area of skin directly behind his balls and sucked his head at the same time.

"Female . . ." A warning, a plea? Only one way to find out. Tanya did it again. He grunted threading his fingers through her hair. His hips jerked as she took him as deep as she could.

"I'm going to . . ." He growled. "I'm nearly . . ." The hand in her hair tightened clasping her to him before he removed it fisting it at his side.

Tanya picked up speed. His body turned to stone. Zane groaned as hot cum spurted into her mouth. She struggled to swallow the copious amounts. Just when she thought he was finished another hot spurt, less this time. He growled threading both hands through her hair in a gentle caress. She slowed, easing the level of suction.

"Where did you learn to do that?"

She released him and shrugged. Her cheeks heated. She really shouldn't have done that. "It's a human thing I guess."

She glanced up at him. His brow was furrowed. "I enjoyed it very much."

"I'm sure you did."

"I didn't think I would like anything human."

It was probably as close to a thank-you as she would get. They were so glaringly different. Something he seemed to highlight at every turn. "Sure thing. How are you feeling?" She rose, feeling a bit shaky. It was his turn to steady her, which he did with a hand to her waist. Once she had regained her footing he released her. He took a slow step towards the faucet and turned off the water using his good arm. His movements were careful, deliberate.

"Still so damned weak," he spat out the word. "If I had a little more strength, I could repay you."

"No need really. I shouldn't have done that anyway." She turned to leave. Zane gripped her upper arm and turned her back to face him.

"While you are with me, you are my female. Do you understand?"

She swallowed hard and nodded not trusting her voice.

"I will take you to my bed. I will take care of your needs. Am I clear?"

She didn't respond. How could she agree?

"Even though I enjoyed the feel of your mouth on me . . ." His gaze turned hungry. "I have a feeling I will prefer your tight pussy clamping down on me as you come. Your gasps of pleasure will be nectar to my ears."

What the . . .

Her female bits screamed yes. Hell, her whole body practically begged for him to do it now. There was no way she could go back to Brant if she allowed Zane to make good on his threats though. She would never be able to look him in the eye. Brant, with his dimpled smile and easy way. The powerful king had left all the control in her hands. Had promised her long walks on the beach and candle lit dinners, and she couldn't wait to do all of those things with him. To make love to him again. To feel how his powerful body would surge into hers. She had never felt the way he made her feel. Guilt rose in her. Soft fabric brushed over her skin bringing her back to reality. Zane pulled the towel more securely around her.

"We need to get dressed. My phone was destroyed in the fight. It's a ten mile hike to the castle." He wiped the moisture from his body in long easy strokes.

"I have a phone."

His eyes widened. The tension eased out of his wide shoulders. "Gods be thanked. Just for the record, I would've made the ten miles on foot."

Tanya shook her head and giggled. "No doubt in my mind. I'm not so sure I would've though."

Zane made a choking noise which she realized was a laugh. From the sounds of things, those muscles never got worked. The slightest half smile appeared on his face. She was in so much shit. The man was a sight to behold when he was angry which seemed to be most of the time and he was utterly . . . beautiful when he smiled.

Just as quickly as the smile appeared, it left, his face hardening once again. "Get dressed and fetch me that phone."

"You need to stop bossing me around and you can try and say please once in a while."

"Female, we do not have time for niceties. I am certain that the elf king will send more males as soon as those do not return." He gestured to where the fallen pixie . . . elf lay. "I may not be able to fight them off this time."

"Oh shit. Why were they after us . . . me anyway?"

"With you gone, there won't be any more vampire heirs. Long term, our people would end up destroyed. There is no love between the different species. Enough talk, get that phone." Taking slow deliberate steps, he walked to where she had left her bag.

Tanya handed him the device.

Zane pushed a few buttons, holding the cell phone to his ear. "Female, fetch me clothes from the closet next to my bed." His eyes looked in the direction of the loft.

"Please." She added as she moved towards the stairs. He grunted something unintelligible.

Zane barked orders at someone on the other end of the line. Tanya finally gave up on trying to find any underwear, she settled on black jeans, a grey t-shirt, boots and socks. As an afterthought, she grabbed the leather jacket that was on the bed.

Zane stood at the bottom of the stairs, in a wide stance, naked as the day he was born and seemingly quite comfortable. She handed him the garments and he nodded in . . . thanks? "The guys will be here in five so best you"—his gaze moved across her skin—"get dressed." Using his good arm, he stepped into his jeans. Tanya rummaged in her bag pulling out a fresh pair of jeans and a light blue top.

"I would prefer it if you wore something else."

She choked, "Excuse me?"

"I like the look and feel of your skin. Make sure that you keep certain parts covered or I will be forced to beat my men when they look at you."

She looked down and felt heat rise in her face. Her nipples protruded from the thin cotton. She may as well have been completely topless.

"What I don't understand is why you insist on wearing such manly clothes? Even that first day in the square . . ."

"Jeans are hardly manly." She was secretly thrilled that he liked the way she looked and couldn't believe he actually remembered her from that day. The only other thing she had with her besides her pajamas was a yellow dress that tied at the back of her neck. The only problem was that she didn't have a strapless bra. In hind sight she didn't know why she brought the thing in the first place. She stuffed it back in the bag.

"Wear it," a low vibrating growl. Goose flesh rose on her arms and her first impulse was to obey him.

"I can't. I don't have the correct underwear."

"You will not be needing underwear."

A thrilling spark of awareness coursed through her. Why did she have to keep reminding herself of Brant? His warm smile. Great hands. Tanya felt like groaning in frustration.

"Your men will have an eyeful if I go braless."

His dark eyes narrowed. "They wouldn't dare look since it would be the last thing they ever got to see. Put on the dress."

"Fine." She ground her teeth. She would do as he said but he was not going to get into her panties. There would be no sex. "I *am* going to wear panties."

"No underwear."

"Why not?" She placed her hands on her hips.

"Covering up like that isn't natural. It would please me if I knew your pussy was naked and waiting for my attention."

Much to her annoyance, Tanya made a strangled sound. That did it. She was going to wear undies whether he liked it or not. Aside from Brant, there was another reason why sex with Zane would be a bad idea yet she couldn't seem to remember why right now. "Face the other way." Damn, her voice was breathy.

He grinned. Zane was unbelievably attractive when he smiled. So much so, she decided right there and then that she would do everything in her power to keep him scowling.

He shook his head. "Are you shy sweetness?"

"Yes, I am." No use lying.

"No need. You are my female. Very soon there will be no inch of your skin that I have not tasted."

Tanya coughed trying to dislodge the lump of sheer desire that had lodged itself in her throat. "Um . . ." She licked her lips. "It's a human thing. Please humor me, Zane."

"Mmmmm," another deep rumble. "I think I could grow to like the sound of my name on your lips."

Heat swept through her. Zane turned, he had only just pulled the jeans over his hips and seemed for the moment to be focused on fumbling with the catches on his pants.

Quicker than she thought possible, she pulled off her own soaked jeans and bra. She pulled the dress over her head leaning forward so that her hair would be out of the way to tie the neck straps of the dress. There was a bit of a built-in bra that helped keep everything together, but one hint of a breeze or any more sex talk from Zane and her nipples would be all over the place. She shrugged to herself. Nothing much she could do about that. Tanya risked a quick glance at the vampire king. He was still struggling one handed with his jeans. Tanya pulled off the wet panties, replacing them with a new pair. Full cotton briefs damn him. What the vampire bully didn't know wouldn't kill him.

She finished getting dressed, still feeling irritated at him for making her go braless. "Oh for goodness sakes turn around and let me help you."

He sighed, turning slowly. A look of sheer frustration

marred his features. The look soon turned heated as his gaze drifted over her. "Much better. Don't ever wear underwear around me again."

Things were quickly moving in the wrong direction. "Did you say you had a first aid kit?" She decided to try and move the conversation to something else.

"No time."

"There's always—" Her sentence was cut short with the sound of a vehicle pulling up.

"My men." He sat on the sofa. "Help me with my boots."

"Please." She paused a few seconds waiting in vain for a bit of politeness that wasn't forthcoming.

Tanya suppressed a sigh and pulled his socks and boots on and had just done up the clasps when footfalls sounded on the outside deck.

She turned in time to watch four big vampires enter the cabin.

"Piece of shit *elves*." The first one to enter spoke saying the word like a curse.

Zane looked her in the eye then gestured to his t-shirt lying beside him on the sofa. His eyes softened for the barest second. This time she did sigh as she picked up the garment holding it out for him.

"They were after our chosen female. Tried to assassinate her. Lance, I need you to let Brant know about the attempt. The human needs round the clock protection. I'm not sure I can trust him and his puny brother to protect her. Their whole coven are like a bunch of pussies."

"Stop that." She swatted him on the side of his good arm. "What did I tell you about speaking badly of those who can't defend themselves?" Tanya stood moving away a few feet.

Zane managed to look sheepish for half a second before

frowning at her. "Just calling a spade a spade. Now get your delectable ass over here and help me up before I spank you."

"You wouldn't dare."

A ridiculously sexy smile slid into place, one that dared her to defy him.

"You're lucky you're hurt or I'd so tell you to go to hell."

Zane's eyes darkened. "I'm disappointed." He held out his hand, which she clasped. His gaze stayed on her cleavage the whole time she helped him up. "Mmmm . . ." He whispered in her ear as soon as he made it to his feet, "I like the dress."

"Lance." The big head guard immediately came to attention. "Have Charlotte meet us when we arrive. I want her to measure my female so that she can have more of such items of clothing."

"I must say my lord . . . that dress does enhance . . ." His eyes had dipped to her boobs. Tanya felt like putting a hand across her chest. She could just imagine how she must look.

"What does it enhance?" Zane interrupted, his eyes blazing. "Are you checking out my female?"

Lance looked down, eyes solidly at the floor. "I would never dream of it my lord. I will let Charlotte know."

"Good. Let me make something very clear. This human might look good, and I know that she smells amazing. Let me catch one of you with even half a finger even crooked in her direction and I will take the whole damn arm. Do I make myself clear?"

A series of mumbles and nods of agreement rose from the men. All hardened warriors in their own right.

"Griffin and Ross, you stay and clean up. I want them on spikes. Ten feet high. We need to send King Katar a little message." Using his good arm, he pulled her towards him. He was so tense it felt like his body had been carved out of granite.

"Spikes as in?"

"Do not concern yourself female, but know that I will do whatever it takes to keep you safe."

Unfortunately she could guess. Dead bodies and spikes. The elf king would get his message alright. She was just glad she wasn't Griffin or Ross at the moment.

Chapter THREE

LANCE AND ANOTHER BIG guy climbed in to the front of the vehicle, Tanya slid in next to Zane in the back. She tried to readjust her boobs without anyone noticing and then pulled on the hem of her dress trying to cover as much thigh as possible.

"Leave it alone." Zane pulled her onto his lap. The sliding motion had the dress riding way up. "Much better." His low growl had her nipples tightening and darned if he didn't notice. She watched in horror as he palmed her breast, making a low rumbling noise as he did it. Everything in her tightened. It felt so good. *Too good.*

Tanya tried to wriggle away. Zane hissed. His face contorted in pain. She realized she'd knocked his shoulder.

"Stay still, Ysnaar."

"It serves you right. Stop groping me."

"I haven't even begun to . . . grope you. If you'd like I could . . ." His eyes had moved back down to her chest.

"No that's okay. What does Ysnaar mean anyway?"

"The direct translation is feisty one. I have never met a female like you before. You want me, yet you keep pushing me away." He frowned as he spoke.

"I do not want you. I am a one man kind of woman and since I already slept with Brant . . ."

Zane snarled. His fangs lengthened. His irises flashed red for a second or two. Tanya cowered, covering her face with her hands. His body shook beneath her as he snarled a second time.

His little outburst was over before it began. His warm hand cupped her chin. "Do not ever be afraid of me. I would never harm you."

"Don't do that again."

"I can't promise that I won't react that way in the future, but I'll never hurt you." His eyes were locked with hers. "I don't like the thought of another man touching you, let alone rutting with you." He released her chin and looked outside the window for a few beats. "I've never cared before. I've even shared females in the past but the thought of you with him . . ." Zane shook his head, his dark eyes bore into her. "I don't understand it. Must be because Brant is a birth enemy or it could be because you are my future mate."

"I'm not your future mate. I'm not even sure I want Brant as a mate. I didn't ask for any of this."

"The system isn't fair. Hell, life isn't fair. Yet it is important that you know that the future of one of our covens is at stake. You must choose or we will fight to the death for you."

It didn't seem right or fair at all. It didn't matter which way she turned, which vampire king she chose, one of the covens would be doomed without an heir regardless.

Zane chuckled, the sound sad. It chilled her from the inside out. "It gives me hope to hear you say that you have not yet chosen Brant."

"I don't understand. Surely there will be strong vampires

born to your coven. They may not be of royal descent, but surely they will be able to lead your people."

Zane skimmed his hand over her skin stopping only when he was under her dress, on the side of her thigh. "That's the problem, all of our males are dominant and strong, they will all vie for the position. It is not in our blood to submit unless faced with royal blood. Once I am gone, an all-out war amongst the males is inevitable." He casually caressed her skin as he spoke. Were all vampires good with their hands? Goose flesh broke out on her skin as he slid higher in tender circles.

"I see. Why couldn't a female lead?"

"We lead with both mind and fist. Females are not as strong physically. Any female that tried to take the throne would be slaughtered."

"That's barbaric."

He shrugged and winced at the movement.

"Don't vampires heal quickly?" She looked at how his shirt stuck to the area. His wound must still be bleeding. It was hard to tell though because his shirt was black.

"This would normally heal within an hour or two, but the poison has slowed the process." His eyes narrowed. "It may be barbaric"—he raised his eyebrows—"but it is the way of our people and not about to change any time soon." She had to suppress a shiver as he circled higher.

"You're doing it again." His hand stilled, he gently squeezed her flesh.

"Doing what?" she asked.

"Telling me you want me with your body."

Shit. She swallowed hard. "I am not . . . my body is not." Her nipples were hard, her panties damp and he'd barely touched her. What was it about him that had her libido running wild?

Zane looked down at her chest. "Did you drop pebbles down your top?"

Damn this blasted dress. She was so finding something else to wear when they got to his place. "I'm cold."

He chuckled and sniffed at the air. "I can smell your arousal."

She gasped. These stinking vampires and their heightened senses. "So sue me, I think your head guard is cute."

The car swerved. Lance managed to get the vehicle back under control before they careened off the road.

"Oh really?"

"Yes really." She winked at Lance when he nervously glanced in the rear-view mirror.

"So if I do this, it wouldn't affect you at all." With ultra-speed, his hand skimmed up her leg clasping her ass. Tanya moaned. The moan turned into a squeal as her underwear was ripped off. Here one second and gone the next.

She shoved her legs together. "Hey!" His hand squeezed her very naked butt.

"Much better. I told you no underwear."

"I disagreed. You can't have everything you want. It doesn't work that way."

He pulled her closer to him. Tanya anchored her hands on his chest, but only so she didn't hurt his shoulder.

"Yes it does."

Tanya wanted to argue some more but something hard nudged her from below. Feelings of guilt and desire warred inside her as she realized it was his cock.

She had to stay strong. Deep down, she quite liked Zane. She even enjoyed their sparring way more than she should. She obviously was attracted to him, but Brant was the vampire for her. If she slept with both of them it would create major problems. Brant might never forgive her. How fun would that be? Living out the rest of her life with a pissed off vampire who fucked her whenever he needed a new heir. *No thanks.*

"I can tell that you were spoiled growing up. Vampire females might open their legs at the click of your fingers but... newsflash... I'm a human."

His whole body tightened and his jaw worked. "You don't know me, therefore you may not assume anything about me."

Oopsie, it seemed she had crossed a line. "Do vampire females turn you down?" If she was one of those hussy vamps she wouldn't hesitate to jump Zane at even the smallest crook of his finger.

His lips twitched. At least he looked a little less angry. "I can have my pick of the females," he paused. Why did she hate the thought of that? Zane came across to her as a virile male. He had sex regularly, she had no doubt.

"I was not spoiled. Far from it." He looked outside. Focusing on the view of the dark, thick forest. His thoughts far away. Something that Stephany had said came back to her. Her friend had mentioned Zane having had a difficult childhood.

"You act spoiled sometimes. I'm sorry if I made the assumption that you were spoiled as a child."

His midnight eyes softened as they landed on her. "I am the king. I'm used to my coven obeying my every command."

"I'm not a part of your coven. I am not yours to command."

His face lit up in a smile that had her insides belly flopping. "It is a new and intriguing concept, yet I feel that I am entitled as you are my female."

"I'm not yours."

"You are mine until you go back to Brant." His face hardened at the mention of his enemy.

"Even if I was yours. It would be as partners. Equals. You need to try and wrap your head around that."

"Female . . ." His hand moved from her ass to her hip. It somehow felt more intimate. " . . . I will try." Not much, but coming from him, it meant a lot.

They turned onto a dirt track that cut between the trees. The thick forest suddenly opening into rolling lawns. Tanya had a ridiculous urge to rub her eyes. Perched on the highest hill was an honest to God stone castle. Just like the ones from the story books she had read as a little girl. The ones she loved so much that they had sparked her love for books, which ultimately had led to her dream of buying the bookstore. The stone castle had three towers and a flag. The only thing missing was a moat and drawbridge. The large iron and wood doors were open.

"And how is it that you mocked Brant about his mansion?"

"This is way better." Zane winced as he exited the vehicle. He waited while she did the same.

The castle, just as the cabin had been, was practical. It might lack flash but it was comfortable. Homey even. Passages were long and wide. The rooms were big and airy. There were a number of both male and female vampires there. The place was busy.

"Does your whole coven live here?"

"A large number do but no not everyone. The West Tower is mine." Zane moved slightly ahead of her, moving to the right and up a winding stair case. Tanya noticed how his hand sought support from the wall every few steps. Zane paused more than once as they made their slow ascent. Sweat dripped from his brow and his skin had paled by the time they made it to his . . . chamber. She struggled with a better word. An old fashioned version of a loft maybe. There were large windows.

A wooden trussed ceiling and shock horror in the form of a four poster bed with carvings of massacres in the dark shining wood.

What the hell was wrong with the man? She noticed an elevator in the far corner. Why had he insisted on walking?

Zane stripped out of his shirt and jeans. Her face heated. The air caught in her throat. She looked away.

"Female." She turned. Zane was between the sheets on the large bed. His broad chest had her mouth-watering. Aside from Brant, there was another very good reason why she shouldn't have sex with this man. Make that scary vampire. Yet, the more she got to know Zane, the more she realized he wasn't that scary after all. The problem was that the very good reason she shouldn't have sex with him kept evading her. Brant seemed very far away as well.

She swallowed hard. Not sure of what to do. If she joined him in bed, they would end up having sex.

"Female." He sounded irritated this time. "I promise not to . . . grope you. I need you close right now." He worked his jaw for a second or two. "Please," so softly spoken she barely heard him.

"Are you okay? Do you have a first aid kit? We need to do something about your shoulder."

"I need"—he paused like he was thinking about confiding in her—"sleep. Join me. I won't be able to rest unless you are next to me."

Zane needed more than just sleep. For whatever reason, he didn't want her to know what that thing was. Tanya looked down at the material that covered her body. A thin summer dress was all that would be between them. In his current condition, she couldn't turn him down though.

Tanya nodded, noticing how the tension in him eased. She

slid in next to him. His arms banded around her pulling her in close. Within minutes his breathing turned rhythmic. She tried to move but his hand tightened on her waist and he mumbled something incoherent, so she stayed still. He nuzzled his head into the back of her neck. Warm breath tickled her skin.

Tanya felt wide awake. His big body enveloped her and his musky scent surrounded her. Zane was very different from what she had expected. Sure, he was the fierce warrior but he had a . . . softer side. He demanded and issued orders as casually as he drew his next breath. His men seemed to obey without question, yet there was a small part of him that reminded her of a small lost boy.

Lying there, snug against him, her body felt so tightly wound. Part of her was a little disappointed that he hadn't wanted to take it further. That he hadn't tried anything. The bigger part of her was happy he hadn't though. Her will power was at zero.

Chapter FOUR

THERE WAS A KNOCK on the door. Tanya woke with a start. The sun was low and much less light shone through the drapes that hung in billows over iron rods.

"Enter." Zane lay on his back, the sheet rode low on his hips. An enormous erection tented the light material. Tanya made to stand.

"Stay." He tucked her into the crook of his arm.

A supermodel walked in. Long, blond hair that fanned her shoulders. She had lithe, tanned legs and wore a short silk robe tied loosely at her narrow waist. "Your highness." She gave a curtsy.

The leggy vampire was clearly naked beneath the robe. Hard points spiked the soft, shiny fabric. Commando was clearly a vampire thing.

"I'm here to measure the human for her new wardrobe." It was only then that she noticed that the vampire had a tape measure in one of her hands.

"Fine." He released his hold on her, wincing as he moved to sit upright. His wound had knitted but still looked angry and red, like it might pop open with even the slightest provocation.

"Hi, I'm Charlotte. Please come and stand over here."

Tanya looked back at the woman who gestured to the area directly in front of her. Tanya pulled her dress down firmly. It wouldn't do to have all her lady bits showing. She tried to run a hand through her hair as she sat up but it was a tangled mess. Damn, she was too scared to look in a mirror. Especially with this beauty queen in the room.

She ran her fingers through the knotted mess a few more times in a last ditch effort as she moved to stand in front of the vamp. Charlotte smiled. "Stay still while I . . ." She surrounded her breasts with the tape and shook her head. "Nope . . . it would work better if you took the dress off. Let me help you."

A sound of horror escaped Tanya's lips. "No, that's fine. I'm not wearing a bra so you should be able to—"

"My measurements won't be accurate. Let me . . ." The vampire took a step toward her, hands raised. Tanya realised in horror that she planned on undoing the knot that tied the dress around her neck.

"No!" It came out a little harsh. Charlotte ignored her taking another step. Eyes firmly fixed on the material that wound around Tanya's neck. The vamp was quick, her hands were on the knot before she knew what was happening. It was a perfectly natural response when she slapped the other woman's hands away. Charlotte's eyes widened.

A chuckle caused her to break eye contact with the striking blonde. Zane clasped his shoulder for support as he continued to laugh. "Leave the human, she seems to have modesty issues."

More like having this ravishing creature measuring her through her clothes was bad enough. Tanya didn't like taking her clothes off for anyone, let alone a crowd. Especially when said crowd had perfectly sculpted bodies.

"Fine, but I will not be held liable if the garments do not fit her perfectly." Charlotte wrapped the tape around Tanya's breasts. "Wow, you will make a very good mother."

Tanya felt her cheeks heat. Next the vampire put the tape around her waist and then hips. "Child birth should not be an issue."

Tanya made a choking sound, slapping her hand over her mouth until she could compose herself. "Has anyone ever told you that it's bad manners to point things like that out to a person? So I'm a pound or two overweight. Big deal." She felt her cheeks grow warmer this time in anger. Charlotte looked at her as if she had suddenly sprouted horns.

Zane chuckled, the sound ending on a moan. "You're killing my shoulder female. Charlotte was offering you a compliment. Wider hips and fuller breasts are a good thing. Very few vampire females are capable of birthing young, their hips are too narrow."

"I noticed," she couldn't help but mumble.

"You are very lucky, my lord. I like her," Charlotte smiled. "I have never met a human with nerve."

Tanya felt pride surge. So the woman was both beautiful and sweet. Tanya changed her mind about the sweet part less than a second later though, when the female vampire removed her own robe. This time it took a little longer to get the choking fit under control. The vampire seemed to have acres of smooth creamy skin. Although much smaller than her own, the blonde's breasts were bigger than most vampires' that she'd seen, with raspberry tips that looked ripe enough to pick. To make matters worse, she was clean shaven down below. Is that how vampires liked it?

"What do you need, my lord?" Was it Tanya's imagination or had the female's voice grown husky.

Tanya glanced at Zane who was looking at her. Their eyes locked. "I will take everything I need from my female."

Tanya swallowed. It seemed she sat on a precipice. Did she let this bimbo into her . . . Zane's bed or did she do what needed to be done herself?

"My lord . . ." The blonde sounded incredulous. "You need blood if you are to heal. Sex will also help. The human is weak, she cannot possibly . . ." Charlotte walked towards the bed as she spoke. The vamp had an ass so tight Tanya was sure she used it to crack nuts. Right now she hated the bitch even if she was trying to, for lack of a better word, help Zane.

"I said I would take everything I needed from my female. You can leave now."

"The poison must be worse than we suspected. You're not thinking straight." Charlotte put a knee on his bed, stretching her hand towards where his erection had been. No bulging sheets in sight at the moment though. For the first time his eyes flashed to Charlotte staying firmly on her face. The vampire's hand inched closer to his cock.

"Touch him and . . ." *And what?* What could she possibly do to this super human woman?

"You heard my female. I assure you I am fine. My female is more than capable of taking care of me. Thank you, Charlotte. Now go before I get angry." His voice took on a sharp edge.

Charlotte nodded. She paused for a few seconds before standing and donning her robe, just as she reached the door she turned back. "Call me if you need me."

"He won't need you." The words were out before she could stop them.

The vampire's eyes lowered as she spoke. "You will be leaving come morning." She wasn't trying to be mean, just stating a simple fact. The door thudded shut as she left.

Anger bubbled up inside her. "Will you call her once I've gone?" Tanya spun to face Zane. The question was so unfair. She had no right to ask it. Wishing she hadn't because she knew she would hate the answer.

"I might. I might call someone else. You will be snug in Brant's arms, so what concern is it to you?"

"None." She lied. "I was just wondering," she mumbled. The thought of him taking Charlotte or one of the many other willing females left a bitter taste in her mouth.

"Come here."

"No." This whole situation was so screwed up. Brant was the one for her, yet the thought of Zane fucking Charlotte, of him drinking from her . . . why did she feel so jealous? She had no right to be so torn between the two kings.

His jaw tightened. "Are you insisting I remain faithful while you are with Brant?"

Everything in her screamed to tell him yes. To force him to do just that, but she couldn't. It wouldn't be right. Especially since she could never choose Zane. Brant had decided on her from the start, while Zane had taken another. The only reason she was here right now was because Zane's chosen was dead. And there it was. The one thing that had eluded her. The most important reason why she could never be with this king. The dead woman had looked nothing like her, was nothing like her. The only reason she was here right now was to give this man future heirs, his true chosen was gone.

"No, I don't expect you to remain faithful."

"Don't look so upset. Is it that Brant has promised this to you?" His eyes narrowed. "Brant is a fool. How many times do I need to remind you of that?"

"You can be such an asshole. Why is Brant a fool? People should be faithful to one another while they are courting. It's the right thing to do." She folded her arms across her chest.

Zane smiled. "This is not a normal situation. I will be faithful to you while you are here, but if you choose to go back to Brant all bets are off."

"That's blackmail."

"That's life sweetness." He cocked his head.

"You're such a jerk, I wish I had never gone down on you. Wrapped my mouth around your slut of a cock."

Zane chuckled. "You will be doing that again very soon but first I want to plough your tight sheath. I cannot wait to make you come."

Tanya felt her jaw drop. "No freaking way. I don't have sex with sluts."

"Sex is perfectly normal and perfectly healthy." He yanked the sheet off his body. One times humungous cock jutted up. "I need it to get well."

What the hell had she agreed to? She wanted to tell him to call for Charlotte but the words stuck in her throat. Brant would never forgive her, hell, she would never forgive herself. She'd only ever had sex with two people before Brant. The first was a giant mistake. Although the second had been a mistake too, they had been in a long term relationship. She was about to have sex with two different men in the space of twenty four hours. Yet she couldn't think of any other way out of this.

"You can't drink from me." It was technically the one thing Brant had asked her.

Zane's eyes darkened. "My shoulder will not heal until I drink. I'm as weak as a new born whelp."

"No blood."

Zane shook his head. "Fine, but that will mean that we have to stay in this room. In this bed until our time is up. As much as I had hoped to be able to take you like a man, it seems I will have to rely on you." His eyes narrowed daring her to defy him. "Straddle my hips so that I can touch you. You will need to ride me."

A zing of need shot from her pussy. It raced through her whole body leaving her feeling a little shaky.

"No," the barest whisper.

"Your body says yes." His eyes softened, "I need you." It must've taken considerable effort for him to say those words. "Straddle my hips. Once I touch you, any doubt will evaporate."

That's what she was afraid of.

"I know you want me." A low growl that had her channel turning slick with need even though she still thought he was a big, fat jerk.

"The only reason I want you is because you have a good body."

Zane threw her a half smile and sniffed the air. "Mmmm." A low rumble of approval as he scented her arousal.

"Stop that. It's not fair. The problem is that sex would complicate things."

"It seems to me that they are complicated already."

"There's more to all of this than sex. It would be wrong."

His whole body tensed. "You rutted with Brant, yet you deny me my most basic of needs."

"I sucked you off just a few hours ago. You've had your fun damn it. Now leave me alone."

"As much as I enjoyed your mouth, I haven't felt you shudder with your release. I haven't heard you scream as I drive into you over and over again. I haven't yet established whether you like it hard or soft. Maybe a combination of both," his brows arched. "Can you come with just g-spot stimulation or will you need me to rub your clit while I fuck you?" Juice trickled down her left thigh forcing her to close her legs tightly. It only increased her arousal. "I want to lick that wetness from between your legs, stick my tongue so far up that sweet little pussy . . ."

Tanya was on the verge of running to his bed, of impaling herself on his hard cock when a knock sounded at the door. She couldn't help but to groan in frustration.

Another knock. "There has been an incident sire."

Zane's eyes flared for a second. "We will finish this shortly. Enter." Zane growled as he pulled the sheet across his hips.

Lance walked in. He inclined his head in Tanya's direction without actually looking at her.

"This had better be important."

Lance was dressed from head to toe in leather. He wore a long jacket. "The north fence was breached."

"When?" Zane pulled himself into a sitting position. A pang of guilt hit her as she noticed how he struggled with the simple task, his right hand clasped his left shoulder for support.

"Less than five hours ago."

"Around the same time we were attacked."

Lance took a step forward. "I think we should discuss this in your office," he lowered his voice.

"Whatever you have to say, you can say in front of my female."

"Sire, she goes back in"—he glanced at his watch—"less than fourteen hours."

"This affects Brant and his coven just as much. We need to get word to him. The incidences are related. They must be. What did the trackers find?"

Lance's eyes narrowed. "I think it would be better if you saw for yourself. It's . . ." He cleared his throat, ". . . concerning."

Zane looked at Tanya. His whole demeanour changed. He looked pissed. "You'll need to call Charlotte."

Crunch time.

Lance could sense the tension in the room because he remained still making no move to do as Zane had instructed. Tanya squirmed as Zane's head guard turned to face her. "Sire, are you sure?" Both males stared at her.

"Charlotte won't be needed." No freaking way could she stand by while he drank from another female. Not while she was here. What happened after she left was out of her hands, but right now? Brant would understand . . . she hoped.

Lance visibly relaxed.

"Give me five minutes." His eyes started glowing and sharp fangs extended. "Make that ten."

Her heart rate increased. *Shit.* It was too late to change her mind but she could make sure that it was on her terms. Lance left. One second there and the next gone. She hadn't even heard the door shut.

"Come here."

She shook her head and Zane fell back on the bed. "What is it now?"

"You don't get to touch me."

Zane smiled. "Not even if you beg?"

"Especially not if I beg. No touching. You can drink but that's it."

The straining erection was back. His jaw locked, his muscles bunched. Zane nodded once.

"I want to go with you when you inspect the . . . fence."

His brow creased. "It's too dangerous."

"I'll be with you and your men. I don't want to sit in this room. Please, Zane."

His eyes clouded in thought. "My scouts will have checked

the area. Lance wouldn't risk me if he was worried about my enemies still lurking. Only if you promise to obey my every command once we are there."

"I promise, I will."

"I mean it female, my every command."

She sighed in irritation, "I said yes."

"We don't have much time. Come here now."

Her nipples tightened as his deep voice washed over her. She knew she should probably hate the way he ordered her around, but in situations like this it aroused her to no end. Tanya lay down on the bed next to him.

"Sweetness."

She turned her head to face him.

"I'm a little bit of an invalid at the moment. I need you to lie on top of me." When she tried to do as he said he grunted, his face taut.

"You bastard," Tanya slid off him.

"What have I done now?" His mouth formed a tight smile.

"You're hurt worse than what you let on."

His face turned serious. "Maybe worse than I thought. Once I have some blood though, I'll be fine."

"How do we do this?" She positioned herself on all fours crouching forward until her neck was at his mouth.

Chapter FIVE

HER SOFT SKIN WAS so tantalizingly close. Zane had to work hard to keep from lunging at her. He had more restraint than that though. The scent of berries had his nostrils flaring and his fangs extending further. Zane had to suppress a groan when he caught the perfect view of her deep cleavage. Her hard nipples were like two pointed barbs under the thin dress. It seemed to him that they were fighting to cut their way to freedom. His dick hardened up a whole lot more at the thought of their lush weight. He'd never imagined that overly full breasts would entice him so. *Round, plump, soft.* He couldn't wait to be inside her, to watch them bounce as he took her. Couldn't wait to hear her screams as she came. He suspected that a female as filled with passion as Tanya was, would let herself go in the moment. Zane couldn't wait to make her lose it. He would have her soon. Very soon.

His lips touched her skin and she jerked away. "No touching. Fangs only."

"Hold still then." He bracketed her hips with his hands.

"Hey." She waggled her hips.

"Need to keep you still. We don't have much time so I'm

going to drink hard and fast." He couldn't help himself as a chuckle escaped. Tanya would be sorry she ever made the no touching rule. "You might want to hold on female."

Zane didn't wait for her reply. He sank his fangs into her, loving the way she gasped as he entered her body. He closed his mouth on her soft skin and sucked, hard. Tanya groaned. The sound interlaced with both pleasure and frustration. She closed a hand on his bicep as he drew deeply a second time, her nails biting into his skin.

Her essence filled him. Her taste so divine that his cock grew even thicker. Surely his skin would burst if he expanded any more. She was panting and mewling, sounding more frustrated than pleasured. Zane wished she would stop being so damned stubborn. He longed to pleasure this woman, wanted it more than he'd wanted anything in his whole life.

Another heavy draw and her pants turned to ecstasy filled groans. Moans of . . . pure unadulterated pleasure. His eyes flew open as she jerked in his arms. He had to clamp his hands more firmly at her waist to keep her in place. *The little minx.* Her fingers were firmly between her legs with her dress bunched in a V where her hand and stomach met. Her fingers worked frantically pumping in and out of her pussy. Her thumb circled her clit. He growled and drew in another mouth full of decadent blood.

Two could play at this little game. Leaving one hand on her waist, he used the other to fist his cock. Zane sucked slower, delaying the process. He had to be careful not to take too much. Palming his shaft harder, he pictured how tight her sheath would be. She was a small human after all. He could just imagine taking her slow and easy or fast and frantic. It didn't matter, he just knew he'd find utter rapture between her luscious thighs.

The taste of her blood on his lips, the sound of her moans, his imagination did the rest. Zane tugged faster. One more hard suck at her neck and she cried out as a second orgasm took her. He watched her hand thrusting into her glistening pussy. It was enough to bring him over the edge. Hot semen jetted from him marking her stomach and chest. A feeling of possessiveness grabbed hold of him. This female was his. He would fight dirty to ensure that he got her.

It was with extreme reluctance that he retracted his fangs. He licked at the wound on her neck. Tanya groaned, as did he. She sat upright, running a hand down her dress as she was in the habit of doing every so often. Her face crumpled as her hand came away sticky. "You pig."

"Did you expect me *not* to watch? Not to like what I saw?"

Crimson darkened her cheeks, she straightened her shoulders and pushed out her chin. "Not watching would've been the gentlemanly thing to do."

"I'm glad I'm not a gentleman then. Watching you please yourself is one of the most erotic things I have ever seen. I have burned the moment to memory and will replay it often in your absence."

"What the hell am I supposed to wear now?" She huffed, pouting her lips as she placed her hands on her hips.

Zane picked up the phone next to his bed and speed dialed Charlotte. "My female needs something to wear." He paused as Charlotte explained the various options. She knew what he liked and how he liked it.

Tanya mouthed the words underwear several times. Zane tried to suppress a smile and failed. Did she ever give up?

He shook his head at her. "That will do nicely." Zane spoke into the mouthpiece before putting the phone in the cradle. Warmth rushed through his veins, he could actually feel his energy levels rise as her blood in his system countered the poison. Looking down, he noticed that the wound was less severe. His healing flesh no longer looked swollen and inflamed.

"I have my jeans, I don't need anything else."

"No jeans."

"You're insufferable." She stomped her foot.

Zane stood allowing the sheet to fall away. Her cheeks flushed further, this time with arousal. He noticed how her eyes tracked the length of his body. How her lashes fused as her eyes grew hooded. She was attracted to him. That much was clear. It didn't take long for her eyes to flash with anger though. She didn't want to want him. Well too bad. He would have her before she went back to Brant.

A knock sounded. Zane pulled on a pair of leathers and buttoned them up. Normally his nakedness in front of the female vampire wouldn't bother him, but he got the feeling his human wouldn't approve. "Enter."

Charlotte walked in holding a number of garments. "They're mine so I hope one of them fits. I will have a wardrobe ready next time you are here."

Tanya had pulled the sheet against her soiled dress, she nodded once at the vampire, her demeanour stiff.

"Thank you. You may leave," he addressed Charlotte.

The female had angered his Tanya. He got the definite impression his female wouldn't want Charlotte to hang around. The female inclined her head at him and then Tanya before leaving.

Two of the dresses were little more than sheaths, similar to the one Alexandra had worn at the club the night previously.

Her body fat would need to be in the minus in order to pull off such a dress. She huffed, if she got any angrier smoke would start to come out of her nostrils. One was a very pretty floral number with triangles so small she'd have no hope in hell of fitting her breasts in it. The last was a stunning shade of green that she knew would complement her coloring. The top was a boob tube and it had a flared skirt that would cover her to about mid-calf. Hopefully, the elastic would fit around her boobage. Maybe, just maybe though, it would work.

"Is there somewhere for me to change?"

"You are my female. What part of that don't you understand?"

Zane infuriated her. "I am not yours damn it. You are never going to see me naked, get that into your thick skull." She knew she wasn't being fair but she felt so embarrassed at what had happened that she had decided to blame him for whole thing.

"Your bra was see-through in the shower and I had a great view of your pussy not five minutes ago. Your hand was a little in the way, but . . ." That did it. She flew at him fists, nails and all. Zane let her slap him and pretend claw at him for a few beats before grabbing her wrists and shoving her up against the wall.

Trapped between hard brick and hard unforgiving male, her breathing hitched. *Only because she was afraid.* It had nothing to do with his scent or the hard nudge at her stomach. "I will humor you female because for some reason your feelings are important to me, but do not push me too far."

She swallowed hard and nodded, not trusting her voice. Zane leaned in, so close his breath mingled with hers. So close that his nose brushed hers as he leaned in a fraction more. Their gazes locked. His eyes burned. He was going to kiss her and she couldn't wait. His eyes dropped to her lips, which she licked in anticipation.

Just as she was sure he would do the deed, he pulled back. "Get dressed. We need to go."

Damn but she hated the disappointment, hated her desire for him even more. He was such a jerk. Firstly, because he made her want to kiss him. Secondly, because he didn't damn well kiss her.

When she turned to him, he was fully dressed in leathers just as Lance had been. He looked every bit the warrior and acted every bit the king. "You have one minute and then I'm coming to get you. Understood?" He didn't wait for a reply. Instead, he strode from the room shutting the door behind him.

Tanya pulled off the sticky dress. The audacity of the man to come all over her. What the hell was his problem? There was a small, teeny, tiny part of her deep down inside that was secretly thrilled Zane had been so turned on by her. Then again, she huffed, he was a man and anything with boobs and a pussy was normally enough. She pulled the green dress up over her body. A bit of a tight fit around the girls, but it seemed to fit alright. Next she grabbed her toiletry bag and headed for the restroom. She readjusted her boobs and gave herself the once over. Not too shabby. The green really worked against her complexion and the shape of the dress accentuated her curves in a good way. Her hair was a mess. Tanya unzipped the bag and quickly tried to tame it. Next, she put paste on the toothbrush and had just started on her teeth when Zane walked in. His big body took up the entire door frame as he leaned against the jamb. Despite his warnings, he folded his arms across his chest and waited for her to finish.

He followed her back into the bedroom where she decided

to push her luck by applying some mascara. With her lips puckered, she prepared to apply a coat of lip-gloss.

"You don't need all that crap."

"Us humans enjoy it."

"I'm not human," he growled.

"Well I am." She ran the lip-gloss over her mouth. Applying a second coat for good measure. "It's not like you kiss me or anything anyway, so why would you care?" *Oops,* she hadn't meant to say that. His brush off earlier must have affected her more than she had thought.

Zane frowned, he opened his big leather trench coat and stuck his hands in the pockets. "I don't kiss females."

"As in you don't like it or . . ."

"I've never had the inclination." He moved his weight from one leg to the other even though both feet stayed on the ground.

Her mouth dropped open. After a few seconds of fly catching she snapped it closed. "You've never kissed anyone before?"

Zane shook his head.

"You're missing out you know?"

His mouth pulled into a thin white line. "I doubt it. Let's go."

Chapter SIX

After driving about a half hour, which took them deeper into the country, they arrived at the area in question. Male vampires were everywhere. More piled out of vehicles both in front of and behind them. The big vampire, Ross, approached them as they pulled up. Zane grabbed her hand as she slid from the vehicle. "Stay close."

"I take it the area is secured," Zane spoke softly.

Ross seemed surprised to see Tanya but quickly composed himself. The big vampire cleared his throat. "Yeah. I sent scout parties out over a two mile radius. All is clear."

"I take it they chose this spot because it's furthest from the castle."

"That would be my guess. They were good to keep the prints to their side of the fence. It was pure luck that one of the guards spotted the area at all. If you'll follow me." Ross walked in the direction of the fence, crouching at a specific area. He gestured to the barrier. "If you take a really good look, you'll notice how the wire has been welded back together."

Tanya gasped, sure enough, there was a definite thickening where the wire had been re-joined. The line was half a meter in a line perpendicular to the ground. It wasn't something you would see unless you were specifically looking for it.

"Take a look around." He pointed at the dirt on either side of them." Red dust with patches of grass. Nothing unusual.

Zane let out a pent up breath as he rose taking her up with him, their hands were still clasped. "Damn. The bastards were here." His eyes followed the dirt to the grass beyond.

"I don't see anything." She knew she should keep quiet.

"That's the problem. This ground was swept. It's too smooth." He walked her a few feet up the side of the fence. The ground had a very different look. Nowhere near as smooth.

"Oh, wow."

"That's not the worst of it," Ross's expression was grave as he spoke.

"I was afraid of that." Zane angled her back to where they had been standing, he used a hand on her lower back.

Ross clasped the fence, his eyes solidly on the ground on the other side. "What do you make of that?"

Zane dropped her hand and mimicked Ross. Tanya did the same. There were definite prints on the other side. Zane gave a sharp intake of breath. "Not a fuck." Tanya felt tension radiate from his body. His hands were white knuckled on the wire. Tanya turned back to the churned up earth, not sure of what it was she was supposed to be seeing. Over to the right was a definite indent of a huge paw.

"An animal?"

"Not bad, human," Ross said. "Try shifter. Too big for a regular wolf."

Now that he had highlighted the fact, she realized that he was right. She could most likely fit both her splayed hands inside the print.

"Motherfuckers were here together," Lance's voice boomed from behind them.

Tanya shrieked, grabbing at her heart. Stupid vampires and their ability to sneak up on a person. All three men looked at her. Zane slid his hand around her waist. The show of . . . *affection* . . . more like possessiveness shouldn't be endearing, yet, it was. She got the feeling Zane didn't normally touch women in public, at least not very often. If ever. Silly man had never even kissed before.

"Are you sure they were here together and not on separate occasions?"

Lance raised his eyebrows. "You're seriously asking me that?"

"I'm being hopeful. Besides, it's never good to assume." Zane narrowed his eyes at the other vampire.

Lance inclined his head slightly. "I had our best tracker take a look and Griffin was one hundred percent sure. Wolves and elves. They seem to have joined forces."

Zane shut his eyes while using his free hand to pinch the bridge of his nose.

"There are more tracks once you get into the cover of the forest, they go on for a few hundred feet," Lance paused as Zane turned to look at him.

"Go on," Zane growled.

"I'm not sure of the reason for the breach, but I would suspect they chose this fence because it's furthest away from the castle. It's also the part of our perimeter closest to the forest. I suspect that they entered our territory to check if they could get away with it. With the intention to scout our land in order to plan an attack." Lance lowered his voice, his eyes darting around the clearing. "They would have been watching for us, but they are long gone by now."

"I think you may be right, Lance. This changes things. Let's follow their tracks, I want to know what they were up to."

"I assure you there isn't much to see. They entered, walked for a few hundred feet under cover of the trees, turned and made their way back. Exiting through the same cut in the fence." Lance gestured to a long belt of thick forest that wound its way as far as the eye could see.

It wasn't lost on her that the forest was the very same one that she had looked on earlier from Zane's tower at the castle. The werewolves and elves would be able to hide in the thick foliage. *Were they really planning an attack?* Tanya shivered not liking the answer that formed in her head. Surely they couldn't be doing this over little old her. Then again, if what Zane said was true, by taking her out of the picture it would mean the end of the vampire line. It would be a very good reason to remove her from the picture. Tanya couldn't help it, she suddenly felt vulnerable, exposed out in the open like this. She stepped in closer to Zane who instantly put an arm around her, pulling her in to his side. He and Lance were discussing ways to fortify both the castle and the perimeter. Zane put his hand up to Lance midsentence, silencing the tall vampire. He turned his dark, concerned eyes on her. "Are you okay? Cold maybe? You're shivering."

"I'm a little cold. I'm not as thick skinned as a vampire." The sun was setting, streaks of pink lined the horizon. Even with the sun disappearing, the weather was mild. A warm breeze tickled her skin. She wasn't cold, rather she was scared shitless of becoming a werewolf snack. Or possibly a new pair of pixie boots.

Zane removed his coat and slung it over her shoulders. He wore a black t-shirt and had an array of weapons attached to his body. Even in this setting, and in this moment, he was a sight to behold.

"You stay in the vehicle. Ross and the others will protect you in my absence."

The thought of leaving his side sucked. She shook her head. He must have seen or sensed her panic because he added. "My men will protect you with their lives."

Tanya looked down. A thin summer dress and sandals, hardly correct attire for traipsing off into the forest. When they got back, she would be having a little chat with him about what she did and didn't wear. Panty-less with little summer dresses was fine for the castle, but she had to draw the line at outdoor adventure.

"I won't be long." He wrapped both his arms around her and squeezed. Tanya nodded.

Zane took the time to tuck her back into the vehicle before setting off with Lance and three others. The rest remained with her. Ross sat at the driver's seat with two men flanking each side of the vehicle. The rest spaced themselves at regular intervals in the clearing.

"Why are the other species doing this?"

"Power," was Ross's only response.

"What does wiping out the vampires gain them?"

Ross shrugged his big shoulders. "The various species have always been at war. This would be a simple way of gaining the upper hand."

She couldn't help but smile at his politically correct answer. "And by this, you mean my death."

"Or worse, young human." He turned to look at her, his expression grave. "You will need to speak to Zane about such things. I am not at liberty to discuss such matters."

"Why not?"

"Zane is your mate and king, besides, I like my tongue

where it is." Ross smiled.

"You're joking right?"

The smile turned into a wide grin and he shook his head. "Couple of days, a week maybe, it would grow back. Although we regenerate from most wounds, we still hurt."

Would Zane really do such a thing? She remembered how he'd had the dead elves put up on spikes in order to send a message. Unfortunately, the answer was a resounding yes. Zane was ruthless. He seemed cold hearted at times, yet there was a definite . . . vulnerability about him as well.

The sun dipped a bit more, skirting the horizon. Zane and the others had been gone for ten or so minutes. Ross and the rest of the men surrounding her were a bundle of fun. She sighed, crossed her arms on the seat in front of her, and rested her head against her arms. She lay like this for a few minutes.

Movement. On the other side of the fence. Their side. Tanya leaned forward trying to discern what it was. With the light fading fast, shadows could be playing tricks. Another definite shift in the foliage. There was something out there and none of the vampires seemed to have picked up on it. They seemed more focussed on her and the direct surrounds. At least half were facing in the direction Zane and Lance had left in. Tanya was about to say something when the shifting shadows took shape. It was a man astride a giant wolf. No, not a man, an elf. The elf had a bow at his back. The beast was a charcoal smudge of color that blended perfectly with the shadows. Now that she could see him more clearly, the hairs on her neck stood on end. She knew she should scream but it was if the air had evaporated from her lungs. The creature had massive jaws. It was muscled and fierce looking. It was five times the size of a normal wolf. Anyone with any knowledge of folklore would be able to tell that the creature was no normal wolf. It was just too darned big. She'd bet money that its eyes would have a human quality.

They stopped their approach. As much as she wanted to believe that it was her imagination, both species had their eyes trained on her. The wolf crouched and the elf pulled his bow free. Finally, she managed to drag a much needed breath into her lungs. Neither the beast nor the elf moved, with just their presence they seemed to be issuing a warning.

At long last, one of the vampires noticed the intruders and sounded the alarm. The beast did a one eighty. The elf absorbed the move with ease staying astride the powerful creature as it leapt back into the foliage, disappearing from sight in less than a second or two.

She realized that she was panting. One of her hands clutched at her neck. Tanya had never been this afraid before. She was alerted of movement by the sound of vehicle doors slamming as vampires piled into the waiting SUVs. A vampire shoved in next to Ross. The remaining males ducked into the other vehicles.

"Buckle up." It was the only warning she got as Ross pushed his foot flat on the gas as he followed the first vehicle as it took off in a spray of sand and gravel.

Tanya scrambled for her belt and clicked it in. "What about Zane?"

"He's a grown ass vamp," was the only answer she got from Ross.

"We can't just leave him."

He glanced back, his knuckles white on the steering wheel. "Just following orders my lady. Keep your head down."

Tanya had only just ducked her head below the line of the window when the SUV screeched to a halt. The belt dug into her. Adrenaline surged.

"Tanya!" Zane bellowed her name. The door opened. She

barely had a chance to turn her head, Zane ripped the belt, tearing it like paper between his fingers. "Tanya," he breathed out her name on a sigh of relief. His chest heaved against her ear as he yanked her into his arms after ducking in next to her. He buried his head into the crook of her neck and squeezed her hard. The vehicle took off but Zane held her in place.

She couldn't help but moan after a few beats. "You're cracking my ribs."

He eased his hold and she slid down, her head on his chest. "I thought I'd lost you. Ten lashes for all of you when we return."

Tanya gasped, "No it wasn't—"

"Yes, sire."

"Please don't do this, they—"

Zane cut her off, "You could've died. They fucked up. They will be punished."

"We will take twenty sire."

Zane's muscles relaxed somewhat even though his mouth was a thin white line. "I would make it fifty but I need you all on duty. Ten cuts."

"Thank you, my lord." Ross kept his eyes on the dirt track ahead. Dusk quickly turning inky black in the wilderness.

Tanya realized with a start that their lights weren't on even though they travelled at a neck breaking speed.

"What is it? Did you spot something?"

Zane glanced out each window in turn like he could actually see into the encroaching dark. "You're a vampire," she stated in awe.

Zane's brow creased.

"The whole no headlight thing was concerning but I forgot you can see in the dark."

Ross coughed, clearly trying to mask a laugh. Zane locked

his jaw and turned hard eyes on the rear-view mirror. Ross got the message and zipped it.

His arms tightened and he pulled her closer to him. "Next time you will remain at the castle," he sighed. "No, that won't do." A long pause. "I can't trust your safety with anyone else, you will stay at my side at all times."

She could feel Zane's heart beat beneath her ear. Fast and strong. Tanya felt she needed to remind herself that the big warrior was worried because his potential future heirs were at stake. This had nothing to do with any feelings he may have developed for her. This was a good thing though. Tanya might not choose Zane in the end and the thought of hurting him on top of the impact to his coven didn't sit right with her.

Damn, she took a few mental steps back. Since when had mating one of the vampire kings become a choice? When had her feelings changed? The thought of turning Zane down and taking Brant didn't seem as clear cut anymore. She buried her head deeper into his chest. Her head hurt thinking about it. Right now was not the time to make a decision so important though. Not after her near miss, and for a second time today. Using the ostrich head in sand approach was convenient right now and she'd use it damn it. It didn't help that Zane smelled so darned good.

They drove back much quicker than the journey earlier. Must have been traveling even faster than she realized. The castle was pretty jacked, with all the modern necessities. Three large garage doors opened in unison, they lead into an underground parking area housing at least twenty vehicles. The doors clanged shut behind them. Tanya tried to pull away but his arms tightened around her, holding her in place.

"Everybody out," he spoke softly.

"Yes, sire," Ross answered. "Move out!" He yelled to the

guards as they exited the SUVs.

"Secure the perimeter. Nobody enters unless instructed." Zane's deep voice so commanding that she felt the need to obey even though he hadn't directed the orders at her.

"What's going on?" *Shit.* Was she in trouble? Maybe he was upset with her too. Maybe he was about to dish out his version of ten lashings on her. *Like hell.* She'd done nothing that would warrant it.

As the door closed, leaving behind an eerie silence, his hands bracketed her waist. Zane pulled her up and against him.

"Straddle me," that same low commanding voice. "Do it now."

She did as he said. Her naked pussy hit hard cock encased in soft leather. His eyes were locked on hers. Dark, fathomless. They burned her up from the inside.

"I nearly lost you," a low growl that had her insides turning to jello. He leaned forward, his mouth a mere inch from hers, his eyes roamed her face landing on her mouth.

Do it.

Everything in her begged. Screamed. Thank God he obliged, slanting his lips across hers. The barest brush. *Firm, yielding, delicious.* The brief touch doing things to her that she never thought possible.

Brant.

She couldn't possibly . . . needed to tell him that this was a bad idea . . . the hands at her waist loosened their grip, they fisted the material at her hips instead. One sharp pull and her breasts sprang free from the tight elasticated confines.

His eyes darkened, narrowed slightly, willing her almost to defy him. She took a deep breath to do just that when his graze dropped to her chest.

Zane made a noise, something between a strangled moan

and a growl. For long seconds he just stared. His cock twitched against her core. When he moved, it was quick, her nipple was in his hot mouth before she had a chance to blink. Sucking softly, he used his tongue to swirl around her tight nub. Her clit throbbed. She ran her fingers across the close cropped hair on his scalp. The plan was to push him away. It really, really was.

Zane suckled her a second time, this time almost to the point of pain, raking his teeth across her sensitive flesh as he pulled away. Her fingers dug in, not wanting him to stop. Zane administered the same treatment to her other breast. When his thumb rubbed across her clit, she cried out in both surprise and pleasure.

"I don't think—"

His lips covered hers as he sank a finger into her pussy. Again the kiss lasted all of a second. His thumb stayed on her clit in a delicate slip and slide motion that had her arching her back. All of her well thought out reasons for not having sex with him left her. Sanity became a thing of the past as she palmed his impressive cock through his pants.

Zane hissed, inserting two fingers into her slick folds. She could feel how wet she had grown. Her sense of urgency rising to levels way into the red zone. He shifted her in his lap and removed his hand from her cleft. Zane yanked his pants open. What started as a moan of frustration ended in a groan of pleasure as his cock breached her opening.

His eyes locked with hers. "You are mine," a low growl as he thrust into her from below. Taking her to the hilt in one easy motion that left her panting with both ecstasy and pain as her body fought to accommodate his size.

"Mine," he growled again as he plunged back into her. His eyes burned with hunger as he continued to plough into her.

His hands solidly on her hips as he kept her firmly in place while he fucked her with savage determination. She screamed as each thrust hit her sweet spot. The muscles in his neck stood on end and his mouth was a tight line. Her orgasm hit seconds later, causing her eyes to pretty much roll back in her skull with the intenseness of the sensations that racked through her body. Intensified by the fact that he kept up the tireless thrusting and the brutal pace. Her back bowed and her head fell back as a second even more powerful wave took her. This time he roared as jets of heat filled her.

When he finally slowed, she sagged against him, both of them were breathing heavily. "I'm not letting you go back." Zane's chest heaved.

Part of her wanted to breathe out a sigh of relief as the choice had been taken from her, but a bigger part forced her to pull away from him. Brant would be waiting for her. Tanya's next thought was how angry and hurt he would be at her indiscretion.

"What about Brant?"

His lips pulled back in a silent snarl at the mention of his birth enemy. "After today, it is safe to say that we are at war." His hands squeezed her waist. It wasn't lost on her that his still mostly erect shaft was still inside her. "Brant cannot protect you. The continuity of our race is at stake."

A loud crack sounded, followed by another and another. Between the harsh noises . . . eerie silence. Zane's punishment was being carried out. At the next loud crack of the whip she started, pulling in a deep anxious breath. Zane pulled her closer. "It's not your fault."

Tanya shut her eyes trying to keep the tears inside. It *was* all her fault. Whichever way she turned, it could only end in disaster.

Part 3

Love & War

Chapter ONE

XAVIER PAUSED AS HE leaned forward to open the door to the SUV. His nostrils flared right before his whole body tightened. By now she knew vampires well enough to know that he could scent Zane on her. He would know that they had recently had sex even though she had showered before leaving.

The big vampire shook his head slowly as he opened the door.

Tanya slid in praying that she wouldn't have to explain herself to Brant's head guard. To Brant's brother. It was bad enough that she'd soon have to face Brant. She was so screwed. She buckled up, letting her face fall into her hands as they pulled away. Another vampire sat in the seat next to Xavier. There were two vehicles ahead of them and another three behind them.

"You do know that I've been assigned to your wellbeing?" Xavier kept his eyes on the dirt track as he negotiated the trail.

"Yes," she paused trying not to sigh. "I know."

"You're making it difficult to keep you safe. You do realize that don't you?" his eyes never left the road as he spoke.

"How is it my fault that the elves and the wolves are after

me?" *What a complete jerk.*

Xavier gave a humourless chuckle. "It's not the other species that I'm afraid of."

They turned up a sharp, twisting incline. Xavier handled the vehicle with practiced ease. Tanya waited for a few beats once the track straightened but much to her frustration, Xavier didn't elaborate further.

"Is there another enemy I'm not aware of?"

Another humourless chuckle. "You have no idea. Really?" He hauled the vehicle sharply to the left, more sharply than what was required. The seatbelt tightened across her chest and she was yanked to the side.

"You rutted with my brother's birth enemy."

Tanya cringed. To make matters worse Xavier sniffed at the air. "From the scent of your essence I would say he drank from you too."

She gasped. "You can tell all that from the way I smell."

"What? Had you hoped to keep it a secret?"

"No." Her cheeks heated. "I would never lie about something as important as that. Brant will understand. He would never hurt me."

Xavier sighed heavily. "I've never seen my brother besotted before. He talked about you the entire time you were gone. He missed you damn it." Xavier hit the wheel. The manor house loomed ahead. "He has started work on your little store. Upgrades to the book section and a whole coffee shop. I realize that Zane invoked Mate's Lore, but I had hoped you would've had some sense of loyalty."

She gasped using her hand to stifle the sound. What had she done? Brant had trusted her. A mere twenty-four hours away from him and she'd fucked another man. Not just any other man, but his enemy.

"Brant wouldn't hurt me," she repeated because what Xavier was implying was too crazy for words. He might never forgive her but he would never hurt her. No way.

"Not on purpose but when he gets a nose full of Zane," Xavier shook his head. "You reek of him." They pulled up to the manor house and Xavier shut off the engine, his gaze still facing ahead. "He might just lose his mind. He won't know what he's doing. I will do my best to keep you safe." He turned dark eyes on her and she shivered. Just when she was sure he must hate her, his eyes softened. "I know it's not really your fault. I'm thankful I haven't had the urge to mate. I'll never go down that road if I can help it."

· ⊂*⊃ ·

Brant could scent Tanya on his birth enemy. It made him want to gouge Zane's eyes from his skull. Made him want to tear off his arms and beat him with them but that would only worsen the situation. Zane was here to discuss their female's safety. *His* female's safety. Just because he scented Tanya didn't mean they had . . . he mentally shook his head. It wasn't the right time for that train of thought and with Tanya on the way he would soon have his answers. It wasn't fair of him to expect her fidelity. At least she was safe, that was what was most important.

Brant paced across the Persian rug at the foot of his desk. His office was spacious with dark mahogany. A space he always enjoyed. Most likely because it was his and his alone. A sanctuary he could go to if he needed to think, work, plan. It irked him that Zane was in his space but it was the best place for a private conversation. "You're sure the two species are working together." He glanced at Zane who stood with his arms folded across his chest.

"My men saw the elf king astride the alpha. They have had more than one opportunity to kill the female . . ."

Brant couldn't help it, he snarled at the thought of losing Tanya and snarled at the vampire that would've been responsible for her death.

Zane unclasped his arms, his hands falling into tight fists. It wasn't lost on Brant how the vampire king had widened his stance. "I am here because I want to keep her safe. The female's wellbeing is of just as much importance to me as it is to you."

"You want heirs."

"As do you."

"I want more than just offspring. I want to share my life. I want her to be happy." Brant felt frustration rise within. Zane was not capable of any type of emotion let alone love. He would never be able to give Tanya what she needed, what she deserved.

"Write a god damned love song. We're here to discuss her safety or there will be no heirs for either of us."

Brant grit his teeth to try and stop himself from retorting. The other vampire was right, but he didn't have to like it.

"The alpha still needs a mate. I think that he plans on taking her for himself."

Brant took in a deep breath letting it out slowly. The thought of a beast laying a single claw on Tanya made his blood sizzle, his veins burn. His skin grew tight. "Destroy our people and take our queen? He can't fucking have her."

"I feel the same. We are very much on the back foot. Neither of us can mate with her until the new moon. Nine whole days. The alpha doesn't have that problem."

"Why did you invoke Mate's Lore in the first place?" Brant fisted Zane's shirt grinding his teeth so hard he was sure they would crack.

"Get your hands off me," a low growl.

Brant held on for a second longer. "If it weren't for Tanya, I'd take your head."

"You would try."

That's where Zane was wrong, it wouldn't be easy but he would win in the end. Brant had a reputation of being the 'just' king, the 'honorable' leader, he was also greatly underestimated which suited him just fine. "You should have left us alone. Tanya and I would've been mated. The future of our people guaranteed."

"What? Your little coven against two species? I think not."

Zane was right. The elves and the wolves would've attacked regardless of whether Tanya had mated one of them or not. They saw an opportunity and had taken it. He would do anything to ensure that Tanya did not become collateral damage.

"Just for the record, I wanted the female from the start." Zane locked his jaw for a second, looking to the left of Brant. He stuffed his hands into his pockets. Zane turned his gaze back on Brant.

He wasn't sure he wanted to hear what Zane had to say.

"I didn't want a repeat of what happened to our fathers. I knew you had your sights set on the female so I chose another."

His heart stopped beating for a second even though blood rushed in his ears. Zane had wanted Tanya from the start.

"It's why I chose the way I did. I wanted to avoid another war." Zane's eyes narrowed.

"Bull fucking shit."

"Listen up asshole, I didn't have to explain this to you but you asked why I invoked Mate's Lore and so I'm telling you. I wanted the human from the start. I should have fought you for her then."

"The only reason you invoked the lore is because you killed your human."

Zane took a step towards Brant, his whole body had tightened like a coiled spring. Brant secretly hoped Zane would come at him. The longer he spent in the same room as the bastard, the more he wanted to feel his bones crack beneath his fists.

"Someone is spreading untruths about me. The human took her own life. It had nothing to do with anything I did or didn't do."

"It seems human females are in a habit of offing themselves on your side of the fence. Can't say I blame them."

It was a low blow with the expected results except Zane moved quicker than he anticipated and managed to plant him straight in the jaw. Thankfully the blow wasn't direct as he was moving away, so although it hurt like a bitch, his jaw remained intact. Brant kneed his enemy in the stomach enjoying the grunt Zane made and the way he hunched over for a split second.

Tanya took in the familiar decadent décor. Her mind going at a thousand miles a minutes. So much for not letting her out of his sight ever again. After they had fucked, Zane took her back to his tower. After a light supper she had fallen asleep, exhausted from the day's events only to have woken alone in his bed. She hated the disappointment. Hated that she felt it in the first place. Zane hadn't so much as said goodbye to her when she'd left. Tanya had pretty much thrown away her future with Brant and for what, a roll in the hay with one times dickhead.

"Are you okay?" Stephany smiled at her, concern in her

eyes. They had said their hellos. Tanya had noticed how the blond vamp's nostrils had flared just before they embraced. Everyone in this whole damned coven would know her and Zane had slept together.

"Do you want to talk about it?" Stephany asked as they made their way into the living room. "I take it you got along well with Zane?" The blonde gave her a mischievous smile. Tanya realized that she'd missed her easy companionship.

"Don't joke, Brant is going to go nuts when he finds out. Where is he anyway?"

"It's Mate's Lore, he may not like it but he will need to deal. He's just in a meeting, he'll be out . . ."

Confusion set in. What did Mate's Lore have to do with her indiscretion? There was a crash as something toppled over followed by a loud grunt. A heavy bashing noise and another muffled crash.

"Nothing to be concerned with." Stephany had plastered a fake smile onto her face.

"Who's Brant meeting with?" Panic rose in her. Zane hadn't been there to say good bye and Brant wasn't there to greet her. It didn't take a rocket scientist to know where the kings were and that they weren't getting along.

"Stay out of it human." Xavier tried to take a hold of her arm, but Stephany swatted his hand out of the way.

"Leave her alone. They need to sort this out and like it or not she's involved."

"I have been assigned to keep her in one piece. Getting between the kings is no place for a puny human."

"Go." Stephany blocked Xavier. Tanya rushed in the direction of the noises. The grunts and thuds growing louder as she made her way to a large oval door. She pushed down the wrought iron handle and opened it. Brant and Zane had each other in a lock. Brant pushed Zane and his back collided with the wall. A picture frame crashed as it hit the ground.

"Stop!" She knew she should be afraid, but watching the two of them kill each other was not how this was going to end. She moved in as close as she dared.

"You shouldn't be around humans," Brant growled as Zane pushed back until the back of Brant's legs connected with a large desk in the center of the room.

"Like it or not. She's just as much mine as she is yours." Zane snarled, he head butted Brant with a sickening crunch.

"No!" She screamed not giving a damn if they hurt her. She inserted herself between them, her back against Brant. "Stop this." Zane had a bloody gash in his forehead.

The room reeked of blood, sweat and testosterone. Heavy breathing turned to loud sniffing. "You fucked him."

Her eyes were locked with Zane's, whose irises turned dark and stormy.

"Oh shit," said Zane.

"You rutted with my female." Brant's body turned to stone behind her. He lunged for Zane knocking Tanya to the side as he did. She fell to her knees landing hard. Thankfully she was wearing jeans or her knees would be a mess. She scrambled further out of the way as Brant took a second swing at Zane's head. Brant had lost his mind and it was all her fault. *Why couldn't she have kept her panties on?*

Zane tackled Brant knocking him to the ground and flat on his back. "It's Mate's Lore." He punched Brant twice using his arms and body to hold him down. "We are required to rut. You know that."

"I know," Brant growled. "Don't have to like it though. I can't stand your scent on her. It's making me . . ." He snarled, his eyes were glowing. "I can't take it."

"Calm down. You need to put your own scent on her."

It seemed that Brant was allowing himself to be restrained by Zane. He had to be since they were pretty evenly matched, or they had been when she had first walked in the room.

Zane looked her way. "Take your clothes off."

"What? No—"

"He needs to rut with you, needs his scent on you to calm down." Zane swallowed hard. Sweat beaded on his forehead and his biceps bulged with the exertion of keeping Brant restrained.

Brant bucked underneath him managing to pull an arm free. He fisted Zane's shirt pulling him almost nose to nose. "Get the fuck out."

"Like hell." Zane shoved Brant back down. "You might hurt her."

"I would never—"

"Do you think I want to watch you fuck her?" His face was contorted in rage. "I will stay. Female"—Zane kept his eyes on Brant's—"take your clothes off right now."

Shit. *This wasn't happening.*

"Do it," Brant's voice was tense.

Shit. *This was happening.* Had everyone in the room lost their minds?

"I can't possibly. You can't expect me to . . ."

Xavier burst in through the partially opened door followed by Stephany and Lance.

"Get out," Zane growled.

"You heard him," Brant's voice held that same level of authority.

"But—" Xavier started to argue.

"Out!" Both kings said simultaneously. Xavier stopped mid-sentence. Lance dropped his eyes and nodded tersely.

Stephany had the audacity to smile. She freaking looked at each of the kings and then at Tanya, a wide grin appearing on her face. The bitch. Lance put a hand to her back as he ushered her out of the room. Was it her imagination or did Stephany stiffen under his touch? There was no time to think on it because both kings turned to look at her as the door closed.

"I'm so sorry, Tanya. Please understand." Brant panted like it was difficult for him to speak normally. "I need you to take your clothes off and you need to do it right now." Brant was apologizing to her when she was the one that had caused all of this in the first place. She shook her head preparing to argue.

"He would never forgive himself if he accidentally hurt you. He's not in full control and needs to get his own scent on you so that he can calm down enough to think rationally." As if in answer, Brant growled low and deep. Not the kind of growl that aroused, but rather the kind that caused fear to spike inside her. "Please, sweetness. I'll talk you through it. Neither of us wants to see you hurt." Zane kept his eyes on her.

"I'm sorry, Cenwein . . ." Brant said between clenched teeth. "Zane's right. You need to do as he says."

"I'm right . . . where is a recorder when you need one?"

"Fuck you." Brant broke a hand free and punched Zane, who laughed. Brant's fist connected with Zane's nose in a spray of blood that quickly subsided.

"Blood. I like the look on you." Brant pulled his fist back to punch Zane again but the other vamp was too quick and blocked the blow pushing Brant back down with a hand to the chest.

"Try to stay calm. I won't bait you again."

"My need to kill you is beginning to override my need to remove your scent from my female." Brant spat the words at Zane, his big body growing tenser by the second.

"Wait. Please don't kill each other. Stop!" The thought of the two warriors coming to blows and possibly injuring each other, or worse, had her forgetting all about her modesty. She pulled off her shoes and unzipped her jeans, which she shoved down her hips. After a moment's hesitation, *this wasn't happening,* she pulled down her panties. The ones that she'd painstakingly dried the day before. Her cheeks heated as both vampires stared her way.

"Okay, maybe rutting is a better idea." Brant gave a low growl this time laced with arousal. Normally the sound would leave her wet and aching but not with two sets of eyes staring at her. God this was so embarrassing. Brant's eyes were hooded with arousal, they turned hard and terrifying. "Your scent on her is stronger now that she's naked." He turned hard eyes on Zane.

"Sweetness, get your delectable ass over here."

Brant snarled.

"I'm going to sit behind him, I'll hold his arms. You straddle him as soon as I'm off. The sooner his cock is inside you the better."

"I can't believe you just said that to me. This is so fucked up." She went down on her haunches next to them.

"Don't over think this, sweetness." Zane cupped her cheek for a second.

"Take your hands off her," Brant growled. "I'll make it up to you, Cenwein." He sounded pained.

"Ready?" Zane winked at her. "You can do this."

She nodded once, not trusting her voice. As soon as Zane moved, she took his place. The moment her pussy touched Brant's clothed cock, he went from semi to fully erect.

"I need you, Tanya," Brant whispered. "You know I would never hurt you." A complete contradiction since Zane held both of Brant's arms to the ground above his head.

"Take him, sweetness," Zane coaxed.

Tanya licked her lips, fumbling with the catches on Brant's suit pants. Brant hissed as his cock sprang free. She positioned herself over him, his big head at her entrance. She struggled to get even the tip of him inside her.

A thumb brushed up against her clit. "Close your eyes." It was Zane. He held Brant's arms with one hand. Brant was clearly allowing himself to be restrained at this point.

Brant snarled, his eyes were glowing so bright that she was sure they'd be able to light up a dark room. "Get your filthy hands off her."

"She's not ready for you. You do want her to have pleasure too. You don't want to hurt her. I don't trust you enough to let you go."

Brant cursed. "Do it." He locked his jaw as Zane's thumb moved over her clit in a lazy circle before dipping into her once. She tried not to react, not when both men were watching her so intently.

"Close your eyes," Zane's deep, husky voice had her pulse quickening. She did as he said. It might be easier if she didn't have to see them. Zane's finger was slipping and sliding over her clit. Her pussy clenched, against all odds, she could feel herself growing wet. He pushed two fingers inside her. She groaned, unable to stop the building need that clawed at her. Brant growled. A vibrating rumble of arousal. Zane removed his fingers only to start back on her tight nub. So soft, she rolled her pelvis to try and grind up against him. Needing more. Instead of fingers, her clit met with hard cock. Tanya ground herself against Brant. Ground herself against his velvet clad steel.

"That's it, sweetness," Zane's voice was tight. Was he just

as aroused? She kept her eyes shut. Didn't want to break the moment. She burned with the need to come, she rubbed herself harder against Brant's shaft. He groaned.

"Take him, sweetness."

She positioned him at her entrance and this time he slipped in easily. Tanya eased down on his hard length panting as he slowly filled her. Loving how she stretched to accommodate him.

Brant pushed up from below. She cried out with the pure ecstasy as he fully sheathed himself in her. She swallowed hard rocking her hips, keeping him deep. Loving how he felt against her.

Tanya eased up and pushed back down. Brant groaned.

"That's it, sweetness," Zane's deep voice rolled over her.

Up and down, she leaned forward ever so slightly until she found that angle that hit her just right. She whimpered as she slid back down on him.

"Faster," Brant urged her. "You feel so good."

Tanya opened her eyes looking down at Brant. His lashes were at half-mast. She did as he asked upping the tempo while still ensuring that she kept him deep and hard. She mewled each time she slid back onto him. Brant thrust from below keeping the rhythm she had set.

"So good." His eyes were still glowing. "Wish I could flip you over and fuck you hard."

She gasped at both his crude words and because he had chosen that moment to thrust into her with added ferocity. Tanya was appalled to find she enjoyed the dirty talk. Brant tensed underneath her, fighting to free his hands. He managed to break one free, which he used to yank her sweater tearing it half way up her front.

Zane chuckled as he secured Brant's hands once again.

Although she wasn't moving, Brant continued to thrust into her, the deep friction seemed to catch all her nerve endings. She moaned.

"Looks like someone wants a look at those stunning tits. Can't say I blame him."

"Watch your filthy mouth." Brant grit out through clenched teeth while keeping up his assault from below.

Tanya lifted her gaze, catching Zane's heated look. *What difference did it make?* She pulled her sweater over her head and unhooked her bra. Zane's eyes almost bugged out of his skull and Brant made the sound a wounded animal would make.

"Gods how I want to touch you." Brant was no longer moving. Both vampires stared like they'd never seen a naked woman before.

"So god damned sexy." Zane's eyes narrowed on hers then moved between her chest and her face.

"Close your fucking eyes!" Brant sounded pissed. He looked even angrier.

"Shut it. You're the one who gets to fuck her. Any more lip and I'll knock you out and finish this myself."

Brant fought against the restraint. Tanya needed a diversion so she sat back more firmly onto his cock. Up . . . down . . . up . . . down. Harder and faster with every bounce. She concentrated on her own pleasure, needing an orgasm more than her next breath. The incredible slip and slide of his cock taking her closer and closer with every sweet thrust.

"That's it, sweetness. Just a little more."

Brant made a noise of agreement. She cried out as a finger brushed against her clit. Zane was holding Brant with one hand while he leaned forward and stroked her clit with the other. His face was taut with desire.

Brant growled something between pleasure and a warning.

"Oh yes," she cried. Her orgasm building as his finger picked up momentum over her tightening nub. When Zane pinched her clit between two fingers while Brant fucked her harder from below, it was as if she had died and gone to heaven. Just the thought of both men touching her, bringing her to completion, was enough to keep her screaming as waves of pleasure rushed through her. She barely registered Brant jerking beneath her as he found his own release.

Warm arms bracketed her, hot kisses were planted on her cheeks and mouth. Tanya opened her eyes to Brant's warm, dark chocolate stare. "I'm sorry I put you through that."

"It's okay." How the hell did she confess that although afraid at first, it had been the most erotic moment of her life? How even now she wanted a redo. This time she could sit on Zane's cock while Brant squeezed and tweaked her nipples.

Zane.

She looked over Brant's shoulder. The big vampire stood behind them. Shit, he looked angry. Eyes dark, body tense, brooding expression. His gaze softened as she caught his eye.

"That was . . . fun. Left me with one hell of a hard on . . . but fun none the less."

Brant growled. "You sick bastard."

Zane sort of smiled. "You would have one too if our roles were reversed and you can't tell me you've never shared before."

"Tanya is different and you know it."

Shit, she should've known that vampires would be into this sort of ménage shit. All that free, natural mumbo jumbo. In the end she'd loved what had just gone down just as much as they had, but the thought of sharing these men in return made her green-eyed-bug-monster pop out.

"As much as I would love to fist my cock during round

number two, better yet, I could . . ."

"Don't say it." Brant held up his hand.

Zane folded his arms. "You're right because, my hard-on aside, I believe we have a conversation to finish."

Brant lifted her off him. Her blood heated as Zane let his eyes slid down the entire length of her stopping in all the naughty places. His leather pants bulged at his crotch. Part of her wanted to giggle while the other part wanted to embrace her feminine side. No contest, she thrust her chest out loving how his lashes practically fused. His chest expanded with a deep breath. Zane shook his head in disbelief. "You surprise me female. You would love to ride my cock right now wouldn't you?"

She gasped. "I so would not." There wasn't much venom in her voice and his answering grin said it all. Tanya tugged on her panties, feeling her cheeks heat under his gaze. She concentrated on dressing while ignoring the vampires.

It scared her how Zane seemed to be able to read her like a book. How could she deny it with any credibility when he spoke the truth? Tanya pulled her jeans over her hips and did up the zip and button. Her bra went on next, she adjusted the twins into the cups. Zane groaned and repositioned himself in his pants. When she looked up, both men were staring at her.

"Have you never seen a woman dress before?"

"I've never been turned on so much by the act before. Then again I'd have normally taken care of this by now." Zane grabbed his hard crotch.

Brant growled. "You sound like a caveman."

"What can I say? This female brings out the animal in me." Zane threw her a half smile. He was such a jerk. Even knowing this, why did she want him so damned much?

"She is mine. If you so much as lay a finger on her I will—"

"Yeah. Yeah." Zane held up his hand. "In less than twenty three hours though, she will belong to me again. Know that I will rut with her . . ."

Brant snarled and took an aggressive step towards Zane. This was quickly turning into another brawl. So far it seemed that Zane had a handle where Brant was liable to lose it at any moment. Tanya put on her sweater, wincing as she took in the damage. It was her expensive cashmere sweater. Becky had bought it for her birthday. Tanya didn't own very many nice things and would never be able to replace it.

Brant took another small step towards Zane. His hands were fisted at his sides. She had to do something. Tanya put a tentative hand on Brant's broad back. He jerked at her touch. It was possible, even after he had taken her, that he didn't really want her anymore. Not as someone to share his life with at any rate.

Zane choked out a humourless laugh. "It's best you come to terms with it. Expect it after my next time with her. We will rut. The female will enjoy my touch. We are highly compatible."

Brant growled a low menacing sound.

"Calm down. From what I have seen, she enjoys your touch also. Right now we need to decide how best to protect her and since she is both of ours for the next nine days, we need to decide what is best together."

Chapter TWO

HER HAND WAS STILL on his back. A warm weight that helped center him. It had been a very long time since he had felt this out of control. He almost felt like a teenager again. Not the king he was. The strong methodical leader. Coming inside her should've had him thinking rationally and although it helped, it wasn't nearly enough. He needed to drink from her. The need was not physical. After taking from her two days ago it would be a few more days before his body would require him to partake again. One small mouthful would do it. More than just blood, he needed to be close to her. Needed to make love to her, to worship her body. Eradicate Zane from her mind. Hell, from both their minds.

Brant hated himself for what he'd put Tanya through. She was a sweet, delicate human, not used to the ways of his people. It was perfectly acceptable for vampires to share. It even happened on occasion that two males would mate with one female. The thought of Zane watching Tanya ride him, taking her pleasure from him had added to his own enjoyment. Let the bastard see his female take what she needed from him. It made his blood boil when Zane had laid his hands on her though. So much so that he had to turn away the first time. The only reassurance he had was that he had his cock buried in her and not the other way around.

"Our female is in danger," Zane said. Brant looked back at the big bastard. The thing he needed most of all was the arrogant king gone. Brant took a deep breath, he took a step back feeling his female behind him. Her reassuring heat at his back.

"What do you suggest?" Brant asked. "You sound like you already have a plan." The bastard would have everything mapped out. Brant knew without a doubt it would be self-serving because just as the other species had taken advantage, so would Zane.

"Your little manor house is very beautiful. I hear you used the best architects and designers and it's turned into quite the creation."

"Out with it." Any more of this and Brant was going to flatten his nose.

"It was never built with defense in mind though. Quite frankly it's an attacking enemy's wet dream."

"It also has passages within the walls. A bunker below my suite with two exits. One in Freelax Forest and another at the statue a hundred feet before the lake."

Zane cocked his head. "You used local builders, so all of what you have just said could become public knowledge with the right incentive."

"I used professionals who would not be easily swayed. I paid them royally for their silence." His irritation grew.

"The kind of persuasion I'm talking about would not need to include money. There are many ways to empty a vein. A well placed dagger and they would sing like birds."

"What are you proposing?"

"You could take one of the wings at the castle during your time with the female. That way she would remain safe, unless of course you are able to move your coven back into Starwood."

Brant flinched at the mention of the castle he had abandoned so many years ago. His mind recalled the amount of blood that had been spilled inside its walls. To him, it represented the long arduous war. Terrible times. Even if he wanted to go back, he couldn't. Its walls had been breached and never repaired once the war ended. The castle wasn't liveable. Zane already knew this. He bit down on his tongue until he tasted blood. He so wanted to tell the bastard what he could do with himself.

"I will take care of my female. I do not need you or your castle to defend her."

Zane narrowed his eyes. "I disagree. She is vulnerable. My offer is perfectly acceptable. I will not interfere when it is your time with her."

Yeah right, next he'd tell Brant that flames would not scorch. Zane would like nothing more than to have Tanya under his roof permanently. The arrogant bastard would do everything in his power to make it difficult for Brant. Would stack the chips firmly against him.

Bottom line, he couldn't trust Zane. Tanya was in danger but he doubted it was as bad as what the other vampire was making it out to be. Even if it was, Brant could protect his female. She would be taken over his dead body.

"I said I can protect her and I meant it. She stays here with me in her rightful place as queen of this coven."

Zane growled. It felt good to see him on the back foot. The arrogant shmuck ground his teeth narrowing his eyes even further. "Think carefully because if something were to happen to her I would kill you with my bare hands." He lifted his arms and splayed his fingers till they resembled claws. *So freaking dramatic.*

"No need since I would die defending her. I will take care of what is mine."

The hand at his back clutched his shirt. "Stop this. I've had enough of listening to you two as if I'm not even in the room. To make matters worse, you're treating me like some possession." She moved in next to them. "I am a person with my own mind damn it."

"Tanya is right." Brant slid his hand onto the small of her back. "She should have a say."

Zane crossed his arms over his chest and glowered down at Tanya. "You would be safer with me human."

Her whole demeanour changed, her succulent lips went into full pout mode, her hands went to her hips and her chin tilted up. "Nothing happened while I was at the manor house before. I'm sure I'm quite safe. Brant will take care of me." She moved in next to him and he had the ridiculous urge to fist pump the air. A small victory but one that moved towards making Tanya his queen and he'd take it.

Zane kept his arms folded. Although he didn't move a muscle, his whole body seemed to bristle. "You cannot make a decision without the full facts."

"Don't go there Zane. We don't even know if our concerns are warranted." Brant pulled Tanya in closer.

"The wolf alpha is looking for a mate. Chances are good he has set his sights on you."

Zane was an even bigger bastard than he thought.

Tanya gasped. Her eyes welled with tears. "But. . . . no, he couldn't. Surely he wouldn't."

Brant willed for Zane to shut the fuck up but the dickhead

carried on. "He can and he will. What better way to not only prevent future vampire heirs from being born but also to fuck with us at the same time? It would cause chaos. Internal war would be a given. Our species would become easy pickings."

"It's not going to happen because Brant will protect me," Tanya sniffed. She wiped away a tear.

Zane shook his head and scrubbed a hand over his scalp. "You are wrong female. The alpha will take you if he gets even the smallest chance. He'll mate you. Do you want to be fucked by a beast?"

Tanya sobbed and his last bit of resolve evaporated. Brant punched Zane. A beautiful, truly satisfying crunching sound filled his ears. He felt bone crush under his fist. Zane hesitated only for a split second, then he chopped at his throat using the side of his hand. Brant had been expecting retaliation, so he stepped back avoiding most of the force. It still hurt though and he struggled to draw breath. Brant threw a solid right aiming for Zane's nose. Nothing like a double whammy to end a fight. Zane blocked. Tanya screamed for them to stop but he ignored her since she was far enough away not to be in immediate danger. Their vampire guard spilled in and pulled them apart. It took three men to pull him away from the bastard. He took satisfaction in the amount of blood that gushed from Zane's nose.

"You are wrong." Zane fought against the vampires that held him, his face twisted in rage. "If she is taken, I swear to God. I swear to God . . ." He repeated as they wrestled him to the door. "I'll kill you!" He shouted as they pulled him from the room. "You will fucking die!" he screamed from down the hall.

Brant pulled Tanya into his arms. She shook as tears cascaded down her cheeks.

"It's going to be okay." He rubbed her back trying to still the shaking of her shoulders as she sobbed.

"Did he mean it?" Tanya finally lifted her tear soaked face. "He couldn't kill me if he tried."

A sad sounding giggle ended on a hiccup. "No. Did he mean it about the alpha coming for me?"

Brant pulled in a deep breath. "Zane was only speculating, but it is possible."

"Oh God." She covered her mouth with her hand. "Just when I thought it couldn't get any worse." She buried her face into his chest. Her little hands fisted the shirt at his back. Brant needed to protect his human at all costs.

"I'm so sorry." She wiped her nose with the back of her hand. He took a crisp, folded hanky from his pocket, it was embroidered in gold with his family crest.

"Hey." He cupped her chin once she finished wiping her nose. She refused to meet his gaze. "What do you have to be sorry about?"

"I had sex with Zane." Tanya ended the sentence on a sob. Fresh tears ran down her cheeks. Brant had to work to stop himself from breaking something just to make himself feel better. Seeing her like this destroyed him.

He sighed using the pad of his thumb to wipe away the tears. "I should apologize. I didn't explain Mate's Lore to you properly. The truth is, I couldn't stand the thought of Zane . . . touching you. I had every reason to believe that he had killed his chosen and was afraid of losing you. I guess I also have a possessive streak a mile long . . . when it comes to you that is."

She shook her head. "No, I shouldn't have had sex with him. It's not right . . ."

"Cenwein"—he brushed a wayward strand from her face—"it's perfectly normal and perfectly acceptable. We are to share you until the new moon. That means in every way." He cupped her chin forcing her to look at him. Her big fearful eyes almost brought him to his knees.

". . . . But you almost went crazy when you smelled him on me."

"I had selfishly hoped that you would rebuff Zane. I was wrong to have wanted it. You have nothing to be guilty about. I'm a weak asshole. I'm so sorry I made you feel this way. I'm even sorrier that I couldn't keep it together when I scented Zane on you." The thought of the arrogant bastard touching his female rubbed him the wrong way. He had hoped that he would have been able to deal with being confronted with the inevitable, but he had been wrong. Even now, her underlying scent was still intermingled with that of Zane's.

He needed to put some distance between them because the need to take her again rode him hard. More than just that, he wanted to mark her body with his semen like an animal. To drink from her and to request that she do the same from him. His little human was not ready for such a big step though. He was also still a little concerned that he might hurt her. Even though he had told her that he wouldn't, he knew he may accidentally do just that. He still didn't fully trust himself.

"You're apologizing to me. This whole situation isn't right." She shook her head.

"We have both chosen you and it is normal that you feel attracted to both of us. Does he treat you well? Does he care about your . . . needs?" Brant forced himself to relax his hold on her. Tanya needed to come first in everything. He had made her feel this way and he would be damned if he allowed her to have any more discomfort because he was a selfish idiot.

"Oh my God. Are you asking me if he . . ."

"Yes. Does he treat you right both in and out of bed? I need to know."

Tanya smiled as she recalled her time with Zane. Brant was sure she didn't even know she was doing it. It made his chest tighten.

"He's a big, fat jerk. The man is unbelievably bossy. Zane can be hard, he is ruthless."

Brant couldn't help himself, he growled. Tanya put her hand on his wrist. "But there is a softer side to him. He has feelings and emotions and he does care, even if he pretends that he doesn't."

Brant touched the fresh marks on her neck and she winced even though there would be no pain. "I know he drank from you and that he rutted with you." Her lashes fluttered as her eyes looked down.

The thought almost sent him into a rage but he put a sharp rein on his emotions. Tanya came first. "I told you that you have nothing to be ashamed about, Cenwein. Now tell me, Zane seems to . . . care about your wellbeing. Has he been good to you and put your needs first?"

Chapter THREE

How could she tell Brant that the sex had been explosive, that they had taken what they needed from each other like animals? Rutting was the right word to describe their coming together.

"Yes," she whispered.

"Good." He strode away from her towards the door. "I need to meet with my guard. We must prepare . . ." He paused at her sharp intake of breath. His eyes softened. "As a precaution only. I would rather that we be over prepared than be taken by surprise."

She nodded trying not to shudder as she recalled how the wolf had looked at her. At the time she had thought that he was sizing her up to make a meal out of her. After hearing Zane's views, maybe he was looking at her with a different kind of hunger. Tanya tucked the thought firmly into the back of her mind. It wouldn't help if she worried about something she could do nothing about, she trusted Brant to keep her safe.

"I have doubled the guard within the manor walls and have men doing perimeter patrols. You can spend some time with Stephany. Xavier must accompany you though." Brant pulled a sheathed knife from a drawer in the large mahogany desk. It was small. With one easy motion he slid the blade clear. It looked sharp. "A silver dagger, the hilt is made from bone. Silver is deadly to non-humans. Make sure that you go for the throat." Brant's words made her feel a little faint, but after her ordeals the previous day she made sure that she took note. "It may be necessary to stab into the abdomen to bring down the enemy first. The throat is where you need to aim if you are forced to kill though. Another kill zone, but I would avoid this one, is the heart. It can be difficult to get to because of the ribs. You would need to stab from below angling your blade like this." He demonstrated bringing the knife up in an arc. "The blade is small but do not be fooled, it is capable of doing major damage. I need you to promise me that you will keep it close at all times and that you will use it if need be."

She nodded as she took the knife from him. Brant covered her hand with his much bigger one. "Do not hesitate. If you are in danger, use the blade." He released her.

They walked side by side to the main living area. Stephany's face lit up as they approached. Brant kissed her forehead and headed to the waiting men at the entrance.

The moment the men left the manor house, at least all but Xavier and York, Stephany turned to her, her cobalt eyes blazing. "Out with it. Don't leave out one single detail."

There were just too many emotions coursing through her, she didn't know how she felt about everything that had taken place. Although Tanya needed to confide in someone, she just couldn't right this second. "I really need a shower."

At first Stephany looked disappointed, then she smiled broadly "And you must be hungry?"

She had already eaten but she nodded anyway. "Yeah, I am." Anything to buy a bit of time alone.

Stephany walked with her. When she tried to enter the suite that had been allocated to her, Stephany gestured towards the door that lead to Brant's bedroom. "Your things have been moved. The King's orders." They walked in, Tanya deposited her bag on the bed.

"Make yourself at home, I'll be back in a little while with something to eat." The female vampire smiled at Tanya as she closed the door behind her.

She walked further into the room. Plush carpet beneath her feet, a crystal chandelier hung from the high ceiling above the king sized bed, a gold guild mirror took residence on the far wall. The room was certainly fit for a king. Tanya removed her tattered sweater, and the rest of her clothes trying not to recall how they got that way. She made for the bathroom.

After a hot shower, she opened the big dressers that lined one side of the suite. The first two were filled with men's clothes. *Brant's things.* The next two were full of women's clothes. *Hers.* The ones Stephany had bought for her, except there seemed to be more now.

What she really felt like wearing at the moment was her old worn out Harley Davidson T-shirt and sweatpants, but those were still at her old apartment. She'd have to talk to Brant about having her things brought to the manor. Then again, maybe she should wait to find out where she ended up living in the end. Back to that irritating indecision. She brought her fingers to her temple and massaged. One of the kings was going to end up losing. No heir, no future, extinction of their coven. The massive weight of her choice settled more firmly onto her. She needed to talk about it, but Stephany was far from objective since she would want Tanya to choose Brant.

She grabbed a pair of boxers that she'd seen in Brant's closet, one of the plain white t-shirts, and some comfortable cotton underwear. She planned on staying behind these four walls for a little while for some much needed peace. Tanya dug in her overnight bag and pulled out her cell phone.

Her best friend answered after the first ring, "Why has it taken you so long to call?"

"Nice hello." Her mouth pulled into an involuntary smile and already she could feel some of the weight lift.

"So what's it like to shag a vampire?" Becky would have seen the whole choosing debacle on the local news station. By now everyone in Sweetwater would know, little old Tanya Milan had been one of the human females chosen. Becky had been so pissed that she wasn't permitted to attend the ceremony. Her feisty little friend would have loved to have had a chance at one of the kings. One of *her* kings.

"Confusing."

"What's confusing about it? Do they do it in some other kind of way?" It felt so good to hear her friend's voice. The stress seemed to melt away from her.

"No." She couldn't help but giggle.

"Please, oh please just tell me the sex is good." There was an expectant pause at the other end of the line.

Tanya couldn't help but recall how Brant had thrust into her while Zane had toyed with her clit. She groaned, "Mind blowing."

Becky screamed directly into the mouthpiece so that Tanya had to hold the phone away for a few beats. "I knew it, I just knew it. Why do you sound so glum?"

Tanya filled her in on the events of the last few days, having to hold the phone away from her ear every so often.

"You are shitting me. They are going to bounce you between them for the next nine days? You get to have sex with both men till the new moon?"

"Yeah."

Another scream.

"Stop that, you're giving me a headache. It's not as great as what it sounds. I need to choose at the end of the nine days and one of them will end up with no heirs. There won't be a future king and that coven will be doomed." Tanya sighed.

"I take it you like both kings?"

Tanya paused. She had been so sure that Brant was the one and if she was forced to choose right now she would go with him, but Zane was quickly creeping under her skin. He might be a big bully and a jerk, but he had a vulnerability that brought out the protector in her.

"Yeah, I guess I do."

"If they're sharing you now, why not indefinitely? You could have both of them. Problem solved." For a half a beat, Becky's suggestion made complete sense. She even felt her heart pick up a beat at the prospect of not having to choose. Then reality came crashing back.

"Weren't you listening? They're enemies. Up until a few years ago, they were at war. There's still a lot I don't know about their history but you should've seen them fighting this morning. I'm talking fists, blood, the whole nine yards. I don't think it would ever work." Surely if such a solution was even half feasible they would've thought of it.

"They were actually physically fighting over you?" her voice was filled with awe.

"It's not as great as what you would imagine. I'm not talking love taps. If the others hadn't been there to intervene, they may've ended up killing each other."

"Over you. How romantic."

Tanya laughed. Right now she wished she had some of Becky's easy going nature. Her friend took everything in stride. It was one of the reasons they were such good friends. They helped balance one another.

"I still say you should keep them both. Sounds like the perfect solution to me. There are worse things than being the filling in a vampire sandwich." Becky laughed at her own joke.

"You didn't just say that?"

"Yeah I did. When are you inviting me? I would love to meet your *men*."

"I don't know Becks, humans are kind of off limits and don't get invited . . . ever." Tanya moved the phone to the other ear. She sat on the edge of the bed and looked out the window. Leather clad guards patrolled the surrounding lawns in pairs.

"I promise to keep my hands to myself. Then again, I wouldn't be able to resist all that muscle. Why are humans off limits?"

"Apparently we break easily."

A long pause, "Are you telling me you're in danger?"

"I'm fine, don't worry about me." She tried to answer immediately and to keep her answer simple, but obviously something had given her away.

"Don't give me that, I'm fine bullshit. Out with it."

"They're big, seriously strong and drink blood, there is some risk, at least until I'm mated. Then apparently I'll become stronger or something."

Her friend huffed. "Mmmm, well come on new moon I say. I'll seriously have me some vampire steaks if anything happens to you though, and I will be coming to visit soon. They can't keep you away from your bestie."

"There are other issues at the moment that would make your visiting difficult. The vampires are kind of at war with the elves and werewolves" She paused deciding not to worry her friend by telling her everything. "It's a little unstable at the moment."

"No ways. You're in danger from all sides. That's it, I'm coming to fetch you." Becky was being impulsive as always.

"Calm down, I'm perfectly safe," she lied. "Brant and Zane will protect me. I'm surrounded by dozens of royal guard. I'm fine."

"Ooooh, in that case, lucky you. Now do yourself a favor and convince your men that a vampire sandwich is the way to go."

Tanya laughed. She only wished it could be that simple. They said their goodbyes and Tanya promised to call Becky again soon. Next, she called her aunt who didn't even know that Tanya had been chosen or that she was missing. Once the old lady had been filled in, she reassured her that she was safe and that everything was fine. Aunt Sally invited Tanya and her new boyfriend round for lunch on Sunday and Tanya had to carefully decline. Aunt Sally didn't seem to fully understand that her niece was about to become a vampire bride. She said her goodbyes promising to call again soon.

Tanya stretched herself out on the huge bed. After ten minutes, she rummaged in her overnight bag and pulled out a book. The latest release from her favorite romance author. One of her guilty pleasures, she loved to read. The problem was that she battled to concentrate on what she was reading and kept having to flip back a page or two to reread the section before. She had too much on her mind at the moment. On the verge of giving up, there was a knock at the door.

"Come in."

Stephany breezed in, a silver tray in her hands covered in everything. Eggs, delicious smelling crispy bacon. There was toast and pancakes with syrup and grated cheese. A pot, of what smelled like, freshly brewed coffee and a tall glass of orange juice. Tanya's stomach growled.

"Sounds like I am just in time." Stephany glanced down at Tanya's tummy before putting the tray on the bedside table. "May I?" She gestured to the spot at the end of the bed.

Tanya nodded and Stephany sat, the bed dipped as she did so.

"I heard that Zane had nothing to do with his human's death. She took her own life, that had to have been really difficult for Zane considering his past."

Tanya tried to stop herself from reacting, but a strangled gasp still managed to escape.

"You didn't know about the suicide?"

"I knew that she had died and that Zane was not responsible, but I wasn't sure of the exact circumstances. What happened to Zane before I mean?" Tanya suspected his hardened exterior and that vulnerable edge had something to do with it.

"Oh no. You need to speak to him yourself. Like I said, he's had it tough. I take it you must have gotten along well with him." Stephany pointed at the tray, "Eat."

"Just because we had sex doesn't mean we got along." Tanya sat up tucking her legs underneath herself. She snagged some bacon.

"Were you compatible?"

Tanya didn't answer, not sure what the female vamp meant. Stephany must have registered the confusion on her face because she added. "Did you enjoy the sex?"

Tanya almost choked on the piece of bacon she was swallowing but managed to compose herself. "Sheesh, is nothing sacred around here? Why is it so important about how much I enjoyed the sex anyway?"

"It is the first and very important test on whether you would make a good pair. I hope that you enjoyed Brant more."

"Oh God . . ." She let her head drop into her hands.

"Oh no, does that mean you didn't? I had heard that Brant is an attentive lover, that he—"

Tanya made a sound of disgust and put her hand up to stop the vampire. "No stop. I don't want to hear about Brant with other women."

"Does it make you feel jealous?" Stephany had perked up significantly.

"You know it does. Remember Alexandra?" *Oh shit.* She'd forgotten all about the female. "Please tell me Brant didn't drink from her while I was away?"

Stephany smiled broadly and shook her head. "No, Alexandra has moved out and is no longer in Brant's service. He was very angry that she nearly struck you and that she used the fact that he drank from her to goad you."

The news improved her mood somewhat, yet the nagging thought that Zane was probably with one of the other female vampires of his coven ate her up from the inside. She knew she had no right to ask for his fidelity. She doubted very much that he would give it to her anyways. Knowing Zane, he would go out of his way to sleep with someone while she was gone just out of principle. Her cheeks flushed as she remembered how intently he had watched Brant fuck her. Zane was so going to have sex with someone else.

"Why the glum face? Alexandra leaving is good news." Stephany cocked her head, her eyes brimming with concern.

"It's Zane," she mumbled.

"What of Zane?"

"Brant has sworn to be faithful, but . . ." She couldn't bring herself to finish the sentence.

Stephany chuckled. "Don't be so worried. Zane might rut with others in your absence, but he wants you."

"No, he needs me. There's a big difference." It irked her that Stephany was so indifferent about Zane's promiscuity.

Stephany looked thoughtful. "I haven't had much interaction with Brant's birth enemy but for what it's worth, I've never seen him act out like he did. I think that he does have feelings for you. The sex must have been good."

"It's not all about sex."

"No, but he is a male so it is very important especially early on. Zane is as red blooded as they come. I am certain he will bed another female, but I can also assure you without a doubt that he would prefer to have you."

It didn't make her feel any better. She was going to give him a big piece of her mind when she saw him again. If he thought she was going to end up choosing a cheating son of a bitch, he had another thing coming. If he had so much as put a finger on another female, she would tell him what to do with himself.

The memory of finding her ex in bed with another woman still stung. The wound was just too fresh. Troy still had the audacity to blame her. She had put on too much weight, she was too flabby. He had needs that she wasn't fulfilling and he was forced to look elsewhere. If she lost some weight, toned up a bit then he wouldn't have to look at other women. He'd even talked about her getting a breast reduction and some lipo. No freaking way. She wasn't changing and she would demand fidelity. She hadn't asked for any of this.

"I see that the thought does not make you happy."

"I don't want either of them drinking or having sex with other women. I don't want to have to choose either," she whispered the last sentence.

"I am sure you will make the right choice when the time comes. I am afraid that they will fight regardless of the outcome."

"They said they would only fight if I didn't choose." She felt her panic levels rise.

"There is too much at stake. Neither will walk away."

"Why can't I just have both? I'll have heirs for both covens and there will be no need for anyone to lose." She felt a tickle on her cheek and her hand came away wet when she wiped at it. Damn, she was crying and couldn't seem to stop. "Surely we could make it work somehow. I can't choose between them and I don't want to see either man die by the hand of the other."

"Oh my God, you love them both."

"It's too soon for that. I care for both of them and for both covens."

Stephany laughed, she scooted towards Tanya and grabbed her into a rib cracking hug. "You are a genius. Brant and Zane are kings first, their alliance to their covens. All decisions must be in the best interest of their people. They would have to make it work." The female vampire finally released her and she took in a big lungful of air. Stephany continued really excited. "This could work. Oh by the gods, this could be the answer. You must speak with Brant when he returns."

"You saw them this morning. How they were tearing into each other. I can't see how it—"

"We'll work something out. You would need to bear both of their heirs." She clasped her hand. "It wouldn't be easy but if you are willing then"—she smiled warmly—"I know this could work." She squeezed. "Now, eat your breakfast and then let's get you ready. My suggestion would be to rut with him first. Men are always more agreeable after their needs have been met."

Tanya gasped.

"Don't act all coy, you know I am right. Brant will be the more difficult of the two to convince. If he agrees, then I am sure Zane will too."

"What makes you think that?" Her heart sped up. Maybe this could work after all.

"Am I right in saying that Zane watched Brant rut with you?"

"How do you know that?"

Stephany touched her nose.

"You freaking vamps and your damned sense of smell." The vamp would've smelled that she and Brant had sex.

"The three of you were in the room together and unless Brant knocked Zane out, it means he would have watched the two of you . . ."

Tanya slid a hand over her eyes and wished she could block her ears as well. It felt weird talking about this.

"I am right about him watching?"

Tanya shrugged.

"Yes or no?" Stephany's voice took on that commanding edge that vampires could do so well.

Tanya shrugged, she narrowed her eyes at the vamp not wanting to answer but she needed Stephany's help. No one knew Brant like she did. "He held Brant down because he was freaking out so much. Brant could smell Zane on me. Zane touched me during . . . you know."

"Brant let him?"

"He wasn't happy about it, but yeah he did."

"This could work. Brant already considers you to be his mate, his queen. We'll find a way to convince him. For the sake of our species we have to."

Within an hour, Tanya had eaten a good deal of the tray of food. There were at least a half a dozen dresses strewn over the bed.

"For the love of blood, this is it." Stephany removed a red number from the closet. It had long sleeves and a high neck with a single pearl button that would clasp at the back of her head. Judging from the length, it would fall mid-thigh.

"Um, it's stunning but more for going out at night."

"Who cares? I know Brant won't. Take off the bra."

Tanya looked down at her underwear and her cheeks heated. "I'd rather not."

"Why so shy? Nothing I haven't seen before and anyway I assure you I'm not into females."

"I didn't realize vampires swung both ways."

Stephany arched her eyebrows. "We may be non-humans, but we're similar in a lot more ways than you would think. Time is a wasting, off with the bra already."

"Fine." She reached behind her and unhooked the clasps letting the cups fall away from her breasts. She had a whole drawer full of stunning underwear she might never get to wear at this rate. Tanya picked up the red dress marvelling at the sensual feel of the fine fabric between her fingertips. This wasn't an off the rack item, that was for sure. She caught Stephany gawking at her breasts as she approached the mirror. For a second she felt the urge to cover up.

"All I can say is, you had better have twins with a rack like that." She whistled under her breath. "No wonder the boys are fighting for your attention."

To think Tanya had actually considered a breast reduction for a half a second after she dumped Troy's ass. "Yeah, yeah, I'm perfect baby making and feeding material."

"You are perfect. Those boys won't be able to think straight with you anywhere near them. Our rules be damned, all of our males will be rushing to town to seek human females for themselves."

"Don't be ridiculous, have you seen yourself? You vampire females are stunning."

Stephany's face clouded. "My hips are too narrow. I could never carry a child to term. I have been advised to be permanently sterilized, but since I don't rut I've decided not to bother. I would have loved children." She looked wistful for a second before snapping out of it. "Put the dress on already."

Tanya pulled the garment over her head. Stephany did the button up for her. She swallowed hard when she saw herself in the mirror. The dress hugged all of her better areas like the swell of her breasts and the narrowness at her waist. The length hid her upper thighs and showcased her great lower leg. Silver heels completed the ensemble and Tanya had to admit she'd never felt sexier.

"You chose this for me, didn't you?"

Stephany nodded, "I knew it would work perfectly on you."

"You know so much about me, yet I feel like I know nothing about you. Why have you chosen to be celibate?"

Stephany narrowed her eyes as she put her hands on her hips. "Nosey human." She laughed. "It's quite a boring reason actually." She paused seeming to gather her thoughts. "I accidentally mated with someone twenty one years ago. We couldn't be together. End of story."

Tanya felt her eyes widen. "Boring my ass. Why couldn't you be together?"

"Let's just say he was from the wrong side of the tracks."

"He was a human wasn't he?" her voice had turned high pitched with excitement.

Stephany smiled down at her like a mother would to her insolent child. "No. Let's leave it at that shall we?"

"No way. You get to know all about my . . . difficult situation. Tell me who he is." The infuriating vampire pursed her lips. "Tell me or you're in the dark from now on."

"Fine. It was another vampire. Someone from Zane's coven."

"Lance." Suddenly it all made sense.

"How do you know?" Stephany cocked her head.

"I saw the two of you this morning. You reacted to him like I've never seen you react to anyone before. Normally you're so cool and collected. I noticed how he got to you."

"Really?" She ran a hand through her short platinum hair. "I'll have to work at schooling my emotion more."

"Do you love him?"

Stephany choked out a negative sound while shaking her head. "Hardly. I don't even know him. It was a one night stand gone bad."

She racked her brain for a moment trying to recall how the whole mating thing went. Realization dawned. "He drank from you during . . ."

The female vampire looked sheepish. A blush crept up from under her collar.

"Oh my God"—Tanya held her hands over her mouth—"you drank from him."

"It was a complete accident. I don't know what came over me." Her hand went through her hair. "The war had only just ended, things were still very strained between the covens. There was no way either king would've accepted the union. Both of us have high level positions within the royal staff."

"So what? You just went your separate ways and that was that?"

"Pretty much."

"My word, that's so romantic." Tanya clutched at her chest. "Let me guess, you have never been able to find another male that does it for you, and you are both pining for one another?"

Stephany rolled her eyes. "Please! I did a ridiculously stupid thing. I can't trust myself to be with a man and technically I am a mated woman. I prefer to stay away. Much less complicated." Her eyes narrowed and hardened up. "As to Lance pining after me. If rutting with anything in a skirt counts as pining then sure thing."

Tanya rubbed Stephany's arm. "I'm so sorry. What a jerk. That sucks. You need to get laid girlfriend. I doubt you would make the same silly mistake twice."

Stephany threw her a look that told her she was full of it. "Not happening sister."

"I think you're still hung up on a certain vampire and that's why you're staying away from all males."

Stephany's eyes widened. "Wrong. Let's move on. I don't want to continue this conversation."

"Fine." She huffed wanting to goad Stephany some more, but the female had confided in her. Which was something she didn't think the other woman did very often. She wanted to be Stephany's friend, wanted for them to be able to confide in each other.

"Let's do your hair and make-up although I have to confess, I don't have much experience in either."

"No, the dress is over the top already. I'll run a brush through my hair and put on the basics." Tanya made her way to the mirror and picked up the hair brush. Once she was done, she put on some concealer, lip gloss and mascara. Simple, almost as if she wasn't wearing any. She remembered Zane's dislike for make-up and wondered if Brant felt the same.

Female vampires, with their porcelain skin and dark, thick lashes didn't need artificial help.

They went on to play several games of chess. Stephany had never played before so she taught her, Tanya won the first round. Once the female vamp got the hang of it, Tanya lost the remaining games. At four games to one, Tanya called it quits.

Lunch was salad and turkey sandwiches with plenty of juice to wash it all down. She shouldn't be hungry after such a big breakfast but she still managed to eat a good deal of food. Card games next, Stephany beat her hands down at poker, but Tanya was the clear winner at black jack.

Stephany kept reassuring her that Brant would be back soon, but there was no sign of him or his closest royal guard.

Dinner was the most delicious pot roast Tanya had ever had the pleasure of tasting. It was served with crisp vegetables. Stephany enjoyed the meal with her, reminding her that vampires did partake in human food and drink from time to time. They did not follow a strictly liquid diet. After the meal, she brushed her teeth and reapplied her make-up.

"I'm sure he'll be here any minute. I'm sure we have a game of monopoly around here somewhere." Stephany plastered a smile on her face.

"No please, I'm all gamed out. I think I'll read a bit. I'm sure you're right, he'll be here any minute." She tried to plaster the same fake smile onto her own face, but truth was she was worried. Was Brant safe? Why was he staying away so long? Had the events of this morning shaken him so much that he was feigning being busy so that he didn't have to see her? "Have you heard anything?"

Stephany shook her head. "I tried calling, but his phone keeps going to voice mail. I wouldn't worry, the estate is huge so they have a ton of ground to cover."

Tanya nodded.

"Well, have a good evening and call me if you need me. I'm just down the hall."

"I will. Please let me know if you hear anything."

Stephany nodded.

Her book was still on the bedside table where she'd left it earlier. She was going to read the romance novel and get into it even if it killed her.

Chapter FOUR

THE ROOM WAS DIM, with only the side table lamp illuminating the space. His human lay on top of the blankets. She was on her side, legs curled towards her chest with a book clutched tightly to her breasts. He removed the paperback, the cover brought a smile to his lips. A half-naked male, the title said Demon Shifters. Brant shook his head while placing the book on the side table.

The dress she was wearing was open all the way down her back, it hugged her ass and accentuated her full breasts. His blood heated and his hands itched to touch her. Brant let out a pent up breath. He was worried how seeing her again would affect him. She still carried the faint undertones of Zane's scent, but for some reason seeing her in his bed made it easy for him to push that fact aside.

It had been a long hard day. What he needed right now was a hot shower. He would not touch his future mate until he had prepared for her. He undressed, making quick work of his clothes and made his way to the bathroom. He turned the faucets on and entered the cubicle, allowing the hot water to massage his skin. Taking some shower gel, he lathered himself including his hair before rinsing the suds from his body. Now that he had seen Tanya, he couldn't wait to touch her smooth creamy skin. He brushed his teeth. Using one of the fluffy white towels, he dried off and strode back to his suite. She was exactly as he had left her. There was a tiny snorting sound and he realized that she was snoring ever so softly. His mouth drew into a smile.

His little human was adorable.

Right now, he wished he hadn't been away for so long. There were many things that needed doing though and he had needed time to think things through. The current situation was not of Tanya's making. This had to be very difficult for her. Brant would do everything in his power to keep her happy. He would have to find a way to tramp down this possessive streak as well, even if it killed him.

Brant slid in behind her. Soft ass pressed up against a very hard part of him. Taking his time, he trailed his fingers down the length of her spine nuzzling into that soft spot at the back of her neck. Tanya whimpered.

Brant carefully brushed her hair to the side, so much skin, where was he to start? He took her earlobe into his mouth and nibbled and sucked alternately until she moaned. Next, he moved to the sensitive patch just below her ear. His delectable human arched back into him, mumbling something incoherent ending on a sigh. Even in sleep she was highly sensual. It was when he ground his hard cock against her perfectly rounded ass that her eyes sprang open in a gasp.

"I missed you." Brant slid his hands around her cupping her exquisite breasts loving how her nipples turned to stone beneath his palms.

So responsive.

"You were gone so long." Her voice held no trace of sleep,

it held a husky tone that made him harden up a whole lot more.

"I will make it up to you, Cenwein." He rubbed himself up against her ensuring that sweet contact was made with her entire slit, honing in on where her clit would be nestled. The sound she made told him he had hit the spot. The intoxicating scent of her arousal filled the air. His human arched her back in such a way that had his hands overfull with her lush mounds while her ass came up flush against him.

Taking the hem of her dress, he slowly tugged it up, wanting to see the material bunched at her hips. Up and up he pulled until the soft globes of her ass came into view.

No underwear.

Without realizing it, he had moved back to get a better look. His little minx pushed her ass out even further.

"Christ." He swallowed hard. Her pussy was the perfect shade of flushed pink. His mouth watered. His entire body tightened in anticipation. Her slit glistened with her arousal. "So pretty." Brant couldn't help himself. Ever so slowly, he slid a finger from her opening across her entire slit settling on her swollen clit. Her nub tightened under his ministrations. She whimpered. Brant loved the little sounds of pleasure.

"I need to taste you."

"Yes," she whispered sounding so needy that he was tempted to ram himself into her welcoming flesh, knowing that he could make her come with just his dick. Instead, he flipped her onto her back. She didn't realize it but her legs had fallen open. Her eyes were half-mast. Her cheeks were flushed. Placing a hand on each thigh, he opened her further.

Swollen, glistening, the scent of her arousal almost took him over the edge. His fangs ached to descend and he clenched his teeth to prevent it. His little human squirmed in anticipation. Her hips tilted towards him as if to urge him on.

Brant lowered his head, not sure where to start first. He had to taste her, needed to sample her sweet pussy. One swipe of the tongue across her opening, Brant closed his eyes to savor the taste.

Tanya whimpered, bucking her hips as he made contact. "Please," a needy cry.

He went in for a second taste, this time he speared her opening with his tongue pushing himself as deep as he could go. Only once his little human was begging in earnest did he move to her clit, sliding his tongue over the bundle of nerves ever so slowly. Next, he inserted a finger into her tight sheath. Brant pumped in and out at a leisurely pace feeling her excitement grow as her body tensed in preparation for her orgasm. He picked up speed, adding a second finger. Her head was thrown back, she clawed at the sheets and came apart on a high pitched scream.

So fucking expressive, his dick throbbed.

His cell phone rang. It was on the bedside table where he had left it when he'd come in earlier. Brant had to stretch to reach it. The screen showed that it was Xavier. He answered with one slide of the thumb. "Yeah?"

Xavier chuckled, "I take it your mate is fine."

"You have no idea just how fine."

Xavier chuckled and ended the call.

Tanya had propped herself up on one elbow. "Who was it?" Wide, chestnut eyes looked at him with concern.

"Just Xavier checking up on you."

"Oh." Her cheeks heated. "He heard me. Oh shit." She nibbled on her bottom lip for a second. "Half the hall probably heard me."

"The only other vampire on this wing is Stephany. The sounds of our love making are to be expected."

She groaned, falling back onto the bed and covered her face with one hand.

"I adore the noises you make. Don't stop making them." As he talked, he moved up her body loving how she locked her legs around him as he drew eye to eye. Brant lowered his mouth to hers. She moaned as their lips meshed. He deepened the kiss keeping the pace slow and easy. The tip of his cock nudged at her slick opening. So warm, so welcoming.

"I had promised myself that I would take you slowly, that I would savor each and every thrust."

"Sounds good," a little breathless.

"I don't have the willpower." He drove into her hard knowing she would be ready for him. She cried out, automatically lifting her legs higher onto his back so that he would be able to take her deeper. Using one hand to grip her thigh, he splayed the other on the mattress next to her head. "Feels so good."

"Yes," she cried and he thrust into her again. Her velvet sheath so tight it almost hurt. A few more glorious thrusts and already his balls were pulling up. No female had ever had this effect on him. The need to feel her soft flesh against him almost overwhelmed him. Brant jerked at the fabric covering her. It came apart easily, giving him access to what he wanted.

Soft, silky skin. Hard nipples that speared his chest. Brant continued to thrust, working hard to keep his release at bay. He grit his teeth. Sweat beaded on his brow. He was grunting with every stroke but couldn't stop himself from doing it.

His human was perfect in every way.

The desire to drink from her rode him hard but he was able to tramp it down, but only just. His balls were so tight. It physically hurt to keep from coming. Brant slid a hand between them using it to strum on her clit. Tanya screamed as her pussy clamped down around him. He roared as his semen filled her with hot jets. Brant turned his head as he jerked into her ensuring that she rode out the pleasure right to the very end. Keeping his weight on his hands, which were now both on either side of her head, he watched as her eyes fluttered open.

"You destroyed my dress."

"I'll buy you more."

Her eyes narrowed in mock anger. "You'll be more careful in the future."

"That might entail you walking around semi naked from now on. Something that allows for easy access and for the record, I like the no underwear thing."

She smiled. "Now you're sounding just like Zane." Her eyes widened as she realized what she'd just said.

It wasn't easy to school his reaction. The thought of Zane having easy access to this beautiful woman. Of the bastard king . . . of his female . . . best he not torture himself.

"I'm sorry I . . ." Her face had clouded.

"You have nothing to be sorry about." It was with reluctance that he pulled himself from her warm body. His cock had decided that it was ready for round two. Although he would take her again before she went back to Zane, she would need rest first. He planned on taking her just before she left, with no chance of a shower. Let that bastard get a taste of what Brant had felt yesterday morning. He knew that Zane would scent him on her either way, but if she didn't shower his scent would be so much stronger.

He brushed his lips against hers. Pulling her into his chest, he found for the second time that night that he was amazed at how well she fit. How right it felt to have her in his arms. "I'm sorry I was gone so long, I will make it up to you when you come back. I believe I owe you a candle lit dinner and a long walk."

"We also need to get to know each other better." Tanya lifted her head to look him in the eyes, her eyebrows bobbed up and down. Brant chuckled.

"Oh we've hardly even brushed the surface on that one."

She smiled wickedly, her tongue skimming the expanse of her bottom lip. "I think someone wants to continue now." She gestured to his engorged cock.

"You are an unmated human. You should rest first before I take you again . . ." His words ended in an astonished groan as she slid down his body and took the head of his cock into her mouth. Her full raspberry lips surrounded his head. Her wicked tongue did spectacular things to the slit at the top of his shaft. Oh by the gods it felt good. Vampire females didn't go down on the males because their fangs got in the way. Not so with his human. One of her blunt teeth raked against him and he groaned loving the sensation.

"Cenwein," he choked out.

She released him and he fisted his hands to stop from pulling her back onto him.

"You were saying?" Her sultry voice was almost his undoing. Tanya smiled, so sexy it could almost be termed predatory. Then, her gaze moved back to his engorged head which she took back into her warm, wet mouth. This time she took him as deep as her throat would allow. It was his turn to fist the sheets, to make ridiculous grunts and moans as she sucked him. Never in his wildest dreams had he ever imagined something could feel so good without actually being inside a female's body. Something about seeing Tanya's mouth surrounding him, watching her head bob up and down. Seeing the sway of her breasts as she took him deep, suckling at just the right degree of pressure.

Tanya picked up speed, her tongue sliding across his rim in an arch that had his balls pulling up. She laved a second time before deep throating him. He so wished he could delay his pending orgasm but his body was reacting to this erotic woman. His human. His future mate, come war or blood rivers. He would do anything to ensure that she stayed at his side. It was on that thought that he erupted, shouting his release, not caring if the whole manor heard him. Incredible how she swallowed him down in greedy little gulps. It almost had him coming a second time. He moaned when she used the tip of her little tongue to lick him clean.

"Better?" Her lips were slightly swollen. The raspberry color had become overripe.

"By the gods." He was panting heavily.

"Don't tell me you've also never had a blowjob?"

He felt his hackles rise. His blood ignited. "Also?" This time it was a struggle to repress the turmoil he was feeling and the word was out before he could think.

Her face crumpled and she covered it with her hand as a sob escaped her.

Brant felt like a jerk. "Hey." He threaded his hand through her hair and used the other to pull her to him. She refused to meet his gaze. "I'm sorry. It just slipped out. I'm a possessive jerk. It is perfectly normal that you would . . . pleasure Zane while you were with him. You need to get to know him better, check for compatibility."

She made a growling noise. "Is that all this is to you? Sexual compatibility? Heirs?"

"You know that it isn't." He cupped her face using both his hands. Her lashes glistened with tears and her lip quivered as she spoke. It made him feel like he'd been stabbed in the heart with a silver tipped arrow. "The reason I'm so possessive is because I'm developing feelings for you. I want a relationship, a union. I want a family."

"I want the same, but I don't want to choose. I don't think I can. Stephany said that—"

"Stephany?" He really needed to have a word with his trusted assistant.

"Don't be mad at her, right now she is the only friend I have. Please?"

Everything in him softened. How could he refuse her anything? "I understand. In eight days' time you will need to choose though Tanya. Best you be prepared."

She sat up fumbling with her dress, she was trying to cover herself from him. The dress refused to cooperate so she finally wrapped her arms around herself. "And what if I choose Zane, would you walk away?"

"No," Brant growled the word unable to fully control his emotions. He banded his arms around her and pulled her to him crushing her against his chest. "He won't have you. I won't let—"

Her little hands were splayed on his chest, they pushed so he released her. "Exactly. If I choose you. Do you think that Zane will let me go?"

Damn, he hated where this was going. He could guess what she wanted to ask of him and hoped she wouldn't do it. It was the one thing he couldn't give her.

"I don't want to choose."

Part of him wanted to leave it there but that would be cowardly. "What are you saying?" He ran a hand through his hair and felt his jaw lock.

"I could mate both of you."

His blood turned to acid. His vision swam. His fangs and claws erupted. Brant could feel that his eyes were glowing. He leapt from the bed to the far side of the room and before he could stop himself, had fisted large holes in the wall.

The door crashed open and Xavier entered. Tanya yelped and grabbed for a sheet.

"Get the fuck out!"

"You are unstable my lord." Xavier took several slow steps towards him as he spoke.

"I am fine."

His brother's eyebrows arched as he glanced at the holes in the wall and back. "I see that."

"I won't harm my female."

Xavier looked down for a second or two before lifting his eyes to meet Brant's. "For the record brother, I think that the human is on to something."

Without thinking, he punched Xavier square in the jaw, just managing to hold back at the last second so as not to inflict too much damage. Tanya screamed. Stephany crouched next to his fallen brother, her eyes blazed. He wasn't sure when his assistant had arrived.

"Have you completely lost your mind Brant?" she asked calmly.

"Is that how you would speak to your king?" He realized he was being a dick but couldn't stop himself. The thought of this arrangement continuing beyond the new moon was unacceptable. Brant turned his gaze on Tanya who sat in the center of his bed wide eyed, sheet clutched to her. Just by looking her way, he felt his demeanor soften. Felt everything in him soften. "I hope that you will choose me," he paused. "But know that if you do not, I will kill Zane to have you."

Silent tears tracked down her cheeks as he spoke and he longed to go to her to give her some measure of comfort, instead he picked up his pants and strode from the room.

Chapter FIVE

TANYA CLUTCHED THE SHEET tighter around herself. She sobbed openly, not able to stop the tears that kept rolling down her cheeks. She had tried and she had seriously failed. It couldn't have gone any worse.

"Will you deal with this?" Xavier directed the question at Stephany.

"Leave it with me," Stephany answered.

"I'll be outside the door."

The bed dipped as the female vamp sat beside her. She placed a cool hand on Tanya's shoulder. "He's only acting like this because he cares. That big idiot actually has feelings for you. They both do."

Tanya shook her head, only wanting to cry harder at Stephany's words.

"It would be easier if they didn't. It would put them in a better position to think about this objectively." The other woman sighed.

"This is supposed to help me how?" She hated how whiney her voice sounded.

"Oh, Tanya." The vampire rubbed her back in firm circles.

It was oddly comforting. "It's not over yet. You need to be strong. The good news is that you have eight days to convince them that this is the best option. You heard Xavier, even he agrees."

"How am I supposed to convince birth enemies to share a mate? Might as well invite the wolf alpha to join us."

Stephany laughed and Tanya did as well, only the tears kept coming so it sounded a little on the hysterical side.

"You are a resourceful female. I know you can do it. Keep in mind that you are in the driver's seat. Don't let them try and convince you otherwise."

Tanya managed to get herself mostly under control, she used the sheet to blot her eyes and nose. "I don't think so." She shook her head and sniffed. "They are damned head strong. I had thought that Brant would be the more reasonable of the two but he's proving me wrong. He can be so gentle, so loving, yet he has this side to him."

"Brant has always dreamt of having his queen, of his family, the white picket fence and all that. He's clinging onto a dream and needs to face reality. Zane hasn't had an easy life. I don't think he expected much from the mating and therefore won't be as disappointed. Like I said earlier, he will be the more agreeable of the two." Stephany removed her hand. "Let's get you in the bath."

"It's the middle of the night." She glanced at the clock. "Make that early hours of the morning." It was just after half past four.

"Nothing like a calming bath and then it's back to bed. Brant will want to see you before Zane comes to collect you in a few hours, and I'm sure Zane has missed you."

Tanya noticed how a naughty smile graced the vampire's lips. She groaned just thinking about the whole mess.

Hopefully her vampire kings would be able to keep their fists off each other. How the hell was she supposed to convince them that this threesome should continue? And even if by some miracle they agreed, how would she cope long-term being shuffled from one king to the other? Her head hurt thinking about it.

Stephany made for the rest room. Tanya heard the sound of rushing water. Sheet still firmly around her, she followed the vampire. She was pouring something that smelled nice into the swirling water. "Get in." Her friend gestured to the soapy water.

Tanya let the towel drop and removed the dress.

"How strange." Stephany's eyes were fixed on the juncture of her thighs.

What the hell! Instead of responding or covering up like she felt like doing, she climbed into the tub letting the water do it for her.

Stephany realized that she'd been staring and her cheeks turned red. "Um, sorry about that. I've never seen a human fully naked. Vampires don't have any hair down there." Her eyes widened. "Don't get me wrong, you have very little, just a tiny strip but it is strange to me."

"Actually, if I didn't see a beautician regularly I'd have a lot more than a tiny strip. Damn, do you think Brant and Zane would prefer me to wax it all off."

Stephany's brow creased. "You could take it all off."

"Yeah. No problem."

She shook her head. "I think they might like it. It makes you human. They seem to be attracted to that fact."

"Okay, so the landing strip stays."

Her crease deepened. "Landing strip?"

"It's what it's called. If I were to take it all off it would be called a Brazilian." Tanya felt her lips pull into a smile.

"I'm just glad I don't have to wax. Does it hurt?"

"It gets better once you get used to it. I almost died the first time, but it's worth it."

Stephany's head whipped up about three seconds before Xavier marched into the room. Tanya shrieked pulling her knees up to cover her chest.

Xavier's eyes stayed on Stephany the whole time. "Our perimeter has been breached." His jaw worked. "A horde of elves and three or four wolves are on their way to the manor house as we speak. Brant is missing. You need to come with me now." For the first time, he turned dark eyes on her.

"I need to get dressed." Her heart raced. If anything happened to Brant she would never forgive herself.

"No time," he growled.

Stephany grabbed a little silk robe. She must've caught the look on Tanya's face because she added. "What? I wanted you ready for Brant's apology."

Xavier turned away from the tub. "Hurry. We don't have much time."

Tanya had barely rubbed the water from her arms when Xavier growled low and deep. "You really need to move or I will be forced to put you over my shoulder just like that."

She shoved her wet body into the silk robe, which clung to her like a second skin. It barely covered her naked ass. She had only just tied the cord when Xavier grabbed her and pulled her through the bathroom.

"What about you?" she shouted in Stephany's direction.

"I'm a big girl. I can take care of myself."

There wasn't any time to argue, so she allowed herself to be dragged into the suite. Asking to stop to put panties on didn't seem likely to go over well so she bit her tongue instead. Her dagger was on the side table next to the bed. Tanya only just managed to snag it as they walked past. She put the sheathed blade into the side pocket of her robe.

Without missing a stride, Xavier reached into his vibrating pocket and pulled out a phone. "Yeah." A pause. They kept on walking. "I have her. I'm on my way as we speak." Another pause. "Of course, my lord."

"Let me speak . . ." She let the sentence die as she watched Xavier shove the phone back in his pocket.

"Brant is safe. He will meet us at the cellar entrance. You are to go underground until we have the situation under control. Chances are good that they are here for you."

Her heart was already racing from the exertion of keeping up with him, but somehow it managed to kick up another gear. Zane's words came back to haunt her. Tanya would rather die than end up mated to the alpha. With one hand firmly on her robe in an attempt to seal it shut and the other clasped with Xavier's arm, she worked harder at keeping her legs moving one foot in front of the other.

Shouts from outside. A bloody scream.

She gasped.

"They are here," Xavier stated unnecessarily as he picked up the pace. Okay, forget the panties, a sports bra would have been awesome. They rounded the corner and nearly collided with two elves.

"Fuck," Xavier snarled. He head butted the closest male who crumpled on impact. The second elf had time to prepare. He was a big son of a bitch with golden hair down his back. The elf pulled a long, thin blade.

Silver.

A shiver raced up Tanya's spine as the elf lunged for Xavier, who side stepped the deadly arch easily. "To the study. I'm right behind you!" Xavier shouted as he punched the elf. Xavier yelped as the blade sliced his forearm. "Now!" He shouted punching the elf a second time.

At first she was frozen to the spot, too afraid to move so much as a muscle, but hearing Xavier shout snapped her out of it. Her choices were stick around and become the next Mrs Wolf or run and save her naked ass. She ran for the study. It was funny how big the manor seemed all of a sudden.

The robe be damned, she pulled the knife from her pocket and removed it from the sheath, shoving the sheath back into her pocket. Both her fisted hands pumped as she pushed herself to run faster. She reached the head of the stairs just as a lone elf stepped up. "Well, well, what have we here? If it isn't the human." His crystalline eyes dropped to her chest.

Oh shit.

She flashed a look down. Her robe gaped, the silk edges barely covered her nipples which protruded through the thin fabric anyway so not much use.

The elf whistled. "Not really the alpha's cup of nectar. He likes um tall and lean." He flashed a glance at her face before dropping his gaze back down. "I'm sure he'll gobble you up anyway. I on the other hand think you're quite lovely." He took two more steps towards her, still focused on her chest.

She did something really slutty, but in this instance necessary since her life was at stake, and pulled her shoulders back as far as they would go. Her right breast sprang free. The elf's jaw dropped as she took the last small step to get close enough to stab him. She couldn't remember anything Brant had told her about where to aim. She almost expected to be stopped and didn't think her ploy would work, but the knife sank home somewhere just below his collarbone. The elf screamed and tried to grab her. She knocked his hand away and kicked his shin, which sent him flying down the stairs. They were long and steep and by the time he landed at the bottom he wasn't moving. At this stage Tanya was half way down, she didn't stop to check if he was dead when she reached the bottom. Instead she jumped over him. Trying to fix her robe while she ran.

"Tanya!" Brant roared.

Thank God. She could breathe a little easier. He wore a pair of leather pants, his chest was bare and covered in blood. There was no time for any type of greeting. He clasped her hand a little too tightly and they made for his study. They ran into elves twice more, the silk clad males had made it through the outside security. The first time there was just one and Brant dispatched him easily. The second time there were three. All with those same, thin deadly looking knives. Brant took a slash across the chest getting in close enough to give the first of the group an uppercut to the nose. With a sickening crunch, the elf collapsed falling to his knees. Brant had to put the elf to his back in order to take on the remaining two. Blood gushed from the fallen male's nose, he swayed threatening to topple over. It didn't stop him from reaching for his knife though. The elf went on all fours and shuffled in the blade's direction.

She glanced at Brant who was working hard to avoid the silver while trying to down his opponents without the help of any weapon of his own. Although he was holding up fine, the fallen elf was in a perfect position to take him down if he managed to reach his knife, which was inches away from his fingertips. She looked down at the bloody knife white fisted in her hand. She had to protect Brant just as he was protecting her. Tanya planted the knife into the side of the elf's neck. The one thing she clearly remembered was Brant telling her to pull the blade clear after a stab. She gave the hilt a jerk towards her and the blade slid clear. Blood sprayed from the small wound. Tanya shrieked as nausea clutched her stomach, causing her to gag. When she turned back, the elf lay face down in a growing pool of blood. The elf was dead. It had to be. She sobbed clasping her hand over her mouth to keep from screaming.

Xavier stepped in next to Brant, using what looked like a samurai sword. He made quick work of the last elf. Brant staggered. There was a puncture wound to his left bicep and a second slice across his chest. Tanya couldn't help but to make another sobbing noise as she rushed to his side. Brant leaned on her for the first few strides before rising up to his full height. Xavier led the way. Brant pushed her in front of him, his hand staying on her waist as they ran. The front lobby was teaming with vampires in full combat. The elves surged as they caught sight of her. A large menacing wolf growled, it's back a mass of wounds. It took a vampire's arm into its massive jaws. The vampire screamed as the jaws closed in a loud snap. The male vamp pierced the wolf with his sword and the beast collapsed.

"This way," Brant urged her through the study door. He closed and locked it behind them. Xavier used a key to open one of the drawers in Brant's large mahogany desk. *What was so important?* There was a crash at the door.

"Hurry," Brant growled unnecessarily.

Once the drawer was open, Xavier fiddled inside for a second or two. There was a creaking noise and the desk slid to the side revealing a gaping hole. She could just make out several steps leading down and then the dark swallowed anything more. Using his good arm, Brant pulled her against him so that only her tippy toes still touched the ground. She had to pull on the robe to keep her ass covered. By now Xavier had pretty much seen her naked, but she'd be damned if she'd allow him more of an eyeful than he'd already had.

There were loud bangs on the walls. "Good thing we blocked the entrances in the hidden passages," Xavier said as they descended into the darkness. "The brick and concrete was reinforced with silver, so good luck to those bastards."

Tanya whimpered. Shit, she couldn't see a thing. Brant pulled her higher up against him and she wrapped her legs around his middle. Right now she was liable to have them all falling to their deaths if she tried to negotiate down the path. She looked up at the small square of light above just as the desk slid shut.

Pitch black.

She doubted she would see her hand in front of her face if she tried. Tanya wrapped herself tighter around Brant. "I have you," he said.

They levelled off onto what felt like flat ground and Brant let her slide down beside him. She kept her arms around him, afraid to take even the smallest step on her own.

"Zane was right, we have been compromised. They will know about this cellar," Xavier said. There were some clicking noises and another sliding sound from above. "That should take care of the study entrance."

"Good thing I ordered for the passage way from the fountain to be sealed. That only leaves the forest entrance," Brant's chest rumbled as he spoke.

"I have our elite troops surrounding the entrance and archers on the perimeter. Rest assured, I will head there myself and will protect our king and queen with my life." This was the first time that she had been referred to as the queen and it felt good. "Your human did well today. She is worthy of our people and will give you strong heirs."

Tanya wished she could see facial expressions, but it was just too dark.

Brant moved forward a step and then she could feel the warmth of Xavier and the brush of fingers across her arm at Brant's back. They were embracing. Brant grunted.

"Have your female look at that."

"I will be fine. You stay with Tanya, I will—"

"No brother. You are the king. Without you or the human female, our coven would crumble."

Brant laughed. "Hardly. You would step in to take my place."

Tanya sobbed. "I know it's selfish, but please don't leave me."

Brant tightened his arm around her.

"You have a nose my lord. You need to stay with her," Xavier sounded stern. What did having a nose have to do with it? Could Brant scent something?

"What is it?" she asked.

Both men ignored her. "Fine, but take care of yourself brother. Our queen needs a guard," said Brant.

"Nothing like a bit of target practice," Xavier chuckled. Retreating foot falls were her only indication that he was leaving.

"Right, there is a first aid kit around here somewhere." Brant moved and she stayed at his side as if glued.

"Um, Brant. Please tell me there's a light in here."

A low chuckle caused another vibration through Brant's chest. "I'm sorry, I forgot that you can't see in the dark. There must be one somewhere, as humans designed this place." He tucked her in closer and moved in one direction and then the other. He reached and there was a clicking noise as the room lit up. Although not all that bright, the sudden blast of light caused her to scrunch her eyes shut while they adjusted. The room was small with a double bed to the side and a free standing toilet in the corner. Oh God, she prayed she wouldn't need to go any time soon. Her cheeks heated just thinking about it.

Brant released her and pulled a first aid kit from the shelf. The walls were lined with shelves filled with blankets, clothes and cans of food. There were vents in the ceiling and various other items that one would expect to find on a camping expedition or during a siege.

Siege.

Panic rose up in her but she shoved it down. They hopefully wouldn't be trapped in here for long. Brant seemed tense, his eyes had a worried look, they kept darting upwards. Maybe he could hear something that she couldn't.

"Is everything okay?"

"I should be with my men. There will be casualties" His jaw worked.

She cast her eyes downwards, guilt burned in her gut.

"No, Cenwein, this is not your fault." He brushed her cheek with his knuckles. "Xavier was right, my place is at your side."

"Give me that. Sit on the bed." She took the first aid kit and followed him, taking a seat next to him. Tanya opened the latch and rummaged through the kits contents until she found a bottle of neat alcohol and a pack of swabs. She opened the bottle and poured some of the contents onto the swab using it to clean the wounds on his chest. The cotton pad quickly soaked through with blood so she repeated the process several times. Either the chest wounds weren't as bad as she had thought or they were already healing. She guessed the latter.

Once she finished, she removed a tube of antiseptic cream but Brant shook his head. "That won't be necessary, I don't get infections."

"Okay." She dropped the tube back into the kit. Next, she

took the half empty bottle and moved to the puncture wound on his arm. "This is going to hurt."

Brant smiled, nodding once. If it hurt, he didn't give any indication, not so much as a twitch of a muscle. She poured a second time over the wound, ensuring that the liquid went into the puncture. Tanya used the swabs to mop up the leaking fluid and to clean the wound. There was a crepe bandage in the kit that looked like it would fit well on a wound of that nature. She pulled out the sealed pack.

"Don't bother, I will be healed within the hour. Let's get you cleaned up."

She looked down and noticed for the first time that the front of her robe was splattered with congealing blood. Tanya made a gagging sound but managed to keep the contents of her stomach down. She tasted bile. Her right hand was also covered. She'd been so busy with Brant that she hadn't noticed. The memory of the blood pumping from the elf's wound came flooding back.

"You did good, Cenwein. Don't blame yourself. He would've killed both of us without hesitation."

"Actually, he would've killed you and taken me to the alpha. I might've killed another one just before you came. It . . . he said that I wasn't the alpha's type but he would take me to the beast anyway."

Brant growled and his eyes glowed. "The wolf is as good as dead. His people's heads will roll and stakes will be erected. Both the shifters and the elves will bleed for this." He stood and paced the small space. "He will not have you."

"Leave their people out of this. Please don't harm innocent women and children. Please Brant."

"By trying to take you, he puts this coven and the future of our species in danger. Innocent vampire women and children will die. I will not allow that."

"Please," she pleaded.

His demeanor softened. "Do not concern yourself, Cenwein. I will do what is needed to protect you, to protect this coven. I am not in the business of killing innocents and will do what I can to avoid it, but those bastards need to be hit where it hurts. I will do what I have to."

A tear rolled down her cheek. Damn. She was crying. Again. This was becoming an irritating habit. Brant pulled her against his warm chest.

"Alone with the female for five minutes and already she is bawling like a baby. Can't say I blame her," Zane's deep baritone voice filled the small space. Brant tensed, the wall of his chest turning to stone.

"You weren't invited." Brant released her. He probably didn't realize it, but he pushed her behind him. Tanya had to tip her head to see past Brant. Leather clad, his muscles had freaking muscles and his dark eyes blazed. Zane pulled a backpack from his shoulders placing it on the ground.

Zane caught her staring and winked. "I invited myself. Had an interesting chat with Stephany outside a few minutes ago."

Brant growled and pushed her further behind him.

"The female wants to choose both of us."

Brant choked out a humourless laugh. "Not happening."

Tanya stepped to the side.

"Suit yourself." His eyes landed on her sweeping down the length of her. Damn, the arrogant jerk could have her hot and panting without so much as a touch. She immediately felt guilty. Tanya was fast developing feelings for Brant. He could be warm and tender, so thoughtful. He was also a deadly warrior. Brant growled louder this time.

"The sun has risen." Zane smiled looking like a predator. "The female is mine." He removed his jacket sniffing deeply. "I believe she is coming into heat."

Tanya gasped. She wasn't even mated yet. She wasn't sure she even wanted children.

"Touch her and I will kill you."

Zane locked his jaw, his eyes narrowed. They stood like this for what felt like a very long time. "If we fight in this small space the female will be hurt, is that what you want?"

"Bastard," Brant spat the word. "You know I don't."

"If our covens were to join, we would be much stronger against the other species." As Zane spoke, he removed a sheath from his back and several other blades that were strapped to his body. He threw the weapons on a pile next to the backpack. "My guard are attacking as we speak. The battle will be over within the next few hours. United we would make a terrifying force. Separated we may be defeated. Neither of us would have the human."

Brant's hands closed into fists at his side. "We are enemies Zane. It would never work."

"We need to find a way. An arrangement that would work for both parties."

Tanya was sick of being treated like she wasn't in the room. "Three parties. I would need to have a say."

Brant turned his eyes, moving them over her face. "You will be queen. You will have a say in all regardless of how this goes." He turned back, his voice deepening. "I highly doubt it would work."

"There is only one way to find out and since we're stuck in this room for the next few hours . . . forced to play nice . . ." He threw a wicked grin her way. Zane removed his shirt, he moved to the bag on the ground gracefully lowering himself onto his haunches and removing water.

Next, he pulled out a whole string of condoms. "The choice is yours, sweetness. If one of us manages to impregnate you, the alpha will no longer be interested in taking you as a mate. But if you would rather wait . . . ?" he tossed the string of silver foil her way and, to her surprise, she caught it.

Part 4

Wild Heat

Chapter ONE

IN ONE FLUID MOTION, she caught the long foil strip while never once taking her soft chestnut eyes from his. The condoms didn't look right in her hand. His future mate should never have a need for them.

His female wore a short, thin robe. The blue silk barely covered the top part of her thighs only just managing to conceal her sex. The fact that the robe was spattered with blood had his heart racing. He clenched his fists at his sides, unused to the emotions that coursed through him. She was, after all, the future of his coven and if anything happened to her his species would be in ruin. That must be why he felt this way. It was the only logical reason he could come up with.

The female scented strongly of Brant, telling him that she had most likely rutted with his enemy recently.

Enemy. Shaking his head, he couldn't help but to think of the implications of what he was encouraging to happen. If things worked out, he would have to try and think of Brant in different terms. He had to admit, even though Brant could be a bit of a . . . pain in the ass, he'd never truly hated the male. It was his birth obligation to do so. What amazed him the most though was that he wasn't offended by the scent of the other male on his female.

Watching this enticing human take her pleasure from Brant had almost made him lose his load straight into the tight confines of his pants like a juvenile youngster. Especially hearing the female's scream as she was dragged over the edge with his fingers on her clit. She was some female, so soft, yet hard in all the right places. So tight that his dick twitched just thinking about it.

His eyes dropped to her breasts, jutting points stabbed at the soft robe. One pull on the tie and she would be all his. He took a step towards her just as she threw the condoms onto the ground.

"Good choice, sweetness." He unsnapped the first button on his pants. Brant growled low and deep, a definite warning. Zane kept his eyes on the female.

"I'm not having sex with a cheating bastard." She laughed but the sound held no humor. "Been there done that. I even have the t-shirt." A sharp pungent scent rolled off her, it hit him square on. It radiated off his female. The sour aroma of pain.

The need to draw blood hit him and adrenaline surged. Zane was on Brant in a second. It was only the sound of the female screaming that kept him from pummelling the other male. Instead he gripped Brant by the throat. "What the fuck did you do to her?"

Small, useless taps rained on his back. "Let go of him you brute." The human insisted on punching him even though it would be hurting her more than him.

"You have three seconds to get your hands off of me." Brant's eyes had narrowed. They were glowing.

He heard his female grunt as her little foot connected with

his calf. Zane decided to let go of Brant before the human did herself damage.

"Not him you idiot!" she shrieked.

Zane took a step back so that he could see the female as well as keep Brant in his line of vision.

"Don't do that again," Brant spoke through clenched teeth.

"Who hurt you?" Zane kept his eyes on his birth enemy even though he was addressing his female. Their two covens needed this union, but he didn't necessarily need to like the male in front of him. They just needed to get along enough to make this work.

"*You* hurt me you bastard!" the female spat at him.

Confusion clouded his thoughts for a few beats.

The human made a sound of frustration and pulled the robe more firmly around herself, crossing her arms over her chest. He couldn't help it when his eyes dropped to the deep cleavage the motion had created.

"Don't you dare look at me like that. Especially since you already had your fill of the females at your coven. I'm sure Charlotte was in your bed the moment I left. The spot barely cold." Her eyes blazed, her lips pouted, her cheeks flushed.

She was jealous as hell. Zane barely managed to keep himself from grinning. So she was quite happy to go from one king to the other, yet didn't want him rutting with any other female in her absence. Zane shook his head. "I told you that only once we are mated will I agree to a monogamous relationship."

She stomped her foot and her hands flew to her hips. "I won't have it. You can turn and leave right now. I might be a little bit plump and just a human but I deserve some sort of respect, and I won't have the other vampire women laughing behind my back because you can't keep your dick in your pants." She stomped again. "If I walk in on you with one of them I swear to God . . ." A tear tracked down her cheek. It felt like someone fisted his heart making it hard to breath, to think.

"Look what you did." Brant took a step toward her but Zane shoved the other male to the side.

Zane picked her up even though she kicked at him. "Stop, Ysnaar." He pulled her flush against him, their faces separated by mere inches. She struggled in his arms still kicking at him. "Stop. I haven't been with another female."

She stopped kicking but tears still coursed down her face. "You lie." She sniffed, "You're just saying that because you want to fuck me."

"He's telling the truth," Brant grunted. "I don't scent another female on him."

The female let out a sigh, her eyes fluttering closed. She let him pull her closer and he buried his head in her soft hair. "Thank you," he said in Brant's direction.

"Let's get something clear, I didn't set the record straight for you. I did it for her."

"Fair enough." Zane pulled back while narrowing his eyes on hers, they were red rimmed. "What's this about being plump and human? If Brant didn't hurt you, then who did?" Zane couldn't keep the growl from his voice.

The female sniffed a few times. She drew back and used her hand to wipe her face. "It doesn't matter."

"It does matter," Brant said.

"It was nothing. Nobody."

"Bullshit." Zane set her down. "Tell me . . . us." He added the last while trying to keep the irritation from his voice at having to include Brant.

"My ex-boyfriend cheated on me. I walked in on them.

Like I said it was nothing."

Zane heard Brant's teeth crack as he ground his jaw just before letting out a low growl of his own. "An idiot," he said, his eyes firmly on his female. "What happened?"

"Troy said it was my own fault. I put on a few pounds after meeting him and just couldn't shake them. I like cupcakes far too much." A stain of pink crept up from her collar. "He said that my thighs were too thick, that I"—she swallowed hard—"had cellulite and that my breasts were"—her lip quivered—"too big."

"Bull fucking shit," Brant snarled. "I will find this human and rip his—"

His female giggled through her tears, she put up a hand. "No, don't bother I don't even remember what I even liked about him to begin with. To think I wanted to have them made smaller." She cupped her lush curves making his cock harden behind his zipper.

Zane made a strangled groan, he couldn't help himself. "Make them smaller? Too big? . . . No fucking way. The human must have been brain damaged. I couldn't bring myself to touch another female. Not after having you." His eyes roamed over her body, moving over each and every curve. "I am going to rut with you now female. Would you like me to use a condom?"

"I'm not ready to be a mom."

"We'll keep you safe from the alpha, no need to rush into anything." Brant said, and Zane could hear that the male was trying to keep his voice even as he spoke.

"Bull, we are here to cement a partnership that will lead to a mating in eight days and the joining of the covens. Should one of us impregnate our human now, it would seal the deal. No way to back out before the new moon. That bastard wolf would be forced to retreat. They're already on the losing end." Zane pointed up to the battle that was taking place above them.

"I am not a means to seal a deal. If they're already on the losing end, you won't need to . . . impregnate me. Just a few days ago I was single and now I have . . . well"—she turned from him to Brant and back again—"two of you and I don't know if I could deal with a baby to add to it all . . . I kind of think we need to get used to this first. Try and see if it'll work between us."

Zane could see the internal battle raging in Brant. The male pursed his lips together in a thin white line, though a low rumble still managed to escape. As much as he hated it, his respect for Brant grew. This whole thing was torture on the other king. The whole possessive number he had pulled yesterday meant that he already viewed the human as his mate as well.

"It's simple," Zane said. "The covens come first. That means the three of us together is happening whether we like it or not. Do you want us both sweetness, or would you prefer to choose come the new moon?"

———·C✳·———

Two sets of dark eyes bore into her. She swallowed hard, not really wanting to answer. Earlier today she had been so sure yet when faced with reality, she wasn't so sure any more. "I don't want the two of you fighting over me. I don't want to watch either one of you die at the hand of the other. I also don't want to be forced into mating a wolf. In addition, I don't know if I'm ready to be a mom."

"What *do* you want Tanya?" Brant took a step towards her, his eyes softened as he spoke. "For the record. You would be pregnant for twelve months and wouldn't show for the first six. Pregnancies are rare and it normally takes an average of four years for a vampire female to conceive. Humans have had a much better success rate, although we don't have much to go on since it is only the kings that have been permitted to take humans as mates."

"Twelve months?"

"This is the same for vampire females," Zane added.

She'd heard that pregnancy was hard on a woman. One of her regulars at the store was a farmer's wife, Sandy. She devoured books and with a limited budget, could only afford reused ones. Tanya had a whole section in her store dedicated to second hand. She still remembered the day that Sandy had skipped into the store and announced her pregnancy. She'd been so excited, smiling from ear to ear. Not long after, she came in looking a lighter shade of green due to morning sickness, except Sandy complained that hers lasted all day long. The sickness soon evolved into back pain and headaches, not being able to sleep at night and the need to pee all the time.

Sandy had visited less and less often as her pregnancy progressed. Tanya could clearly remember the day Sandy had brought the baby to the store after she had given birth. She had never seen someone look at something with such love and adoration before. Sandy had said that being a mother was worth it in the end. Tanya had felt a little broody looking at the little one's chubby cheeks and tiny little hands that had clasped her automatically when she had put her finger close. When she'd brought up the subject with Troy, he had shot her down immediately. It would be different with the vampire kings though.

Brant had said that he wanted to be a father. Zane seemed to only want heirs and was treating this whole thing like a business arrangement. The thought of carrying another life, of raising a child scared the hell out of her. It also sent a jolt of excitement through her. All of this was so unexpected.

"What do you want?" Zane mirrored Brant's question. "I know that you are compatible with both of us and that you wanted to rut with both of us yesterday."

She scrunched her eyes shut. "You didn't just say that?"

"We need to be honest and rational about this. Admit it." Those dark eyes stayed with her.

She held Brant's gaze, it had turned hard. He nodded. "Be honest, Cenwein."

"It was a little embarrassing at first, but I'll admit that I enjoyed it." She looked away, unable to maintain eye contact. "I liked both of your hands on me." She felt her cheeks heat.

"You want us both," Zane said. It was more of a statement than a question.

"Yes," she whispered.

"You want both of us to mate you come the new moon."

"Yes," another whisper.

"I'm going to have you now." Zane tore at his pants, removing them quickly while somehow managing to advance on her at the same time. He picked up the condoms at her feet tossing them distastefully to the other side of the room. With one light tug, her robe fell in a blue arc at her feet. He touched his hand to her belly. "I cannot wait for your womb to quicken with my seed." Brant snarled but stayed where he was. Zane's lips twitched. "Fine," he sighed. "With royal seed. That alpha won't get you, but this will be the best way to ensure your safety. More importantly we need this to secure our union with no means for escape." His eyes softened. "You will make a good mother." He glanced Brant's way and her eyes tracked his.

Brant looked like he was barely managing to keep a handle on his emotions. His jaw worked. He eventually nodded once. "It would be for the best, Cenwein." He tried to smile. "I look forward to seeing your belly swollen with our child."

"Cenwein," Zane said, his eyes tracked her naked flesh. "I can see why you call our female that . . ."

"Don't you dare think of calling her that—" Brant's eyes were so dark that they looked black.

"Relax . . ." Zane held up a hand. "I prefer Ysnaar myself."

"She does tend to want to claw your eyes out a lot of the time," Brant smiled. It was tight and didn't quite reach his eyes.

"You should see her when my dick's inside of her."

Tanya gasped. Brant snarled, taking a step towards Zane but somehow managing to hold back. "Watch your dirty mouth."

"Stop being so freaking uptight. There's nothing like a bit of dirty talk to liven up the party." Zane bobbed his eyebrows up and down. His cock jutted from his body.

"What does it mean? Cenwein?" she asked trying to defuse the situation. Also, it was something she had been meaning to ask.

Brant's eyes softened. "It is a type of flower. Exquisitely rare and beautiful, yet very delicate. One touch and the flower dies."

"I'm hardly delicate." She laughed ending on a snort.

Zane wrapped his hand around her waist. "Oh, yes you are. The funny thing is that although we use the term Ysnaar to describe a feisty individual, it is also a type of flower. Strikingly beautiful, just as delicate only full of deadly barbs. You do have bite to you and I like that in a female. I have found it to be rare in a human."

"Oh happy days, you at least like something about me."

"I do like that trait. There are other things I like too though." He paused, his eyes dipping to her chest. "Now the time for talk is over." He sniffed the air. "The scent of your heat grows stronger." This time he nuzzled into her neck and Brant rocked from one foot to the other, his fists were clenched at his sides.

"How did you know I was coming into heat?"

"Like I said earlier, I ran into Stephany outside the entrance to this place. She was the one who gave me the condoms. Told me where I could find you. She must've scented it on you earlier."

Fantastic. Stephany had orchestrated the whole damn thing. She held Brant's eyes. "You really need to have a little talk with her."

His lips twitched, but didn't break into a smile. Zane bent down, he picked up his discarded shirt and a bottle of water. He opened the water and poured some onto the shirt. Using careful strokes, he cleaned the blood from her neck and hands. Reapplying the water to his shirt at regular intervals. Once he seemed satisfied with his work, he used the dry side to mop up any remaining water on her skin.

"You weren't hurt," again a statement.

She shook her head. It was times like these that she glimpsed a different side to him, one that gave her hope, one that told her he cared and that this was more than just the future of his coven to him. It was also about his future too. One with her. Hopefully one in which he would be happy. Maybe he could even grow to love her. She hoped the same for Brant and prayed that she wasn't alienating him by wanting this.

When Zane was done, he threw the shirt down and set the water on the ground to the right of them. He stood, towering over her and put his hands on her hips almost waiting for an invitation, which was strange because Zane had always come across as a male that took.

"Tanya," Brant's pained voice cut into her like a knife. She looked up and saw the stricken look on his face. Every muscle was roped and bulging. Especially the ones on his neck. They were corded and strained.

She couldn't hurt him like this. She pulled away from Zane's embrace and stumbled in her haste to get to Brant, thankfully he was there to catch her. Brant wrapped her in his arms. "I'm sorry, it's okay," he whispered for her ears only.

"No, it's not. You don't want this."

"It doesn't matter. At least this way I get to keep you even if I can't ever have all of you. You'll be happy. It's all I need."

"Are you sure?"

"Yes. It is for the best." His tender eyes held hers. Why did this have to be so difficult?

"Okay." Her eyes pricked. Before she could think on it, there was suddenly heat and then hard male behind her. One part in particular. It hardened up a whole lot as it made contact with her lower back. Zane put his hands on her hips rubbing up and down her upper thighs.

"We'll make this work, sweetness," his deep baritone voice caressed her. One of Zane's large hands rounded her belly, dipping down and immediately zoning in on her clit. God, but the man was good. She had to suppress a moan since she was still in Brant's arms. Her breathing must've changed because he tensed taking a step back. Her hands stayed on his shoulders. Brant glanced down and when his eyes lifted they were hard, narrowed. His jaw tensed and locked. Tanya wanted to say something, but what could she do or say to help him through this?

He moved to the far wall. Taking up a stance that reminded

her of a marble statue. His eyes followed them as Zane ushered her to the bed. She couldn't take her eyes off him either. Even while Zane's hand remained on the bundle of nerves between her legs, or even as he picked her up and positioned her on all fours.

Crouching over her, Zane slipped a finger inside her while his thumb stayed on her clit. Tanya had to work hard to suppress a moan as she tried to concentrate on Brant's face. His eyes were glowing, his body so tense that she was sure he would sprain something. Her orgasm built inside her with a speed that surprised her considering the situation. When Zane inserted a second finger, she couldn't help the whimper that escaped. Brant growled, low and deadly but he didn't move so much as a muscle.

As hard as she tried to resist, it was useless, Zane was just too good at zoning in on all of her sweet spots. He knew exactly how to touch her and went about the task with relentless precision. Using his other hand, he palmed her breast squeezing almost to the point of pain. It felt so damned good.

"Fucking sexy." His words surprised her, he wasn't the type to dish out compliments lightly. Or possibly ever. Zane nipped at her shoulder, continuing his ministrations on both her pussy and her breast. "Come for me, sweetness," a rough growl that sent her over the edge.

Eyes squeezed shut, she rode his hand trying to hold back a cry and failing dismally. Rough hands grasped her hips. Zane thrust himself inside her balls deep in one motion. She cried out, her pussy still clenching from the orgasm. Not giving her time to catch her breath, he continued to ram himself into her. No sooner had she rode out the rest of her orgasm, did the build of her next one begin.

Brant snarled, his face was contorted in rage but her body

didn't give a damn as it tightened with her pending orgasm. "You feel so good." Husky, deep, she loved the sound of Zane's voice.

She didn't think it was possible, but Zane picked up speed and her core hummed. The first flutters contracted her pussy walls. Zane had her caged underneath him. His hands kept her anchored in place. There was a sharp pinch at the base of her neck followed by an explosion of blinding pleasure. Her back bowed. She screamed as he sucked a second time. Her body shook, her mind blanked, everything in her stopped. Her breath caught in her lungs. All she could do was feel. Zane jerked inside her, grunting as he found his own release.

There was a loud thud and Zane was no longer behind her. She turned her head, feeling dazed. Brant stood behind her with Zane on the floor, his lip split and bloodied. Brant looked pissed. His eyes glowed, flashing red for a second. He snarled, his long, wicked looking fangs gleamed. On the ends of his fingers, sharp looking claws had taken the place of his nails. She had to stop herself from backing away. From telling him to stop. It took every ounce of strength she possessed to stay still as he closed the small distance between them.

Brant pushed her into the mattress, her breasts and the one side of her face pressed firmly down into the soft material. One hand held the back of her neck while the other grabbed her hip. His claws dug into her flesh. They would leave marks for sure. She whimpered but knew instinctively that it would be best to keep still and to remain calm. Brant was still somewhere inside the vampire that clung to her. He might not be himself right now but he would never hurt her.

"Easy," Zane said. His voice even and calm. At least if Brant did lose it Zane was right there.

"Fuck you," an inhuman snarl as Brant sank into her. He

growled as his balls slapped against her ass. There was a sharp pinch in the same area Zane had bitten her and she orgasmed hard as he sucked. The fact that she was restrained with his dick, unmoving yet deep inside her, had her coming even harder on the second draw. Brant withdrew his fangs and licked her neck. Her groan ended on a cry as he began to move in long, hard thrusts. He grunted with each languid stroke. Not letting up on the grip on her neck and hip. How in the hell was it possible? She physically hurt from the rough sex both vampires had doled out, yet another orgasm started its slow build again.

Brant continued to fuck her hard, yet he didn't increase his speed. It kept her on the edge. Every muscle clenched in expectation. Her body was slick from the exertion. She was panting and mewling. On the verge of begging when he bit her again. It was like a freight train hit her. Her mouth went slack, her eyes widened before squeezing shut and her pussy clenched so hard that she was sure she would hurt him. Another suck had every muscle in her body contorted under his heavy weight. She felt hot bursts deep inside as Brant came, they urged her to higher limits.

Somewhere in the distance she thought she heard a shout, but blood rushed in her ears making it hard to hear. A meaty thud. Brant ripped both his hands and fangs away from her neck. His whole body seemed to vibrate with a low growl. The spot at her neck throbbed.

"Enough," Zane's deep voice finally penetrated her rational mind.

Brant clasped her hips with both hands, his cock was hardening up and he began to rock into her. "No"—she moaned—"I can't."

"I said enough. Let our female rest. I'll let you have her first next time."

"Generous of you." Brant continued to thrust. She moaned because it hurt, but damn it somehow it managed to feel good as well.

"She is human and needs to rest." Zane's voice had dropped about three octaves. Another deep thrust. There was a loud crack and it was Brant's turn to hit the floor. Tanya collapsed. She grabbed for the blanket at the foot of the bed as Brant leapt to his feet. The two vampires clashed chests, snarling into each other's faces. They looked like the non-human version of rabid dogs about to fight. Tanya felt too drained to try and stop them. She wrapped herself in a blanket while moving as far away from the males as possible.

Zane backed down first. "The female will be hurt if we fight."

Brant moved into the empty space still snarling.

"Tanya will be hurt. You need to stop." This time the statement seemed to snap Brant out of his crazed state. Weird how just a few hours ago this had seemed like a good idea, right now she felt like she might have made the biggest mistake of her life.

Chapter TWO

Zane tossed some clothes her way. A set of sweats that were so big that she had to fold the waist and sleeves to get them to sort of fit. Then he grabbed a bottle of water and sat down next to her on the bed.

"Are you hurt?" Zane asked as he handed her the water.

"I'm a bit bruised and I have a couple of scratches," more like claw marks, "but I'll survive."

"Let me see." Zane moved the hoodie of the sweatshirt and leaned in to examine the back of her neck and throat. She thanked God that he stayed away from her hips, which had taken the brunt of the assault. When he pulled away, his mouth was set.

"It's fine," she shrugged.

"It's not fine. We were too rough, but it won't happen again." Zane turned to look at Brant who sat on his haunches back on the far side of the room.

"It won't happen again," Brant repeated leaning his arms onto his thighs. "I won't watch you rut with her again though. This will only work if we remain separate. We'll have to find a way to share." More of the same shuffling from one coven to the other. She sighed.

"You need to move to my castle. We agreed it would be best," Zane added more gruffly.

"As a short term solution. Separate towers. I'll only agree on long term if we build on neutral ground. Something fit for both covens."

"Fine, but how do we share the female?"

Brant shrugged.

"For now we'll stick to the current arrangement, but when she's in heat—"

"We'll take turns. One cycle she's mine and the next she's yours." Brant stood in one graceful motion.

Zane chuckled. "Fine, but since this is my twenty four hours with the female I get to spend the rest of the time with her. I get to have her first cycle. You can consider what just happened as a gift. Happy fucking birthday!"

Brant snarled. His eyes glowed. "Like hell."

Zane chuckled some more. "On occasions like this, the three of us will have to try and get along."

Brant growled something incoherent.

"Let's hope our seed takes and we won't be faced with this problem again for a while."

Brant nodded once while sliding back down onto his haunches. His head hung, he looked defeated. Tanya wanted to go to him, but didn't dare. She had no idea how he would react. It hurt. She'd really banked on a future with him. It looked as if she would remain torn between the two kings with one who saw her as a business arrangement and the other who wouldn't be able to hold feelings for her because he had envisioned a more normal relationship. Her hand tightened around the bottle that Zane had given her earlier, she opened it and drained half the contents.

"Are you hungry?"

She shook her head but her stomach growled. Zane smiled, a sexy grin that had her nipples tightening. Other parts responded with a throbbing ache. Her body was telling her that she was ready for round two, yet her mind responded with a hell no knowing full well that her body didn't know what it was talking about.

Zane tore open a silver foil package and offered her a biscuit. Tanya took the snack and nibbled. Not bad. The second pack had dried fruit in it. Between the biscuits and the fruit, she ended up enjoying it and felt much better even though she was still exhausted.

Tanya yawned. She'd spent half the night waiting for Brant to come home and her morning had started long before dawn.

"Sleep, Ysnaar. We will need you again soon. The scent you give off during this time will make a male lose his mind with need. Vampire female's only go into heat twice per year."

"Really? Because with us it's every month."

Brant growled, the sound more frustrated than angry as he spoke. "We have to go through this once every moon cycle. Sleep, Cenwein." His body tightened as he looked in Zane's direction. "I get to take her first."

"Calm the fuck down. You can have her first so long as you go easy."

"Don't tell me what to do." Brant's lips curled back into a snarl that had her feeling a little hot. *Must be all the testosterone flying around the room,* she thought.

"Actually, Brant, everything feels a bit tender. You will need to take it slower." She didn't like picking sides, but her body wouldn't take much more of what had been dished out previously.

"I'm sorry." Brant averted his eyes and Tanya longed to

wrap her arms around him.

"I know you are," she added. "It felt really good at the time even if it hurts a bit after."

"You smell so good and seeing him rutting you made me want to lose my mind." Brant growled again. The sound evoked a feeling of terror this time even though she knew he wouldn't really hurt her.

Brant's nose twitched. "You have nothing to fear."

"I know."

Zane chuckled. "Watching us rut made you want to lose your mind . . . don't you mean lose your load?" He pretended to hump the air.

Brant growled, "Like fuck. Fuck you!"

Zane chuckled a second time but thankfully dropped it. He turned to her and said, "Sleep." Zane adjusted himself in his pants, a pinched look came over his face. He sat on the edge of the bed, but within a few minutes was up and pacing. "Oh, to hell with it," he said. There was a rustling noise. When Tanya looked, his pants were in a heap on the floor. "I'm sorry female but I need to take care of this and I realize that you are too sore." He gestured to his engorged shaft, turned and walked over to the toilet and palmed his cock. His back was to them with his tight ass in full view. Zane used one hand to lean against the wall. His elbow moved back and forth with increasing speed.

"Really?"

"It is extremely difficult for us to scent you and not be heavily turned on." Brant spoke while keeping his eyes averted. "I will need to do the same once he is finished. It will be better this way. Maybe we can be gentler if we take care of ourselves first. You sleep." Brant's cock jutted up against his belly.

"Like hell," she whispered. "This shouldn't be happening, but I'm feeling really turned on anyways."

"It's the heat." Zane grunted, his hand still moving back and forth.

Tanya took off her sweatpants and walked over to Brant whose eyes started to glow as she stood in front of him. "I've never felt this turned on before," she added.

"You've never been around vampires before during this time. Never rutted with our kind." Even though his hand was still wrapped around his member, Zane had stopped fisting his cock. He had turned and was watching her and Brant intently. She straddled Brant, who put his hands on her hips. She winced.

"Shit, I'm sorry," Brant's brow furrowed as he took in the scratches on her hips.

"Put your hands on your thighs and leave them there." Tanya unzipped her sweater knowing it would be shredded if she didn't. "If you so much as lay one finger on me then this stops. Do you understand?"

Brant swallowed hard, his eyes on her breasts, he nodded once.

"Good." She took his shaft in her hand and guided it to her opening. It stung a little at first but she was soon riding him, chasing yet another orgasm. He felt so good inside her, filling her. His face was taut with desire, his eyes dark. They studied her, moving from her face to her bouncing chest. It felt so good to be in control but when he thrust into her from below, she came undone on a long wail. Brant grunted, right there with her. As soon as she slowed her movements, Zane picked her up off of Brant.

He used the wall to anchor her. "Wrap your legs around me, sweetness." She did as he said. "Good girl." He grunted as he entered her in one swift motion. "I'm already close." He grit his teeth while fucking her with exquisite slowness.

She moaned, feeling yet another orgasm build. "Oh God, me too."

"How you holding up?" Zane whispered between rugged pants.

"I'll be sore and sorry for myself later . . ." She moaned. "Feels really good right now though." She moaned again as her body tightened. "How long will I stay this way?"

"I"—he grunted—"don't"—he groaned—"know."

She just knew there was no way she would survive too much more of this. That thought quickly dissolved as his finger brushed her clit. It wasn't long and she was coming apart again. Between his deft strokes and skillful fingers, she didn't stand a chance. Zane grit his teeth, growling low as he found his completion. His eyes never left hers.

Brant growled pulling her away from Zane the moment he stilled.

"I can't," she whispered. "I mean it this time."

"You will sleep with me," Brant said, his eyes on Zane.

Zane's eyes hardened but he nodded. Tanya picked up her sweatpants and headed for the bed. She could deal with her males later, right now she needed to sleep. Yawning, she moved to lie between the sheets. Brant pulled her against him, leaving his arm tightly around her middle. It was hard to believe that it was possible, but his hard erection dug into her lower back.

"Can you move that please?" It would be hard to fall asleep with his dick throbbing against her. "You might bruise me with it."

Brant made a sound of disagreement. "I can't," he paused. "I feel a little bit better when I am pressed up against you."

How could she argue with that? It was actually kind of sweet in a weird way. "Fine," she huffed, sure that she would never fall asleep. Above them a battle raged, another one raged just as fiercely right here in this room. She glanced over at Zane who sat with his back resting against the wall, a stony expression on his face.

Tanya awoke some time later to the sound of a loud grunt. She turned to see Zane hunched over the toilet jerking as he found his completion. As soon as he was done Brant planted a kiss to the back of her neck and slid from the bed taking up Zane's position, dick in hand.

"Is it really that bad?"

"Worse." Zane's chest rumbled against her as he took Brant's place in the bed, he pulled her against him. The familiar feel of an erection dug into her.

"You can't be horny already?"

"Wanna bet?" Zane grinned. "Don't worry, sweetness, we will wait until you are ready again."

Brant grunted. Tanya glanced over feeling a bit like a voyeur. Legs set apart, ass pinched, arm moving back and forward in a rhythm that had her mouth turning dry. That familiar need resonated from between her thighs, but she was just too sore to be able to act on it.

"Think of our female's tight sheath," Zane threw at Brant.

"Shut it," Brant bit back.

"Think of her lush tits against your chest, of her little pants and moans as she's about to cum."

"I said to . . ." He grunted, his ass jerking as his hand pumped harder.

"I know. Impossible not to cum isn't it?"

Brant finished up. He used a bottle of water to wash his hands. "I can fantasize about Tanya without your help."

Zane chuckled, he trailed his finger along her arm. She was tempted to drift back to sleep but pulled herself up instead. She glanced at Zane. "Tell me about growing up. Where are your parents?"

Zane tensed. "I think we can save that for another time." He looked at Brant like he expected the other male to say something. Brant put on some pants and took up his position on his haunches at the wall.

"I might be pregnant with your child. I need to know more about both of you if we are to make this work."

"Female," he paused. "It is done whether any of us likes it or not. In eight days we will officially mate, hopefully your womb will quicken before then. It must work between us." Zane pulled away rising to a sitting position.

"I want to know more Zane." She sat in front of him, putting a hand on his chest. Feeling the warmth of the skin somewhere in the vicinity of his heart. Again he glanced at Brant. Maybe she should've brought this up when they were alone, but at the same time they were in this together. All three of them. She didn't want to have to go back and forth for the rest of her life.

His dark eyes settled on her. "My mother was not technically my father's first choice. He wanted a female that he couldn't end up having and chose another at the ceremony. It didn't work out," he paused. "Although he chose my mother, she always knew his heart had been set on another. She could never come to terms with that." Tanya wanted to know more about why he couldn't have the female he really wanted but didn't want to interrupt. His eyes clouded for a second. "She was never happy. A fragile, timid human. My father tried hard to please her, but by the time I was born they had drifted apart and had even taken up separate rooms." His mouth became a thin white line. He seemed to be composing himself. Tanya wrapped her hand in his.

He squeezed. "She wasn't a very good mother. Thankfully there were many females at the coven to take care of me. She would spend days in her room. She cried often. I can only ever remember her hugging me once. I fell and skinned my knee. Even though it healed almost immediately, I cried. She comforted me while telling me that life was unfair. It was the first and the last time it ever happened. I saw her less and less and when I did, she had a vacant faraway look. On my sixth birthday I was told that she had died."

Tanya gasped, "On your birthday?"

Zane smiled humorlessly. "I only found out much later that she had taken her own life. Cut her wrists in the bath. How cliché. Couldn't even wait one more day."

She could see how much he hurt. "Look, Zane. I realize that by some sick twist of fate that I also am not your first choice. I'm really sorry that she died the way she did, and that your first choice died. That they both died . . ." Shit. She was babbling, she took a deep breath. "I'm so sorry about . . ."

Zane cupped her chin. "Be still, Ysnaar. You are nothing like those humans."

Brant cleared his throat about to say something it seemed. Tanya was just turning toward him when Zane's hand tightened on her chin. He moved forward and kissed her. It wasn't fumbly like before. His soft lips caressed hers for a brief second before he slanted his head in the opposite direction. She made a sound of frustration as he pulled away altogether.

"I thought you liked to kiss, sweetness." Zane whispered.

"I do, but there's more to it than that."

He looked confused. "Kissing is the touching of lips. Have I missed something?"

She couldn't help but to smile. "Kissing me like you just did was really great."

"I don't see the problem then . . ." His eyebrows had drawn together.

"Let's use sex as an example." She said watching his delectable lips form a sexy, half smile. "A quick brush of the lips is great. It's similar to rubbing your dick along my slit. Feels good right?" His eyes turned a little hooded and he nodded. "But not as good as thrusting into my pussy."

He rolled his eyes and covered his ridged shaft with his hand like he was about to shoot off at any moment. "Careful, sweetness, I don't have much control at the moment and you're still sore."

"Yes, I am. So no ideas."

"I still don't understand what you're—"

She leaned in cutting his sentence off with her lips and tongue, which she swiped across his lips. Thankfully he caught the hint and opened. He was a quick learner and it wasn't long before he took the lead groaning as their tongues swirled together.

Zane was panting when they finally broke apart. "Another human concept that I really like and want to do often." She was about to kiss him again when Zane tensed up pulling her behind him. Brant jumped to his feet grabbing one of the swords that Zane had discarded earlier.

Then she heard the sound of footfalls. "It's me." The sound of Xavier's voice punctured the room. Two arrows jutted from his back and his face and torso were covered in blood.

"Oh my God," she whispered.

"Do not be alarmed, my queen. They are merely flesh wounds." Xavier must've seen the look of confusion on her face. "The arrow tips are not poisoned," he added.

Zane stood, donning a pair of pants. "Casualties?" he barked.

Xavier blinked several times. It was as if he raged an internal war. "Only four when we were taken by surprise. None of your men, although Lance is badly wounded." Xavier hung his head. "He may not make it."

"What the fuck happened?"

"Back the fuck off." Brant turned glowing eyes on Zane.

"What happened?" She asked also needing to know.

"Stephany was taken." Xavier said, head still facing the ground.

"What the fuck happened? Who took her? I'll fucking kill them!" Brant raged.

Tanya clasped his arm trying to give him a measure of comfort, but he brushed her off.

"They took Stephany, my lord. Lance was nearly killed trying to save her. As for the rest of us, we had to choose between you"—He turned his head to look them each in the eye. His teeth clenched as they landed on Zane—"or her. I would choose the same way again if given the opportunity."

"You did the right thing," Zane said.

"Oh my God. How can you say that? Poor Stephany." Tanya felt tears cascade down her cheeks. She'd never cried so often in her whole life. Zane wrapped an arm around her.

"We'll send a party after them right now," Brant growled.

"Already done. Vampires from both sides." Xavier looked at them both in turn.

"Good. If I leave right now," Brant said taking a deep breath. "I'll be able to catch up to them."

"No, my lord. You need to stay with the queen." He raised his eyebrows.

"Zane can take care of her, I will find Stephany." Brant

strode down the tunnel and within seconds it was too dark to see his retreating back.

Tanya buried her head into Zane's chest and cried. She felt guilty because although most of her tears were for her vampire friend, some of them were for herself. Zane thread his fingers into her hair.

"Why did they take her?" she gasped. "You don't think the alpha will mate with Stephany do you?"

"Stephany is already mated, so I highly doubt it."

"It's not like her and Lance are truly together." She sobbed harder.

"That is true," his deep voice rumbled through her.

"How would the alpha even know that she was mated?"

"He would scent it. Then again, Lance has not left his mark on her in many years."

She sobbed even harder.

"It would be unwise to speculate. Wolves and vampires do not mix anyways, so I am sure he has not taken her for that reason. We will soon know his intentions though. Brant may just get her back before the wolf makes it back to the rest of the pack and into shifter territory. Problem is, the bastards are fast and really good at hiding their trail. Brant might get lucky though."

At the mention of Brant's name, she clutched onto Zane hiccupping as her tears came down faster.

"He will get over himself."

"No, he won't."

"Sweetness . . ." he caressed her back. "Look at me."

She shook her head, unable to stop the tears.

"Tanya."

The use of her real name had her pulling back. Red nose, snot and all.

"He will get over himself. This is a big adjustment."

"How is it that you don't mind? Don't you care either way? Is this all about heirs to you?"

His eyes softened turning to melted, rich chocolate. "I care, Ysnaar. For whatever reason, I don't mind as much as I thought I would. I enjoyed watching him rut with you."

She gasped, "Really?"

Zane nodded. "Yeah, really. Problem is that Brant doesn't feel the same, so we'll need to keep things separate . . . It will work out in the end," he shrugged.

It made her feel hot remembering their earlier encounter. Especially now that she knew Zane had enjoyed watching. A shiver raced through her and her pussy gave a little throb of both need and soreness.

Zane chuckled, the sound coming much easier than the first time he had laughed for her. He sniffed in her direction. "You amaze me, female."

She giggled stopping as soon as she thought of Brant. "He can't even look at me right now, let alone . . ." She sniffed and bit her lip trying to hold back another wave of tears.

"Like I said, he'll get over it and if not then it's his loss."

She tried to smile even though half her heart felt like it was raw and bleeding.

Chapter Three

Brant strapped the last of the weapons to his back. A long samurai sword capable of doing much damage. He pulled on a leather jacket and started running in the direction that Stephany had been taken. He could scent the group of both covens' best warriors on her trail.

It was indeed a wolf that had her. Damn it to hell. He could smell its musty animal scent. Wolves were much faster than elves. He picked up the pace some more. Xavier's breaths came in ragged pants next to him.

"Are you sure you are sufficiently healed brother?" he glanced in Xavier's direction.

"Yes, my lord. Yet, I think I should stay and protect your female. Hells, I think you should stay with your female for far more important reasons."

"We have had this conversation."

"She is in heat, my lord."

"I had noticed. Zane will stay with her." It almost physically hurt to say the words.

"It increases his chances of impregnating her each time they rut."

"I know that," Brant ground out.

"For the future of our coven, you should return."

"She can't take it."

"Tanya is a strong human." Xavier didn't turn his head when he spoke.

"She is an unmated human female. Next time will be different. Right now one of us is too much for her. Let alone both."

"There may not be a next time, my lord."

"If she has Zane's child," he paused trying to compose himself. Brant shook his head, "You know what? I do not believe that she will fall pregnant. Human women are more fertile, yet it can still take months. If by some small chance she is pregnant and the child is Zane's"—It killed him to say the words—"I will make sure that I impregnate her as soon as she is fertile again."

"That could be years."

"I am a patient man." He pumped his fists, willing his legs to go faster.

"You love her."

"I don't know, maybe."

"You fucking love her."

Brant rolled his eyes, "Yes. I do."

"Fucking kill me if I ever fall in love."

Brant turned to face his brother, slowing down for a few beats. "I will." He laughed. "It isn't what I thought it would be. Not at all what I expected."

"Three's a crowd and all that."

"Yeah. It's weird though. I hate Zane, yet I am turned on when I have to watch them fuck even though I detest that another male is touching my female. It's a nightmare."

"Too much information brother." Xavier held up a hand.

"I need help with this. I don't have much experience in this type of situation."

"Fine."

"He's not as bad as what I thought. I think he really cares for Tanya. Might even love her."

Xavier tripped. "You're shitting me."

Brant slowed down while his brother regained his footing. "I hate sharing her. It kills me, but at the same time I am turned on by watching them. What the hell is wrong with me?"

"I don't have the answer. I have shared a few females before but none I felt strongly about. If it helps any, I enjoyed watching them being fucked too. It is an erotic sight, like a live action porno. One of the biggest perks about going second is a fully lubed pussy."

Brant choked out a laugh. "Really? Who's giving too much information now?" They jogged in silence for a few beats. "You've never felt anything more for a female?"

"No. I've liked a few and lusted after many, but nothing a good rut wouldn't cure." Xavier turned his grey eyes on him.

"You're lucky brother. Love sucks." He sighed. They continued along the trail, the scent of their comrades growing stronger with each footfall.

Damn it all to hell, he may've been turned on watching them rut but he had hated watching them kiss. The sight had been enough to bring his blood to a boiling point. If Xavier hadn't arrived when he had, Brant would've intervened and would only have been satisfied once Zane's lips were smashed to a bloody pulp.

Even though his fists still itched to punch the bastard, he felt a pang of guilt at not setting the record straight about Zane wanting to choose Tanya at the ceremony. He had been about to rectify the situation when their female had started the whole kissing thing.

Their female.

The need to hit something returned, so he picked up the pace.

Right now he had to focus on the task at hand. There was no doubt in his mind that Stephany would survive this, but the sooner he had her back the better. He had grown up with the female, she was an important part of his royal staff and Tanya had grown to like her. By blood, he considered her to be a close friend.

Brant spotted the team of males converged ahead at the banks of Sweetwater River. As he ran towards them a ridiculous image hit him, so out of place at that moment that it had him stumbling for a micro second. He pictured Zane and Tanya rutting. Not being there drove him insane, he used the image to push himself faster and to fuel his resolve to bring Stephany back.

———⸺———

"I thought that you said you wouldn't leave me again." Tanya knew she sounded like a whining child, but she couldn't help herself. Stephany was gone God only knew where. Brant had left, putting himself in the line of fire and now Zane wanted to leave her too. She was scared, confused, really upset and didn't want to add lonely to the list.

Zane put a hand to the small of her back, pulling her against him. "You will be safe. York and Griffin have been assigned to protect you. I need to check on Lance and the rest of the wounded. I also want to check in with the hunting party."

"Brant," even saying his name brought fresh tears to her eyes.

"Yeah." He took a hold of her chin. "I told you it would

work out, at least we won't have to fight to the death anymore."

"It could still happen."

Zane pursed his lips, causing her heart to skip several beats. "Charlotte will be here soon. She can keep you company." He chuckled when he caught the look on her face. "Don't tell me you're still mad at her for offering to rut with me."

"Why the hell is that funny?" She found herself smiling which irritated her even more because the thought of half-naked Charlotte made her want to hit something. "She's so freaking sexy and one of the biggest hussies alive."

Zane tensed, his eyes narrowed and his face took on a stern edge. "You are sexy." His eyes tracked the length of her body heating with every second. "With hips made for holding. Legs designed to straddle a male's hips." He made a strangled noise "Breasts that fill my hands, and I have big hands." His eyes darkened. "That makes them just right. Not too big. Just right." He rumbled, his voice heating her from the inside. "Your mouth is soft, your teeth blunt . . ."

"Wait a minute . . ." She held up a hand. "You find my blunt teeth sexy?"

Zane gave her a goofy grin. She would've bet cold hard cash a few days ago that she'd never see the like grace his face. Her heart clenched at the thought that she had put the smile there.

He leaned in a little closer, "Your blunt teeth felt so good against my shaft when you did that thing with your mouth."

"It's called a blowjob and if you stay . . ." She put her hand on his crotch finding a huge erection.

Zane hissed and moved away from her touch. "Don't tempt me female. I can't. Your mouth would not be enough, I would need more." His eyes hooded. "Because the best part of all is that your pussy is so tight." He all out growled, so low and deep that her insides did a flip flop. "I don't know if it's a human thing." He advanced on her, pushing her up against the wall, caging her in with his big body. "It almost hurts to be inside of you."

"I hope it's a good pain." She goaded knowing the answer.

"The best. The way your pussy walls clench around me when you come." His eyes were glowing, his erection hard against her tummy.

"Maybe we could . . ." She licked her lips feeling more excited by the second. Her clothes felt heavy and scratchy against her skin.

"No, Ysnaar, as tempted as I am to bury myself in you . . ." He took a deep breath. "I need to go and you need some rest." Although he stared at her lips, he kissed her forehead instead. "I won't be long." Coming from Zane, the gesture was so sweet. It threatened to start up her crying all over again.

Charlotte arrived two minutes after Zane left. Tanya watched her enter from her curled up position on the bed. The vampire wore a long summer dress. It wasn't a particularly flattering cut or color, yet the vampire still looked ravishing.

"Hey." She smiled looking genuinely pleased to see Tanya. As she walked up to the bed she stopped, wrinkled her nose and took a step back. "Yucky."

"What is it?"

"You need a serious shower. I'm afraid that crusty old blood, sweat and semen do not smell good together and in this case loads of semen." Her nose twitched again. "Oh my God, you're in heat. On second thought let's get some pillows under your feet." She walked over and tried to prop some of the throw pillows under Tanya's legs.

"What the hell are you doing?"

"I've heard that human women are ultra-fertile. Do you feel any different yet?" Her face was lit up in sheer excitement. Charlotte adjusted the blanket around her feet, tucking it in at the edges.

Part of her wanted to slap the other woman's hands away while the rest of her wanted to feel some excitement right along with her. All she really felt was pressure and just as in everything else, she felt torn. She wanted to give her vampire kings heirs and to be a mommy, but she wasn't sure that she was ready. At twenty seven she was older than what she thought she would be when she had her first child. She tried to stand.

"Don't you dare move. I'll have some food and drink sent up. You rest."

"I'm perfectly fine." She tried to sit up, but Charlotte gently pushed her back down.

"You are so lucky. My hips are too narrow for childbirth."

Tanya had to fight to keep her eyes from rolling.

"I was sterilized when I became sexually active. Not the nicest procedure."

She felt sorry for the female. "Why couldn't you have a C-section?"

Charlotte laughed. "We heal too quickly and using a silver blade would kill the unborn child. We have tried various methods but none have been successful. There are a few that can bear young but even then, normally only one child. Sometimes, if they are truly gifted then two children are born to a mated couple during their fertile period. Considering only nine percent of all mated vampire couples reproduce though, our population is in a steady decline."

"That's nuts."

"You will be expected to bear many young." Charlotte

pulled a blond strand behind her ear and grinned broadly like she had just told her all her wildest dreams would come true.

"Excuse me? Did I hear you correctly?"

Charlotte nodded, her blond locks bounced with the rhythm. "Hopefully, one every two years as long as you are fertile." She beamed.

"No freaking way."

Charlotte turned pale, her hand went to her throat. "Our species is on the decline. It would be your duty as our queen. The previous queens failed us. Not you too." She grabbed Tanya's hand and squeezed. "Please."

"There has to be another way. Why can't some of your men mate with humans?"

Charlotte giggled. "Our males are too strong. They are too ferocious in bed. They have sexual appetites no human could match. You must've realized that by now."

"What are you trying to say? I am a human unless you didn't notice."

Charlotte shrugged, suddenly finding non-existent pieces of lint on her dress. "I noticed," she mumbled.

"Are you saying that I won't be able to please Zane?"

"I'm sorry, I shouldn't have said anything. Me and my big mouth." Her blue eyes flashed up for a brief second before looking for more lint.

"No way. Don't you dare play that card. Out with it."

"Rumor has it that you are to mate both kings and from the scent of you . . ." She looked up from under her long, thick lashes.

"Yes. It's true." Tanya was fast losing patience.

Charlotte finally lifted her eyes, they were filled with . . . pity. "You can't possibly satisfy them both. I doubt a human could satisfy even one of our vampire males."

"Bullshit I can't. I'm supposed to get stronger or something once we're mated."

Charlotte smiled and nodded. "Oh yes, I had forgotten about that. It only happens with royalty so it is the major reason why humans don't mix well with our males. You may get stronger but not strong enough to handle two males. I'm sorry, Tanya. Maybe if you chose one or two females to assist you. I would be willing—"

"No!" She responded a little louder than she had intended. "I don't need any help, thanks for offering."

"Sex is a bodily function just as any other. Whether drinking, eating or breathing. It would not mean that your males didn't care for you."

"Stop, Charlotte. I will satisfy my males on my own."

"If you change your mind," Charlotte lifted her eyebrows.

"I won't." She thankfully sounded way more confident than what she felt. Her whole body ached. What if it took days to recover? Would one or both kings seek out one of the vampire females during that time? No freaking way. She wouldn't accept it and they both knew it. Her males had hands and could take care of themselves.

"I heard one of Brant's coven was abducted."

"Yes. Stephany."

Charlotte gasped. "Oh my God, no wonder Lance almost died trying to rescue her."

"You know about the whole . . . situation?"

"Although they managed to keep it a secret for many years, these days everybody knows that they are mated. Lance is crazy about her."

Tanya's heart sped up. "Strange way to show it. He's been sleeping with anything in a dress."

Charlotte's eyes turned serious. "You must be mistaken. He

might rut with quite a number of our females, but he never sleeps with them."

Tanya had to giggle. "Sleeping is a human term for rutting."

Charlotte cocked her head to the side. "Strange word to use. I told you it's a bodily function like any other. A close friend of mine was highly compatible with Lance. They used to rut often." *Too much info.* She felt like telling Charlotte to shut it. "He called out Stephany's name once though, right at that moment. Let me just tell you"—Charlotte paused—"this vampire friend of mine was pissed. She'd kind of been hoping all along that she and Lance might hook up. Informally of course since he is already mated to Stephany. Lance never rutted with her again. He's a rut only kind of guy and never sticks around for small talk."

"Wow." She felt a little like a school girl talking behind her hand on the playground.

"Yup. I think he wants Stephany even if he won't admit it."

"I really hope Brant gets her back. I only hope that alpha doesn't try anything with her while he has her though."

"Nah, I wouldn't worry about him forcing himself on her if that's your worry. Wolves and vampires have never been overly fond of one another. He might kill her though."

Tanya gasped into her hand, feeling her eyes prick with tears. "They wouldn't." She knew as she said the words that non humans were ruthless. "They must've taken her for a reason. We'll give them whatever they want for her safe return."

"That is not for you to decide. If their demands were to put you or our coven in jeopardy . . ." She shook her head.

"I don't understand all of this."

"We're in the middle of a war. There isn't much to

understand. Thankfully the covens have joined forces, once again the vampire species will be a force to reckon with and that's all thanks to you." Charlotte squeezed her hand. "I am here for you human. I will help you in any way, whether to run your bath, give you a massage . . . I have heard that a woman's back can ache during pregnancy."

"Hold up. I may not be pregnant, in fact chances are good that I'm not."

"You humans are like breeding machines. I am sure you are with child."

"Stop, Charlotte. You'll jinx me." She found herself laughing despite her worries.

"Rubbish. Vampires don't believe in superstitions. It would be so amazing to have the sound of a child's laughter grace our court. Chubby cheeks and sweet innocence. You will let me hold him?"

"Or her."

Charlotte narrowed her eyes. "Or her. A pretty little girl with Zane's dark eyes," she sighed.

"Or Brant's."

"Oh no . . . Zane will sire the first child. I would be willing to bet on it." Charlotte's eyes had widened to the size of small plates.

"Again with the bets. Let's first wait to find out if I'm pregnant."

"I'll bet that you are."

"Stop already. Let's wait and see. How long before we know?" She flinched at the desperate tone in her voice. All this excitement was catching. Hopefully it wouldn't be too long before she had an answer.

"Can be as soon as twenty four hours, but certainly within the next three days. You'll get thirsty except nothing you drink will quench your thirst."

Tanya felt her stomach turn. "I forgot about that. I'll want blood."

Charlotte laughed. "It's not as bad as what you think, in fact, you'll crave it and will enjoy drinking from the kings. Don't pull such an ugly face." She laughed again.

"I just can't imagine it."

"It's great. The sex is phenomenal when both of you drink from each other as well. Hopefully you will continue to crave blood after you have had the baby."

"I'm going to take a nap now. Maybe you can come back in an hour or two." All this talk of drinking blood made her feel a little queasy, and frankly she just needed some time alone. Charlotte was sweet in a backward way, but she didn't feel like keeping a brave face. What she needed was a shower and some sleep.

Charlotte smiled warmly. "That would be good for the baby."

"Stop."

"Sorry," she winced. "Just remember, I am here for you. If you change your mind about helping out with . . ."

"I won't." She tried not to sound like too much of a bitch because the infuriating woman really was just trying to be helpful.

"Eat something first."

Go away.

"I'm really tired."

Charlotte narrowed her eyes. "Fine, but I'll be back in an hour or two to check on you. I'll bring food."

Tanya nodded. Charlotte grabbed a second blanket from the foot of the bed and tucked her in. If she really was pregnant—her heart rate increased at the thought—she wasn't sure she could handle twelve whole months of being coddled like this.

Once Charlotte had left the room, she put a hand to her belly. A baby. A tiny little person who would be her responsibility. To raise, to love . . . she found that she didn't mind the idea anymore really. In fact, she was starting to wish it was true. One little piece of hope amongst all this chaos.

Chapter FOUR

THREE DAYS LATER, BRANT still hadn't returned. Tanya was worried. She took another bite of her third cupcake. Vanilla with strawberry butter icing. The treat made her feel at least a little better. Zane had assured her that Brant and the rest of the vampires in the hunting party were fine. They were trying to find out where the wolves were holed up at. The problem was that they were a nomadic species, and although they had their borders and territories, essentially, they could be anywhere. With miles of open country and a mountain range, there was a vast territory to cover. That had to be it.

Zane hadn't spent much time with her. Scouts had been sent to monitor the elven territories. There was even talk of retaliation. Tanya was too afraid to ask if it was true. The thought of Zane or Brant, or both, heading up a war party had her gut twisting sharply and bile rising in her throat. He had given her regular updates on Brant, but so far the hunting party had come up empty handed at every turn.

Although Zane had slept with her every night for a few short hours, he hadn't so much as tried to kiss her again. Charlotte's words kept ringing in her ears. Was he getting his needs met elsewhere? She'd played their conversation over and over in her head and he'd never sworn fidelity. He'd said that he would be faithful only once they were mated which, technically, hadn't happened yet.

She took another bite, closing her eyes as the sweet icing melted in her mouth. *Nothing like cake for breakfast.*

"Well?" A familiar feminine voice.

"Well what, Charlotte?" She opened her eyes wishing she'd kept them closed. The tall vampire wore a tight floral dress that barely covered her ass. Tanya could feel that she had put on a few pounds since coming to live with the vampires. It was from all the delicious food and being waited on hand and foot. Aside from making a few decisions about the up and coming mating ceremony, she hadn't really done much of anything else. Her boobs felt tight in her bra and her jeans were just a little too snug.

"Are you craving blood yet?"

Was nothing sacred in this place? She shook her head, taking another big bite of a fourth cupcake. "I told you, chances were slim. Leave it alone please."

"You can try again soon enough."

"We will thanks." Tanya tried to keep her cool, she realized that the vampire was only trying to be nice.

"For the love of blood." Charlotte's eyes widened and she cocked her head, listening for something.

"What is it?"

"Something is happening."

It wasn't long and Tanya could hear footfalls. Both kings rounded the corner with a large portion of the royal guard behind them. Brant had stubble, his hair was wind swept. He had never looked better.

She squealed and ran to him, somehow managing to forget

how upset he had been with her when they had last seen each other. He smiled as she approached catching her when she launched herself into his arms. He pulled her close, kissing her like they were alone. She wrapped her legs around his hips, locking her feet at his back. She blushed when they finally broke, catching the faces of all the males behind them. York smiled and winked.

"Leave!" Zane roared. "Now!" The men filed out. Brant released his hold and she slid down his body. He kept his arm around her.

"You too," Zane added in Charlotte's direction. She did as he said, a frown marred her otherwise perfect features. They were now all alone in the large dining hall. Just the three of them.

Brant's arm tightened on her. "I know it is your time with the female, but it has been three days."

Zane's demeanour tightened and for a second she thought that he would argue. "Fine, but she must be returned before nightfall." Zane remained stiff. "I am sorry about your assistant."

Stephany.

"What happened Brant?" She whispered not really wanting to know but needing to all at the same time.

Brant shrugged his broad shoulders. "I don't have much to say. They definitely have her. We don't know where they are or why they are keeping her. I could spend the next six months searching and would probably find nothing. We have sent a message requesting her safe return. If they comply, we will put an end to the war. United we would destroy both parties. The elves must have heard about the joining of the covens because they have already sent their apologies and are no longer in partnership with the wolves."

"Or, so they say," said Zane.

Brant nodded. "It is fair to say that the wolves are on the run. My hope is that they accept the olive branch and return Stephany." His eyes hardened. "They would be fools not to." He hesitated for what felt like forever. "Are you . . . ?" He looked down at her belly and she wished the ground would swallow her whole. Heat flushed her cheeks.

She shook her head. "It's not looking good."

"Her thirst would've been upon her by now." Zane's deep voice rumbled through her.

Brant let out a breath. He somehow seemed relieved but she thought that must just have been her imagination.

Zane growled. "At least we get to have a little more of that heat fun." He bobbed his eyebrows.

Brant stiffened.

"Come on. Our female is scented of the heavens. Your heat made me so damned horny that I totally forgot to sample the goods." He licked his lips throwing her a devilish grin that had her clit tingling. "I won't forget next time."

"Come, Cenwein. I have missed you." Ignoring Zane, Brant pulled her into the crook of his arm and headed for the west tower. She turned her head as they walked away catching Zane's frown.

"Nightfall," he growled after them. "Go easy." He added using a softer tone. And just like that, she was back to being a possession.

———・C✱⊃・———

Brant craved his female with a need that scared him. He couldn't help but to feel relieved that she wasn't pregnant yet. Odds had favored Zane to be the father of the child this time. He didn't look forward to going through the heat experience again though. It didn't matter that he was turned on by watching them rut, three was a crowd in his opinion.

They marched through winding staircases and long hallways. He knew this castle like the back of his hand since it was an exact replica of the one that he had grown up in. Even though Xavier and York trailed them like shadows, Brant was tempted to stop in one of the darker side passages or to slip into one of the many chambers along the way. His desperation to be inside of his human mounted with every step. Somehow he managed to hold back. He had taken her like an animal the last time they were together and he'd be damned if he was going to do it again.

"How are you feeling?"

It was possible that she was still sore. Tanya had only just entered her heat cycle when Brant had left. Zane would have rutted with her many more times. For some strange reason his human didn't scent like she'd been rutted recently though. Maybe Zane had hurt her and had not had her since the heat.

"I'm fine."

He felt his brow crease. "Are you sure, Cenwein, because"— they entered his newly appointed suite and he closed the door behind them—"I really need you, but I don't want to hurt you." He pulled her flush against him feeling each soft curve melt into his chest.

"I swear I'm fine and I need you too." She pulled her t-shirt over her head, her hair becoming a wild tangle about her face. She cupped his jaw and covered his lips with her hot mouth.

He moaned while pulling her over to the bed, allowing them both to fall. Brant caged her body with his own. He took in her flushed cheeks and half-mast lids. Her lips were glistening and plump from their kiss. "By the gods you are beautiful. I have missed you." He reached for the clasp between her deep cleavage wanting a taste of her ripe nipples. With one deft move, the bra fell away. Deep curves, jutting points, soft succulent heaven. He feasted until she was clawing at the sheets, he kept up the onslaught until she was begging. The scent of her arousal surrounded them. His cock throbbed. "I need . . ." Brant unbuttoned his pants, tearing them down. He tried to be gentle but ended up ripping her jeans in his attempt to get them undone.

"Brant," she chided.

"I told you to wear less. May as well get rid of them . . ." He ripped them off completely leaving her bared to him. "I'm not sure if it's possible, but you are more beautiful than when I left you."

She gaped at him. "More like chubbier from all the cupcakes."

"I will buy you more." He palmed her breasts and then moved between her parted thighs where he rubbed his cock against her slit. "So wet."

"I told you that I needed you. Enough fooling around." She ended the sentence on a groan as he nudged into her opening.

"Is this what you need?"

"Yes," she whispered, her eyes closed as he slid the rest of the way home. Brant took his time. Concentrating on each and every thrust, he concentrated even harder on not coming. Her greedy sheath clenched his shaft in a way that had his balls pulling up.

His little human threw her head back. She dug her nails into his back and drew her knees up higher on his torso, taking him deeper into her heavenly pussy. He loved how she rocked against him, matching him thrust for thrust. Loved the sting on his back as she clutched him tighter.

He grit his teeth, fighting against the inevitable. He slid his hand between their bodies and frantically circled her clit. She came apart just as he was losing control. It felt so right to be back in her arms like this. Brant didn't share well. Right now, just like this, was how it was meant to be between them. He wasn't sure how they were going to make this work. Closing his eyes, he lost himself in her.

Still breathing hard, he turned onto his back and pulled her into his arms.

"I needed that," she panted.

"Me too." He ran a hand down her back. "Are you feeling okay?"

"Stop that. I'm fine." He felt her stiffen for a fraction of a second.

"What?"

"Nothing." Vampire, human, it didn't matter, any female that answered like that was hiding something.

"Tell me."

Tanya lifted herself off of him, leaving her chest against his and her eyes firmly on him. Her mouth was cocked to the side in thought. "Why did you push me away before you left? Why didn't you say goodbye?" She bit her lip.

"Let's get something very clear. It wasn't you." He cupped her chin. "I hurt you, yet I still wanted to have you again. If Zane hadn't pulled me off you, I may have"—he paused having to compose himself—"I may have killed you, Cenwein."

"You didn't."

"I could have. I hated watching the two of you kiss. I hate that you are getting along so well. It's so selfish and so wrong of me."

"It's not."

"You didn't ask for this. I need to find a way to come to terms with it, but know that it is not you."

"Okay," her voice was timid. "You still could've said goodbye."

"I wouldn't have left. The thought of leaving you . . ." He took a deep breath before letting it out slowly. "I needed to at least try and find Stephany. I hope you understand. If I had so much as looked at you, I would have stayed and would not have been able to forgive myself. I still feel responsible for them taking her."

Tanya's lip wobbled and she bit down on it, her eyes filled with tears.

"Please don't cry, Cenwein. Stephany will be returned. The wolves can't run forever, we will eventually find them and make them pay." Blood will flow.

"I hope you're right."

"You'll see that I am."

"I'm glad you're back." She smiled through her tears and he had to kiss her. His cock filled. This female would be the death of him.

"Up you go."

Her face scrunched in confusion.

"I believe I owe you a long walk."

She bit her lip. "Is it safe?"

"We'll have to stay close to the castle and we will be surrounded by guards, but if you're game then so am I." He only prayed that she would agree. If they stayed in bed, he would take her again. As compatible as they were, he wanted to get to know her in other ways too.

Her face lit up. "That would be great. I've been stuck inside for days."

They dressed quickly. Tanya wiggled herself into a dress that had his mouth watering. Black silk with splashes of red and royal blue. It had built in triangular cups for her luscious breasts and fell to just above her knees. He hadn't seen her put on any underwear. It would be better if he didn't check because, either way, they wouldn't end up going anywhere.

They walked through the castle and out into the fresh mid-morning air. The weather in Sweetwater was mild this time of year. A warm breeze picked up tendrils of her hair, which held an auburn tinge in the sunlight. They made small talk for a few minutes while walking hand in hand before he finally asked her the question that had been on his mind.

"How did your parents die?"

"Car accident. My three year old brother Sam was also with them." She frowned as she spoke.

"I am sorry, Cenwein."

"I wish I could say that it was a drunk driver or that the roads were wet, but the truth was that my dad was driving way too fast. I'm sure they were fighting again."

His chest tightened.

She squeezed his hand. "It's okay. It wasn't easy those first few years, but I have learned to get on with it. I have my aunt. She's old and a bit ditsy, but she loves me in her own way."

Brant wanted to say that she was a part of a new family now and that life would be smoother, but the words died on his tongue. He would have to try harder to make things work.

"I remember them arguing all the time. They never outright said it, but I'm sure I was an accident being that my folks were still in college when I was conceived." She sighed. "I think my mom never forgave my dad for having to give up on her dreams of becoming a big shot lawyer. She ended up working as a legal secretary instead. He still got his medical degree though." Her eyes darkened with the memories. "I think they were planning on divorcing when she fell pregnant with my brother. Talk about double bad luck." She sort of smiled.

"Don't refer to yourself as bad luck."

"I didn't mean it like that." She folded a piece of hair behind her ear and pulled her lip between her teeth. "It wasn't fun living in a house with two people that didn't get along. I didn't realize how dysfunctional we were until I stayed over at a friend's house and saw what a real family was all about." She smiled. "I remember how weird it was seeing two people who actually loved each other. There were no arguments. They talked. With my folks, it was either fighting or they went their separate ways."

They walked together in silence for a long while. Brant wasn't sure how to comfort her. He was not about to make promises that he couldn't keep. Their situation was difficult to say the least.

"I don't want that for my kids. I'm afraid that it's going to happen though."

Brant let out a pent up sigh. "It is not going to be easy and I can only speak for myself . . ." He paused considering his words. "I will try." It was the best he could do.

Tanya squeezed his hand and smiled up at him like he'd given her the best gift. He felt like a jerk, like he should be doing more but it was still all too new. Maybe in time, he thought.

His sensitive hearing picked up footfalls. Someone strode towards them with purpose. *Brilliant.* It was Zane. His face was a mask of determination. Brant's first reaction was to demand why the other male had interrupted after promising he could have Tanya for the afternoon but after the conversation he had just had, he held his tongue. Brant halted. He increased his hold on his human's hand and turned to face the approaching male trying hard to keep his emotions in check.

Zane inclined his head as he came to a halt. Brant noticed how his hard, almost black, eyes softened as they landed on the female.

Zane held out a leather pouch. "This came for you. It reeks of wolf." He added glancing back at Tanya.

Brant could scent the heavy wolf musk. The stench offended him and he had to fight not to growl. He took the pouch. Inside was a crisp white envelope, his name in neat cursive. Brant would recognize the handwriting anywhere.

"Stephany," he whispered tearing it open. Beneath the wolf stench, Stephany's scent was apparent. The note was short and written in the same handwriting.

"What does it say?" Tanya stood on tippy toes trying to read over his shoulder.

"Stephany wrote this. She was taken by accident and will be released in due course. She is unharmed and we shouldn't worry." Emotion churned in his gut. "Why didn't she call? I don't trust this." He crunched the white paper in his hand.

"It is at least something. You say she wrote it?"

He nodded once.

"They may not have cell signal if they are deep in the mountains. The pouch was left hanging on the front gate at Manor House. Our scouts found it. I think she will be released. What use is she to them anyways?"

As much as it irked him, Zane was more than likely right but he would not be able to rest easy until the female was returned. She had been his faithful assistant . . . and friend for many years. Tanya was fond of her. Brant grit his teeth. The alpha would kneel before him and swear allegiance or so help him and his species.

"There is more." Zane ran a hand over his scalp. "I received word from the elven king, Katar has requested to meet. He would like to give his apologies and wants to swear allegiance."

"It might be a trap."

Tanya tensed next to him, her breathing and heart rate increased and she grabbed a hold of his arm.

"I realize that. I suggested neutral ground. I will attend alone. You stay with the female."

Although evenly delivered, it felt too much like an order for his liking. Brant felt everything in him tighten. His first reaction was to tell the other male to go to hell, but he paused instead until he had a handle on his anger. "Fine." He tried to keep his voice neutral. "But take some of my males with you and keep me updated."

Zane's eyes narrowed, his jaw tensed. He nodded once. "I'll prepare and leave within the hour. I figure the sooner I get there, the less chance they have to prepare an ambush."

Tanya gasped. "Do you have to go?" She took a step towards Zane, her hand still in Brant's.

Again his eyes softened as they landed on the female. The bastard was in just as deep as he was. It was at least some consolation. "I do, Ysnaar. To refuse such a request would insult the elven species. It might cause the war to flare back up." Zane probably didn't realize it but he had taken a small step towards Tanya as he spoke.

It took major willpower, but Brant released her hand. The moment he did, she closed the space between them and Zane and put his hands in hers.

"I will be gone for a few short hours. Back by nightfall," Zane stated.

"Take care of yourself."

Zane chuckled. "You are a major incentive to come back quickly and in one piece. I will be back by nightfall. Make sure you are ready for me."

Zane had the sexiest voice and when it dropped as low as it was right now, it did strange, wonderful things to her insides.

"I'll be ready."

"When I say ready, I mean naked and in my bed."

Tanya laughed. "What if you're late?"

"I won't be."

She heard Brant shuffle behind her but then Zane leaned in and kissed her. Quick but deep and so full of promise that it had her toes curling.

Zane released her and looked back at Brant. "I'll be in touch." He touched at his pocket which most likely housed his cell phone.

Brant looked pissed. He swallowed hard, his Adams apple bobbing. He nodded, his jaw locking.

She watched Zane walk away. He barked orders to several of the vampire guard who picked up pace beside him. Tanya felt her eyes prick but refused to cry. He would be back soon and Stephany was safe. There was reason to celebrate. Her lip wobbled so she bit down on it.

Brant put an arm around her. "He'll be fine." She turned into his chest, burying her face into his shirt. A tear managed to escape. She sniffed, fighting harder to maintain control.

"I hope you cried when I left too." His arms banded around her as he spoke.

Tanya laughed. "Like a little baby."

"Good." He stroked her back. Tanya could hear that he was smiling.

She laughed harder.

"Thank you for behaving. It was nice to see the two of you working together."

"It was not easy, we are both too dominant as is our nature."

"You could be friends."

He chuckled. "Slow down a bit. We have to first get used to not being enemies. Like I said, it will take time and I will try."

"Thank you." She reached up and kissed him. He tensed up for a few beats before returning the kiss. It was soft, sweet, and comforting rather than sexual. Brant broke the kiss leaning his chin on her head. He hugged her tight.

"Can we go back to my tower now?" His voice was a low growl that she'd come to recognize as arousal.

"You can't tell me you want sex again so soon?"

"It has been days, Cenwein." His lids hooded.

"Okay but . . ." She hesitated. How did she tell him to go easy because Zane would need her later?

"You're thinking of him. He's had you for three days. Had you for your heat. I will take it slow." His eyes had narrowed and she could tell that he wasn't a happy camper.

Tanya shook her head. "Zane hasn't touched me since you left."

"Why the fuck not?" He took a deep breath. She could tell that he was trying to calm himself. "What game is he playing at anyway?"

"I don't know why. He hasn't . . ." It was weird talking about this with Brant. "You know, been with anyone else? I've been a bit worried."

Brant cocked an eyebrow. "Oh no, you're not going to use me as some kind of bloodhound to keep tabs on him. You can ask him yourself."

Brant turned and walked in the direction that they had come from. She had to work to keep up. "Wait, Brant. I'm sorry. It was wrong of me."

"Damn straight it was wrong." He stopped dead and she walked into his back.

"It's just, I was talking to Charlotte earlier."

His brow creased in confusion.

"One of the females in Zane's coven, and she said that I wouldn't be able to keep up with two male vampires. She even offered her services."

He made a sound of frustration. "How many times do we need to tell you that we don't want another female? I know I can speak for Zane on this one. We only want you. Neither of us will rut with another female. Yes we have a high sex drive but we're mature males. If you are not available for whatever reason, we will deal. It might mean severe arm cramp but we'll deal."

She choked out a laugh.

"You don't strike me as the type of female that would believe everything she hears." He folded his arms.

"Not normally. I don't know much about vampires though. She was really convincing."

"I don't want to get into it with you, but as kings we've had our pick of the females. We've had sex whenever we wanted and mostly with whomever we wanted. Don't look at me like that."

"Like what? Like you're a male slut?" She couldn't keep the smile from her lips. Tanya realized that they had a past and had come to terms with it.

"Okay fine. We were male sluts, but have since been reformed."

Tanya slipped her hands around his waist. "Let's go back to the tower. You have to promise not to tear my dress."

"I can't promise that."

"I'm not wearing panties," she whispered.

Brant growled dragging her in the direction of the castle, then he made a sound of frustration and picked her up throwing her over his shoulder. Tanya squealed. One hand clamped firmly on her ass, he picked up the pace and she couldn't help but to giggle in excitement.

Chapter FIVE

Zane exited the vehicle. The elves were already there. Neutral ground. Wide open space for miles. An ambush of any sort would not be easy. Especially considering that the elves favored the bow as their weapon of choice. He felt out of sorts not having Lance at his side. Another few days and the warrior should be back on his feet. He had taken over fifty arrows to the chest and back. Four of those had been direct to the heart. It was a miracle that he had even survived. Zane had to suppress a growl. It was the elves that had nearly put him in his grave. He'd bet big money that this whole plan had been Katar's. The wolves were too dumb to have come up with it on their own.

The elven king called a welcome in his native tongue as they approached. His long robes flowed to the ground, they swayed as he stood. Zane was shocked to see the grey at his temples and how he hunched slightly. The big male at his flank was the spitting image of his father. Katar must have looked just like this male when he was in his prime. Tall, plenty of lean muscle, hair that shone like pure spun gold. The male wore a silk robe, as was customary with the eleven species.

Thank fuck he hadn't been born a pussy. On occasions like this, he much preferred leather and the measure of protection it afforded.

The king must've caught him staring. "This is my son Keto and my daughter Esral."

Zane felt himself relax as he turned to face the female. If Katar had brought his daughter, then he did not mean to fight. The elven princess was a tiny thing although he could see that she was a mature female. Her hair was so long that it touched her thighs. Her eyes were wide and shone a beautiful blue. Like the sky on a clear winter's day. Although she was highly attractive, he found that she did nothing for him, unlike his little Ysnaar. His human was lush, sexy . . . he snapped himself out of it realizing that the princess held out her hand. He took it, trying to be gentle as she felt like she might break under his touch. Shivering, she lowered her eyes.

"Can we offer refreshments?" Katar asked. A smaller male appeared carrying a tray of golden goblets.

"No, thank you."

"Your men perhaps?" The old male raised an eyebrow.

"No. Why have you called me?" Enough with the bullshit. He wanted answers and needed to see the old king on his knee before accepting a truce.

"My mate has been gone six months now." His blue eyes filled with unshed tears. "I am a fool."

"Father," Keto's eyes had narrowed.

"Be still. I allowed myself to be swayed. An old fool." The last he muttered more to himself. Katar shook his head. He seemed to be trying to pull himself together. Some of the elven guard shuffled in the background. "My mate was everything to me. Aside from her many attributes, she was also my most loyal and trusted advisor." He smiled for a few beats. Managing to look the picture of sorrow. Zane found himself feeling sorry for the old king.

"Esme was wise. She understood my people and the different species like nobody's business. Never once gave me bad advice. I know that it is probably unwise to admit this, but under the current circumstance I feel I can be honest" He swallowed motioning to the male with the tray of goblets. Once he had taken a drink, he continued. "I am lost without my Esme. We should never have listened to those beasts. I would like to offer my apologies and if it's not too late, my allegiance to the vampire species."

Zane noticed how the younger male's lips had pulled into a thin white line. How his hands had fisted at his sides. His eyes were narrowed shooting poison tipped arrows his way. It was clear that Keto did not feel the same way as his father.

The old man's eyes shone with sincerity and for now Katar was the leader of the elves. The elven king lowered his gaze as a sign of submission. "As a peace offering, I would like to offer you my most valued possession."

"Father, please." For the first time, Keto turned his head towards his father.

"Be still. You have done enough." He added, "This is my will."

The younger elf turned his eyes back on Zane, his jaw clenched so tight that Zane was sure he might crack some teeth.

"Please accept as a token of peace my beloved daughter."

Griffin made a choking sound and many of the guard, on both sides, shuffled nervously.

"She is a virgin and fully mature. She will make a good mate."

How the fuck did he respond? To outright refuse would be

seen as denial of the elven allegiance. It would be taken as an insult.

"Thank you, Katar. I will graciously accept, but know that it is unnecessary and if you wish to reconsider..." Zane hoped that he had not offended the king.

The old man smiled. "I insist—"

"Father, the vampire said it is unnecessary."

Vampire. Who the fuck was this young buck's vampire? Surely the bastard wasn't referring to him? Zane bristled at the younger male's attitude. His hands itched, wanting so badly to turn to fists. He wanted to punch some respect into the insolent little prick.

"Be still. It is the last time I will ask this of you."

This time Zane heard how the male ground his teeth together. Keto nodded once before staring at the floor. His knuckles turned white at his sides.

The female said nothing. Her little hands were clasped in front of her, her eyes to the ground.

"I would like for you to have Esral. The ultimate token of peace, of a species united."

Fuck.

The covens were much stronger united. They would win a war against the elves, but at what cost? The last thing Zane wanted was another war. Why had the old man chosen such a public place to make the offer? He could've talked some sense into him in private. Those around them grew restless. The old man's eyes hardened. Even the princess lifted her big orbs, they pleaded with him.

"Thank you," he managed to choke out. "We are honored." Already his mind rushed at finding a way out of this.

"I insist that she mate with royalty. She is a princess and should be treated as such. You would slight me if you were to give her to a commoner."

This was the king's way of locking him in. *Double cluster fuck.* Tanya was going to have his nuts. There was no way he was going to mate with this female. No freaking way. Aside from not needing another female, he happened to like his nuts right where they were. He would find a way out of this. Zane would call a meeting in a few days and discuss it with the elven king in private.

The king smiled. "Esral will make a good mate, she is stronger than what she looks . . ."

For the first time the female showed some real emotion by gasping. "Father, please."

"Now that it is settled." The old man moved to kneel. He held his hip as he bent.

"Wait." It was Zane's turn to narrow his eyes. "Your son will kneel on your behalf."

"Yes, but . . ." The elven king looked worried. He glanced from Zane to Keto and back.

"I insist," Zane growled softly. "I require your allegiance, but also that of your heir. You have given me your daughter. He can kneel." Zane gestured in the direction of Keto, but didn't take his eyes off the king. He could feel the animosity rolling off the elf prince.

"Do as he says." Keto didn't move. "Do it," Katar added raising himself higher and pulling his shoulders back.

Keto dropped to his knee while inclining his head, in less than a second he was back on his feet. The youngster could not school his emotion well. A mask of anger contorted his features.

As was customary, Zane and Katar shook hands at the wrists. The old man's skin felt like paper beneath his grip. Katar smiled. "And so it is done."

"It is done," Zane repeated holding to tradition. All gathered from both sides and repeated the phrase. Zane noticed that the elven prince didn't utter a word. An insult, but for the good of both species he would let it slide.

After a short goodbye, which was mainly for the benefit of the princess, Esral picked up a silk tie bag. It was small considering that it held all of her belongings. Zane took it from her. The bag weighed nothing. They climbed into one of the waiting SUVs, Esral beside him. Zane had been tempted to put the princess into one of the other vehicles but that would potentially have hurt her feelings. She seemed nice enough. They pulled off in the direction of his castle.

"When are you going to mate me?" She pulled her golden hair behind a pointed ear.

He was shocked by the question as she seemed like a shy little thing. "I haven't had much time to think on it."

"What's to think about?" Her blue eyes shone.

"Well"—he paused—"shouldn't we get to know each other a bit first?"

Her brow knitted. "What purpose would that serve?"

For the love of blood, his little human had turned him into a pussy. Zane had to suppress a smile. Just thinking of his female had his cock filling. "You are a virgin. We shouldn't rush into anything." He needed to tell her that he had no intention of ever mating her, but this didn't seem like the right time or place. Zane also found that he again didn't want to hurt her feelings.

"I think that right now would be a good time. Tell your men to stop the car. We can go into the wooded area." She gestured to the forests to the right of the moving vehicle.

"It would be best if we waited. Your"—he swallowed hard—"first time should be in a bed. It should be special." Fuck he really sounded like a class-A pussy. The thought of bedding her left him cold though. Zane had to buy time. Once he managed to talk to the king in private, he was sure he would understand.

Esral smiled, flashing him her teeth which all had sharp little points. He had to suppress the urge to clutch his dick. Thank the gods his female was human. "It is customary for our people to mate under the open sky on the earth as nature intended. I am ready for you." Esral lifted her robe. Unfortunately, he reacted instinctually and looked just as she parted her thighs slightly. Even though she had a pleasant floral scent with earthy undertones, her hairless pussy held no appeal. He had grown to love Tanya's strip of fuzz. The way it looked, it's silky feel. It seemed that no other female came even close anymore. Esral must've sensed his indifference because she pulled a sleeve of her robe from her shoulder until a surprisingly full pink tipped breast sprang free. Griffin let out a choking sound, his eyes glued to the rear view mirror.

Zane leaned forward and carefully pulled up the silken fabric until she was properly covered.

Her eyes filled with tears. "I was told that I am fair. That males would not be able to resist me. That I would find a mate easily and that he would not be able to resist if . . ." A tear tracked down her cheek.

"You are beautiful."

"Well then . . ." She reached to open her robe.

"Stop."

Once again her eyes filled. "It is important that I am accepted and that we mate soon, or my people will think that I'm defective. If you send me back, I will be ridiculed. Destined to live a life of solitude."

Zane rubbed his eyes and then scrubbed his hand over the

stubble on his head. "I am to be mated to another in a few days."

She nodded. "Okay, well then our information was incorrect. It was understood that you had lost your future mate. We have the wrong king. Then I will mate with Brant. Please take me to him."

Zane shook his head. He needed to put an end to this right now. "Brant and I are to mate with the same female."

Her chest rose and fell at an alarming rate and her eyes filled with horror.

"I will explain this to your father in private. He will understand."

"No," she sounded shrill. "You can't take me back." Her eyes filled with tears. This time she covered her face with her hands and cried softly.

He had little experience in dealing with hysterical females. Zane pulled out his cell phone and dialled Brant.

"Yeah."

"We have a little situation," Zane said.

"Did they refuse to swear allegiance?"

"No, they went a little overboard. Katar has given us his daughter."

"What? Why?" A low growl.

"As a mate. He wants to secure the partnership between the species." A pause.

"You told him we are to be mated?"

"We are not mated yet. There is one female and the two of us. Katar would never have understood."

"Fuck," Brant snarled. "You're right. If you had refused, he would've seen it as an insult. Get your ass here, we'll discuss it then." Brant sighed. "We're in so much shit."

Zane had to chuckle. "Tanya will not be happy."

Brant made a sound of agreement.

"Inform her before I arrive with the princess. We'll meet in the dining hall in ten."

"You want me to tell Tanya? You were the one that fucked up," Brant whispered.

"You would've done the same," he growled.

"Fine." Brant ended the call. The princess continued to weep softly.

———·⊂✱⊃·———

They'd had a fantastic day together. Brant had taken her back to his tower and had worshipped her body. First with his mouth and hands and then by making slow, sweet love to her.

They'd gone for a picnic on the grounds and had talked for hours. He'd had to take a call at one point and then everything seemed to fall apart. He'd insisted Zane was fine while they packed up and headed back to the castle. Zane had called a meeting so they made their way to the dining hall.

Brant had paced for a few minutes before finally telling her what had happened.

"The elven king did what?"

Brant took a deep breath, cleared his throat and spoke louder this time. "Katar gave his daughter to Zane as a token of his allegiance."

"Why would he give ..." Then the reason hit her, "... oh."

"Didn't he explain that he's already ... taken?" Tanya asked.

Brant shook his head. "The king is old school. All he knows is that there are two kings and only one chosen, so therefore he has given his daughter. If Zane had refused, it would've been seen as a major insult."

"I thought Zane couldn't mate unless with a chosen female."

"He can mate, he just can't have heirs." Brant ran a hand through his hair and then jammed his hands into his jean pockets. "He is not going to mate her so don't worry."

This was wrong on so many levels. Just then the door opened and a tiny woman walked in, Zane followed close behind. She had to be at least one and a half heads shorter than Tanya and at least four dress sizes smaller. The princess had big, blue red rimmed eyes. Such a pretty little thing.

"This is Esral," Zane said avoiding eye contact with her.

"Why has she been crying?"

"I told her that I am not going to mate her." Zane turned his gaze on Tanya.

The elf female hiccupped rubbing a tear away with the back of her hand.

"Of all the insensitive brutish things." Tanya put her hands on her hips. The princess cried harder. Damn these non-human men. "You are a bunch of boorish"—she walked to the princess and put an arm around her shoulders—"bullish, insensitive . . ."

Zane's brow furrowed. "Do you want me to mate her?"

Really?

Tanya couldn't help it when her finger pointed at the big vampire. "You did not just say that, Zane." She wagged her finger at him and he had the good grace to look sheepish. "No, you will not bloody well mate with her. Unless you want to that is." Her eyes narrowed and her heart raced.

"I said I did not. You are all I need."

She felt herself both soften to Zane's words and anger as the princess' shoulders shook beneath her arm. "You are all a bunch of barbarians and should be ashamed of yourselves."

"This isn't our fault." Brant moved in next to Zane.

"Not your fault?" She paused clenching her teeth. "You

vampires don't hold a little ceremony every century or so where you force young women from their homes, their families, to mate with and raise your heirs?"

Brant shuffled. Zane's eyes narrowed.

"It's barbaric and wrong. The elven king gave you his freaking daughter. You have to see that as wrong on some level as well. Females are not possessions to be shuffled from one to the other, here to scratch an itch and raise your children. We have feelings."

"We know that," Brant said.

"Our females are prized. The mating thing is to secure our partnership . . ." Zane stopped when she narrowed her eyes on him. "You are right. We will relook over the rules of the choosing ceremony."

"I want one of you to mate me. I can't go back. I told you I will be seen as defective to my people," Esral sniffed.

"Who brainwashed you into believing that load of bull?" Tanya shook her head. "You are a beautiful and intelligent woman. You don't need to mate with either of these males. You don't have to mate with anyone. You are free to choose."

"No, she isn't," Zane spoke softly. "She has to mate vampire royalty or her father will see it as an insult and declare war."

"You can talk some sense into him," she paused. "Better yet, let me meet him and I'll talk some sense into him."

"Sense . . ." Brant looked flustered. "Cenwein, you can't talk sense into him. He won't get it. Age old beliefs and traditions will not fall away because you say so. I hear you and I agree, but he's not—"

"Call him, set something up . . ." Hang on just a minute, she thought. "Unless you want to mate her, Brant."

He pulled in a breath, his eyes wide. "No, that's not what I meant. I thought I made myself clear earlier when I said that you were the one for me . . . us," he quickly added.

She held up a hand to stop him and ushered the elf female to a chair. "Sit." The princess sank into the soft fabric looking defeated. "Can I get you something to drink?"

Esral shook her head.

"Don't mind if I do," Tanya said to herself. The freshly squeezed orange juice looked so good. There was condensation on the glass jug. Rivulets of water ran down the sides. Tanya poured a glass and downed the contents.

"I'm not calling him," Brant said.

"Please don't," Esral pleaded.

"You don't need a man to complete you. You can stay here as long as you please. Until you meet someone you want to be with that is."

"You'd allow me to stay?" Her voice was filled with awe. Her eyes held hope.

"Yes, Esral. For as long as you need. We can be your new people."

"Cenwein, it would still mean war. Unless the princess mates with royalty . . . wait a minute." Brant laughed. "I have the solution. Why didn't I think of it sooner? Xavier is royalty."

The male stood by the door. "No freaking way," he said as he shook his head.

"You must. You are a prince and royalty so technically if you were to mate the princess . . ."

Xavier shook his head, his grey eyes darkened. "I've always been happy that I wasn't born as heir, because I wouldn't have to be saddled with all the bullshit. I have other plans and they don't involve a mate."

"You are royalty and will do what is best for the people." Brant's even voice brought chills to Tanya's spine.

Xavier's mouth pulled into a thin white line.

"You may be royalty but you are not a king. Katar says that she is stronger than she looks. Although not as fertile as humans, the princess should get you young." Zane said.

"Did you not hear a word I just said?" Tanya narrowed her eyes at Zane. She turned to the princess. "Esral, it is your choice. You don't have to mate him or any other." She swallowed, her mouth feeling dry. "You don't have to have . . . young. You can decide."

"No, she can't." Brant looked frustrated. "If she is not mated by vampire royalty it will be considered an insult. According to Esral, the mating will need to take place soon. No pressure." He added looking at Xavier who had turned a lighter shade of ghost.

Esral shook her head. "I have to say that since hearing your female talk of having a choice, I like the idea of being able to choose my own mate. The male doesn't even want me." Esral looked at Xavier. Her lip wobbled. "I need time to think about it."

"That's not what you said to me when you were disrobing in the vehicle."

"Disrobing?" Both Tanya and Xavier said together.

Zane threw up his hands. "I didn't ask her to. I told her to stop."

"I'm sure you did," Tanya narrowed her eyes at Zane.

"I'm done talking. You mate her ASAP." Zane pointed at Xavier and Esral in turn. He strode towards Tanya picking her up in one easy move. Her breasts flattened against his chest. "I may have to keep telling you over and over while we rut, you are the only female for me." The way his eyes heated told her his words were true, except at that moment her eyes were pulled to the pulse at the base of his neck.

Her mouth felt dry.

So thirsty.

She licked her lips, feeling sharp little fangs instead of canines. Holy shit. Still carrying her, Zane moved towards the door in determined steps.

"You'd better come with us." Tanya met Brant's eyes. "I need to tell you something important."

Part 5

Red Lust

Chapter ONE

She licked her lips, feeling sharp little fangs instead of canines. *Holy shit.* Still carrying her, Zane moved towards the door in determined steps.

"You'd better come with us," Tanya met Brant's eyes as she spoke. "I need to tell you something important."

Zane stiffened and stopped walking. "You are mine. He had his turn." Zane gestured to Brant with his head since his arms surrounded Tanya in a firm grasp.

"Didn't you listen to a word I just said?" Tanya paused trying to let her words sink in.

"I listened." Zane took another step towards the door.

"I'm referring to the part about not being a possession and having a mind and a will of my own."

"You are mine." He tightened his hold. "I will have you now." She pushed at his chest, trying to get him to release her. He ignored her completely. "As to having a mind and a will." Zane chuckled, he put his lips against her ear. "You won't mind when I lick your pussy and you will scream several times when I make you come hard."

Tanya made a sound of frustration. Irritated by how her

body responded to his crude words.

Brant took a step forward. "*The female* wants to discuss something with both of us."

"The female? Not you too, Brant." She said trying to throw him the dirtiest look she could muster.

"I'm sorry, Cenwein. You know I don't mean it like that." He scowled at Zane.

"Fine." Zane strode out into the hallway. Brant followed close behind. "You will need to make it quick or Brant will get a show."

Brant's face tightened, his eyes darkened. "You're acting like you haven't just spent the last three days with her."

"I haven't rutted her since we were in the basement, so forgive my sense of urgency." Zane rubbed a hand down her back clasping her ass. He made a strangled sound as he felt that she wasn't wearing any panties. Tanya had to keep from gasping as his fingers skimmed her slit. Zane made an approving rumble while pulling her dress down over her naked flesh and then anchoring his hand on her ass.

Tanya wrapped her legs around his waist. Her tongue felt like it was stuck to the roof of her mouth and her eyes kept straying to the pulse at the base of his neck. Was it just her imagination or was his musky, manly scent stronger making her mouth water for a taste? *Just a little kiss to his neck.* One little tongue swipe across his skin. Who was she kidding? The thought of sinking her newly formed fangs into his skin had her blood rushing, had her pussy turning wet. The sight of Griffin and York trailing behind Brant had her biting her teeth together to prevent herself from doing it.

"Hurry," she whispered.

"Needy little human." Zane chuckled. "Can't wait to scream my name?" He sucked in a deep breath. "Can't wait until I'm balls deep inside you?" He groaned picking up the pace. "I sure as blood can't wait, Ysnaar." Tanya clenched her teeth all the tighter.

Zane reached the winding stairs, taking three at a time. Tanya clutched her arms around his neck and locked her ankles at his back. "I've got you." His chest vibrated against hers.

Not even winded, Zane deposited her on the bed before unstrapping various weapons from his body. Brant entered, closing the door behind him.

"Take off your clothes and talk fast." Zane's eyes were on her, his lids half-mast.

"Slow down." She held up a hand.

"Do you have any idea what torture it was to lay next to you and not have you?" Zane pulled his shirt over his head as he spoke.

"About that." Brant's hands fisted at his sides. "What game are you playing at? Why didn't you rut with our female?"

"Stop calling me that." Standing, Tanya put her hands on her hips, trying to make herself as tall as possible. *Yeah right.* Next to these two she was a wilting flower and loved it.

"You don't mind when Zane calls you female," Brant growled, his eyes narrowing.

"You are you and Zane is Zane. I don't like it when you call me female. It feels different coming from you."

"Take your clothes off," Zane repeated on a growl.

"I'm thirsty," she blurted.

Zane rolled his eyes while grabbing the phone. He barked an order for several different types of beverages to be brought up. "Hurry," he added before punching the disconnect button.

"You don't get it. I'm really thirsty." She tried again hoping they would get it this time.

"Answer me Zane?" Brant's eyes darkened.

"I wouldn't have liked you rutting with her in my absence, especially during the heat. We need to try and make this work. That means respecting each other." Zane unbuttoned his leather pants. "It nearly freaking killed me. Thought my balls would explode."

"I would've rutted her."

"I guess that makes me the better male." Zane's eyes narrowed, his whole body tensed.

"No, it makes you a pussy." Brant took a step forward.

"Next time I will take her."

"There won't be a next time," Brant snarled.

Zane took two steps towards Brant, putting them chest to chest.

"Stop!" Tanya tried to talk above all the growling and snarling.

"It might be best if you stepped out of the room so that we can work this out." Brant growled at her, not taking his glowing eyes off of Zane.

"I'm pregnant."

Brant's head snapped in her direction. His wide eyes caught hers. In a flash, Zane was in front of her. He picked her up, cradling her against his massive chest like a child. "What do you need? How are you feeling?"

"I'm thirsty," she whispered feeling so ashamed.

"No problem." Brant removed his shirt.

"Leave." Zane tightened his grip on her, making it hard to breathe.

"My female needs me." Brant clasped her hand.

"*My*, Ysnaar needs blood, which I am perfectly capable of giving her. You can go now," Zane spoke softly. Each word came out sounding like a threat.

"Stop," she managed to choke out. "You're holding me too tight."

Zane released his hold on her, but only just.

"I will drink from both of you."

"I'll go first." Brant put his other hand on her back.

"The fuck you will," Zane snarled, his fangs had extended. Brant's eyes glowed brighter.

"Stop it. We'll toss a coin or something just do it quick, I'm so freaking thirsty."

"In the drawer, bottom one on the right," Zane spoke to Brant. He caressed her back. "I can't believe it." When he pulled her back he was grinning. God he was gorgeous when he smiled like that. "I bet I win the toss."

Tanya punched Zane on the arm.

"I bet the child will be mine," Brant said as he moved items about in the drawer. He was also grinning.

"No chance," Zane growled clutching her to him. Tanya groaned and he eased up his hold again.

"Griffin," Tanya called. She'd had just about enough of these two bull headed males. "Griffin, get your ass in here."

The guard walked in together with a female who deposited a tray of jugs holding numerous types of juices, she could probably sense the tension in the room because she walked straight back out.

"Yes, your highness? What can I do for you?" A confused expression graced Griffin's handsome face.

"Get your vein over here." She tried to keep herself from smiling.

"Get the fuck out!" Zane snarled.

"Or die!" Brant added just as harshly.

The poor vampire turned ashen and left without another word.

"Toss the coin and call it," she instructed Brant.

"Hey. Why does he—"

"Shut it." She looked up at Zane who ground his teeth together but did as she said.

"Do it." Tanya looked at the coin in Brant's hand.

"Heads." He tossed, caught the coin and slapped his other hand over the large, gold disc.

While everyone looked on, he slowly removed his hand. "Yeah!" Brant fist pumped the air. These great big warriors could be just like over grown children. "You get to drink from me first."

"Oh, God. I'm so thirsty, yet the thought of drinking blood still makes me feel queasy."

Zane slowly released her so that she slid down the length of his hard body. Brant's eyes were still glowing, his shirt in a crumpled heap on the floor. Her new fangs throbbed just looking at the vast expanse of exposed skin. Rock hard abs and a strong broad chest to match. The need to drink almost lost out to the need to drool. Within two steps, she was in his arms. Brant bracketed her waist with his hand and lifted her easily. He turned his head to the side allowing her easy access to his neck. He smelled so good, clean, manly, mouth-watering. Her stomach gave a little lurch, but the need to drink overrode any queasiness in the end.

Tanya kissed his neck, next she gave a languid lick on the patch that looked the most inviting. Her whole body tightened in anticipation. It reminded her of how she felt as she neared an orgasm. Her fangs throbbed as she sank them into his flesh. She moaned as the first trickle of blood hit her tongue. The perfect combination of sweet and salty, just as intoxicating as a shot of alcohol after a lick of butter icing. Maybe more so. Brant moaned as she took a second pull, he ground his straining erection against her core. The throb in her fangs had eased, though now it was replaced by a throb deep inside her core.

———⸺·C✻⁀·⸺———

Tanya ground herself against Brant, who responded by curling his hips so that his cock would be positioned just right. Zane's own erection hardened up a whole lot more. He needed to be inside this female almost as much as he needed to draw his next breath.

Patience.

Not something he was used to. Not something he liked. Especially since Brant continued to insist on being a dickhead. Zane couldn't believe he'd forgone rutting with Tanya as a show of partnership, of wanting this damn thing to work. The other male kept throwing it in his face and chances were good that he wasn't going to change anytime soon.

Hearing her sensuous moan, Zane's gaze was brought back to the erotic sight of his female drinking greedily. Gulping down mouthfuls of blood that had his own fangs extending. The visual made Zane glad that Brant had won the bet. But if she continued to drink like that, she wouldn't want from him.

Zane moved in behind her. Brant's eyes were closed. His jaw slack. They were grinding against each other in earnest and from the sound of Tanya's frantic, little moans, she was on the verge of orgasm. Zane almost felt bad for breaking them up.

"Come, Ysnaar. It is my turn." He slid his hands onto her hips.

Brant's eyes shot open. He glared daggers at Zane.

Zane gave a half smile and shrugged. Tanya made a sound of protest as he pulled her away. The little minx licked at her lips. Her eyes were a brighter shade. Not glowing exactly, but close to it. Her cheeks were flushed. His female was glowing and looked half dazed. Zane felt a sense of pride at the thought that the baby inside her could be his. "Are you still thirsty?" he asked noticing how her eyes were glued to his neck. "I swear you've done this before."

"Yeah," Brant said. "She knew exactly where to bite."

"Very thirsty," Tanya answered. She ran her tongue across her lip.

"Good," Zane growled. He pulled his pants down freeing his cock. He took a hold of her dress and ripped. The fabric parted easily. Her heavily curved breasts were his at last, his to admire. The top part of her dress gaped.

"You didn't just do that." Although she sounded gruff, she was smiling.

"You have other dresses."

"You guys need to stop destroying my clothes. I liked that dress."

"I like you naked more," Zane said catching Brant's heated gaze. His cock peeped out at the top of his jeans. He growled in the direction of the other male. Zane wasn't about to invite Brant to join them.

News of his female's pregnancy was fresh, and a feeling of possessiveness gripped him. Brant's eyes narrowed as Zane pulled Tanya's dress over her hips. A thin strip of fur, a glistening slit. "Drink." He growled putting his hands on her hips and pulling her up against him. Her legs closed around him. He nudged ever so gently into her wet welcoming heat. His female whimpered.

Zane sat on the edge of the bed. His dick buried inside her. Using his hands, he lifted her as he thrust into her from below. Balls deep, he paused waiting for her to accommodate his size.

His little human sniffed at his neck, the sensation almost making him come. A small sting as she sank her delectable little fangs into him. It felt amazing, his hips jerked with a mind of their own. She whimpered and mewled with every thrust. His female didn't mess around, she sucked hard almost making him lose his load with each pull. Her sheath clutched at him. Her silken walls tugging just as hard as her mouth. With a snarl, he sank his own fangs into her. Tanya came instantly on a scream. Her pussy clamped so hard that he found himself finding his release on a deafening roar.

So fucking good.

Zane fell back taking her with him, his cock still buried inside her. After a few beats, she turned her head to the spot Brant had occupied.

"He's gone," Zane said. He'd heard the male leave as he moved to drink from his female.

When she turned back, her eyes were clouded. Zane hated that she felt pain. He leaned forward and kissed her, tasting his own blood on her lips.

Something he could get used to fast.

She smiled as he released her. Pulling her closer, his greedy human sniffed at his neck. "I want to do that again. Maybe we could stay here for the rest of the evening." She gasped. "I know, we could stay here for the rest of our lives. Share blood and live on orgasms." She giggled licking at his neck. "I only wish Brant could"—she huffed and her eyes dropped to his neck—"never mind."

Tanya nuzzled his skin. "You need to stop, Ysnaar." He chuckled. "You've had too much already." He ignored her previous comment, not wanting to talk about the other male.

She pulled back a little. "Oh no, is there a limit?" Her lips were glistening. Her eyes still on his neck.

"You need to get used to taking blood. It's new to your human system. Take it easy. Too much of a good thing and all that."

"I feel fine." Her lashes fused. She pulled a lush lip between her lips and pulled herself onto her elbows wriggling in a way that had her nipples rubbing up against his chest.

"Stop that or I'll change my mind."

"That's the plan."

"Sex, yes." He paused, flipping her so that she was on her back with him over her. Zane pulled her arms above her head. Tanya nipped at him but he pulled just out of her reach. "Blood, no."

She made a sound of irritation which quickly turned to a groan as he rocked inside her. "I believe I promised you multiple orgasms."

"You also promised to use your tongue on me." She lifted her eyebrows.

He pulled almost all the way out. "The night is young, Ysnaar." His female's eyes drifted shut and her mouth slackened as he slid back into her. Slow and easy.

―――・(*)・―――

Leaving his female satisfied and napping, Zane went in search of Lance. Upon entering his suite, he faltered halting mid-step. Charlotte's robe rode low on her hips. She faced Lance, who was still bedridden although he wouldn't be down for much longer.

"I said no." It pained Zane to hear how soft and weak his friend's voice sounded.

"Rutting will make you stronger." Charlotte said, yet she still pulled her robe back over her shoulders and fastened the tie.

Poor Charlotte, he thought. Even though she was infertile, she was considered one of the most desirable females in the coven. Yet, she wasn't having much luck in the male department lately.

"Thank you," Lance added almost whispering.

Zane had never known his head guard to be quite this polite. It worried him.

"My lord." Lance greeted turning his face to him only after he had spoken.

Charlotte gave a semi curtsy. "If you change your mind." She looked in Lance's direction.

"I won't."

Confusion marred her features, Charlotte was not used to being denied. She nodded once and left the room.

"You should've taken her up on her offer."

"I was tempted, but I hate lying here while Stephany . . ." His lips tightened. Pulling a second pillow behind his head, Lance struggled to pull himself into a semi upright position. He was breathing heavily by the time he finished. His skin was pale and there were dark circles under his eyes.

"It won't be long before she is released. The wolves would be fools to harm her."

"Within a day or two, I will be well. I will find her."

"You will do nothing of the sort."

"I will seek out my mate and bring her back to her rightful place at my side." Lance's eyes glowed, his biceps bulged as his hands closed to tight fists.

"Enough."

Lance closed his mouth into a thin white line.

"Trying to find her would be futile. Our best trackers failed, as will you." Zane pulled a chair up next to the bed. "If she is not back within the week, then we will act."

"A week is a long time. So much can go wrong. I need my female. Three days or I will—"

"Quiet. You are not being rational. Since when do you care so much about what happens to the female?" Zane was fast losing patience.

"My female," Lance growled.

"You accidentally mated her twenty years ago, you ignored each other ever since it happened, and now you want to claim her as yours?" He couldn't help but to point out the hypocrisy there.

"The moment her fangs breached my skin during the new moon, she became mine. When our blood flowed as one, she became my mate."

Zane held up his hand. "Spare me, I know how it works." He knew he was being a little insensitive but *fuck,* maybe one of the arrows had pierced Lance's head. "Twenty years Lance. I gave you leave many years ago to take the female. Why now?"

"With all due respect, my lord. It's none of your fucking business."

Zane chuckled. "Glad to see you haven't turned into a complete pussy."

"Stop that," Lance smiled. "You look weird when you laugh."

Zane smiled. "Having a female has been good for me."

Lance narrowed his eyes. "I hear you will continue to share her with Brant. Again, with all due respect . . ." Lance paused waiting for permission to continue.

"Yeah, yeah." Zane motioned for him to get on with it.

" . . . a three way mating. What the fuck?"

Zane arched his brow. "It's a bit tricky." He wasn't sure he was still game. Since his female had become pregnant, he didn't feel as up to sharing. If her pregnancy affected him this way, it would be twice as bad for Brant who hadn't been able to share well from the start.

Lance chuckled and winced. "Tricky." He smiled "I'll bet, one female and two cocks. Especially when the cocks happen to be attached to two dominant, arrogant males. It must be all fun and games."

"A whole, big bundle. Tanya is with child."

Lance's eyes lit up. "Wow. You are to be a father. Good news."

"It could be Brant's," he bit out.

Lance's face turned hard. "It will be yours, my lord."

"The covens are one, so it doesn't matter who the father is."

Lance raised a brow. He clearly thought the sentiment was flawed. Zane really didn't mind either way. Tanya was pregnant with royal blood. It didn't matter who the father was. Yet, he had begun to mind that he had to share his female especially considering Brant insisted on being so thick skulled. Best he think of something else, his human wanted both kings so he would just have to deal. "If you are not going to rut, then make sure you take blood more often."

"I will," Lance said.

"Rest assured that Stephany will be back soon." Zane felt his lips pull into a smile. "I don't think she will fall back into your arms though my friend."

"I will have her in my bed in no time."

To think Lance had had the audacity to call him arrogant. Zane shook his head. "There is nothing more dangerous or difficult to appease than a female who has been slighted. You mated her and dumped her."

"She mated me," Lance said.

"It takes two, so don't give me that bull. She may have bit you first but you bit her right back."

"The best sex I've ever had," Lance sounded wistful.

"Whatever. The details are not important. You mated her and left her. Haven't tried to see her or speak to her since."

"I've spoken to her," Lance looked a bit panicked.

"Traditional functions don't count. You never sought her out yourself with the specific intention to talk things out. Did you call even once?"

Lance shook his head.

"You are so fucked, or in this case not. You won't be getting any for a very long time." Zane chuckled.

"Want to bet? One week of courting and she'll be mine."

"A whole freaking week. Have you gone soft?" He was fucking with the other male, a week would never be enough. Hell, it might take years.

Lance's jaw tensed. "She is mad."

"You won't get anywhere near her any time soon, maybe not ever. The covens talk. She'll know how many females you bedded while she has remained celibate. You can be thankful that you are not a human though, or your dick may've fallen off a long time ago. I am the king and yet even I have not bedded as many females as you."

Lance grunted. "I am a male, I have needs. Rut with the same female too often and she begins to think that you are in a relationship."

"Excuses. You should've gone to Stephany."

"Oh yeah, and that would've gone over well. You and Brant birth enemies . . ." Lance said as he shook his head. "They were dark times of mourning. Both your fathers lost in battle. Levels of hate still ran high." His eyes clouded in thought.

Zane shrugged. "You gave the impression that you didn't care. If the female had meant something to you, you would've fought for her. You never did."

Lance winced. "I managed to convince myself that she was nothing to me. Lived the lie for so long that I believed it myself." He scrunched his eyes shut for a few beats. "Watching that wolf take her though. Not being able to protect her. It made me realize what she means to me. I will find a way to win her."

"About that, you ran into their range, making it easy for the archers to take you out. Don't pull a stunt like that again. You should've died from your wounds."

"The only thought I had was of saving Stephany. I would do it again." His eyes narrowed.

Zane nodded and found himself smiling. "I would do the same if it came to my female."

"You have grown fond of her."

Zane nodded. "You could say that."

"Aren't you worried about hurting her? She is human after all, and we know how fragile they are. It must be difficult to rut whilst being so careful."

Just thinking about being with his female had his body tightening. Some places more than others. "In many ways it heightens the experience. Humans are stronger than we give them credit for, yet at the same time they are so soft." A low rumble escaped him.

Lance gave him a look that told him he was full of it. "If you say so."

"You need your rest if you are to be well when your female returns." Zane stood. "You're going to need your strength for sure."

"For rutting." Lance had a dreamy look on his face. Scary, Zane had never seen him this way.

"More like for walking on your knees." Zane laughed as Lance's eyes widened.

Chapter TWO

A ROAD TRIP. *HAPPY days!* Brant was taking her out and she couldn't wait. She wore a dress and underwear. The boys would have to come to terms with the fact that she couldn't walk around commando all the time.

Her only hope was that her sexy turquoise underwear stayed in one piece. The dress was beautiful, also in a dark turquoise blue. It had sequins embroidered around the neck line and it made her feel beautiful.

"Please don't rip this dress."

Brant threw her a half-cocked smile. So drool worthy it was crazy. His eyes moved down her body. "You look great." His dark orbs zoned in on her curves, heating more and more as they roamed. "I'm afraid I can't make any promises."

"You can and you will."

"Only if you promise to undress quickly before we even make it back to the room, because once that door closes . . ."

"That would mean my undressing in the hall." She put her hands on her hips. "I'll give your men an eyeful."

He growled. "They can close their eyes."

"Then again, it's not like Xavier hasn't seen me naked." She chewed on her lip for a bit reminded that Xavier wasn't outside their door at the moment. "How is he doing? Have he and Esral mated?"

Brant chuckled while shaking his head. "I don't know if I should be really mad at you or agree with everything you said," he paused. "She refuses to give him the time of day. They do need to mate, Cenwein, or it will mean trouble."

"She is free to do as she wishes."

"You explain that to her father and the rest of the elves."

"No problem."

His eyes narrowed and he walked to her, putting his hands around her waist. "You could probably pull it off. Then again . . ." he shook his head. "Katar is old, highly traditional and set in his ways. There is something I need to talk to you about"—he paused squeezing her hips—"I have a favor to ask."

"Yes?" She got the distinct feeling that she wasn't going to like whatever the request was.

"Please talk with Esral. She's been holed up in her room since she arrived. Won't eat or talk to anybody. I think she might feel differently about you though."

"I'm not going to talk her into mating Xavier."

He cupped her cheeks. "My brother isn't that bad."

"He's freaking hot, but mating with someone is a major step."

Brant's eyes narrowed. "You think my brother is hot? Are the two of us not enough for you?" The edge of his lips twitched in amusement.

She laughed. "More than enough you idiot. Just stating a fact."

"Please talk her into giving him a chance."

That poor girl.

"Please, Cenwein. It's not healthy for her to be stuck behind closed doors."

"I'll talk to her." She smiled while thinking that Esral must be lonely and afraid. She probably needed someone to confide in, and Tanya had an inkling of what she was going through.

Brant kissed her. One quick, soft touch of the lips. As he pulled away, his eyes dropped to her mouth and heated. "Ah, hell." He dipped back down cupping her chin and taking her deeper. His cock pressed against her lower stomach. He growled as he released her, his eyes glowing. "How are you feeling?"

"Tired and a little sore."

"Bastard," Brant spat the word.

"Hang on just a second. It was my fault." She felt her cheeks heat. "The whole drinking thing kind of made me really horny. You should've stayed."

He shook his head. "Zane would not have wanted it. Even if he had, threes a crowd, it's not for me."

Pain welled.

"I'm sorry, Cenwein."

"Work on it. I don't like this arrangement."

His eyes narrowed and his body tensed. "What is it that you want? One big cosy suite? A double king sized bed?"

"Double king." She laughed, snorting a little. He gave a small smile before seeming to remember that he was irritated with the conversation.

"Forget the double king thing. I'm never sharing a bed with that asshole. I prefer it when it's just the two of us."

"Only it's not just the two of us, Brant, and I don't know how long my moving from one bed to the other can go on. We are going to be a family." She touched a hand to her stomach. It was funny how quickly her attachment to the baby had grown. She felt silly, it wasn't even a baby yet, just a clump of cells really and yet she couldn't help but to feel warm and fuzzy at the thought of the life growing inside her. "I want the little one to grow up in a loving home. I don't want the bickering and the fighting. All the back and forth."

His jaw clenched. "Give it time. There is no rush."

She nodded. It was wrong of her to expect miracles overnight, at least her men weren't attacking each other anymore. So, in their own way, they were making progress. It hurt her to see Brant upset though. It wasn't easy being pulled in two directions either, but for now she would get on with it.

Thankfully she had a mating ceremony to arrange, it would keep her mind occupied on other things. Tanya felt excitement bubble up inside her, she was allowed to invite Becky. Her best friend was going to die when she heard the news. It wasn't easy convincing Brant to let her fragile human best friend to come through to the coven for the ceremony. Though Zane was fine with it.

"Let's go and see Esral and my brother." Brant smiled. "He's never been turned down by a female before. Even though he pretends he doesn't care, I suspect he's taking it hard even if he won't admit it." He took her hand as they walked from his suite.

Xavier stood outside a closed door in one of the long hallways. His hands were clasped in front of his big body. He turned his head as they walked up. His expression remained solemn.

"Still not interested?" Tanya noticed how Brant's mouth twitched as he spoke.

Xavier must have noticed too because his body tensed as he shook his head. "She won't speak to me and sends her food back uneaten. Please, can we stop this madness? The princess does not want to mate me and I am happy to oblige her."

"Did you speak with her about it?" Tanya asked.

"She won't let me in, just shouts through the door for me to go away." His eyes darkened. "Since your little talk with her yesterday"—he motioned to Tanya—"she feels like she should have an opinion and does not want to be forced into mating. Like I said earlier, it suits me just fine in the end though. Brother please can we stop this now?"

"You *must* mate her. You must convince her." Brant stated slipping his arm around Tanya's shoulder as he spoke.

"It's wrong to expect people who don't even know each other to make such a commitment. I'm against this. At least with the choosing ceremony, the whole thing is based on scent and chances of compatibility are high. That's not even the case in this situation." Tanya addressed Brant.

Xavier grunted, his mouth a tight line.

"I realize her father expects her to mate with royalty, but if you are not willing then maybe Griffin would agree. The princess is very pretty, Griffin won't stop talking about her. I think he might even have a little crush on her," Tanya added the last to prove a point.

If she had thought that Xavier was tense before, she had been wrong. His whole body tightened to where she thought he might tear a muscle. "What the fuck does Griffin know?"

"He was in the vehicle when she was transported back," Brant said.

Xavier's eyes narrowed, "So what?"

"The princess disrobed for Zane to try and seduce him. Griffin caught an eyeful," Brant replied.

"I will hit Griffin until he loses his memory. Problem solved." Sheesh, in this moment, Brant's brother looked very much the deadly warrior he was. "I think the princess' modesty should be protected."

Brant chuckled. "I think you have a thing for the princess."

Xavier shrugged. "She's a nice piece of ass. I wouldn't mind rutting her, but mating . . . not so much. If . . . and it's a big if . . . I ever decide to mate, it will be with a vampire female."

Tanya gasped, she punched Xavier on the arm. Her knuckle made a cracking sound on impact.

"Careful human, you might break something."

"You are the one that needs to be careful brother." Brant stepped up to Xavier so that they were inches apart. "Tanya is your queen and you will address her as such. If she so much as breaks a nail, I will take you down. Are we clear?"

"Yes, my lord. Apologies my lady, but for the record the queen hit me. Why would I be punished if she hurt herself?"

Brant relaxed a little taking a small step back. "It's how it is. Do not provoke her."

Xavier nodded.

Tanya shook her head and had to suppress a laugh at how sheepish Xavier looked before she could speak again. "It shouldn't matter what species she is. Esral is a person with feelings and not just a tight piece of ass. She is also a virgin and deserves respect."

"I assure you, my lady, that if I were to rut with the princess it would be because she was begging for me to do so." The edge of Xavier's mouth lifted.

"I've heard rutting is difficult through a closed door." Brant chuckled. Xavier quickly lost his smile.

This time Tanya hit Brant, who irritated her by laughing harder. Xavier looked even more pissed.

"Forget your freaking dicks for once. This is not about sex."

"Um"—Brant smiled—"I hate to break it to you, Cenwein, but mating and rutting go hand in hand." His face clouded before he appeared to turn to stone, shutting his emotions down. He was obviously thinking about their own mating that would happen in a few days' time, which she knew didn't enthuse him since three was a crowd in his opinion. In order for her to mate with both males, they would need to all be together.

"Yeah, but you first need to win her over. Let me go and talk with her. Her opinion in this is important. She might not find you attractive, Xavier."

He snorted, "As if."

"Arrogant much?" She lifted her eyebrows and gave him what she hoped was a scathing look.

Brant laughed. "You go and talk with Esral"—he put a hand on her back—"I'll have a little chat with my brother."

Tanya walked over to the door, she knocked and announced herself. There was a tell-tale sound of a key turning in the lock. She couldn't help but to give Xavier a self-satisfied smile. *Arrogant, full of it jerk.* She thought a little bit of grovelling would do him good.

Esral smiled a small, unsure smile. She was wearing another robe. It was slightly darker than the one she had worn the day before. Her large eyes were still red rimmed with dark smudges underneath them.

"I take it that you didn't get much sleep."

Esral shook her head. Her lip quivered. "I am a failure, defective."

"Stop saying that, you are not a failure. I thought you understood that after our talk yesterday. You are a beautiful woman. You should never have been given away by your father."

"Every day since I first really understood the way of our people, I prayed that things would be different but still resigned myself to my fate. It is the way of our people."

"By fate, you mean being given in marriage?" Tanya asked.

"Marriage?" Esral's brows pulled together in confusion.

"Marriage is the same as mating. You would be forced to mate with someone?"

Her mouth pulled to the side in thought. "I don't know that force is the right word."

"Being given to someone against your will after being brainwashed into believing that it is perfectly fine is force in my book. Just because you didn't run away screaming doesn't make it right or consensual." *The nerve of some species.* They called humans puny and weak, but at least most of her species had made progress with regards to women's rights.

"I used to pretend that I was one of the commoners. It's only the high born that suffer from this fate. Males included," she huffed. "Our high born males are all a bunch of arrogant idiots." She paused for a few beats. "I was glad when my father told me that I was going to be given to Zane. Very scared, but glad. I had hope for the first time. You see"—she blushed—"I'm already twenty four, truth is my father should've given me to someone by now but all the eligible males are terrible."

"Arrogant idiots."

"Oh, yes. I had hoped that there would be a spark between Zane and I. Like I said, I was really scared at the thought of having to mate a big, scary vampire but anyone other than the high born elves would've been an improvement. Besides, I had seen his picture and thought he was attractive. You are lucky." Her eyes welled. "I just want to feel like a normal female for once. The girls in our village go on dates and get to have fun. They get to choose who they spend their lives with and I want that."

"You can have all of that."

Her eyes lit up, "I can?" Her shoulders slumped and she

shook her head. "My people would not understand."

"What did I tell you? You're one of us now."

"I would disappoint my father."

"He will eventually understand. It sounds like he loves you very much. He tried to give you what you wanted in a roundabout way."

Esral sort of smiled. "He does love me. Maybe in time. What were you saying about the vampire males?"

She may as well just say it. "Vampires are highly sexual and might try funny business with you."

"By funny business you mean they'll want to rut with me?"

Tanya nodded and Esral laughed. "It is a normal bodily function. One which highborn females are denied while the males can run after every village girl they like." Her face flushed in anger.

Tanya prepared to argue. It wouldn't be good if the virgin elven princess moved from bed to bed.

Esral laughed. "I can see by the look on your face that you don't like the idea of my rutting with the vampire males."

"I think that being a virgin is something special. Sex should be special. I was an idiot and don't want you to make the same mistake that I did. It was my senior year in high school and one of the jocks took an interest in me. Little old plain Jane me . . . I couldn't believe it. Taylor was so popular, I thought he was a hunk at the time, but what he really was, was a grade-A asshole."

"Ass . . . hole? He was a hole? What is an ass?"

Tanya laughed. "It's another way of saying arrogant idiot."

Her mouth rounded in an "o" and she gestured for Tanya to continue.

"Anyway, it turned out that the asshole only wanted into my panties. He saw a self-conscience young lady and used it to his advantage. I had that nagging voice in the back of my head that told me sex for the first time in the back of his pickup was not the actions of a guy that really cared, but Taylor was a sweet talker. He literally charmed the pants off of me."

"I have heard that rutting for the first time can hurt?"

It had hurt like a bitch when Taylor had shoved himself into her before preparing her first. *The bastard.* She really hadn't had much luck with men, at least until Zane and Brant. What a cruel twist of fate to throw two really great males at her. If only they could all get along.

"Your silence speaks volumes." Esral had wide eyes and looked a little nervous.

"If you are with the right male, it won't be so bad."

"Sex must be good though since everyone seems to want to do it all the time. I'm so curious to find out what it's like." She smiled.

"Sure it's good, but that doesn't mean you should just jump into bed with anyone just to appease your curiosity. You don't need to have all out sex, you could fool around a bit."

"Fool around?" She shook her head, her eyes clouded in confusion.

"Have they kept you wrapped up in cotton wool?"

"I don't understand the question."

Tanya made a sound of frustration. "You can touch someone and they can touch you back. Touching can feel good too. First, I would suggest a date or two. If you really like someone, you can kiss. If you really really like them, you can let them touch you a little. Take your time though. You are still young. No sex. Virginity doesn't seem to be a big deal for vampires. Sex is considered . . . like you said earlier . . . a normal bodily function. If you allowed it, you would be on your back in no time." Tanya worried for the innocent elven female. The vampire males would have her for breakfast quite literally. "I'll talk to Brant about letting you go on a date."

"Please do. I would love to go out with one of the gorgeous males." Esral crossed her legs under her while smiling broadly. Then her face turned serious. "I will think on what you said about being a virgin though. I don't think I could rut with just anyone anyway. Too many years of . . . what did you call it . . . brainwashing. I was always taught to save myself for my mate."

Tanya didn't know what to say to that. On the one hand staying a virgin for her mate wasn't a bad idea, but it was ultimately Esral's decision. She didn't want to fall into the same trap of telling her what she could and couldn't do. So she took the safe route and changed the subject. "You need to eat something or you'll waste away."

Esral grimaced. "They keep bringing me dead things."

Tanya laughed. "You mean meat?"

"That's what I said, dead things." She wrinkled her nose. "Disgusting. I only eat food from the earth."

Tanya nodded. "I'll have something brought up. Would you like new clothes? I really like your robes, but maybe you would prefer garments that would help you to fit in around here a little better."

Her eyes lit up and she gasped in excitement. "Really? That would be wonderful. I would love something like what you are wearing and blue . . ." She raised her eyes in thought. ". . . jeans. Did I say it right?"

"Yeah you did. What size are you?" Esral shrugged. "Okay. What size underwear?"

"No idea. Unmated females are not permitted to wear underwear."

"Fucking barbaric." Tanya couldn't help the anger that coursed through her veins. She would take it upon herself as queen of the freaking vampires to change some things around here. She would also make it her mission to talk to their species allegiance partners about some of the outdated, sexist practices that were still normal to them and carried out. "I will have Charlotte come and measure you. You'll get underwear, dresses and blue jeans. I'll talk to my males about the whole dating thing. They won't like it, but they'll like it even less when I withhold sex, so don't worry your sweet little head."

Esral nodded. "Thank you, Tanya."

"We'll chat later." She slid off the bed. She turned just as her hand touched the door. "Get out a bit. It might take a few days for my boys to agree to the dating thing. It's not good for you to be stuck in here though. Xavier will look after you."

"He's the one that I'm supposed to mate with."

"I told you, you don't have to mate with anyone. He'll keep you safe though." She turned the knob just a fraction.

Esral's eyes narrowed, stopping her from leaving. "The kings want me to mate him."

"Look, Esral, he is royalty so your father's wishes would be granted if you chose to mate with Xavier. It would still be your choice in the end though."

"Good, because I don't think he likes me very much."

"He likes you just fine."

"He refused the mating." She put her hands on her tiny hips.

"Just like you don't like being told who you can and can't mate, neither does he. He was just a bit shocked. Don't let it concern you. He happens to think that you are very pretty." *A tight piece of ass.* "He was very jealous when he heard that Griffin has the hots for you."

"Who is Griffin?"

"He was one of the vampires in the front of the SUV that day you arrived with Zane."

Esral laughed. "The one who saw my breasts in the mirror? I was a bit worried that he would crash the car."

Tanya laughed. "That's him. We'll talk later."

Esral nodded, "Okay. Thank you."

Tanya nodded and left the room. The lock turned as soon as the door closed. She felt that Xavier and Esral still had a chance. Xavier was definitely interested, even if he didn't want to admit it.

"And?" Brant crossed his arms across his chest.

Xavier didn't say anything, but she noticed how his eyes tracked her closely.

"Firstly, she doesn't eat meat. Have them send her fruits and vegetables. Also, I must get a hold of Charlotte so that she can be measured for a wardrobe."

"Pity. Silk looks good on her," Xavier cleared his throat. "I am a male, I did notice her legs under the short robe."

Tanya smiled. "I'll bet. She will still wear her robes but would also like to try some of our clothes. She especially mentioned blue jeans. Anyway, she also mentioned that she wants to go out on a date." She didn't mention the fact that Esral didn't seem too keen on Xavier, or that it sounded like the princess wanted to play the field a bit.

Xavier made a frustrated sound and ran a hand through his hair. "Seriously?"

"What's wrong with that?"

"Date?" Xavier spat out the word like it left a bad taste in his mouth. "I don't date."

"Fine. If Esral leaves the room then you follow her."

Xavier raised his brows before replying, "Yes, my lady."

Tanya purposefully squared her shoulders and strode down the hallway. Brant was soon in stride beside her. "You gave up too easily," he whispered. "What are you planning?"

"Your brother can be an ass."

Brant chuckled. "He has always maintained that he does not want to mate. Hates the thought of being tied down to one female. The whole species thing is also an issue for him, but yeah he can also be an ass."

"What's with the whole—it has to be a vampire female—thing?" Tanya asked.

"I've told you that my father wasn't permitted to drink from our mother. She was only ninety six when she died . . . so really very young. My father—"

Tanya held up a hand. "Ninety six is considered young? . . . She was human wasn't she?"

Brant nodded.

"Ninety six is *not* young for a human."

"If you continue to drink vampire blood, then you will age much slower. All mated couples drink from each other, it strengthens the bond. I've told you before that my father suffered greatly because my mother refused to share this with him. He had to watch her wither away." Brant's shoulders slumped. "He loved her very much and she loved him too but being that she wasn't a vampire, she never could accept blood drinking. Unlike you . . ." He pulled her towards him slanting a quick, hot kiss across her lips.

"What if I don't like drinking after the baby is born?" Her lips began to feel dry just thinking about blood. She was sure she could hear Brant's heartbeat, she could definitely smell his delicious scent.

"You enjoy it too much, Cenwein. I don't have much knowledge of humans, but I can safely say that you are nothing like my mother was. I remember how she struggled to take blood even when she was heavily pregnant with Xavier. It used to make her gag." He slid his arms around her waist. "My father would beg her to take from him after she had Xavier and I could see that she really wanted to drink from him, but she just couldn't. That is why I think Xavier fears being tied to someone who is not a vampire."

"Oh shit, Esral doesn't eat meat, is disgusted by it. She probably wouldn't be able to take blood." Her eyes dropped to his neck and she licked her lips.

"You never know. It is always a toss-up as to whether the thirst will hit. There has never been a vampire elven mating so who knows what would happen there. Or, how it would work out in the end. Try to understand my brother's fear though."

"He likes her."

"He wants to rut with her, there's a difference. My eyes are up here, Cenwein. Since when did I become a blood bank to you? You'll hurt my feelings."

She laughed, tearing her eyes away from his neck to look him in the face. "You became a blood bank after impregnating me. I'm thirsty." Her canines had sharpened up into little fangs. Drinking would have to wait a few more minutes though. "Esral wants to date."

"I'm sure Xavier will come around. He can take her out." His hands were splayed on her back, rubbing her in easy strokes.

"I have my doubts that he will. It's risky, but I think we should have Griffin ask her out. Let the two of them go out on a date."

Brant tensed. He put his hands on her hips. "Oh, no. Griffin is a horny young buck, his dick is still bigger than his brain. Xavier might kill him if he so much as laid a single finger on the princess."

She narrowed her eyes in a suggestive manner allowing a sly smile to form on her lips.

Brant choked out a laugh. "Little minx. You want to make Xavier jealous."

She waggled her eyebrows. "Right now, even though he is interested, there isn't enough of an incentive for him to go after her. I plan on giving him one. We need to get the princess a new, really sexy wardrobe and then let her go on a date with Griffin. Xavier won't be able to think straight I assure you."

Brant's eyes narrowed in thought. "The only problem I have with this plan is that Griffin might end up rutting with Esral. We can be a persuasive species."

Tanya took her lip between her teeth, squealing when her sharp fang broke the skin. Brant laughed. He kissed her all better but as he did, his eyes sprang open, and they were wide and glowing. He broke the kiss. His body hardened and he pulled further away.

"Are you okay?" He didn't respond. "Brant?"

After taking a deep breath, his eyes dimmed somewhat. "Sorry, Cenwein. You just taste really good. Control is still a big issue around you. Even more so now that you are pregnant. I look forward to the new moon." His face clouded taking on a familiar scowl, one that meant he was thinking of Zane.

"I can't wait either." She moved back into him.

"I've been thinking, Cenwein. I don't want to mate you with Zane in the room. I'll take you and then he can have you. We need to keep it separate." Brant released her hips completely.

"Or, Zane can mate me first."

His fists clenched and his jaw cracked as he ground his teeth. "Do you want him first?"

"It's not about who goes first but that's just it, it will become an issue if we keep things separate. I am mating the two of you,

Brant. As Zane has pointed out before, we are in this together. The three of us."

"I want our mating to be special. I want to make love to you, Cenwein. I don't want him watching." He cast his eyes to the floor. Emotion evident on his face.

Tanya took a tentative step towards him. "Oh, Brant. She clasped his jaw. We can make love. We *will* make love."

His eyes narrowed. "I will go first and I will take my time, that bastard can wait."

"Here we go again." She rolled her eyes. "And all along I thought Zane was bad with his dictating ways."

"Please don't compare me to him."

"You're right, I'm sorry." She put her hands in his. "This is new to me too. We will figure something out."

Brant nodded. "I still think it is a mistake to have us all together on that night."

"We are together whether we like it or not. Trying to separate the mating would end in the two of you in a fight."

"Put the three of us in the same room during the new moon and we may end up fighting anyway." His eyes bore into hers.

"Not if I'm naked, plus there's the baby to consider. It would be dangerous if I ended up in the crossfire."

His body remained tense.

Tanya pressed herself up against him. "Promise me that you'll at least try to make it work."

His eyes softened. "I'll try, Cenwein."

"I'm so freaking thirsty." She nuzzled into his neck lapping at the spot where his pulse was strongest, but Brant pulled away.

He surveyed the hall looking in one direction and then the other. "I need to warn you that drinking in public is on the same level as walking around naked or rutting."

She gasped. "Oh my gosh, really? I thought that there was nothing intimate about drinking."

"It can be intimate and when you drink from me it will be, but it doesn't have to be. Changing into your pajamas is not considered an intimate act either, yet it is not something you would do in public."

She giggled. "I guess not. It just strikes me as weird that you fornicate at will. Drink like mad from one another. The females walk around half naked, yet drinking in public is seen as taboo."

Brant shrugged his big shoulders. "Are you sure you can't wait until we get back?"

She shook her head unable to take her eyes off of his neck. God he smelled so good to her. Tanya let go of his hands and clasped his biceps. *So big.*

Brant chuckled, he picked her up and carried her to the nearest door. After knocking once, Brant entered. It was a lounge alcove and it was thankfully empty. He turned and propped her up against the closed door. "Don't want any interruptions." His voice held a gravely tone that cranked up her need.

Tanya closed her legs around his hips and buried her face into the base of his throat. Her fangs throbbed as she sank them into his smooth skin. She drank her fill, sighing as she released him. Brant's jaw was locked, his eyes glowing softly. His rock hard cock pressed against her belly.

"Are you okay?"

"You do crazy things to me." He kissed her ever so softly, and she could see that his fangs had extended. Huge, deadly looking things. "Maybe it is best that Zane be there during the mating. I'm not sure that I'll be able to keep it together." He shook his head looking defeated. "So much for making sweet love to you on the night."

"Don't be silly. We have many years ahead. Many long nights."

Brant smiled. "I can't wait." His dick twitched between their bodies.

"It looks like someone wants to start right now."

Shaking his head, he lowered her. "There's time for that later. Let's get going."

She giggled, "Drinking makes me hot."

"Makes me hot too, but I have something special planned remember?"

"Where did you say you were taking me?" she asked on a sigh.

"I didn't," he grinned. "It's a surprise."

Chapter THREE

TANYA'S HAIR CASCADED AROUND her shoulders. The beautiful dress she wore was the color of the ocean. It hugged her body in all the right places, pulling tight around her breasts which seemed to have swelled in the last few days. So drool worthy, he'd have to work hard to keep from ripping the material from her body once they were behind closed doors.

Her cheeks were flushed and her chestnut eyes were bright with excitement. She squealed as she exited the vehicle throwing herself in his arms for an embrace that had his cock swelling all over again.

Since finding out about the child, he had felt even more drawn to her, more attracted and all the more possessive. Brant pulled her tighter against him, enjoying her scent.

Tanya pulled away rubbing at the tears that ran down her cheeks. "I can't believe you did this. I had forgotten all about the mention Xavier made of it. Oh, thank you." She sniffed reaching up to kiss him. No female would ever taste as good. He pulled her back in for a second scorching slant of the lips, this time deepening the kiss until they were both breathless.

Someone hooted and shouted for them to get a room. For a second there he had forgotten they were in the town of Sweetwater, surrounded by humans.

"It's amazing. Let's go inside." Tanya giggled like a teenager, she grabbed his hand and pulled him in the direction of the store.

When Brant had found out about this little book store, he'd come out to see it for himself. It was easy to see how much it meant to her because her whole demeanour changed every time she talked about it. She'd bought this business with the money that her folks had left her and he wanted her to see her dream of a coffee shop within it realized. More than that, he wanted her not only to keep her little business but to watch it flourish. Since the store was closed in her absence, he'd taken the opportunity to make a few upgrades.

Once inside, Tanya turned in a slow circle with her mouth in the shape of an "o." A loud gasp escaped her and she clasped her hands to her mouth. A tear tracked down her cheek.

"You're not meant to cry."

Her tear soaked eyes flashed to his. "It's just so perfect. Better than I had ever imagined."

Brant had gone with a mix of modern and classic. His little human seemed to like the chandeliers at the manor house, so he'd had two major pieces installed. Bookcases lined the walls from ceiling to floor. There was even one of those ladders that wheeled up and down the wall. He'd have to remember to thank the interior designer. She'd outdone herself.

The desks and tables were restored antiques but the chairs were retro and bright red. The floors were polished porcelain with Persian rugs to add warmth. The kitchen was small but modern. Fitted with the latest gadgets. Brant had handpicked the cappuccino machine himself.

Tanya shrieked as she caught sight of the checkout area. "This is amazing."

"You seemed to like the one at Aorta."

"I love it." She sighed as she ran a hand over the glass surface. The glass slab was a much smaller replica of the bar at the club. It was the first time he was seeing it in the store and he had to admit, it did look impressive.

There was another feminine shriek at the front door that had him cringing as pain lanced his eardrums.

"Becks!" Tanya screamed and Brant had to suppress a real urge to cover his ears. The females both ran towards each other, embracing somewhere in the middle.

They proceeded to call each other names while laughing and hugging happily.

"You look so good, you skanky little whore," said the small, human female. She had blond hair that curled softly in kinks halfway down her back. She was smaller than Tanya but just as curvy. Not that he was interested in any way. In fact the human looked far too breakable for his liking.

"I've missed you so much, Becks." His female gushed. They released one another.

"Only one call since you left, you brat?"

"I've been busy. Stop bitching for once in your life." They were both grinning so broadly.

"Yeah, if cock sucking can be termed busy then yeah you have been."

"Bitch." Tanya put her hands on her hips still smiling broadly.

"Cow." Blond curls bounced.

"Nerd." They both giggled and threw their arms around each other for a second bouncing on the spot all out hug. "This is Brant." Tanya turned her eyes on him. "Come over here."

His human motioned for him to join them. Tanya slid her arm around him as soon as he was at her side. "You are the absolute best. This"—Tanya turned in the direction of the small human female—"is my bestie Becky, but you already know that since you invited her."

He felt his brow knit in confusion but wasn't given an opportunity to react since the little human nudged Tanya aside and threw her arms around him. His body stiffened and he kept his hands at his sides. He wasn't used to this type of show of affection.

"So good to finally meet you," she said squeezing him tight. The female finally released him, and she took a step back. "Ooooh, you weren't lying when you said he was hot. Oh God and big . . . make that enormous." Becky gave him the once over, propping her hand on a cocked hip as she did. "Is the other one just as tasty?"

Brant couldn't help the low growl that was pulled from him.

Tanya put her hand into his and squeezed, her eyes remained firmly on her friend. "Don't be so rude, Becks." His female eyeballed the other woman.

"Rude, smood. You know it's straight down the line with me. I thought Zane would be here as well. He has such an amazing voice." Her big blue eyes were wide.

"I thought . . ." Tanya turned to him. "Didn't you call Becky?"

He held up his hands. "The store was me . . . your friend . . . Becky must have been—"

"Zane called," Becky bounced as she said his name. This little human had to be on something although he didn't scent any drugs or alcohol. "He told me you would be here and to pop by if I wanted to see you."

The bastard.

Trust that son of a bitch to hijack his surprise. Brant tried not to react, he didn't want to upset Tanya in any way.

"How sweet."

"This place looks amazing. You seriously lucked out. Are all vamps this sweet, caring . . . I happened to notice the guys at the door . . . are they all this freaking hot?"

It was almost as if on cue that York entered the store removing his sunglasses as he did. "Apologies for the interruption, my lord. The two of us together are drawing a bit of attention. Permission to wait inside."

"Permission granted."

Xavier's second in command threw the little human a wink and she smiled broadly while thrusting her chest out in a suggestive manner. York's eyes almost bugged out of his skull. Brant could almost hear the thoughts running through the other vampire's head. Ones in which he and the blonde would be naked and sweaty.

"Face the exit." He addressed York ensuring his voice was laced with authority.

York inclined his head and turned around. Becky made a show of checking out York's ass. If he hadn't already agreed to this female attending the mating ceremony, he would never go along with it now. He would have a hard time keeping his men in line with her around. Brant would have to figure something out. Becky would need to be kept safe while in their territory and would need to be escorted back to Sweetwater immediately afterward. There were a number of mated males on his team that he trusted to perform the task.

"Relationships between vampires and humans are illegal," he addressed Becky.

"No one said anything about a relationship. Just some good

old fashioned sex would do me just fine."

York made a groaning sound, he tried to cover it up by pretending to clear his throat. The human didn't scent nearly as delicious as his own female, but he could understand why York was reacting so heavily to her. Her scent was of candied apples. A refreshing combination of slightly sour and shockingly sweet.

Brant cleared his throat. "Sex between our races is not permitted."

"No problem, it's amazing what my mouth can do."

York fidgeted, Brant realized he was adjusting his pants, to accommodate a raging hard on no doubt.

"Not allowed," he growled, still facing York.

When he turned to face the human, she was pouting. "Heavy petting? You have to at least allow that."

"Not happening."

"Behave," Tanya whispered in the human's direction.

"Tanya cares for you and wouldn't want to see you get hurt." He tried to soften his voice.

"For the record, I think that Becky is fully capable of looking after herself." He could feel his female's eyes on him and turned to her. "But, Becks those are the rules and I would appreciate it if you would respect them. I want you at the ceremony, but at this rate you're going to get yourself banned." His female looked at him with pleading eyes and he felt himself soften. She could probably ask anything of him and he'd agree, well, almost anything.

"I'm only kidding . . ." Becky giggled ending in a snort. "Okay, you got me, I'm so not kidding." She turned serious. "Look, I have to say that it won't be easy, but I'd do anything for you . . . you'll still owe me though." Becky narrowed her eyes, and her lips went straight back into pout mode the second she finished the sentence.

"Whatever. You still owe me from the last time."

"I washed your sheets, no harm no foul."

"You had sex in my bed while I was in the house. You freaking owe me." Tanya put her hands on her hips, mimicking Becky. "I had to sleep on the sofa and listen to the two of you"—she made a sound of disgust—"You'll behave or I won't invite you again."

Becky huffed, her curls bounced. "We both know how that ended. My broken heart should've been a leveller."

His female cocked her head not buying it.

"Fine, but this will make us even Stevens." Becky sighed.

His human smiled. Both females giggled loudly and fell back into each other's arms. The whole thing was baffling, but it felt good to see Tanya so light-hearted.

"I'm going out front, we need to get going soon. I'll give you two sometime alone. I'm sure you have . . . female things to discuss."

His female smiled up at him and he leaned down to kiss the top of her head. "We'll be right outside if you need me."

Tanya reached up and kissed his lips.

"York." He grunted as he passed the other male. The guard grudgingly followed him outside.

As soon as they were outside and the door had closed, Griffin turned excited eyes on York. "And . . . does she scent just as good up close?"

"Better. My cock is still hard. Her breasts are so—"

"Stop," Brant growled. "She is a human—you will keep your hands off her. Is that understood?"

"We were only looking." Griffin's brow furrowed.

Brant snarled causing a group of passers-by to shriek and run in the other direction. "Look what you made me do. I don't want you smelling or even looking at her. I don't want you so much as glancing in her direction. The human is off limits. Am I clear?"

Both vampires' lips thinned, York's jaw locked but they both nodded.

"Good." The problem was, he knew that both of them would jump if the human so much as crooked a finger in their direction. Mated vampire males would need to watch her every move once she was in their territory. He could only hope it would be enough to keep the female safe.

"Oh my God, you are so lucky," Becks gushed. "He is so hot and he has that whole brooding thing going on."

"They both have it down pat."

"Tell oh tell, what's a vampire sandwich like?" Becky's eyes were wide and shining. "Sex must be off the charts. Two men, I can't even imagine." She clutched her hand to her chest and did a mock swoon.

Tanya took a deep breath. "Not that it's any of your business."

"Bull freaking shit, if you can't tell your bestie then life may as well end. Why the glum look?" Becky took her by the hand and led her towards a table. "Let's sit." Once they had both taken a seat, Becky said, "Spill, tell me everything."

"I'm pregnant," she blurted. The thought of a baby made her feel warm and fuzzy and so excited that she could burst. The only downside was having to wait a whole twelve months. On the upside though, it would give them a chance to get to know each other. To sort things out between them.

Becky's mouth dropped open. She opened and closed it a few times, which was comical since Becky was never at a loss for words. "Wow," she finally sputtered. "Surely that's not what you're upset about?"

"No. I'm thrilled. It's only been a day, but since finding out I'm expecting I just can't help but to feel excited and happy. I love the idea of becoming a mom, of giving my vampire kings a baby."

"Who's the father?" Her friend blurted in true Becky style.

Tanya shrugged.

She gasped. "You don't know."

Tanya shook her head.

"Is that why you're upset?"

She shook her head a second time.

"Didn't think so. If you're happy about the baby, then what's up? They are taking care of you I hope?" Her face turned stern.

Tanya found herself laughing at the mental image of Becky giving her vampire men a piece of her mind. Her bestie wouldn't hesitate if she thought they were treating her badly. "Relax, they're treating me great. It's just that they're still not getting along and I hate being shuffled between the two of them."

"Honey, it's one of those things I'm afraid. You said they were enemies before, are they still fist fighting over you?"

Shaking her head, Tanya tucked a loose strand behind her ear. "No, but there is still major animosity between them. I had hoped that they would become friends. That, I don't know"—she felt herself blush—"I want that vampire sandwich, but I also want friendship, love, happiness. All the things a girl would want out of a normal relationship. I want them to lead the vampires together."

"Hang on a second. You need to understand that it won't happen overnight. Realistically, it may never happen." Her face was solemn. "It sounds like there has been major progress though. Try to be patient."

Tanya nodded. She was a patient person, well normally anyway. It hurt to watch Brant walk away, to watch his features cloud. It hurt that Zane wasn't here. The mating ceremony, especially the actual mating that would follow, should be something that she could get excited about, yet there was this knot of fear inside her about how the night would go. Would her vamps end up fighting?

"Am I selfish to want us to get along? All three of us? Right now it's only two of us at a time, and either I'm with Zane or Brant and the other is left out. It's not healthy. They are doing their best, but it's only a matter of time before things come to a head. I can just feel it."

"As long as they are trying, you need to be patient. Do your best to keep them both happy."

"It's difficult when I am destined to make one of them unhappy just by being with the other. Do you get what I'm saying?"

Becky squealed and giggled. "Oh my God, you love them both don't you? This has gone beyond caring or lust."

Tanya smiled, sighed and smiled some more. "Yeah I do, very much. I want them both happy and fulfilled. Right now that's not the case though. Zane is much more relaxed about the whole thing, but I'm not entirely sure how he really feels about me. He's definitely sexually attracted to me, but—"

The door opened and Brant stuck his head around the jamb. "Five more minutes. It might not be safe to stay much longer."

"Safe?" Becky asked as the door closed.

"Yeah, the wolves still have to swear allegiance and until then we are still officially at war."

Becky's eyes widened.

"It's fine. I wouldn't be here if there was any real threat. It's just a precaution."

"You were saying how attracted to you Zane is."

"Right, I don't know if he loves me though. Brant is the more difficult one, but I know that it is because he does love me and doesn't want to share me." She sighed. "It's so complicated."

"It's more than just an attraction for Zane. He took the time to call and to organize for me to be here. It was an extremely thoughtful thing to do. If it was just about the sex then he would've bought you lingerie or edible undies or something." They both laughed.

Insecurity, her old friend reared its ugly head. "The problem is that he didn't choose me at the ceremony, Becks. I was never his first choice. It was convenient to call Mate's Lore. It's the only reason anything ever happened between us."

Becky's brow furrowed. "Mate's Lore?"

"Yeah, the whole give me an opportunity to choose between the two kings thing after his true chosen died."

Her friend nodded. "Oh yeah, that. I wouldn't worry too much, he cares. I could hear it when he called, and Brant loves you. Those little looks he gives you are something between wanting to eat you alive and wanting to hug you to death."

"Don't joke, he could do both literally." They both laughed again.

Brant opened the door once more. "Come on, Cenwein, we need to hit the road."

"On our way." She made to stand as the door closed.

"What does Cenwein mean?" Becky asked while pushing her chair back.

"Delicate, beautiful flower. Oh and rare." She smiled broadly.

"Like fuck. You're tall for a woman and—"

"You're supposed to be my friend bitch . . . a little reminder of how big those guys are. I am small to them."

"If you say so." Becky grinned.

"I'll have you know that hips, ass and breasts are considered major assets in the vampire society."

"You're kidding me."

Tanya nodded. "Curvy women like you and I are considered seriously beautiful."

Becky's face scrunched up in a scowl. "Great! They're also off limits."

"Yeah. Please behave when you come out on Friday."

Becky sighed like she was conceding to the most difficult thing in the world. "Fine." She smiled. "Hang in there kiddo. Your boys care. Just be patient, don't try and force the situation."

This time when Brant opened the door, Tanya walked towards him. "At least I'll see you soon," Tanya said over her shoulder.

"I can't wait." Becky gushed as they walked out onto the sidewalk. "Congrats on the pregnancy."

York stumbled, his head whipped in her direction.

"Thank you," Brant mumbled.

They had planned on not saying anything yet. It normally took a week or two for a woman's scent to change. That would be a more natural way of going about it rather than making a big announcement so early on.

"You're with child?" York's eyes were wide and gleaming with excitement. Tanya nodded. The big, burly guard was at her side in a flash, he lifted her off her feet in a bear hug that had her gasping for air.

"York!" Brant barked. The large vamp released her

immediately. "Don't do that again," Brant added.

York grinned. "Such good news. I apologize."

Brant smiled. "We are excited."

"Congratulations, my lord, my lady." Griffin said inclining his head to each of them in turn.

"Let's go," Brant growled. Although he sounded angry, the corners of his lips were pulled into a semi smile and his eyes twinkled.

They said their goodbyes. It was reassuring to know that she would see Becky again soon.

Chapter FOUR

Between spending time with Brant and Zane, both in bed and out, and planning the ceremony, Friday arrived before she knew it.

By now, both covens knew she was pregnant. The vampires treated her like she was made of pure gold. They smiled, bowed, gushed. It irritated her how everyone felt it was appropriate to sniff her though. It seemed that even though she was definitely pregnant, it was only deemed official once a person's scent changed.

"Oooh ,you're a hot one." A familiar voice sounded outside her bedroom door. Tanya smiled to herself, so much for Becky behaving.

There was a knock.

"Come on in," she said while walking towards the door. It swung open. Hand on the knob, Becky was eyeballing Ross something fierce. The vampire looked like he appreciated the attention, even taking a step towards her.

"Don't even think about it," said an unknown vampire male who stood to the right of the door.

"Someone needs to start a petition against these outdated

rules." Ross' eyes tracked the length of Becky's body. "I swear I'd be very careful."

"Not too careful I hope." Becky winked suggestively.

Her friend wore a dress just shy of the knee, but the neckline plunged to the point of indecency. Tanya had to suppress a smile. "Get in here." She grabbed Becky by the hand and pulled her into her room, closing the door behind her.

Becky giggled. "I'm sorry, it's just that I'm not used to so much attention by such seriously hot men. I even have my own guards. Brant was worried it seems."

"Vampires, Becks, they aren't normal men and Brant was right to give you guards."

"I'm not scared of a few vampires." Her friend cocked her head.

"Rules are rules and they must've been made for a reason."

"And, normally I would try and break them but this is your special day so I promise to behave. Please promise to try and see what you can do for future reference though."

Tanya laughed. "Sure thing and as to you behaving, I'll believe it when I see it."

"Pinkie swear. From now on I'll be extra good." Becky threw her arms around Tanya and hugged her tight. "I'm so happy I'm here. I have to see your dress! Where is it?" She did a three sixty around the room.

"I'm waiting for it to be brought up. It's customary for the groom to choose the gown. I'm not sure how my men went about that. There haven't been any major fights that I know of, so maybe they agreed on something for once."

"The man gets to choose . . . ?" Becky made a sound of disgust. "That's just plain wrong."

There was another knock at the door and Charlotte entered a second later. Her eyes were wide and she looked a little pale.

"We have an issue."

"This is my best friend Becky."

"Hi there." Charlotte briefly turned her stormy blue eyes on Becky. "Normally I love meeting new people. Especially humans—not that I've had many opportunities—but we are in the middle of a major crisis."

"What's the problem?" Nervousness caused her stomach to clench and her heart to race. She tried to maintain her composure though.

Charlotte put a large plastic suit bag on the bed. She unzipped it and pulled out a stunning red dress. It had a corset top and ran in an A-line style cut to the floor. The corset was a silk fabric with tiny diamonds sewn into the bodice.

Both she and Becks gasped in unison. "It's amazing," Becks said on a sigh.

"I have to say, Brant has amazing taste." Charlotte hung the dress on the door and went back to the bag where she pulled out a second garment. A black gown. It had a tight fitting spaghetti strap top with twisted chiffon across the breasts. The lower half was more gown like with more chiffon layers. If it weren't for being pitch black, it would've reminded her of a modern fairy-tale wedding dress.

Tanya could feel her mouth hanging open. "Wow."

"They're both amazing," Becky gushed.

"This one is from Zane. What are we going to do?" Charlotte paced. She looked panicked.

Tanya refused to give in to the emotion, it wouldn't help her anyway. The ceremony was in less than two hours. Either way she was damned. She looked from one dress to the other. Both were beautiful in very different ways.

"I'm screwed." She slumped onto the bed. "I've always wanted a fairy-tale wedding dress but I love the little diamonds on Brant's gown, and I think the red would look really good on me." In this instance, she wished really badly that Stephany could be here. Tanya missed her calm presence.

Brant had received a phone call from Stephany yesterday saying that she was fine and on her way home. She'd promised to try and make it for the ceremony, but doubted she'd be back in time. Brant had visibly relaxed after the call. Her vampire friend really was on her way home, but chances were good that she wouldn't be here in time. Giving the dresses another once over, she sighed, maybe she could choose something else.

The tall vampire kept pacing, muttering to herself like a crazy person.

"Charlotte," Becky called.

When Charlotte didn't respond, Becky snapped her fingers in the other female's direction. "Vampire lady."

This time Charlotte did react by throwing up her hands. "This is a disaster."

"Snap out of it. Stand still for a second so that we can think." Becky threw the vampire a disgusted look which seemed to work since Charlotte stopped pacing.

Silence filled the space, seconds became minutes.

Tanya was at a complete loss. The only thing that seemed to make any sort of sense was to ditch both gowns and wear something neutral. The problem was, she'd run the risk of pissing them both off. Which quite frankly they deserved since they clearly hadn't discussed this with one another or even worse, this was some sort of pissing contest. She'd bet the latter. Also, she kind of loved both gowns and didn't know which to choose.

"I've got it. Oh my God, I'm a freaking genius." Becky bounced up and down. "Right, let's see if I get this straight—you always wanted the Cinderella poofy gown right?" She positively glowed, barely waiting for Tanya's nod. "Okie dokie and you love the diamonds"—she motioned in the direction of Brant's red number—"by the way, that cut would put your breasts somewhere under your chin . . . with the right bra that is." She pulled a strapless Wonderbra from her purse and threw it in her direction. The garment landed at her feet.

"I hope you have a seamstress hidden somewhere in this castle, because . . ." She ran to Charlotte taking the black gown from her hands, next she folded the top half down and placed the skirt against the red bodice part of the dress hanging on the door. The result was amazing. "You can wear both gowns. Brant's corset on Zane's poofy skirt."

Tanya found herself laughing to the point of wanting to cry. It was perfect. It looked great, and it would hopefully keep both her guys happy.

Hands on her hips, Charlotte shook her head slowly. "There isn't anyone I know of that can sew the dress in time. We would need someone with a real talent to pull something like that off so quickly." The vamp glanced at the watch on her wrist. "The ceremony starts in less than two hours, which means we have less than that to sort the gowns."

Tanya sank back down onto the bed. They had the perfect solution, but no one to execute it. "Don't you vampires sew?"

Charlotte pulled a face. "Not so much. You humans?" She raised her brows.

"We don't, no," Becky answered. "At least we"—she gestured between herself and Tanya—"don't. Now stop being a bitch and think of something damn it."

Charlotte's eyes widened at Becky's comment and she had just opened her mouth to argue when Tanya's cell phone rang. For a second she was tempted to ignore it. The number was from somewhere in the castle. Since it might be important, she decided to answer. "Yeah?"

"Hi, Tanya," Esral's soft voice came through the earpiece.

"Hi there."

"So sorry to bother you, but I'm not sure what is normally worn for such an occasion. Charlotte brought me some dresses and things, but maybe it would be best if I wore one of my robes instead." The poor thing sounded so unsure.

"Listen, bring the clothes and come to my room. We'll help you. Maybe you can help me with my own dress problems."

"Don't you have anything to wear?" Shock was etched in every word.

"I have two dresses which need to be joined together, but I don't have anyone who can sew well enough to pull it off before the wedding."

There was a long pause. "I am an excellent seamstress. Graduated top in my class."

"You lie!"

"I would never lie about something as important as this. Elves take sewing very seriously. All females, regardless of class, are expected to be adept with the needle and thread."

Tanya had to laugh. "I don't mean it literally. Get your ass over here. Bring the dresses."

"What is this ass you keep referring to?"

"You . . ." she was about to say *crack me up,* but had to stop herself because it would just confuse things even further. "Nothing, just get here." She pushed the red disconnect button. "Esral can sew."

"I forgot about Esral. Oh goody, problem solved." Charlotte clapped her hands. "How long are you staying human?" the vamp's gaze turned on Becky.

"My name is Becky and unfortunately Brant doesn't trust me with your men, so I have to go as soon as the ceremony is over." Becky went into full pout mode.

"More like the other way around I would think." Charlotte's eyes narrowed. "You are tiny. Even smaller than Tanya."

Becky turned her head towards Tanya, her eyes were wide in a mixture of shock and excitement. "I've never been called tiny before."

"All humans are so small and weak. You are also lucky that you make such good breeders. It is a pity that our species don't mix well, or our fertility problems would be solved."

Becky's mouth gaped open. "Breeders . . . did I just hear you right?"

"Yup," Charlotte beamed. "You have nice wide hips, come on heat often and let's not forget your excellent sized mammary glands." She clasped her own much smaller breasts. "And to think I thought I had big ones."

"Well you do . . . for a vampire that is," Tanya said. "And to set the record straight, not all humans are good breeders . . . not all humans have the attributes you described."

"Most then."

Tanya took in Charlotte's lean form. She wore one of those sheaths that the vampire females seemed to love. Her breasts were high, like two ripe peaches. Small, but very much there. Her waist was incredibly narrow with hips to match. A modelling agency's dream candidate. Very different from most humans. It was weird how much the human body was revered by vampires and the opposite was true of humans themselves. It really was a shame that the two were not permitted to mix. "Yeah, Charlotte. Most humans fit the profile you described in varying degrees."

There was a knock at the door.

"I'll get it." Becks had already skipped her way there,

pulling the door open. "You must be Esral. Come on in. Oh my Lordie, what a handsome specimen you brought with you." Becky moved to let Esral in. Instead of closing the door though, she leaned against the jam. "Sheesh, you have amazing eyes. What is your name?"

"Xavier. From your scent I can tell that you are human and therefore it would be against the rules for us to rut."

"More the pity. I might just be in love." She sighed dramatically.

Tanya noticed how Esral's face had turned red, and her eyes threw daggers at Becky's back. She got the feeling that if the princess' arms weren't loaded with clothing, she might just fly at Becky with fists and nails.

"Come back inside. You promised to behave."

Becky took a tentative step back. "Start that petition cutie pie." Her friend looked in Ross' direction.

The male chuckled. "I will human. I most definitely will."

Becky closed the door and leaned back against it. "I really might be in love. Xavier," she said his name on a sigh.

"You can't have him." Esral put her hands on her hips.

"Why the heck not?"

Tanya decided to intervene. "Two reasons. One, it's illegal Becks and two, he and Esral are to be mated or there will be another war with the elves. Please don't ask me to explain because there isn't any time right now. Esral, do you have a sewing kit or do we need to try and find the necessary items?"

The little elf smiled, then she inclined her head briefly in what looked to Tanya like a thank you. "No self-respecting elf female would leave the house without the basics." She put the garments she was carrying down on the bed. After digging in her sack for a few seconds, she pulled out a little leather pouch.

Becky gasped. "You're an elf?" she shrieked. "Oh my god,

you have pointy ears. You are an elf. Hi, I'm Becky. Sorry about your man, I didn't realize that he was taken."

After hesitating for a brief second, Esral licked her lips and stepped forward. "No harm done, he isn't really my man. The elven kind don't venture into human territory so it is only natural that you would find my appearance strange."

"Don't get me wrong sweetie, you're seriously hot, at least you might be under that silky sack thing you're wearing."

"My robe?" Esral's brow furrowed. "Don't you like it? It's my finest garment."

"It's beautiful," Tanya interjected. "I'll tell you what, you get started on my wedding dress while we sort through your clothes. Between my wardrobe and what you've brought, I'm sure we'll come up with something a little more . . . fitting for the occasion . . . not that you don't look stunning."

Tanya directed the elf to the gowns and explained what she wanted. Tanya planned on making Esral look ravishing for the ceremony. Both Griffin and Xavier wouldn't know what hit them when they caught an eyeful of the princess. Hopefully Xavier would get a wakeup call. If not then Griffin would ask her out for sure, which would no doubt spark Xavier's jealousy.

The princess picked up the red gown and smiled. "Easy as a knife through a banana." She took a moment to dig around in her sewing kit and then got to work.

Not ten minutes later, she held the gown up in front of her. "I think this will work great."

The rest of the ladies were still sorting through different potential dresses for Esral to wear. *More like arguing.* Becky wanted to see the princess in a hot pink sheath dress. Tanya felt a long lavender sleeveless gown would look amazing on her. Charlotte had chosen a floral strappy dress with a conservative neckline. It widened out into a flared skirt that would fall mid-thigh. None of them could agree on which dress was right, but they were all in agreement that Esral should definitely not wear the robe.

Tanya felt her jaw drop when she caught sight of her gown. It was even more beautiful now that it was together. "Are you done?" She clasped her hand over her mouth for a few beats. "I can't believe you're done."

The little elf giggled, the sound almost musical. "No, silly. We first need to make sure it fits properly before I do the final stitching."

"Okay."

"Here"—Becky threw her the bra—"don't forget this." She wagged her eyebrows. "I bet you that dress gets you that vampire sandwich you've been fanaticizing about."

Charlotte laughed. "I happen to know that Zane quite enjoys . . ." She froze. Probably caught the dirty look Tanya threw her. "Oops. Sorry, I keep forgetting that humans are more reserved about such things."

"It's not about being reserved, I just don't like to hear about Zane with other females."

Charlotte shrugged. "Let me know if you ever want to know more. I have often been with two partners. There are some interesting things that you should know. Really enjoyable things the three of you could do." Her eyes brightened. "Stuff that wouldn't be possible with just one if you catch my drift. But then again you don't need me to tell you because . . ." She dropped her eyes to the floor. "Forget I ever said anything."

"Charlotte"—Tanya put on her best warning voice—"out with it."

The vampire's shoulders slumped and she let out a sigh.

"You'll just get mad."

"I won't."

The vamp's blue eyes met hers, instead of answering though she crossed her arms and pursed her lips.

"Tell me damn it."

"Fine, Zane is already familiar with the things I was talking about. He'll know what to do and how to do it." Charlotte held her breath.

Although Tanya didn't like that Charlotte had slept with Zane, hated that the female had experienced things with him she probably never would, she managed to somehow school her thoughts. "Thanks for letting me know." She bit her lip trying to keep a tight hold on the emotions coursing through her.

"You're not mad?"

At first Tanya had to force a smile, but when she saw the relief on the other female's face she found herself smiling for real. Her vampire males had a past. Moping about it wouldn't help.

Tanya turned back to Esral, who held out the gown. It was so perfect. Somehow representing each male. Very different yet working perfectly together. Each piece enhancing the other. "Oh wow," Tanya gushed. Esral handed her the garment which she couldn't help but to crush to her chest. Hopefully they would find a solution in their reality. If only it could be as simple as finding a seamstress.

Making for the bathroom, she turned back. "I'll be right out."

Tanya undressed quickly. The bra Becky had recommended was tight, her friend hadn't lied though when she said it would make her boobs look huge. Next she stepped into the gown, holding the silky fabric to her chest.

"Please, can someone zip me up?" She said as she walked back into the bedroom. No one reacted. When she looked up, they were all looking at her with shocked expressions on their faces. "Oh my word, what's wrong?"

"You look . . ." Charlotte left the sentence hanging.

"Freaking amazing!" Becky shrieked. "You'll get your vampire sandwich for sure."

That bundle of nerves in her tummy pulled tighter making her feel a little queasy. Her hands felt clammy and her heart raced. It wasn't that she wasn't sure about mating with Zane and Brant, she was just worried that the males wouldn't behave themselves. They'd barely kept it together during her heat, would they be able to play nice today? It hurt her to even think about it, but she doubted that they could. Brant had already expressed his concerns. Neither male had communicated at all with one another about how things would proceed with the mating. She swallowed hard, her tongue sticking to her palate.

"I need a drink," Tanya said.

"I will pour you a water." The tall vampire made for the table.

"I need a real drink."

"You're pregnant so forget about it." Becky put her hands on her hips.

"I know, but right now a bottle or two of champagne sounds fantastic." There was no way she'd put the baby at risk, but her nerves were starting to get the better of her. At this rate, she'd be a blithering idiot by the time the ceremony started. Tanya took a deep breath, she could do this. She could handle her men. Clenching her fists to stop the tremors, she faced her friend with a smile plastered on her face. Becky raised her eyebrows not buying the act so she turned to the large bay windows instead and nearly fainted. Zane and Brant were on the lawns. *Together.* Heads bowed, inches apart. Brant nodded, Zane did too. Heaven help her, it looked like they were actually agreeing on something for once.

She released a pent up breath. Her heart rate slowed down just a smidgen.

Chapter FIVE

THIS WAS IT, THE moment every girl dreamed about.
Her big day.

The strange thing was that a sense of calm had descended upon her as she stepped onto the red carpet. Tanya had never pictured that she'd ever have her ceremony in the open. Though it was a magnificent setting, with the stone castle as a backdrop and rolling lawns that were swallowed by a dense forest. The lawns were covered in chairs as vampires from both covens were present.

Becky waved from the front. Tanya felt a pang at the thought that her father wasn't there to walk her down the aisle. That her mom couldn't be here to see this. She could just imagine how her eyes would've filled with tears. Her mom could be emotional like that.

Then there was a momentary feeling of guilt that flooded her for not having invited her elderly aunt, but this wasn't the right . . . situation to let her know which path she had taken. It was probably better if the old woman was kept in the dark for now. Little by little she could get her used to the whole vampire threesome thing.

She took a deep breath and clasped Xavier's arm.

"Ready?" His silvery grey eyes met hers and she nodded once, not trusting her voice. He looked straight ahead and tensed. Tanya followed his line of vision. There stood Esral wearing the floral number that Charlotte had picked out for her. In the end Esral had decided between the various options herself. The result was astounding, the princess was petite with serious curves in all the right places. Several sets of male eyes were focused on the little elf. Tanya was sure she spotted drool on the lips of more than one. Xavier must have noticed too because his eyes narrowed and his jaw locked.

"Are you okay?" Tanya whispered.

He nodded once while taking a slow step forward.

There were certain human things that she'd requested, like an escort down the aisle and a wedding ring. Otherwise she'd followed vampire traditions. Charlotte had prepared her for what was to come. At least she hoped the slightly ditsy blonde had told her everything without either leaving something out or embellishing on anything.

Allowing her gaze to travel to the end of the red carpet for the first time, she caught Zane's intense stare. He gave her a quick half smile as she locked eyes with him.

Managing to pull her eyes from the magnificent sight of him, she sought out Brant. His eyes smoldered for a second before he too smiled. Maybe she'd been wrong to worry. She willed herself to smile back, but her lip trembled so she bit down on it instead.

Brant wore a grey suit that fit his body like a second skin. Beneath the jacket was a white dress shirt and tie. Her breathing hitched because they both looked so unbelievably handsome. Zane was all in black. His big body encased in a fitting suit. His tie and dress shirt were both dark, as were his eyes as they tracked the contours of her body.

Tanya took a deep breath as she continued her walk. Each of her soon to be mates were standing at the end on either side of the aisle. Before she knew it, she was taking up position between the two males.

Her males.

She never thought she'd ever be saying those words.

"Welcome," a voice sounded. Tanya had been so focused on Brant and Zane that she hadn't noticed the male at the foot of the aisle. It took some effort to school her reaction because he had grey hair, hunched shoulders and lined skin. A long red velvet robe adorned his tall, bony form, the hem sweeping the ground at his feet. "Yes, child . . ." he said. "We do eventually age."

Tanya bowed her head in respect, feeling bad for her reaction to the old vampire.

The start of the ceremony was very similar to that of a normal wedding, the priest welcomed everyone and all present were asked if they objected to the union.

Tanya held her breath, thankful when no one stepped forward. Brant shifted next to her, he slid his hand in hers and gave her a small squeeze. She turned her head to him and he winked. On the other side, Zane moved in a bit closer, putting his hand around her middle. There was a collective sigh from the crowd behind them. For all accounts and purposes, no matter how unorthodox, this was the royal wedding.

"I need you all to repeat after me in unison. When you speak, it will be each to one and the other . . ." The priest bowed his head, his eyes shut. "Let us begin," he paused. "To you, I give of myself."

They all repeated the words.

"My vein is your vein."

Again they repeated.

"My blood is your blood." Brant squeezed her hand as he spoke.

Zane leaned in so that his deep, smoky voice washed over her as he said the meaningful words.

"Together as one in this life as well as the next."

They repeated the priest's words and her eyes pricked. Tanya turned her head from side to side so that she could look at Brant and Zane. Both sets of eyes were dark and intense. Brant's adam's apple bobbed as he swallowed hard.

"It is time for the ceremony." The old vampire removed a dagger from a sheath at his side. It was a rose tinged gold, bejewelled with rubies. Both men released her. "This will sting." The old priest directed the statement to her.

Great, the part she'd been dreading. All three of them held a hand out to the old man. The priest moved to her first. "Once I slice Brant's hand, you need to act quick as the wound will seal."

It didn't feel right that this would happen one at a time. If she wanted the three of them together in this then it needed to start with her first, so she held out both her hands.

The old man seemed taken back for a beat, but then he nodded in understanding. Closing her eyes, she tried to think happy thoughts but still gasped when the sharp blade sliced through her skin. It was difficult not to react when all she wanted to do was to pull her hand away as pain flared. The priest moved to her other hand and it took everything in her not to blanch or to tell him to stop.

"Wait," Brant said, his brow creased. "You don't have to do this."

She looked down at the hand that had already been cut. It welled with blood and did more than just sting a little bit. It hurt like a bitch, but she had to do this. "We're in this together, all *three* of us," she added with emphasis. Brant's eyes narrowed, but he didn't try and talk her out of it. She reached her hand further towards the priest. Both males put their hands on her back meeting somewhere in the middle. Both stiffened and snapped their arms away.

The knife sliced a second time hurting more than the first, if that was even possible.

Not reacting to his female's pain was one of the most difficult things that he had ever had to endure. There was nothing he could do to help her through this. If only there was some magical way in which he could carry her pain. Zane knew he would if he could.

Her mouth was set in a firm, white line. Determination and pain warred with her delicate features.

"Congratulations"—the Sentinel lifted his watery eyes—"finally a human female fit to be queen." He bowed low to Tanya in the ultimate show of respect even though she was not yet queen. "Now to complete the ceremony." He gestured to both Zane and Brant and they held their hands out to the priest palms up. Almost in one swift motion, he sliced both of their palms. The tiniest sting, a minor irritation. Then again, he had almost died many times and had healed from so many wounds inflicted in so many places. Not to feel pain in this moment was not something to celebrate. Brant didn't flinch either.

Using the same quick movement the Sentinel had used moments earlier, both he and Brant reached for their female. Already he could feel his flesh knit.

"My blood is your blood," they announced in unison.

His female repeated after them.

"With the rising of the new sun, Tanya Milan shall be queen."

"Aren't you forgetting something?" She looked at the Sentinel and then to each of them.

Brant smiled and his eyes flared with understanding. "I have it here, Cenwein." He reached into his jacket pocket at his chest and removed a small blue velvet box.

The rings.

Zane reached into his pants pocket while glancing over at Brant who carefully slipped a band onto Tanya's finger. It comprised of a large diamond surrounded by smaller rubies on either side. It was an alien emotion for him, but for just a second he felt uncertain. What if he'd made the wrong decision? What if she didn't like it? Maybe he should've chosen something new. Something with less ghosts attached to it.

His female turned to him and his throat constricted. She had left her hair down and it swirled around her face on an unexpected breeze. A beautiful smile adorned her face. Holding out her hand, she took a small step towards him.

Pushing down the uncertainty, he squeezed his hand over the ring. It had been in his family for centuries and consisted of a large oval ruby in a simple setting. All of the queens of the past had worn it and it was only fitting that his queen would do the same. Careful not to hurt her, he slipped the ring into place. Her smile widened and her eyes sparkled.

"Good." The Sentinel folded his hands in front of him. "Now"—he paused—"with fang and body it shall be done."

The coven all stood and everyone clapped.

"Kiss her. Kiss her." A tiny human female bounced just to the left of them. Tanya's best friend continued to shout for them to kiss.

Zane couldn't wait to finally mark his female. As dusk

approached, he could feel the new moon calling. His dick twitched. Turning, he watched Brant claim her lips first. Possessiveness struck, the emotion welled until he could be denied no longer. He clasped his female's waist and gave a small pull forcing them apart. Brant's eyes narrowed in . . . hate. Pure and simple, what the other male felt for him went beyond simple dislike. Brant hated him.

Well tough. Brant would have to deal. Zane was done trying to appease the other male where Tanya was concerned. Sick to death of trying to keep Brant's feelings in mind, or of offering to share their female during *his* time with her.

That punch to the face two days ago had been the last straw. Brant and Tanya had come back from their field trip to Sweetwater. The first thing Brant had done was seek him out and flatten his nose. Why? Because according to Brant, Zane had tried to steal his moment when all Zane had wanted was to please their female. Inviting Tanya's friend had been about making Tanya happy. It had sweet fuck all to do with Brant. The other male could get knotted for all he cared.

Zane tugged her towards him. Her soft body fit perfectly against his. Dipping his head, he captured her lips deepening the kiss as his hands clasped her tighter. His gums tingled as his fangs tried to descend. A low growl sounded behind them. Brant's eyes were glowing. Instead of stopping, he wrapped his arms more firmly around his female while still keeping his eyes on Brant.

Mine.

Zane broke the kiss just as Brant took a step towards them. The muscles at his neck roped, his hands were in fists at his side. For a moment he was tempted to take back her sweet lips just to prove a point, but the whole thing would end up blowing up if he did. His soon to be mate would not appreciate a public fight so he held back.

"Let's go," he whispered. Tanya turned her gaze to Brant as Zane ushered her in the direction of the waiting vehicles.

"Sheesh, Charlotte wasn't exaggerating when she said we would leave immediately. Do you feel the call of the new moon?"

Zane couldn't help but to chuckle. "Yeah, Ysnaar. I can't wait to be inside you in all ways. To hear you scream as I make you mine." Her lashes fused and her nostrils flared. The scent of arousal clouded the air around them as Brant stepped up latching a hand around her waist.

Zane had to fight a snarl. With difficulty, he pulled his eyes from the other male's direction.

"I thought it had to be dark?" she asked.

"It will be by the time we get to my cabin."

His female gasped, "Is it safe?"

"The wolves are no longer a threat and will swear allegiance once Stephany is back." Brant smiled down at their female as he spoke. "There will be guards posted. We thought we could use the privacy."

"We wanted to get away. The new moon can be just as hectic as the heat," Zane added. With what they had in mind, being away from the castle would be best. A fight was long overdue. He had been wrong to try and keep things amicable. It was not the vampire way.

Their little human sat between them in the back of the SUV. Neither male dared touch her. As dark descended, Zane felt his resolve slip. His gums ached. His dick was hard as steel. His nail beds tingled, his claws barely contained beneath the surface. The need to fuck rode him hard.

Brant's scent offended him, as did the vicious stares thrown his way. His enemy's eyes blazed, his lips pulled back in a silent snarl. Zane noted that Brant's fangs were extended. Tanya seemed oblivious to the brewing storm. That or she chose to ignore it.

His female made small talk about those that had attended the ceremony. Inconsequential things. He struggled to stay focussed on what she was saying and gave the occasional nod or comment. The ten minute trip seemed to last a lifetime. Brant leapt from the vehicle the moment they slid to a stop. He immediately started issuing orders to the guards that emerged from the three vehicles that flanked them.

"Set up a one hundred fifty meter perimeter radius. Xavier, you are in charge."

Not a fuck. "Ross, you are in charge," Zane barked. There was no way he was allowing his men to take orders from Brant's second.

Brant threw him a dirty look.

"We'll share the responsibility," Xavier said, his voice even. Pity *Brant's younger brother wasn't king,* Zane felt that he was the more reasonable one. Maybe this arrangement would've worked with someone like him.

Ross nodded in agreement. "You heard the kings." They all moved out.

"Fine." Brant turned and made for the cabin. "Stay at your posts. Do not bother us unless you are summoned."

Zane hauled Tanya into his arms, making sure that she was flush against his chest. She squealed, tucking her head into the crook of his neck.

Brant moved ahead of them. The guards would secure the perimeter, Brant would secure the cabin interior and he would make sure that their female wasn't harmed in any way. Although the wolves had released Stephany, she wasn't back within coven territory yet. The wolves had promised to swear their allegiance, but until it happened neither he nor Brant were letting their guard down. Zane halted outside the front door. When Brant emerged, he allowed Tanya to slide to her feet.

The other male removed his shirt. Zane tore his own suit shirt from his body not bothering with the buttons. Their eyes locked for long seconds, neither backing down.

"Let's do this then," Brant growled.

"What, out here?" Tanya asked, her beautiful features pulled in confusion.

"You go inside, Ysnaar," he said not taking his eyes off Brant.

Brant rolled his shoulders. "No weapons."

"No. Are you sure you don't want to concede?"

The other male made a sound that told him he was full of it. "I was about to ask you the same." They took a step towards one another.

"Will one of you please be so kind as to tell me what the hell is going on?"

"We discussed the mating and agreed that it's not going to work. Vampire males . . . especially royalty are too strong. There will be one male to rule the covens. One male will be your mate. There can be only one." Brant said, his eyes softening as they landed on Tanya.

His female's body tensed as she folded her arms. Her cheeks reddened. She chewed on her lip seemingly too angry to talk.

"Go inside female. Close the door. This is between him and I." Zane widened his stance. He was ready for the bastard and by the look Brant gave him, he was feeling just as ready. If only Tanya would remove herself from the direct line of fire then he'd be happy.

Her cheeks reddened even more. Her breaths coming out

in short puffs. She put her hands on her hips. Her chestnut eyes looked like they were on fire.

"Do as Zane says. Go inside. I will be with you shortly."

Zane chuckled. "I will be with you shortly, Ysnaar. Get undressed and wait for me."

———⋅C✼⋅———

That did it.

"So the two of you have finally agreed on something at last? When you were talking earlier . . ." She took a deep breath, trying to stay calm when all she wanted to do was to launch herself at the arrogant assholes. "Did you actually sit down and discuss it?" *Of course they did.* Today on the lawn when she had caught them finally agreeing on something. She was such a freaking fool.

Brant dropped his eyes to his feet.

Zane nodded. "Yeah. We had to. This whole sharing thing, although a sweet sentiment and a great idea in theory, is never going to work. Brant has made that clear from the start."

Tanya ground her teeth so hard that she was sure she'd need dental work as a result. "So, let me guess, you decided you would fight each other and what? The winner gets me."

"It will be for the best, Cenwein." Brant's dark eyes pleaded with her.

"Says who? The two of you?" Tanya folded her arms. Maybe if they were locked around her middle she wouldn't use them to beat some sense into these two morons. Before either of them could answer, she continued. "And the loser. Is this a fight to the death? When I say goodbye to one of you"—her throat tightened and she stumbled on the last few words—"will it be for good?" Her eyes pricked, but she refused to give in. There was no way she was going to cry. She was too damned angry.

"Cenwein . . ." Brant took a step towards her.

"Don't come near me and don't you dare call me that." Thankfully her voice was stronger this time. "So, are you fighting to the death?"

"We will fight until one concedes." Zane turned hard eyes on Brant.

"Neither of you will concede, so one of you will die. You both allowed me to go through with the mating ceremony knowing that you were going to fight. You also both allowed me to think that I had a say in this matter. I meant every word I said back there. All the while the two of you knew that this is how it would end." A tear tracked down her cheek. It irritated her. She wiped it away with the back of her hand and took a deep breath. "I'm wearing both of your rings damn it." She stomped her foot.

"The mating is not complete until fully consummated with body and fang."

"You don't get it." She shook her head. "I didn't ask for you to choose me." She locked eyes with Brant. "I didn't ask you to invoke Mate's Lore." She turned her gaze to Zane. "I didn't ask for any of this. I have feelings for both of you. As far as I am concerned, I mated both of you. One of you is the father of this baby." She let her hand trace the contour of her belly. Another blasted tear escaped. "I refuse to stand by and watch one of you beat the other to death. I won't do it." She started towards the closest SUV. "I care too damned much," she whispered the last, wishing she didn't.

"Where are you going?" Brant asked his voice a little unstable.

"I'm leaving. By that I mean"—she took a deep breath not turning back—"I'm going back to Sweetwater."

"You can't," Zane growled.

"Watch me."

"What of the child?" Zane asked. His voice so soft that she barely heard him.

Tanya turned back, neither male followed her. "I hate to break it to you, but human females are capable of standing on their own two feet. They single-handedly raise children all the time."

"Tanya, please." Brant took a small step towards her.

She swallowed hard. "You've both made it clear that the three of us won't work out. Vampire males of royal descent are too dominant to share. This way you won't have to." She squared her shoulders and walked towards the vehicles. Tears streamed down her face. She refused to look back. It was done, she had made up her mind. So much for this being the happiest day of her life.

Part 6

New Moon

Chapter ONE

Brant stared at Tanya's retreating back. Her posture was stiff, her movements jerky. She made the tiniest little sob as she yanked the car door open.

He pulled out his phone and speed dialed Xavier, who answered immediately. "Get your ass over here. I need you to drive Tanya back to the castle." His brother tried to argue but he cut him off. "Bring Griffin. Do it now."

Tanya exited the vehicle, obviously realizing that the key was not in the ignition. Not ten seconds after he ended the call, Xavier arrived with Griffin in tow. His brother helped Tanya into the back of the vehicle. It wasn't lost on Brant how Xavier threw him a questioning look, he chose to ignore it.

Fisting his hands at his sides for a few beats, Brant jammed them in his pockets. Everything in him screamed for him to go after her.

Stop. Her.

Even if it meant locking Tanya in the cabin. Making her his at any cost. If his mother could read his thoughts, she would turn over in her grave. He had been raised better than that. He wasn't some caveman that would keep a female against her will.

"This is all your fault." Zane moved in next to him, his eyes on the retreating vehicle.

"How do you figure that?" There was no fight left in him. Numbness filled the space that used to contain his heart.

Zane cursed, pretty much summing up the whole situation, then he growled, "We really fucked up."

"Yeah we did but it wouldn't have worked, you know that and I know that." Brant shook his head.

"We should've discussed this before the ceremony. Should've included our female. Tried to make her understand." Zane cursed again, digging the toe of his boot into the dirt. "We should've known that she wouldn't have agreed."

Brant turned to the other male who still faced the area where the vehicle had disappeared from. "Humans don't seem to understand the vampire way. It was my fault in the first place for agreeing to this whole pony show."

Zane turned hard eyes on him. "We could sit here and cry like a bunch of pussies, but frankly I would prefer that we start planning how to get our female back."

"You heard Tanya, she won't allow us to fight for her. Wouldn't take the winner as a mate anyway."

"We need to do something though. I agree that the current setup isn't ideal but at least we had our human. Sharing is better than nothing."

"I refuse to share." Brant snarled, knowing that he was being unrealistic but unable to stop himself.

Zane chuckled. Thankfully Brant's hands were still in his pockets or he would have punched the asshole for sure.

"The way I see it, we have two choices, we share the female or we lose her. Which would you prefer?" His voice was low, his eyes dared Brant to argue.

"I would prefer for you to concede. I will rule with Tanya at my side." The words sounded ridiculous to his own ears and he knew full well that his request would never be accepted, but he had to try anyway.

Brant was rewarded with another slow chuckle. "I didn't realize that you were such a fucking comedian. I would ask the same but prefer not to waste my breath."

They both stood in an uncomfortable silence.

"My only fear is that it may be too late. Even if you were to agree to go back to the *pony show*," Zane threw his own words at him, "she may not accept us back."

"Tanya said that she cares for us. I don't believe she could turn her back and walk away. She will soon realize that she's made a mistake." Brant refused to believe that they had lost their precious female. Tanya would change her mind about leaving them. She had to.

"She is stronger than what we have given her credit for. Our female may care for us, but we hurt her . . ." Zane looked up to the dark night sky. For a second Brant swore he saw the other male's eyes shine with what looked like unshed tears.

No way.

When Zane looked him in the eye again, the glint was gone. A hard edge had taken its place. Maybe he had imagined it? It was the most likely explanation because a bastard like Zane wasn't capable of such strong emotions.

"Tanya has made up her mind about leaving us and about raising the child on her own. It is going to take a team effort to sway her," Zane continued while narrowing his eyes. "I realize that we are too dominant to ever see eye to eye but unless we can at least show a semblance of solidarity, we are screwed. We can figure it out once we have her back."

"I don't need *you* to win my female back." Brant knew he

was being a dick but there was no fucking way he would pair up with the likes of Zane. He would talk Tanya around. Talk her into accepting him—and him alone—as her mate. Even as he thought the words, he knew they would never fly but he had to try. "I'm going after her."

"No," Zane growled.

"You don't get to tell me what I can and can't do." He narrowed his eyes at the other male. "If I want to go after my female, I will."

"You would be making a mistake. Emotions are high. The pull of the new moon will make us volatile."

"I said that I would go after her. You are not invited." Again he knew he was being a dick.

"Our female wants us both. You are welcome to try on your own, but I can tell you right now that you will not succeed. You may even make things worse." Zane made a noise of frustration. "Believe me, I would like nothing more than to drag her back, lock her up if I have to, but it would never work in the long run. If we say what she wants to hear and talk her into staying, then it will just end up falling apart when you and I go after each other again. We both know that future battles are inevitable."

Brant grunted in acknowledgement. Zane, on his knees, was something he looked forward to seeing. The thought of Zane bleeding almost brought a smile to his lips. Brant cursed. "You're right."

"Give her time to calm down." The male scrubbed a hand over his face. "Let's meet at sun up. We're about to embark on the fight of our lives."

Brant nodded.

"The war to win our female back. Like any battle, strategy and unity is what is needed even amongst birth enemies."

Brant locked eyes with Zane for the longest time. It wouldn't be easy, in fact he'd go so far as to say that working together with Zane would be something akin to torture but he would do it. Brant would tramp down on his need to take action right now and focus on winning his female back no matter the sacrifice. His human was worth it.

⸺⸻⚜⸻⸺

Tanya cried the whole way back to the castle. Xavier threw her questioning looks in the rear-view mirror, but there was no way in hell she was going to discuss this with him or anyone else but her best friend. She just prayed that Becky hadn't left yet. They could be taken back to Sweetwater together. Fresh tears cascaded down her cheeks. She felt it was ridiculous how much her tear ducts had been worked ever since that fateful day of the choosing.

How bizarre, in less than two weeks she'd turned into a broken hearted, single mother. Well, worse things had happened to others and she would deal. There was no way she would live out the rest of her life as a possession being shunted from one male to the other, caught between their pissing contests. Even worse, there was no way she would watch one tear the other apart.

Once back at the castle, she headed straight for her suite. "Please find out if Becky is still here." She turned to Griffin as they were about to ascend the staircase.

The male inclined his head. "Yes, my lady."

"Don't call me that!" she snapped a little too harshly.

He inclined his head a second time, "Sorry, my . . ." He pursed his lips, nodded and turned and strode down the hall.

"Are you okay?" Xavier finally asked.

A tear tracked down her face. She shook her head. "No, I'm

not." Tanya forced her legs to carry her up the long winding staircase. Once inside her room, her first inclination was to throw herself on the bed and let the tears rip. Let all her emotions out, but there was no time. Her vampire kings would be here soon to try and talk her into staying. Quite frankly she just didn't have the energy right now.

She was mostly worried that they just might be able to talk her into giving them a second chance. Unfortunately for her, she loved them. If they promised her that they would behave, if they said all the things she needed to hear, she might just do something stupid like actually believe them.

"Becky left already," a familiar voice said. Tanya turned to find Stephany smiling at her from the doorway.

"Oh my God, it's you. Oh, Stephany." To her irritation, more tears managed to escape. At this rate she might die from dehydration. She ran to the female and threw herself into her arms. Like she'd done on previous occasions, Stephany held her while running a hand up and down her back in firm strokes. The action helped to soothe her. The tears finally stopped.

"Why are you not with Zane and Brant? You should be completing the ceremony. By sunup the new moon will be over." Stephany released her.

Tanya took in her big blue eyes. Her short blond hair. She was the same Stephany she remembered, only there were dark rings under her eyes and her face looked sad somehow. "Are you okay? Did the wolves hurt you in any way?"

A definite look of sorrow flashed across her face. So quick that if Tanya had blinked she would've missed it. "What is it? Tell me right now?"

Stephany shook her head. "They were rude. I'm sure you've heard that our species don't get along, but I am unharmed." She paused before continuing, "I'm glad to be back." The funny thing was that she looked anything but glad.

"Are you sure? I feel like there is something you aren't telling me." She watched closely for any sign of emotion but when Stephany smiled, it looked genuine. Maybe Tanya was just reading into things because of her own situation?

"I'm fine." Her friend took her hand. "Let's sit, I want you to tell me what's going on."

"I can't, I need to pack." Tanya tried to pull away, but Stephany's grip tightened.

"Five minutes won't matter either way."

"They will if Zane and Brant are on their way here." She heard her voice catch as she spoke their names.

Stephany nodded once and followed her to the closet. Grabbing a bag from the bottom shelf, Tanya rummaged through the many items trying to find the ones that she'd arrived in and finally gave up. Technically, none of this stuff was hers. She didn't want any of it either. She turned to face Stephany and swallowed hard. All the events of earlier seemed stuck in her throat. Where did she even start?

Stephany kept silent, her eyes on Tanya. After a deep breath, she relayed the events of the last week. The blond vampire gasped and hugged Tanya when she heard the news about the pregnancy. Stephany's eyes turned stormy though as Tanya relayed what had happened after the ceremony. She felt her own anger build inside her again as she relived the events.

"You're right to be mad," Stephany shook her head as she spoke. "Of all the pig headed male things to do. I can't believe"—she took a deep breath—"You were right to leave them there and you shouldn't complete the ceremony at this point, but I think leaving is a mistake. You belong with us, you're one of us. You carry a vampire child. You do realize that your thirst will not diminish?"

"Shit." How could she have been so stupid as to forget something so important? "I have to go. They made it clear that they will never be able to mate me together. They are too dominant and would eventually end up fighting. What happened was inevitable. I guess I should be happy it happened now and not after the mating, or once I had invested more of myself than I already have." Even as she spoke the words, Tanya knew that she was already in hook, line and sinker. "I'll make a plan when it comes to needing blood. I'm sure Becky will agree . . ."

"Most humans are squeamish when it comes to that sort of thing."

"But, I let Brant and Zane drink from me—"

"You are not most humans . . . you are special. I still think that you should stay, move in with me for a while." Stephany took her hand. Her skin was cool.

"I can't. I need to cut myself off from this, from them."

"You can still work this out." The vampire's eyes pleaded.

Tanya shook her head. She grit her teeth and straightened her back. "I wish that things had turned out differently, but one of them will eventually kill the other. It would break my heart." An irritating tear tracked down her cheek. "I won't keep the child from them. I will stay in Sweetwater. The covens will have their heir." If the child turned out to be female, then the covens had a hundred years to resign themselves to the fact that a woman would rule them. She felt many of the sexist outdated traditions needed to change anyway.

"Please, Stephany. Try to understand."

Her friend inclined her head for the briefest second. Her eyes clouded. "It hurts me to see your pain. I do understand why you need to do this though and know that if Becky is unable to assist with your little blood problem, I plan on visiting you often anyway."

She gasped, feeling her lip wobble. "You would let me drink from you?"

Stephany nodded. "Of course. I would be honored."

"Thank you." They hugged. "Please look after Brant and maybe check in on Zane for me." She had to purse her lips for a few seconds, clamping down on a well of emotions that threatened to make her cry. *Yet again.* She was done with crying though. She needed to be strong, if not for herself then for the baby. "I'm ready. Can Xavier take me home?" It was weird how she no longer thought of the little apartment that she'd lived in for the last few years as home. Home was with these people and with her two pig headed males, but that was over. She squared her shoulders and took a step towards the door.

"I will have some of the guard assembled to escort you. We need to get you packed, I will call for help."

Tanya held up a hand. "No, none of this stuff is mine. My things are still at the apartment."

"But these were purchased or made especially for you."

She shook her head. "They were bought for the queen," she paused. "I'm ready to go now." Best she leave before her resolve slipped and she allowed herself to be convinced that staying would work out. It wouldn't. Leaving was for the best, and she knew it.

Stephany's crystal blue eyes softened. "I understand."

"It is my turn to try and win our female back," Brant's voice took Zane by surprise. He had being trying so hard to make out which silhouette was Tanya's that he hadn't even heard the other male approach.

"I know that. I just needed to assure myself of her safety."

"Griffin and York are on duty if I'm not mistaken." Brant raised his eyebrows.

Zane's shoulders sagged. "I just . . ." he paused not wanting to look like a pussy. *Ah hell.* He found he didn't care. "I needed to try and catch a glimpse of her or maybe to catch her scent. I needed to be close to her." He paused again. May as well go whole hog since he'd disclosed this much already. "Truth is, I really miss our human." Zane grit his teeth waiting for an insult or at the very least a laugh at his expense.

Instead, Brant looked down, using his boot to toe the asphalt. "I know what you mean. I snuck past yesterday for the same reasons. We really need her back." His eyes lifted and the need that resonated in the other male's eyes mirrored what he felt deep down. "We've tried everything that the humans recommended on the internet," Brant said.

York chose that moment to approach. "My apologies my lords, I overheard you mention human courting tactics and would be interested to know what you have tried."

"Humans are off limits," Zane growled.

"I have no interest in humans, I am merely curious." The big male bowed his head in a show of submission.

Zane narrowed his eyes at the male for a few beats. The request seemed innocent enough. "We had a truck load of flowers delivered, but our human sent them to that place down the road where they keep the elderly."

"Yeah," Brant sighed. "Sweetwater Old Age Home. I sent boxes of imported Swiss chocolates and Tanya had them sent to an orphanage."

"We even sent a band to sing love songs, but she called the human peace keepers," Zane added.

"Sheesh, it sounds like you have both worked hard to convince her. I'm not sure I understand the giving of plant life as a courting ritual though." York shook his head.

"They even give baby feline and canine animals. It is very strange." Brant's eyes hardened. "Regardless, we will find a way to win her back."

"We have to." Zane ran a hand through his close cropped hair.

"Please excuse me, my lords," York said as he headed back to his post. Zane swore he heard him mutter something about irrational human females. At the moment, he just couldn't disagree with him.

Zane and Brant stood together in silence for a few beats. Zane was stumped and by the way Brant's shoulders slumped, he would bet the other male felt the same.

"If my latest endeavour doesn't pan out, we're screwed for sure."

"It will. By all that is blood, it has to. We will keep trying. Maybe we should do another search on the web . . . plan our next approach." Zane loathed working with the other male, but what choice did they have. At least Brant had stopped being a dick, so the whole process was less unpleasant than it could have been.

Brant nodded. "I'm doubtful it will work, but we have to try."

"Did you ask Stephany for advice on the matter?"

Brant snorted in disgust. A major frown appeared and his eyes narrowed. "She isn't talking to me except to tell me what a fool I've been. She is feeding our human."

Zane had to grit his teeth at the thought of his precious Ysnaar taking blood from another. It was difficult enough to accept that she had taken from Brant. Yet, a knot of anxiety eased. One he wasn't even aware of until right this moment. At least she and the baby were getting the sustenance they needed. "Good," he stated simply.

Brant glanced up longingly at Tanya's apartment. Shadows danced behind the partially open blinds. "Stephany and that annoying human are there now."

"Becky is not so bad."

Brant made a noise of irritation. "The men have started a petition to be allowed to date humans."

Zane choked out a laugh.

Brant managed to crack a smile. "It's not funny. I'm surprised you haven't seen it yet since Ross is the main instigator. The human gave him the idea in the first place."

"I'm sure once he has enough signatures he'll bring the document my way." Zane sighed. "Maybe we should let them have their way. Mating with humans would solve many of our current problems."

Brant's eyes widened. "Are you out of your mind? One human death and we would go back to being persecuted. Do you want to be burnt alive at the stake or beheaded? The humans are well aware of our aversion to silver and with their sheer numbers . . ." He shook his head instead of continuing.

"We are stronger than most vampire males and yet our female still lives."

"You and I understand the ramifications of an accident, particularly when attached to a chosen human female like Tanya. I don't think the others would have the same frame of mind that would allow them to think as clearly in the situation."

Zane put his hands in his jeans pockets. "I take it that you are referring to bloodlust . . ." Something that Brant himself suffered from. "We can make a no drinking during sex rule."

Brant laughed. "That would be like telling a red blooded male not to come during sex. The problem is that the males will not know if they have bloodlust until it strikes, which would only happen when they actually drank . . . it could mean disaster. At the time of the new moon, loss of control could mean many unwanted matings as well." He shook his head.

"You are right. As much as I would like to see our covens flourish with many new births, the risk is too great." He sighed. "I will speak with Ross"—Zane moved towards his vehicle—"I will see you later."

"Pray that my latest attempt works and that our female comes home."

"I will. Let me know either way," Zane growled.

Brant nodded, turning his gaze back to the apartment window.

Chapter TWO

BECKY PEEKED THROUGH THE blinds for the second time in less than a minute. "They're definitely both out there. They are talking to each other."

Tanya huffed, she wasn't falling for it. It was easy to misinterpret a conversation when watching from afar. Just because Brant and Zane were talking to each other, did not mean that they were getting along or that anything had changed.

"Oh my God!" Becky squealed, her eyes focused on the road below.

"Stop it, Becks. They might think that I'm the one peeking through the blinds. It could give them false hope." Everything in her burned to go and take one little, tiny peek. To see her males again. But they weren't hers, not anymore so she held back. Only just.

"You have to see this, they are laughing together."

Without thinking, Tanya rushed over and sure enough the males were both smiling as they talked in what looked like . . . agreement. She had been fooled before though. They had made it clear that it would never work. Instead of taking a step back, she leaned in a little closer. Zane had stuffed his hands in his jeans pockets. His t-shirt pulled tight around his large chest and biceps. Brant's pants hugged his large thighs, and the way his golf shirt lovingly caressed his torso had her mouth watering and her heart clenching. She forced herself to take a step back and then another and another. Once she lost sight of the big vampires, walking away became easier. The ache in her heart increased though. Hopefully in time it would get easier. Somehow she doubted it would.

"They have been getting along much better lately."

Tanya shrugged. "You see . . . proof that it's better without me to complicate things."

Stephany shook her head. "So cynical."

"You can't blame me. A week ago they were getting ready to beat each other to death."

"A lot can change in seven days, Tanya." Stephany eyed her with concern.

"I highly doubt it."

"You are pregnant with their child. Maybe you should give them another chance." Becky took a step towards her and Stephany. She gestured towards the window. "I just saw another truck pull up."

Tanya groaned, covering her face with her hand. "Not more flowers or chocolates I hope."

"They are only trying to win you back." Stephany raised her eyebrows.

"How? By buying me ridiculous amounts of things? Yet putting no thought into it? I am not interested in things."

"I think it's kind of sweet." Becky smiled.

Tanya rolled her eyes. "Fine, let's just say I did go back. I'm willing to bet you that they would be at each other's throats again in a matter of days."

Stephany laughed. "Spoken like a true vampire."

Tanya managed to crack a smile. Her friends were helping her to keep her sanity even if they were both set on trying to convince her to give Zane and Brant another chance. It was easy for them to say that though, since they wouldn't be the ones being shuffled from one male to the other. Stuck in the middle of a pissing contest and liable to have to watch them tear into each other. An image of her males snarling and chests bashing came to mind. She knew that if they really intended to kill one another at some point, then there would be nothing she could do to stop them. The thought of being forced to stand by and watch them kill each other was just too much to bear.

A knock came at the door, thankfully stopping her current train of thought. Great. She knew that there were vampire guards posted outside her apartment day and night and that they followed her to the bookstore every day. She was also well aware that Brant and Zane often came by to see how she was doing. The fact that they came by regularly meant more than the silly things that they kept sending. Both had tried to see her, but she still refused and would continue to do so until she was much stronger. For now, she just didn't trust herself to keep them at arm's length.

Another insistent knock. Becky skipped to the door. "No, don't." Tanya held out her hand.

Becky stopped and looked over her shoulder. "They'll keep coming back until you deal with it, so may as well be now. Besides, I really want to see what they've sent you this time."

Tanya let out a sigh. "Fine, but only because I want this over with." She turned to face Stephany. "Please tell them to stop sending me things. I've just about had enough of this."

The vampire held up her hands. "Oh no, honey. You can

tell them yourself. I'm not becoming the go between."

It was wrong of her to have asked, especially when Stephany was doing so much already. "You're right. I apologize. I'll send them a text message or something."

Stephany smiled warmly. "You should speak with them."

Tanya pursed her lips.

Becky opened the door and greeted two men. After a half a minute of conversation, she turned back to Tanya. "It's a furniture delivery from Brant for a new lounge and dining room suite as well as a new"—she waggled her eyebrows—"king size bed. Maybe they plan on visiting sometime soon."

"Stop, Becks. It's over between us. How many times do I need to keep saying that?"

"Whatever." Becks moved to take the delivery note.

"Don't you dare sign that. You can take it back," she addressed the two men in overalls.

"Um, Tanya"—Becky put her hands on her hips—"I hate to be the one to tell you this, but you could use the help." She gestured to the threadbare couch and rickety dining set.

"I'm happy with my old faithfuls. I'm not taking their gifts. I don't plan on taking them back so it wouldn't be right."

"You are pregnant with their child, so it would be fine to accept their help," Stephany said.

"I am grateful enough for the renovations they did to The Book Corner. Business has picked up substantially. I will be able to support us now." Without thinking, her hand slid to her belly. "I don't need hand-outs. In time, they can help out financially with our baby."

Tanya signed the necessary paperwork, which stated that she would not be taking delivery and closed the door. A dull headache started up, so she put her fingertips on her temples and closed her eyes for a second while leaning her back against the cool wood.

"You need to drink," Stephany said.

"Eeew! Now? Really?" Becky wrinkled her nose.

"You are a big wussy when it comes to the whole blood thing for someone so intent on dating vampire males." Stephany narrowed her eyes at Becky.

"Sex"—she bobbed her eyebrows—"yes, please baby, but the whole blood thing. No thank you."

Tanya couldn't help but to laugh. "I hate to break it to you kiddo, but for vampires sex and blood drinking go hand in hand. I don't know why I'm arguing a moot point since it is still forbidden."

"Not for long." She lifted her eyebrows. "I have it on good authority that the males have started a petition, which they plan on taking to Zane and Brant. Most of the unmated males have signed."

"How do you know that?" Stephany's brow creased with concern.

Becky's cheeks heated and she looked down at the tight t-shirt she was wearing and picked at some non-existent lint.

"Becks!" Tanya used the most authoritative voice she could muster.

Her best friend looked up with determined eyes. "Ross and I have been texting each other."

Stephany gasped. "I can't hear this. I will have to tell Brant, who in turn would need to tell Zane."

Becky put her hands on her hips and cocked her head to the side, her chin lifted. "Tell him. We haven't done anything wrong, or is it illegal to send a few messages?"

Stephany's eyes softened. "No, but no good can come of it because nothing can come of it. You understand that don't you?"

Becky took a step towards Stephany. "Once the kings see the petition, they will overturn these stupid rules. I'm sure of it."

"These stupid rules—as you call them—are there for your safety. What if Ross were to kill you?" Stephany's blue eyes were wide.

Becky huffed. "Please, as if."

"What you don't realize is that a certain number of vampires have what's called bloodlust. They can't control themselves when they taste human blood, it's especially bad during rutting. If Ross has bloodlust, then he could kill you if he so much as tasted a drop of your blood." She sighed. "You will end up dead and his life will be ruined with a good chance of him being executed for his sins as well. You are putting yourself and him at risk."

Tanya had to school her reaction. Brant was affected by bloodlust. He'd said so himself. It hadn't been lost on her how careful he was when it came to drinking. One of the males was always close in case he lost control and he'd never taken blood from her during sex. It was one of the things that she longed to experience during the mating. One that would never happen now. Her heart clenched painfully.

"Maybe it's a risk that I am willing to take."

"Stop," Tanya said. "You can't do this, Becks. It won't end well."

"You two need to chill. We're only texting. I won't see him."

"Pinkie swear that you'll stay away from him." Tanya held out her finger.

Becky rolled her eyes, her blond curls bounced as she walked towards Tanya and clasped her little finger with Tanya's. "I pinkie freaking swear. Are you happy now bitch?"

She smirked. "You just completely ruined my sex life."

"There are plenty of human men out there, you brat."

Becky pouted. "You obviously turned blind, dumb and deaf since returning from Vampireville, but you are lucky that I love you anyway." Becky threw her arms around Tanya. "We'll have to move in together and get some cats or something since we're going to be spinsters."

"So freaking over dramatic." Tanya giggled as they released each other. She tried not to feel depressed at the truth in her friend's words.

Becky picked up her oversized Gucci purse. As a medical doctor with her own practice, she did extremely well and was often underestimated based on her fire cracker personality. The low cut tops might also have something to do with it. Truth was though, she was highly intelligent and dedicated to her field. Tanya was so proud of her friend. "You don't have to leave," Tanya said.

"I won't say anything to Brant," Stephany chimed in.

Becky lifted her eyebrows. "Looks like I'm not going to be getting any action any time soon, so I'm off to buy myself a large vibrator and an extra pack of batteries."

Stephany's brow knitted in confusion.

"Oh, come on already. You vampires act like you're from the dark ages or something. A vibrator is like an extra-large penis, except as an added bonus it vibrates at different speeds."

"They're vampire males, Becks," Tanya said turning to Stephany. "They are normal sized fake penises."

"You have to be freaking kidding me?" Becky stomped her foot. "They're sexy as sin, buffed up the whazoo and they have humungous dicks and I'm banned." She shook her head and huffed. "I'm so buying the one that stimulates both your g spot and your clit. I can't believe you've never heard of them."

Becky shook her head, a look of disbelief on her face. "Stephany is celibate, I'm sure she doesn't want to hear all of this."

Stephany turned her gaze to the floor, she clasped her hands together in a tight knot on her lap.

"Sorry, Steph, I shouldn't have said anything."

"It fine," she whispered but she didn't look in the least bit fine.

"Are you sure? Is there something you want to talk about?" Tanya got the distinct feeling that her vampire friend was keeping something from her.

Stephany looked up and smiled. She looked sad. "I really am fine, thanks."

"I'm here if you change your mind."

Stephany licked her lips and nodded once.

"All the more reason to buy yourself a vibrator. I'll get you one if you want," Becky offered.

"Thanks, but no thanks."

Becky took in a breath, intent on arguing.

"She's good," Tanya intervened. Becky could be a bit overbearing.

Her bestie shook her head. "Your loss."

Becky said her goodbyes and left blowing a noisy kiss at the door before she closed it.

Stephany sank back into the couch looking relieved. Tanya had planned on bringing up what was going on with the female vamp, but decided to drop it instead. At least for now. There was definitely something different about her friend since she had been returned by the wolves.

"You need to drink." Stephany leaned her head to the side exposing her neck. The throb in Tanya's head increased and her teeth sharpened. Her mouth felt dry. In that moment she could hear Stephany's heartbeat, could scent her vanilla fragrance, like freshly baked cookies yumo.

"Thank you for helping me. I hope the kings haven't given you too much flack." Tanya made her way to the couch and moved in next to Stephany.

"Nah, they want you both healthy and would prefer you drank from me."

There was a burning question that kept swirling around in her mind. One she had to ask but didn't know how.

She leaned in and sank her tiny fangs into Stephany's neck. It was weird. She finally understood what her . . . the males had been trying to tell her. Drinking was not always sexual. Tanya enjoyed taking blood from Stephany just like she enjoyed licking the butter icing from one of her favorite cupcakes or sucking on a block of decadent chocolate. Although it was enjoyable, there was nothing remotely sexual about it. Once she had drunk her fill, she released Steph's neck and carefully licked the two leaking holes until they sealed. "Thank you."

"Anytime. I'll be back in a day or two." Stephany rose and retrieved her purse. Either she asked now or she would have to wait for Steph to come back.

She needed to know.

"Who are Brant and Zane drinking from?" She blurted, expecting Stephany to tell her to ask them herself like she did whenever she asked a question about either of them.

Stephany smiled. "You still care."

"You know I do." She huffed. "I left them because I care. Although I really wish my emotions had an on/off switch, they unfortunately don't, so I can't switch my feelings off. Now who are they drinking from? I need to know."

Stephany's brow furrowed. "That's the thing, they don't seem to be drinking from anyone. I assure you that it would be common knowledge if they were. You don't even want to know how many bets are flying around the castle. Who will they drink from? Who will they rut first? Will you come back? How long before they rut with someone else? How long before you come back?"

And that was the second burning question that wouldn't leave her mind. "I take it they're not rutting with anyone then?" She inwardly cringed.

Stephany smiled. "I should be telling you to go and speak with them yourself, but in this instance I think it is important for you to know that they are definitely not rutting with anyone. They have to be drinking from someone, but I don't know who."

"If you don't know about the drinking then you may not know about the rutting."

Stephany squeezed Tanya's arm and shook her head. "You have never in your life seen a more sorry sight. They are devastated at your leaving. They mope around, growling and scowling at everyone that has the bad luck of crossing their paths. It's comical. You may start getting requests from the general population to return to them. Life has become difficult at the castle." She smiled down at Tanya warmly. "I would know if they were rutting and I am certain that they are not. They want only you, Tanya. Remember that."

Tanya felt her eyes prick and she blinked a few times to hold back the tears. "Why did they have to be such jerks?"

"I hope that in time you can forgive them."

"It is not about forgiving them. They hurt me by going behind my back like that. That is something I can forgive, but I cannot watch them destroy each other and they made it clear that their dominance would never diminish. They will never be able to rule together. They told me that the three of us would never work."

"I think that they were wrong. Only time will tell."

"I don't see how time will change anything. They can't change their dominant natures."

Stephany shrugged. "We'll see."

Tanya had to roll her eyes. She refused to allow hope to creep into her heart. It would only mean more heartache for her in the long run.

"Call me if you need me."

Tanya nodded. "I will."

Brant tortured himself for many long hours staring up at Tanya's window. He eventually had to face his responsibilities though so he made his way back to the castle.

His first instinct was to shoulder his way through the closed door in front of him. By entering Zane's private suite unannounced, he would show dominance over the other male. With or without their chosen female, they were still in a predicament over who would take the lead when it came to ruling the newly integrated covens. A fight to determine leadership was inevitable. He sighed heavily. Not something he wanted to think about right now since there was the more pressing matter of getting their female back. While working together to gain back her trust, they seemed to have formed a truce of sorts. Whichever male was working on winning Tanya gave over decision making to the other. They met daily to discuss all pressing matters as well as their game plan when it came to Tanya.

Brant scrubbed a hand over his face and knocked twice on the heavy wooden door.

"Enter."

He turned the handle and strode in. A scantily clad female he would once have thought of as attractive inclined her head, a small smile played on her lips. The room was thick with the scent of arousal. The female sidled past him and closed the door as she left.

Zane pulled a shirt over his head. Brant's blood caught fire as anger coursed through his veins. *The bastard.*

His mind blanked, his vision narrowed until his focus was solely on the other male. He should have known Zane would drop to this level.

Zane's brow creased. "What?" he had the audacity to ask.

"Fuck you!" Brant growled as he launched himself at the male. Zane didn't move to block the punch, which took him square in the jaw. He stumbled backwards barely managing to keep his balance. Using his backward momentum to his advantage, Zane was able to mostly dodge his left upper cut and blocked the next punch easily.

Hot anger boiled inside of him. The emotion blocked his ability to think rationally. Did Tanya mean so little to this arrogant dickhead that he was already taking other females to his bed? It was not something he had felt the need to discuss with Zane. He obviously had wrongly assumed that the other male would take his same stance on the matter.

No other female would do. Not now. Not ever.

Zane's infidelity would devastate his female, would crush her fragile confidence. As much as he disliked the other male and wanted her for himself, her happiness meant everything to him. His rage stepped up another notch, his vision turning a hazy red as he grabbed Zane on his upper arms so that he could anchor him for a knee to the stomach. Zane grunted with the impact. Using his forehead, he bashed Brant hard in the face. Pain blossomed but quickly subsided as his wounds began to heal. The momentum from the knock sent him flying backwards into the closet door. Zane grabbed a hold of his arms. The bastard was strong. He was shouting something, but all Brant could hear was the sound of his own heartbeat ringing in his ears. Brant managed to yank an arm free which he used to punch the other male. Instead of striking back, Zane allowed himself to be hit grabbing Brant's arm as he tried to pull back for another.

"I didn't rut her. I didn't touch her." Zane's words finally registered.

"You lie," he rasped.

Zane's hold on him loosened but he didn't let go altogether. "You would be able to scent our rutting."

Brant tried to suck in air through his nose but clotted blood slid down his throat making him choke. Zane released him and moved back a step. "I could scent her arousal when I entered."

Zane grinned making Brant want to smash his face in. "I have that affect on females." He shrugged. "She came to try and rut with me but I turned her away."

"Did you drink from her?" Another explanation for the strong scent as he entered.

The other male grunted wiping blood from his mouth. "I think you loosened a few of my teeth. Maybe check first before you start swinging. I didn't take from her. We have an agreement. Tanya is the only female I want in my bed."

"Good. I think you may have broken my nose."

"It was a reaction. You might want to straighten it out before you fully heal."

Brant touched a hand to his face, feeling how his nose stood at a slight angle. There was a crack followed by a sharp pain and then some more blood as he straightened his nose while moving to the mirror so that he could check his handy work.

His nose was blue and swollen. He looked terrible, but at least everything was back to being symmetric. Thank blood for his accelerated healing.

"You can't tell me that you haven't had offers since our female left us," Zane said.

He shook his head. "Stephany put the word out that she'll take out any female that tries to rut with me, so they are staying away. She also threatened to cut my dick off with a silver blade if I so much as look at another female." He smiled thinking of the fierce vampire. In a few short weeks, his most trusted assistant and loyal friend had sided with Tanya instead of with him. "Other than to threaten me, she hasn't said more than two words since Tanya left."

Zane sat on the edge of the bed and pulled on his boots. "Since our covens are now one unit, will you ask her to let the females of my coven know that I am off limits also? I'm not tempted by any of them, but it is becoming annoying to tell them to leave and that I am not interested."

Brant chuckled. "What part of her not talking to me don't you get? Ask your assistant to speak to the females of your coven."

Zane lifted his eyebrows. "You are right, Charlotte has not tried to rut with me since our human left. She is not dominant like Stephany though, so I do not think the females will listen to her." He rolled his shoulders a few times before standing while holding a hand to his left side. "I think you may have cracked a rib."

"You'll heal."

"Bones can take a few hours."

"Yeah . . ." Brant cleared his throat. "Sorry about that."

Zane nodded. "I understand. How did it go today?"

Brant felt his shoulders slump. "She wouldn't accept my gift."

"That is bad news. I did another internet search"—Zane gestured to the laptop on a mahogany desk in the corner—"I may have found something we can use . . . apparently diamonds are a girl's best friend."

"How can a sparkling stone be a best friend?"

Zane shrugged. "Humans are weird. As you know plants, food stuffs, stones . . . giving these items is considered courting in their culture."

"It doesn't make sense to me."

"Me either, but I have to try. Did you notice if her ears were pierced? I never saw her wear any ear adornments."

"She never wore anything on her ears," Brant answered.

"I will get her a bracelet or a necklace." His brow was creased in thought.

"Get her both," Brant said.

"You are right." Zane stood. "The trackers checked in while you were out, there have been no more sightings of wolves in any of our territories. I have officially requested that the alpha swear allegiance but have heard nothing back."

"This could still mean war."

"I doubt it. We have the bigger numbers," Zane said.

"They are cunning and have an uncanny ability to disappear though."

Zane shrugged. "Let the cowards run and hide. We have yet another more pressing matter."

The look on Zane's face made Brant want to sit. "I don't want to ask."

"Katar called . . . he wanted to visit with his new son-in-law and his beloved daughter, wouldn't take no for an answer. We will need to go and see him to try and explain things or you will need to convince Xavier to mate her. Time is running out."

Brant cursed. "Tanya promised the elf princess that she could date our males."

Although Zane's expression softened at the mention of their female, his words came out sounding harsh. "Not happening. That would spell war and although I wouldn't mind taking down Katar's son, I don't want to see the elven people destroyed."

"I will speak with Xavier."

"Thank you. I will let you know if Tanya accepts the gift."

Although his chest tightened at the thought of another rejection, he plastered on a half-smile. "I hope it goes well."

From the pinched look on Zane's face, he knew that the other male was feeling it too. A longing, an unrelenting need that only their human could fill. They had to get her back. They just had to.

———⋅⊙⋅———

Tanya put a second batch of muffin trays into the oven. She didn't have long before the lunch rush. Although she currently didn't have a wide selection to offer, it seemed the townsfolk were still eager to see the woman that had somehow managed to escape the vampire kings' clutches. Both men and women alike. Some bought her books while others just sat in the restaurant section and gawked at her while they ate their pastry or drank their coffee. Most just looked, but some actually straight out asked about her time with the vampires. It was something she hoped would blow over quickly because although the money was good, being gawked at on a daily basis was emotionally draining.

Why?

It was the most asked question. Why had she left? Was it bad living with a coven? Had she been hurt? Mrs Marsh from down the road even had the audacity to ask her if vampires had big dicks and if the sex had been painful? Although she didn't like the constant reminder of the life she had left behind, she considered it harmless curiosity.

After closing the oven, she'd gone back to shelving her new book delivery. She still couldn't believe that she'd already had to order new books for the store just one week after reopening. Tanya sighed, realizing that the hard covers in her hands were science fiction novels that had somehow gotten mixed in with this batch of romance novels. She put the books to the side and reached back in to the box, wrapping her hand around a paperback. The cover looked interesting but instead of turning the book to read the blurb on the back like she normally would've done, she shelved it and moved to pick up the next novel. Tanya hadn't felt much like reading lately. A broken heart and a romance novel just didn't mix well. There would be no happily ever after for her and so it hurt to read about others who found happiness.

The next paperback had two muscled males who sandwiched a female. They were in an embrace, pure rapture on all of their faces. She practically threw the book back into the box. Fantasy and reality were two very different things. Something she'd found out the hard way. The doorbell jingled as a man walked in. He looked to be in his early forties and although he sported a small belly, he had wide set shoulders and a muscled frame.

She smiled in his direction and moved to stand as he walked to one of the tables. The two ladies in the far corner continued to talk amongst each other. Since Tanya had just taken them their coffee and cupcakes, she was sure that they would be okay for a bit longer.

"Good morning." She handed the man a single page menu and grabbed her notepad and pencil from her apron pocket.

He took the menu, glancing at it for a mere second before tossing it on the table. "I'll take a grilled cheese and a cup of black coffee."

"I'm sorry, sir, but I don't make sandwiches . . . yet. Maybe a croissant or a custard slice?"

He put his cold, hard eyes on her for the first time. "You women are all the same. Doing everything in your power to upset a man must be built into your genetics."

The words escaped before she could stop them. "Excuse me?" Part of her couldn't believe that a total stranger would say something like that to her.

"You heard me, girl." He spoke quietly, not taking those hard eyes off her once. He didn't seem to blink or even to breathe. "Two slices of bread and some cheese. It aint so hard," he paused. "Why are you back anyways? Did the vampire king not want ya?" His eyes snapped down the length of her, his face pinched. "Can't says I blame him. Looks like you ate all that bread and cheese yourself."

"I think it would be best if you left," she blurted still in shock.

"I'm a paying customer." He picked up the menu. "I'll take one of those custard slices and a cup of coffee." He smiled, but the gesture didn't reach his eyes.

The two ladies at the corner table continued to talk, oblivious to the turmoil that she felt inside. The last thing she wanted was a scene so she nodded once and started to turn but his voice stopped her. "Make sure the coffee is real hot, girly."

She took in a deep breath tramping down her anger.

"Before you rush off . . ." her heart rate picked up a notch. She got the feeling she wasn't going to like what he had to say next. "Did you fuck one of those blood suckers?"

She gasped. Stunned at the crassness of his question.

"Women," he sighed. "You're all a bunch of hussies." He clicked his tongue and shook his head. "I can tell by your reaction that you opened those thighs of yours. You probably fucked more than one of um. It's why you're back isn't it? Couldn't keep those knees together could ya?"

When she looked down, she realized that she had crushed both the menu and the notepad. "Get out," it started as a whisper. "Get out." She repeated louder this time until she screamed the words over and over.

The man smiled. This time it did reach his eyes. His whole face lit up in sheer joy and she had to clutch her hands to her sides to stop herself from smacking him. He didn't move from the chair. Just sat there grinning at her.

Thank God Griffin arrived. He lifted the man like he weighed nothing. It was the asshole's turn to scream. "I'll remove him, my lady, and I'll have a little chat"—he gave the man a shake—"outside." The big vampire talked above the noise, inclining his head once before leaving. Up until five seconds ago, she'd thought of her vampire shadows as annoying pains. Not so much anymore.

She was panting with one hand to her chest. Tanya pulled out a chair and sat trying hard to control the rampant fear and anger that still rolled through her.

"Are you okay?" One of the women who she had served earlier touched her on the arm and she had to stop herself from shrieking at the contact.

She nodded, not trusting her voice.

"Are you sure?"

Tanya tried to smile. "I just need a few moments." An alarm sounded. "That'll be the muffins. I need to get them out of the oven," she added making to stand. "Your coffee is on the house. I'm really sorry you witnessed that."

"Don't be silly. We'll pay. What did he say?" The woman's eyebrows shot up. "Sorry, I didn't mean to intrude. Forget I asked."

"He was really sexist and racist and just a fat jerk."

"That was Carl Jackson. His wife left him a few years ago for another man. Rumor has it that he used to beat her."

"I'll bet," was all she could muster.

"He's a nasty piece of work. Are you sure you're okay?"

"Yeah, thanks."

The older woman smiled warmly at her. "Don't listen to anything he said. I'm sure it was all a bunch of bull." She reached out and touched the top of Tanya's arm.

"I know." But deep down inside, she couldn't help but to think that maybe Carl Jackson was right in a roundabout way.

Donning a pair of mittens, she opened the oven and had just grabbed the tray when the first pain hit.

Deep.

Piercing.

Enough to take her breath. To have her clutching at her stomach. The air in her lungs seized. Her mouth widened and she doubled over as another soul shattering ache lanced through her like someone had shoved a red hot poker into her abdomen. There was a gush of warmth between her legs.

"Are you okay?" It was the lady she had just had the conversation with. "Honey?" Her face was a mask of concern.

"My phone," she managed to get out between rugged pants. She pointed to the counter top and the lady picked up the device.

"Call Stephany. Hurry." She moaned falling to her knees next to the still open oven. Tanya tried hard not to topple over but it felt like the ground was sucking her down. Another sharp pain sliced through her and she landed on her side.

Chapter THREE

THE FEMALE PUT ANOTHER bracelet on the counter. "This one has twenty five, half carat diamonds set in platinum, the stones are . . ." She continued to talk about the diamonds' color, clarity and more meaningless things that meant nothing to him. Once she finished babbling, she placed the jewelry in his hand and he was surprised by the weight of it.

A girl's best friend.

The string of stones were sparkling but he didn't understand the appeal. He preferred his female without any fancy adornments or that stuff she insisted on smearing all over her face. He didn't understand why humans needed all of these things when it came to courting either. If it were up to him, he would've put his human over his shoulder days ago. He would've locked her up in his suite until she agreed to talk to them. Zane sighed. Hopefully the jewels would work, because his patience was wearing thin.

"I'll take it." He put the bracelet back on the velvet fabric. "I'll also take the necklace with the . . . rain drop . . . stone . . ."

The female smiled. "The tear drop diamond. That's a canary yellow diamond, Mr Zane."

"Just Zane." He tried not to growl. "I'm not color blind." Or an idiot. Did the human think that vampires couldn't tell different colors apart? He knew the female knew what he was since she'd started shrieking in excitement the moment he'd set foot in the store. That was up until he'd growled at her, at which point her screams had become shrieks of terror until Ross had managed to calm her down.

Her eyes widened and he worked harder to keep the scowl from deepening. "No, what I meant was that it's very costly. Gosh, both the tennis bracelet and—"

Zane raised a hand and clicked his fingers.

"My lord." Ross stuck his head in around the door.

"My briefcase."

Ross returned a minute later and put the case on the counter clicking open the locks. The female sucked in a breath when she caught sight of the stacks of cash that filled the space. "I'll just wrap these up then and get you your invoice. Are they a gift?" Her smile was wide.

"Yes."

"Whoever she is, she's one lucky lady that's for sure."

He didn't know how to react so he stayed silent while she flitted around behind the counter.

Once back in the SUV, parcel tucked safely beside him, he contemplated heading straight for Tanya's bookstore and was sorely tempted. After a few beats he decided to head back to the castle instead, at least until this evening. The conversation he needed to have with his female was not one that would go down well in a public place. Least of all her place of business. His Ysnaar didn't know it yet but she was going to talk to him even if it meant having his guard entertain her friends while he cornered her. And by entertain he meant tie them up if necessary.

If Tanya tried to run, he'd hold her down until she listened. Pin her under his body if he had to.

The vehicle pulled away just as a human female plastered herself against the side of his window.

"Take me with you, King Zane." She yelled trying to see through the tinted windows.

"Keep going," he addressed Ross. This was one of the many reasons he didn't like coming into town and why unmated males were not permitted here alone. Human females seemed to be greatly attracted to vampires. It was only when his second in command gradually accelerated that the female was forced to let go.

Once they were out of the town confines, the vehicle picked up speed. His pocket vibrated alerting him to an incoming call.

He checked the caller ID before answering, "Brant."

"Our female is in Sweetwater Hospital. She's cramping and bleeding. Thankfully she had a human female call Stephany."

If Zane's heartbeat any faster, he was sure it would explode in his chest. "Where are you?" He growled forcing his fingers to release their hold on the phone.

"Stephany and I just left the castle."

He pulled the device away from his ear. "Turn back," Zane commanded Ross. "Step on it!" he yelled at his second's confused stare in the rear-view mirror.

"I should get there ahead of you." He said to Brant as he put the phone back to his ear.

"Zane . . ." It wasn't lost on him how panicked Brant's voice sounded. "Last we heard she was unconscious. The female who was with her called an ambulance which arrived as she was calling me. You might even make it to the emergency room before her."

"I will be there soon."

"They must do all it takes to save her." Brant seemed to choke on the last words.

"Don't jump to conclusions. I am sure that the humans know what they are doing."

"She carries vampire young."

Zane squeezed his eyes closed for a few seconds. "It is still early. Thinking along these lines will only drive us insane. I will call you when I get to the hospital."

"Please tell her"—Brant made a sound of anguish—"Just make sure that you tell her . . ."

"Tell her yourself. I'll call you when I get there." He ended the call.

"Head for Sweetwater Hospital. Tanya is in trouble."

Ross punched down on the gas. The already speeding vehicle lurched forward. His second spoke while keeping his eyes firmly on the road ahead. "Is it the . . ."

"I don't want to start jumping to conclusions. She had pains and blacked out. Just get us there."

Each minute in the back of the speeding vehicle felt like an eternity. Zane tried hard not to picture what might be going on with his female. What if she had started to scent of her pregnancy? If she had . . . he refused to think along those lines.

There was so little information on human/vampire pregnancies. All human pregnancies he'd ever known, not that there had been many, had all progressed without incident. Miscarriage, even among their species was rare. On those occasions when it did happen though, the female would suffer terribly. Vampire young, seemed to embed themselves securely into the womb lining. The further along the female, the greater the risk but the lower the chance of it happening.

Human females were both better at conceiving and

birthing healthy young. It never crossed his mind that such a thing would befall his precious Ysnaar. He halted himself from this train of thought . . . best he take his own advice and stop speculating. Maybe it was something else. Maybe it wasn't his fetus tearing away from her womb. Causing untold damage to his precious, delicate human.

He roared, the sound reverberating through the closed space. Griffin turned in his seat. "We will be there within a minute, my lord." The young vampire's eyes were filled with anguish and pity.

"Don't look at me like that," he growled. "She is going to make it. Do you hear me? My human is going to pull through this."

Griffin swallowed hard, his mouth a thin white line, he nodded.

Minutes later they pulled up to Sweetwater Hospital. Zane pushed the door open and exited the still moving vehicle. Griffin followed while Ross parked. Automatic doors slid open as he approached the facility at a jog. The acrid scent of harsh cleaning chemicals hit him square on. Though it was the cloying smell of illness, death and decay that caused him to take a momentary, step back.

Breathing through his mouth, he headed down the hallway shouting Tanya's name.

"Can I help you sir?" A tiny human female ran up next to him. "Please, sir." She reached out and touched his arm.

"My female is hurt. She was brought here." He slowed to a brisk walk looking into each of the rooms as he made his way down the long hall.

"Please stop, sir. I can help you."

"Tanya Milan. Where is she?" He tried hard not to growl, knowing how it affected humans.

"Oh." Her eye's widened.

"Don't be afraid."

"You're referring to the young lady who was brought in just a few minutes ago. The doctors are busy with her. I need to ask you to come with me please, sir." She put a hand on his arm, her mouth was a grim line.

Looking down at where their flesh made contact, he growled low and deep. The female gasped, she snapped her hand away and took a small step back.

Smart human.

"Take me to my female and do it now."

The female sucked in a deep breath. "I can't. Like I said earlier, the doctors are busy with her, we don't want to disturb them while they work. It would be bad for"—she cleared her throat—"your female if we did. Please come with me, I don't want to have to call security. We're doing the best that we can. I'll let them know you are here so that someone can come and talk to you." Her eyes were wide and pleading.

Zane could take out their puny human security with one hand tied behind his back. Unfortunately he had to trust that the humans knew what they were doing, that they would save Tanya. The last thing he wanted to do was to place her in harm's way by disturbing the very people trying to make her well.

Zane took a deep calming breath. He nodded. "I will do as you say, but someone will come and tell me what is going on. Know that I am not a patient man."

"I understand, sir. Follow me." She led him back down the hall, turning right before they hit the entrance, stopping at one of several glass cubicles. Within the glass confine were seats which he ignored, choosing to pace instead. Griffin and Ross took up standing positions on either side of the entrance.

"Um, sir." The human looked up at him. He locked eyes with her. "There is a cafe down the hall," she gestured in the opposite direction to the one he'd taken earlier. "If you'd like some coffee or . . ." She let the sentence die as he narrowed his eyes. "I'll let the doctors know you're here."

As soon as she left, he withdrew his cell phone and dialed Brant.

"I just pulled up," Brant said.

"It stinks, so you will struggle to pick up my scent." Zane gave him directions to the glass cubicle and hung up.

Seconds later Brant strode into the small space York, Xavier and Stephany on his tail. "Where is she?" he growled.

"How is she?" Stephany asked. Zane knew by her red rimmed eyes that the unflappable female had been crying. It unnerved him.

"I am waiting to hear," he answered simply.

"Fuck that," Brant ground out. "We need to find her right now." His eyes had a crazed look. Take anger, frustration and an extra dose of fear and Brant was the end result. Zane only hoped that he looked more stable, because he sure as freaking hell didn't feel of sane mind.

"They are sending one of their healers to inform us of the situation," Zane added.

Brant's already tense frame roped and bulged as his hands pulled into fisted knots at his side. "These humans are fucked in the head if they think I'll stand by while my female . . ." His jaw worked, "I swear to God if anything happens to her . . ."

Zane's chest constricted. His breathing hitched and he fought to control the growing panic. Not a feeling he was used to. "We need to wait, they are busy with her and cannot be disturbed. It could mean"—he took a deep breath—"disaster."

"Tanya is a strong female," Stephany sniffed. "She'll get

through this. I was with her yesterday and she did not scent."

"She is a human and unmated at that," Brant growled. "We fucked up. We didn't protect our female. If she had been mated then she would have been stronger and there would've been less cause for concern. What have we done?"

Brant looked like he was on the verge of breaking down. If that happened then blood would flow. *Human blood.*

Zane grabbed him by the bicep. "We can make it up to her. We can make this right. Let's wait to hear what the humans have to say before jumping to any conclusions."

Brant had initially stiffened at the contact but as Zane spoke, his shoulders slumped.

He dropped his head. "She has to make it," he said on a ragged breath. "I need to tell her that . . . I need to speak to her tell her . . ." His chest heaved.

Stephany put an arm around his shoulders.

"We both do," Zane said.

Brant raised his eyes and their gazes locked.

Someone cleared their throat behind them. They'd been in such deep conversation, so buried in grief, that they hadn't heard the human approach. The others turned and Zane moved in next to Brant.

The human male looked to be in his forties. Dark hair greying at the temples, glasses and a white coat. "I'm Doctor Pollard." He scented of their female. On the bottom hem of his coat was a single drop of blood. Zane struggled to take his eyes off the crimson reminder of how their female lay fighting for her life.

"Are you friends or family of the patient?"

"Her name is Tanya and we're family," Stephany answered for them.

"Nurse Michelle mentioned that a man was trying to see

the pat . . . Miss Milan a little earlier, are you"—he cleared his throat—"the father of her baby?" He looked in their general direction.

"Yes," both he and Brant answered, both stepping forward. The doctor's eyes widened in momentary surprise before he masked his emotions. "Which one is it gentlemen? Biology dictates that it can't be both."

Brant sucked in a breath between clenched teeth. Zane could feel the tension radiate off the male.

"Tanya is mated to both of us. We are both responsible for her . . . condition. Continue," Zane said somehow managing to keep his voice even.

"Mated?" The doctor lifted his eyebrows.

"Understand that Zane and Brant are the vampire kings and that Miss Milan is pregnant with a vampire child."

The doctor's jaw dropped open in an all-out gape. He lifted his hand and then dropped it again, opening and closing his mouth several times before he finally grunted something unintelligible.

"How is our female? Speak or die." Brant growled, taking a step towards the human whose already pale complexion turned ghostly. The male took a fumbled step back but didn't run like Zane expected him to.

"Stable, but she has lost a lot of blood." He swallowed hard taking a second step back.

"Speak." Zane felt his own patience wearing thin.

The human flinched.

"We won't harm you," Zane added.

"Unless our female dies, then all bets are off," Brant's voice had dropped several octaves.

The doctor sucked in a shaky breath. "I assure you that I will do everything in my power to keep Miss Milan alive."

Zane nodded. "Continue."

The male looked from Brant back to Zane. "The embryo still has a heartbeat, however it is erratic and very faint. I do not believe that Miss Milan will retain the pregnancy. My recommendation would be to remove the fetal sac before it can cause any more damage to her uterus lining. It is my professional opinion that Miss Milan is experiencing a very early stage miscarriage due to there being a problem with the developing embryo. It should have been a simple bleed with the sac coming away like a blood clot within a slightly heavier menstruation . . . my apologies for the graphics." He blinked a few times while pushing his glasses back up on his nose. "You are vampires, which must explain the current complications Miss Milan is experiencing."

"Our seed tends to embed itself deep into the female's womb."

"Ties in with what we could see on the scan." He nodded a few times. "I recommend surgery to remove the embryo and to stop the hemorrhaging. Any further blood loss could be fatal. I've never seen anything like it before."

"Do it," Brant said, his eyes narrowed at Zane.

"What does Tanya have to say about it?" Zane asked.

"We are keeping her sedated while attempting to stabilize her enough for the surgical procedure. I don't want to wait too much longer though and will begin with the preparations for surgery as soon as you sign consent forms."

"Tanya would want to decide for herself. Can we have five minutes with her?" Zane asked. They had made this mistake before with dire consequences.

The doctor shook his head. "I would recommend—"

"Please. It is not a decision we can make on behalf of our female."

Brant breathed out a sigh, he shoved his hands into his jeans pockets. His jaw worked. "Fuck." He snarled and the doctor stumbled backwards only just managing to keep himself upright by grabbing ahold of York.

Brant roared, anger and frustration etched in his facial expression. "You're right," Brant finally conceded.

"I don't recommend this." The doctor shook his head.

"Wake her up," Zane growled. "We want to see our female within the next five minutes." The doctor nodded and walked away. He shook his head muttering to himself about what idiots vampires were and whether they thought the sun shone out their asses, which Zane really didn't get. The healer obviously didn't realize that vampires had excellent hearing.

"It's too risky," Stephany said. "But I agree that Tanya would want to decide." She ran a hand through her blond hair. "I think that she will choose to keep the child." She shook her head. "Regardless of the cost. I fear for her life." Stephany's eyes glinted with unshed tears.

"For what it's worth, I agree with you and Brant. Tanya comes first." Zane had to swallow down a lump that had formed in his throat. "She means everything to the future of our covens . . . to us." He motioned between himself and Brant.

"As much as I hate risking our female's life, Tanya would want to decide. We have to respect her. Honor her. We went behind her back once and I refuse to hurt her again." Brant removed his hands from his pockets together with his cell phone. "I will contact Isla so that we can be in a better position to help Tanya to make the right decision."

Zane nodded. Isla was a birthing female, the oldest and most experienced of both the covens. After a minute or two of conversation Brant ended the call, his face grave. Zane noticed how the other male's hand shook. Adrenaline surged, the taste of fear so strong he had the urge to gag.

"Isla says that the doctor is right. Our female is showing all the signs of miscarriage." Brant squeezed his eyes shut and took a deep breath. "Vampire females that scent, confirming a stronger embedding, are normally bedridden for several days after such an ordeal as this. Isla does not think that Tanya can survive." His voice cracked and he pursed his lips for several long seconds. "Though she did concede that it does happen on the rare occasion that all the signs are there but the pregnancy holds."

"We can make the final decision once we have spoken with our female. She may not scent." Zane said.

"Make sure that you give her blood. Both of you. She will need it either way. It will give her a fighting chance. Might even help to save the baby." Tears rolled down Stephany's face. Zane wanted to grab a hold of her and force her to stop. It was like she had already decided that Tanya would not make it, which was unacceptable.

"I do not hold much hope for the child. Our female must come first." Zane growled.

"Always." Brant's eyes narrowed.

———⋅C✱⋅———

Tanya sucked in a breath. Her throat was dry. Her head ached. A dull throb resonated from her abdomen. She tried to move but something tugged on her arm. When her eyes finally focussed, she saw the cause for her immobility. There was a snake on her arm. It stretched up and up. Gosh, it had a big water filled head. She tried to smile. *Funny looking snake thingy.*

"She might be a bit groggy for another minute or so. You have five minutes before she goes back under. Any longer and the pain will become too severe."

Why would she be in pain? Had the snake bitten her? She tried to ask but her tongue refused to move.

"Ysnaar." His deep voice caressed her, causing her insides to do back flips which . . . hurt. Damn that snake had gotten her for sure.

"Cenwein." Make that double the back flips and another painful throb. Tanya ignored it, trying to smile, thankfully her lips responded. Turning her head, she managed to focus on the two trouble makers that had turned her life upside down. Although exactly why or how they had turned things upside down she couldn't remember. Having said that, she knew there was something she should be really mad with them about. If that was the case then why the heck was she smiling at them? Maybe because she missed the hell out of them.

"Zane," she croaked. "Brant," sounding a little clearer.

"Shhhh, sweetness, don't try and talk."

"Did the snake bite me?" She needed to know what was wrong with her. It wasn't a snake . . . no not a snake . . . but damned if she could remember.

Brant cracked a smile but she could tell it was forced. His eyes looked so sad. "Cenwein, something has happened. We don't have much time."

The throb in her belly increased and her memories came crashing back. The pain, the blood, the doctors at the hospital. "My baby." She tried to move her hand to her belly but an IV was taped to her arm. Not a snake after all.

"Oh my God, my baby." She sobbed. "Is it, is it . . . ?" She could not bear to ask and felt her face crumple.

"Ysnaar. You are still pregnant. That monitor"—he pointed to a machine next to the bed, it had a green bouncing line—"shows that the baby still has a heartbeat."

The line continued to bounce, Tanya took in a deep breath

trying to slow her racing heart. Her baby was still okay. *Wait just a freaking minute.* Why did Brant's throat work, which was something he did when he tried to push down his emotions? Zane's eyes shone with unshed freaking tears.

"Am I dying or something?"

"No," Brant growled.

"The doctors think that there might be something wrong with the fetus. It's still very early in the pregnancy, Ysnaar."

She shook her head. "It's just stress. I'll take it easy. We'll be fine."

"No it won't, Cenwein. You carry a vampire. If the fetus continues to pull away from your womb it might kill you."

"Stop calling our baby a fetus. We're going to be fine." Her heart raced and the dull ache turned into something more sinister, but she refused to let the pain show.

"Your doctor has advised that you should . . . we should have it removed. Our birthing healer agreed. You are showing all the signs. The blood loss and internal damage would be too much for you to survive. We cannot risk your life, Cenwein. You need to have an operation. Please try to understand," Brant said, his eyes solemn, his skin taut with pain.

She shook her head. "Not happening." Tanya tried to control her breathing, tried to keep herself from shouting. "Don't let them touch my baby please, Zane." She turned to face him. His eyes were grave.

"We don't want anything to happen to you. There will be more children please, Ysnaar. We need to listen to the doctors. They don't think the baby is going to make it."

Pain tore through her. It hurt way worse than the physical pain. There was another gush between her legs and she suddenly felt faint.

"Your eyes are rolling back, Ysnaar." She tried to fight the darkness, the dizziness. Had to stay awake. If she didn't, then they would take her baby.

"Fuck. She needs blood. I'll hold her head, use your fangs to break the skin on your wrist and feed her," Brant growled.

Oh God, her baby. She had to convince them to save their unborn child. Tanya didn't care that her pregnancy was so new. That at this point the little one would be a clump of forming cells. She was in and out of consciousness when she had first arrived at the hospital. One of her moments of clarity was when they had put a monitor on her belly. She had heard the distinct sound of the baby's heartbeat, had seen the green line bouncing just now, evidence that her precious child still lived.

A heartbeat meant life. To her it represented their unborn child. He or she deserved a fighting chance. She didn't care if she died trying because she certainly wouldn't be able to live with herself if she didn't at least give it her best shot.

Stay awake.

She so needed to open her freaking eyes. If she could slap herself she would.

But as hard as she tried, she couldn't get them to open. Something warm was put against her mouth. *Wet and toasty.* It trickled into her mouth and she swallowed.

Blood.

Delicious.

The energy burst was immediate. Not enough to fully rouse her but enough to allow her to close her lips on Zane's skin, to suck down his life giving blood in tiny sips.

"Thank fuck," Brant's relieved voice registered in her tired mind.

"You should feed her too," Zane said, his deep voice washed over her.

Brant made a sound of affirmation. Zane pulled away. She whimpered but the loss didn't last long. From the scent, Brant's skin touched her lips and she sucked greedily even managing to crack open her eyes. Her . . . *the* males stood close, a look of relief crossed Zane's face.

"That's it, Cenwein," Brant whispered.

"That's all the time I can give . . ." A male voice sounded from the far side of the room. Zane and Brant huddled together using their big bodies to block her from whomever it was that had just entered.

"One more minute." Zane turned his head.

"I can't possibly allow—"

Brant cut him off. "Get! Out!" he said on a vicious growl that had goose bumps rising on her arms.

"Fine, one more minute," was the flustered reply. The door closed with a swoosh.

Tanya released Brant's arm. She needed to talk to them about the baby. The fire in her belly increased. She moaned, feeling dizzy.

"Drink more," Brant said.

"Save the baby," she whispered.

"Drink, Cenwein. We can't lose you." His brow was creased. Tanya did as he said, knowing it was the only hope left for the new life that struggled inside her.

All too soon she heard the door *swish*. "We really need to prepare Miss Milan for surgery. It can't wait. You are putting my patient at risk."

As soon as she stopped drinking, the pain and dizziness returned. She could feel herself slipping. "Please." She looked them both in the eye from one male to the other. "Our baby." It was no use trying to fight it, but she did anyway. Her eyes fluttered closed. As she drifted further away she could still hear what they were saying.

"Her scent," Zane's voice cracked.

"I could scent the change when I first entered. The baby is killing her."

"It's faint, but there."

"Fuck. I wish there was more we could do. I wish more than anything that there was another way."

"We need to do what it takes to save our female." She couldn't make out who was talking anymore.

"She'll never forgive us."

No, she screamed, the sound in her own head. It looked as if she hadn't managed to get through to them. They were going to let the doctors cut out her baby and there was nothing she could do about it.

Chapter Four

Her eyes snapped open. White light made her momentarily blind so she closed them. Trying to keep her breathing even, Tanya slowly cracked them open a second time. Taking her time so that she could acclimatize. A machine beeped softly somewhere in the background. Low murmuring voices, footsteps down the hall. She lay in a semi reclined position, the IV still attached to her arm. The sides were up on her hospital bed, caging her in.

Brant slept in a chair to her left and Zane in one to her right. Both males looked like hell. Brant's hair was mussed and Zane had dark smudges under his eyes. Neither looked comfortable. She slid her free hand under her hospital issue gown, holding her breath and was shocked when she met with skin instead of a bandage. Maybe they hadn't operated after all. Maybe she was still pregnant. She couldn't be. Everyone had been dead set on cutting her child from her belly. They had been so sure that she was losing the baby. Maybe they hadn't operated because she had miscarried in the end.

She whimpered. Couldn't help the small sound that escaped her at the thought of the loss of her baby.

Zane stirred, his eyes opened and locked with hers.

It was all it took to start up her tears which rolled down her cheeks, splashing on the gown.

"Ysnaar, thank God." He stood in one swift move that brought him to her side. Then Brant was there too on the opposite side.

"You scared the crap out of us." Brant clasped her hand.

"How long have I been asleep?" She asked not wanting to know the answer to the most pressing question. She wasn't ready to deal with it.

Brant looked at the Rolex on his wrist. "Two days and one hour give or take a few minutes."

"Okay." She swallowed hard. Blinking until the tears stopped threatening to fall. Zane used the pad of his thumb to wipe away a lone tear that had managed to escape. Brant swept a wayward strand of hair behind her ear.

The two males locked eyes.

Zane finally broke the stare and looked at her. "You are still pregnant, Ysnaar."

She let out all her breath on a sigh. The water works started up again but this time they were tears of joy. "Oh, thank God. Thank you for listening to me."

"You could have died. There were a few times there that I nearly changed my mind," Brant said. His eyes dark and churning with emotion.

"For a while I was sure we had made the wrong decision." Zane's brow was creased, he looked ready to kill.

"I'm fine. We're fine." She smiled broadly.

"You're coming home with us," Brant declared squeezing her hand a little too hard.

Tanya winced, glancing down at where he clasped her poor fingers. "Hello! I break remember?"

"Sorry." He eased his hold.

"Brant is right, you are coming home with us and we're mating come the new moon." Zane scowled at her. "Both of us," he growled. She could see that he expected her to disagree and he was right.

"No. Nothing has changed. You are both still pig headed royals. Both too dominant to ever be able to both take me as a mate. Too freaking dominant to both rule the covens. Are you telling me that one of you has conceded?"

They both looked away. Brant's jaw locked. Zane looked sheepish for a few beats before trying to entwine his fingers in hers. The IV got in the way so he stroked the top of her hand instead.

"I thought so," she said trying not to sound so disappointed.

"We will make it work," Brant said.

"Let's give it a little time," Zane added.

"Where have I heard that before? It's not going to happen." She shook her head trying hard not to cry. "It won't be long and you'll be at each other's throats again. I don't want to raise a child under those conditions. I know how it feels to . . ." She knew all too well what growing up in an unhappy home felt like. "Never mind." She didn't have the strength right now.

Neither male even tried to tell her that she had it wrong.

She chewed her lip. So tempted to give them another chance, but how could she? "It won't work."

"At least come back with us. We don't want you working right now." Brant looked over at Zane. "Not after what happened." His eyes turned stormy.

"Yeah," Zane said. "Too much stress won't be good for the baby. Stephany and Charlotte will take care of you. You should not be alone right now." He glanced back at Brant.

"Please, we have discussed this. It would be for the best,"

Brant said.

"I can take care of myself."

"Think of the baby." Zane raised his eyebrows.

"You need rest and care. The doctors will tell you. They have already spoken with us. You need to be in bed for a week . . . maybe more and will need to take it easy." Brant leaned in a little closer.

"At least until we mate, at which point you will grow stronger." Zane narrowed his eyes looking deep into hers.

"There will be no mating." She couldn't disagree with needing bed rest, though she'd be sure to confirm it with the doctor first.

"Please, Cenwein. Just come back with us. The new moon isn't for another week. If we mess up, then you can always change your mind."

"I want my own room."

"Done," Zane said.

"No sex."

"The doctor said that you will be fine by the new moon, but until then it's strict bed rest . . . no sex"—Brant conceded looking miserable—"It would be for the best for both of you."

"It's not about what the doctor said dummy. Even if he'd told me hours of sweaty, hard core sex was perfectly okay, the no sex rule would still apply." His jaw tightened. "I'll go back with you for the sake of the baby, but we are no longer in a relationship and that still stands." It hurt her to say it but she had to stick to her guns. Needed her feelings to be clear.

"We can discuss it."

She never thought she'd ever hear Zane say those words and was momentarily stunned. After blinking a few times, she managed to get her vocal cords to work again. "Unless you can prove to me that you can get along and this can work, all bets are off. And by work I mean double king size bed and all or"—she paused—"nothing. Once I've had my bed rest, I'll go back to my apartment."

The males locked eyes. Something they were doing far too often for her liking because she got the feeling that they were in cahoots to win her back. A short term truce of sorts, all hell would break loose the moment she mated them though. Tanya refused to believe their so called friendship went any deeper than that. She really didn't want to have her heart stomped on all over again. She couldn't take it.

"Did you hear that?" Brant asked.

Zane nodded once. "The part where our little flower made a bet?"

Brant grinned. "Yeah, that would be the very part I am referring to."

"I definitely heard it." Zane raised his brows.

"Wait," she said, her eyes wide. "I didn't make a bet."

Both males raised their eyebrows. "You said that we had to prove that we could get along or all bets were off. I accept." Zane grinned.

"Yeah. Sounded that way to me too and I also accept." Brant winked at her.

"I didn't mean it like that." Once they won the stupid bet it would be back to the same old bickering and shuffling her around until one finally killed the other.

They both turned to her. "Too late to change your mind." Brant smiled.

"We already accepted and, Ysnaar"—Zane's voice had grown husky so she kept quiet not wanting to encourage him—"when we win, you will owe us." His predatory stare bore into her for a few beats before he turned his eyes on Brant. The males actually smiled and nodded at one another. Tanya almost expected them to pat one another on the back. "After the new moon, and our mating, we will stay in bed for several days and explore all the opportunities a three way mating has to offer."

Brant chuckled. "I really like the sound of that."

There was still a whole string of arguments she wanted to bring to the table, but her blasted vocal cords seized on her . . . again. Watching the two of them grinning at each other like old buddies was just plain weird.

"We will win this little bet before the new moon," Brant said.

"Then you will be ours." Zane's voice was so low that it sent flames of heat licking up her spine. "We will claim you in so many ways . . ."

"You will scream my name so often . . ." Brant's voice was just as deep, just as seductive.

"Our name," Zane growled.

"Our name," Brant agreed.

It wouldn't last. She would be fooling herself if she thought that they had a chance. No freaking way. Tanya refused to allow herself to believe.

"I demand to be let through," a familiar voice sounded from the hall. "That is my best friend in there. I'm a doctor dammit."

"Ma'am it's family only at this stage."

"I. Am. A. Doctor. What part of that don't you understand, nurse?"

"You are not Miss Milan's treating physician. I would be happy to set up an appointment for you to see Doctor Pollard to discuss Miss Milan's progress," a woman said clearly distressed.

"Move it or freaking lose it, darling. I'm going in." Becky was using that tone. The one that meant trouble would follow close behind. Tanya cringed. So did Zane and Brant.

"Please." A male voice, she recognized but couldn't quite place, chimed in. "Let her have five minutes. What is your name?"

"Emma and I really shouldn't." The feminine voice had turned a little giggly.

"Tanya would want this female to visit. She is both a family friend and Miss Milan's health advisor. Two minutes please."

"Fine." A giggle. "Two minutes," her voice had turned hard which meant she was probably addressing Becky the second time around.

"Thanks, babe," Becky crooned.

"Anytime," replied the same male voice, only this time husky and full of promise. It was Ross.

"How's that petition coming along?"

"Very well. I hope you're ready for me little human," Ross murmured.

"Oh, you have no idea, big boy," Becky giggled.

Tanya covered her mouth with her hand to hide a smile. Zane and Brant's expressions had both turned stormy.

"We need to do something about that," Brant mumbled running a hand through his hair.

"Yeah." Zane's jaw worked.

"You need to control your male," Brant growled.

"How would you recommend I do that? Cut off his dick, remove his fangs?" Zane chuckled.

Brant shrugged. "Threaten him, beat him, I don't really care . . . he can't have her."

"I will talk with him."

Becky came through the door. She breezed towards them trying to look carefree and happy, but Tanya could see right through it. Her bestie's folks were both surgeons. Their careers were everything to them. Both worked long hours and both believed that appearances were everything. No public showing of emotion. No major outbursts. When it came to almost every situation, Becky defied this rule. It was why she was so out there so . . . utterly Becky. Yet, when faced with difficult situations, she struggled to show emotions. Pain, suffering, serious anger, she plastered on a fake smile and acted like nothing was wrong. Today was no different.

"My friendykins. So glad you are doing better." She waltzed over, shouldering Brant out of the way and kissing Tanya on the cheek. "You gave us quite the scare you little skank. If you were looking for attention then you should've just asked."

Zane growled but Becky ignored him.

"You will be coming home with me. I've already hired a nurse to take care of you while I'm at work and I'll take personal care of you when I am home."

"It's already settled, our female is coming home with us. A healer . . . one of your human nurses, is already in place at the castle," Brant said shoving his hands into his jeans pockets.

"Someone's a little testy," Becky giggled. "Are you sure it's what you want?" She raised her eyebrows. "I'm game for a little sleepover if you are."

"We'll have that sleepover, just not right now. I need loads of sleep . . ." She yawned. Every muscle in her body ached.

"Our female needs to rest." Zane's brow creased. He looked so freaking cute when he was being bossy. Tanya hoped that she was making the right decision.

"You call me if you need me." Becky sounded way too serious, but thankfully it didn't last. "I throw the best sleepovers. I'll invite some male strippers and we can have an all you can eat ice cream buffet . . . on their hot naked bodies." This time Brant's lip curled up to expose a fang when he growled in Becky's direction. Her best friend ignored him flat out. "Any nonsense from these two and you're with me."

"I'll call."

"Do you pinkie swear? I'm not fooling around here. I really could do with some Rocky Road on some rock hard abs." Becky did a great job of licking her lips and bobbing her eyebrows.

"I swear, I'll call you." Tanya couldn't help but to giggle.

"If you decide to go back to these jerks, I need to visit you often." Darn it all, Becky looked serious again. Her eyes stern and fixed on Tanya, her mouth a white line while she waited for an answer. This wasn't normal behavior for her friend. "Often," she repeated.

"Of course you can and I'll visit you too. I'm fine, Becky."

"I almost lost you," Becky whispered, her eyes sparkled with unshed tears. Tanya felt a lump rise in her throat. She knew she had been in a bad way and knew she nearly lost the baby, but she hadn't realized how close she'd actually come to dying. Becky leaned forward, narrowing her eyes. "I would've followed you through the gates of heaven and beat your ass if you had left me. Don't freaking do that again. Not ever. Do you understand me?"

Tanya smiled. "I pinkie swear on all counts."

They locked pinkie fingers and hugged. Both giggled. It was amazing how much better she felt.

There were voices outside the door. It was the same feminine voice from a few minutes ago. "That's my cue. Call me. I want all the slutty make-up details." She turned to Zane and Brant. "For efforts sake boys"—Becky put her hands on her hips—"give the girl her vampire sandwich already."

Tanya gasped, she felt her face heat. She wanted to set Becky straight. She had so not agreed to making up with them, but two sets of intense, dark eyes turned on her. She pursed her lips.

Becky gave her an air kiss, skipped to the door, turned and waved at them with one finger before leaving.

Zane stepped closer, running a finger down her arm. She was going to have to enforce a no touching rule. Brant came up close to the opposite side and thread his fingers through her hair before planting a kiss on her forehead. Zane trailed back up using just the very tip of his finger. Tanya had to suppress a sigh. She would so make the rule . . . tomorrow. Right now her eyelids felt heavy.

"Sleep, Cenwein."

"We'll be here when you wake up, sweetness."

Although her body gave in and she felt her limbs grow heavy as she started to drift off, her mind was in turmoil. She couldn't allow herself to forget that nothing had really changed since they declared that they would be fighting to the death. They were still the same males she had left. It was only a matter of time before they came to blows even if they didn't realize it themselves. Yet she loved them so very freaking much. There had to be a way to solve this dilemma, only she didn't have a clue as to what that was.

Chapter FIVE

Six days in bed. It was enough to kill a girl. *Oops,* she probably shouldn't say that out loud. Zane and Brant would react badly, they'd probably insist that she stay tucked up for an extra few days just to be sure. Charlotte and Stephany would become even more annoying. They'd make her eat more, drink more, sleep more, dress warmer . . . she sighed to herself. One more day and her bed rest would be over.

There was a knock on the door. Before she could answer, Zane put his head around the jamb. "Are you decent?" he asked, his voice low and husky.

"Yes."

"Dammit. I really have to try and time it better." He closed the door. "I can't wait to see all your silky skin . . . make that lick every inch of your body. Slow and careful. I'm going to make you scream and beg." His eyes smoldered as they moved down her sheet clad body. Underneath the sheet, she wore flannels, hardly sexy. "You've been through an ordeal, but there's nothing wrong with your vocal cords is there?" He didn't give her a chance to answer. "I've missed you so much, Ysnaar. Just thinking about your tight, wet little p—"

"Stop . . ." Her breathing had hitched. "I'm still not convinced that this is going to work." Any more talk of what he would do to her and she might just beg him to take her here and now. Maybe she should take Becks up on her offer and have her friend bring her a really large vibrator. Once she got the all clear from the doctor tomorrow, it was going to be difficult not to just fall back into bed with her vampire males. Until they convinced her that they were going to put their dominance aside and work together though she couldn't allow herself to be swayed.

He pulled in a deep breath and his nostrils flared. "Your scent drives me insane." Ever since she'd started to scent of the baby, both males had mentioned on more than one occasion how it drove them crazy with need for her. She needed this to be more than just about being shared between them though, she wanted a partnership involving all three of them.

A vampire sandwich.

Becky wasn't far off. The thought of making love together, drinking together and hell even sleeping together had her toes curling. Tanya sighed. "I take it that one of you conceded and that you are ready to convince me that there will be no more fighting to the death?"

"Our . . . relationship is much improved."

"I need guarantees that I won't have to watch you kill each other in a"—she shrugged—"month . . . a year."

"You know I can't make such a promise." She could give them one thing, and that was that they were honest to a fault even if it was to their detriment.

There was another knock and Brant opened the door. "I'll come back later," he said when his eyes landed on Zane.

"No"—the bed dipped as Zane sat next to Tanya—"come in."

Brant moved to the opposite side of the bed. He kissed her cheek, his eyes dipping to her lips as he pulled away.

"It seems that we still have some convincing to do," Zane said, his eyes on Brant.

"Once the doctor gives the all clear."

"No," she said a little too harshly, only because her body had decided it was all in. Her nipples had pebbled and had turned ultra-sensitive under her cotton pajamas. Her clit throbbed. She knew they would be able to scent her arousal and it irritated her.

"Until you two can prove that there won't be any fighting in the future, I'm afraid I can't agree to anything."

"You know we can't promise that. Give us another chance. We promise to try and not kill each other. I am optimistic that we will succeed," Brant cocked an eyebrow.

"Optimistic,"—she paused—"just as I thought," she huffed. "You promise to try," she made a sound of frustration. "First you take me away from my life, make me fall in love with both of you"—she looked from one male to the other—"You impregnate me. Make me go through a mating ceremony in which I bonded myself to *both* of you. Then you wanted to freaking kill each other while expecting me to carry on with the survivor. It's insane." She ran her hands over her face covering her eyes. "But you're optimistic that you won't kill each other in the future and that's supposed to make it all better," she mumbled into her hands.

Silence.

When she finally uncovered her face, both males looked to be in a state of shock, complete with gaping mouths, pale skin and wide eyes.

"What?" she asked tentatively.

"You love us?" Brant asked. "You love us," he stated while

grinning.

"Say it again," Zane slid his hand onto her belly, shifting closer.

Holy shit. She'd just told them that she freaking loved them.

"No," she shook her head. "That's not the point"—she stopped there because she realized that she was wrong in saying that—"okay, maybe it is the point. I do love you both. Do you really think I want to watch either of you die though? Especially at the hand of the other?" She fixed the pillows behind her head so that she could sit more upright.

Brant cupped her cheeks with both of his big hands. "I just have to say that I—"

"Don't you dare say it." She hit her hand on the bed covers with a light thump, needing to drive the point home.

"—but it is important that you know that I—"

"I said, no. Weren't you listening? Love doesn't change the situation. I don't want to hear it." The last came out sounding a little panicked. Her resolve would crumple if she listened to them . . . listened to Brant swear his undying love to her.

"I'll show you instead." Brant kissed her. Lips warm, tongue seeking. She couldn't help but to whimper as he deepened the kiss, plundering her mouth. She really shouldn't be allowing this, but how could she refuse him? It was a scorching, smoldering, toe curling, heat inducing kiss. Slow, tender, loving.

Brant pulled away and she found herself following him as he moved back. More please, her whole body cried. Zane's hand hooked around her waist, he pulled her so that she faced him.

His dark eyes seemed to look straight into her soul. "I need to show you too, sweetness. I wish I could really show you just how much." His eyes dropped to her mouth a second before he kissed her. *Oh wow.* Her back arched as their tongues clashed. Her breasts mashed against his hard chest. Freaking hell, for a newbie kisser he was damned good at it. Slanting his face left then right. Suckling on her bottom lip before plunging into her mouth with his hot tongue. Her nipples rubbed against him. She dug her fingers into his biceps. Hard, hot male. Where Brant had been tender and soft, Zane plundered.

Both kisses left her breathless. "How did you become so good at that?" She asked as he ended the kiss, then she narrowed her eyes at him in what she hoped was a death stare. "Who have you been kissing?"

"No one." He threw her a half smile. "You told me kissing with tongues was like sex, so I kissed you in the same way I would fuck you right now if I could"—he cleared his throat—"I wouldn't take you slowly, Ysnaar, but I also wouldn't rush. I'd sink deep into your sweet pussy keeping you on the edge until you begged me to make you come." His voice had dropped to a low rumble.

His words had her womb clenching. "So . . . so," she stammered. "You haven't kissed anyone else?" Flip, she hated that she was still so insecure.

"Neither of us is even remotely interested in anyone other than you. We need you back." Brant cuddled up behind her, his breath on the back of her neck as he talked.

She stiffened. They might not be having sex with other females, but they were drinking from someone else and neither male would divulge who that someone was. They refused to take from her, stating that she wasn't strong enough yet.

"What is it?" Zane asked looking at her with such tenderness.

"Who are you drinking from?"

Zane looked panicked for a split second before schooling his thoughts. Brant moved away from her and climbed off the bed. "It's not something you need to concern yourself with," he said. "You need to trust that we are doing right by you."

"Just tell me. I need to know."

"Trust us," Zane said, his eyes wide. He climbed off the bed as well and proceeded to pace.

Tanya folded her arms across her chest. "Out with it. Right now." She looked from one male to the other. Zane stopped his walking and turned to face her. His brow heavily creased.

"It's embarrassing." Brant looked down at his shoes.

"Embarrassing for whom?" she narrowed her eyes at them. "Is there something I should know? Once this gets out, will I be the brunt of all the jokes? Is everyone going to laugh at me . . . did you know the covens are taking bets on who—"

"We are drinking from each other," Zane growled, his hands fisted at his sides. "If it gets out, then we will be the laughing stock of both covens. Hell, not just the covens, of all the species."

Tanya giggled into her hand and immediately regretted it.

Brant made a sound of frustration. "It's not funny, Cenwein. Males do not normally drink from one another. We did it for you."

"Yeah, we knew that you would not want us drinking from any of the females." Zane shrugged. "It was the best solution."

She bit down on her lip until she regained some control. It was hard to imagine the two of them . . . together. "Thank you. I appreciate it. It could not have been easy." Her lip twitched but she managed to keep herself from cracking a smile.

"More like freaking torture," Zane grumbled.

"It wasn't that bad," Brant growled.

Zane grinned. "I didn't realize that you enjoyed it so much. You'd better not ask me to start stroking your dick while you drink."

Brant grit his teeth. "You always have to take things too far. It wasn't ranked as one of the best experiences of my life, but torture . . . really? My female will stroke my dick and I'll be drinking from her from here on out."

"Our female."

Brant took a deep breath, his chest heaved. "Our female," he conceded. Tanya noticed that it took some effort.

Zane glanced at his watch. "Katar will be here any minute. We had best go and prepare. Did you have a talk with Xavier?"

A look of regret crossed Brant's face. "He will do what is expected of him."

Zane sighed and nodded once. "Good. I'll do my best to convince the old king, but . . ." instead of finishing his sentence he raised his eyebrows.

"What's going on?" Tanya asked, although she could guess.

"Katar is here to visit Esral. He won't be happy when he finds out that she is not mated," Zane said clasping his hands in front of his body.

"And the whole Xavier will do what is expected part?" She narrowed her eyes at Brant.

"Don't look at me like that, Tanya. Xavier will mate with Esral." She tried to interject, but he stopped her. "Please, Cenwein. It is something that needs to happen for the good of both species. Try to understand."

"Well, I don't. Esral wants a chance to choose. I think that the two of them will end up together in the long run. A forced mating won't work though, they'll end up miserable."

"It can't wait. They will have to learn to deal. It is their duty. I . . . we will try and convince Katar to give them more time but should we fail, tomorrow is the new moon . . ." Brant's eyes were dark and pleading. "I will do my best, but Katar is very traditional in his thinking so I do not hold out much hope."

"Let me talk with him." It was worth a shot. Tanya held her breath. The males exchanged glances.

"You need to stay in bed." Zane caught her gaze. "We do not want you to exert yourself. Please do not worry. Xavier and Esral may not be thrilled with the news but they have both resigned themselves to the inevitable. As you said, there is an attraction there."

"Yeah, but they shouldn't be forced. Let me speak with him."

Brant shook his head. "Don't worry. We will take care of everything. It'll all work out." He leaned forward and kissed her forehead.

"You need to take care of yourself, Ysnaar, and our baby." Zane crouched over the bed. He pulled down her sheet and kissed her belly, nuzzling into the fabric of her pajamas.

Brant threw her a wicked smile before kissing her lips. He nudged his tongue into her mouth and nipped on her bottom lip.

Zane moved down and buried his head into the juncture at her thighs, he sniffed making a strangled noise. The sudden friction sent desire coursing through her whole body. Brant swallowed her moan while swirling his tongue with hers.

By the time he broke the kiss, she was panting. Her breasts felt heavy, her skin tight. She needed that vibrator or she would end up begging. Having both males touch her like that at the same time was more than she could handle. What she really needed to do was to start enforcing that no touching rule.

"Rest." Brant touched his lips to hers one last time before

kissing her nose. He stood and moved to the door.

"Don't worry." Zane moved back up. He kissed her neck and his nostrils flared when he lifted. "Oh female, I can't wait . . ." He kissed her quick and deep before touching his forehead to hers. "Tell me . . . us again."

"Tell you what?" she felt her brow crease.

"That you love us."

She shook her head. "It doesn't change things. I shouldn't have said anything."

"Have we still not convinced you?"

"No, and my loving both of you doesn't change things. It is in your nature to be dominant."

Zane's eyes clouded.

"I'm sorry," Brant said.

"We're sorry, Ysnaar," Zane let out a deep breath. "We will find a way."

"We'll talk more later. Get some rest," Brant said as he opened the door.

Once the door closed behind them, she reached for her phone and dialed Stephany.

"Are you okay?" Her friend's familiar voice sounded over the device.

"Is that any way to answer a phone?"

A sigh. "Sorry, it's just that I couldn't help but to notice that both Zane and Brant were in your room. I didn't hear any fighting or . . . other loud noises. I was just worried . . . you know . . . just worried. How is the baby?"

"We're fine. Zane and Brant are getting along. It's weird."

"Enjoy it. Don't complain." Stephany sounded incredulous.

"It won't last. I can't risk it." She heard Stephany take a deep breath, preparing to argue no doubt. "That's not why I'm calling. I need you to do something for me," Tanya said.

"Anything. Name it."

———⸺·✳·⸺———

Katar entered the boardroom first followed by Keto. The elven king smiled broadly making a greeting in his own language.

As a sign of respect, Brant and Zane returned the greeting using elven tongue. Xavier stepped in beside them and did the same.

Keto remained silent. His eyes were hard, his jaw tense. *What was the male's problem?* Zane had mentioned that the king had aged greatly, yet Brant was still shocked by his lined face and greying hair.

A look of confusion crossed Katar's face for a brief moment. "Where is your mate? I had hoped that my daughter would be here to greet me. I take it that all is well with Esral?" The old man smiled.

"Esral is well," Zane answered. "Your daughter is slowly becoming accustomed to the ways of our people."

"Have you found her to be a good mate? She is in many ways much like her mother and will serve you well."

Zane cleared his throat, looking uncomfortable.

Brant stepped forward. "Let's be seated. Can I offer you some refreshments?" He gestured to the table which was laden with fruits and pastries. After talking with Esral, Stephany had advised him that elves had a sweet tooth. "Would you like a glass of juice? Wine perhaps?" He motioned to a pitcher of deep red liquid.

"I shouldn't, but why not? It is a celebration after all. The union of our species." Katar looked thoughtful for a second before smiling.

This was going to be more difficult than they'd thought.

Brant poured a glass and reached for a second. "Keto?"

The elven prince narrowed his eyes and shook his head. "I am fine"—he ground his teeth—"Thank you." He said the words like they were a curse.

Katar took a long drink from his glass.

"This is Prince Xavier, my brother," Brant stated.

Katar inclined his head while maintaining eye contact with Xavier.

Brant tried not to shift in his seat. "I am glad that you called this meeting today—"

"Meeting?" Katar shook his head. "Think of it more as a family get together."

It was time to suck it up. The longer they dragged this out, the worse it would be in the end. "Zane did not mate your daughter." Brant had to work hard to keep himself from cringing. He definitely could've worded that better.

Katar's brow knitted. "That means that my daughter has mated with you, Brant son of Taine. It was my understanding that you had taken a mate already."

"Your information was correct. I have not mated your daughter either."

Katar exploded in a spray of wine scented spittle. "What is the meaning of this? I put my beloved daughter's life and reputation in your hands and you disrespect me like this?" He took a deep breath. "When do you plan on mating her?" he turned to address Zane.

"I too am already promised to another, and tomorrow we fulfil the mating come the new moon."

Keto bashed the table with a closed fist, his blond hair flew about his face. "The honor of my sister is at stake. Filthy—"

"Silence!" Katar shouted, his face was bright red. His nostrils flared and his knuckles had turned white on the glass. Brant was worried that it would shatter under the pressure. If the old man cut his hand open on the shards it would flame his anger. Katar didn't seem to realize that he was still holding it.

"By slighting my Esral, you have slighted me. My people." He swallowed hard. "My daughter"—his eyes grew glassy. Katar shook his head, his lips a thin white line—"my beloved Esral will be seen as defective, forced to live a life of solitude. My beautiful, innocent, sun filled child. So full of potential." His shoulders had sagged while he spoke, his eyes drifted to the table.

"We have welcomed her to live among us as one of our own," Brant said hoping that Katar would be appeased.

"What?" Keto snorted. "So that her innocence can be taken by any commoner? Rutted in some back alley like a piece of trash?" His eyes were blazing, his face set in a deep scowl. With a loud scrape, Keto pushed his chair back but did not make to stand. "Fucking unacceptable." Although he glanced Brant's way, he noticed that most of the prince's animosity was directed at Zane. It wasn't the time to think on it.

Katar grunted. "The agreement was that my daughter would mate vampire royalty, anything less would be taken as an insult." His eyes grew hard as he squared his shoulders. "I had not wished to bring war to my people, but you will force my hand."

How should he proceed? Should he inform the king of his daughter's wishes to date and to choose her own mate? The elven king would have little understanding for her desires. Glancing at his brother, he noticed how grim and ashen his expression had become, like he was about to be put to death. Xavier briefly inclined his head in acceptance, his respect grew for his brother. Brant ran a hand through his hair. He suppressed the urge to sigh. "Xavier is royalty, he will mate your daughter but it will happen in due course. It would be preferable if they could have some time to—"

"No," low and evenly delivered. The elven king's eyes narrowed. "Tomorrow is the new moon, the prince will mate her or I will declare war on the vampire species."

"That would not be wise Katar, many would die," Zane stated.

Katar locked his jaw.

"Your species would be hardest hit," Brant added. "It is not our wish to slaughter the elven kind, do not force our hand."

"It is you that forces my hand." He turned to Xavier and locked eyes with him. "Mate my daughter." His voice had a hard commanding edge. For a moment he looked like the man Brant remembered, then his shoulders sagged again and he seemed to age before Brant's eyes. "You have wronged me, both of you." He shook his head.

"We will make this right, Katar, you have my word," Brant said. They could not enter into another bloody war. He did not wish to decimate a species. His female must be rubbing off on him because he wanted what was best for the elven princess as well. She may not realize it, but having Xavier as a mate would be for the best in the long run. Brant knew that his brother would do right by Esral, even if it killed him.

Xavier reached for a jug of wine, he filled the glass in front of him and downed the contents. The buzz from the alcohol would be over in a few minutes, hardly worth the effort. Yet, if he was in his brother's shoes, he would probably do the same.

Chapter SIX

TANYA HAD JUST FINISHED running a brush through her hair when a knock sounded. She was still dressed in her flannels, only she'd taken the time to put on a bra. It wouldn't be right to address the elven king without underwear.

"Come in."

Stephany entered followed by the king. Behind him, trailed a large robe toting, pointy shoes wearing guard. It reminded her of the night the elves had breached the castle in order to kidnap her so that the alpha could mate her. She mostly remembered how she had been forced to kill two of them in order to survive. She shivered, feeling that this may not have been such a good idea after all. Tanya took a deep breath. The fact of the matter was, she'd promised to help Esral and she would damn well do everything in her power to do just that. Tanya swallowed down her fear.

"Ah, you must be Tanya," he locked eyes with her and smiled warmly. "This delightful young lady mentioned that you were unwell." He looked concerned.

"I'm on the mend. Thank you for agreeing to see me. Please"—she gestured to a seat next to the bed—"take a seat."

The king smiled and did as she asked. "Stephany told me that you are to be mated to one of the kings, but won't divulge which one. It's all very cryptic."

"Both." Not that she was going to mate either male. They weren't even together but she wasn't about to go down that long winding road with the old king. It wasn't why she'd called him here.

He raised his eyebrows for a second before chuckling. "Excuse my reaction, elves are a little more . . . conservative. You must be some female to have tamed the likes of those two."

Tanya smiled, but chose not to respond since she would also have to set him straight on that count.

"Stephany said that you were concerned for Esral." His face turned stormy. "I share your concern."

"I understand that a decision was made that Esral is to mate with Xavier come the new moon."

Katar shrugged. "I had hoped that she would become queen. In many ways she reminds me of my late wife. So soft and timid. Fair to behold, yet strong and resourceful. Clever like Esme. I will come to terms with the new arrangement. Princess Esral"—he shrugged his shoulders—"she is a princess already, I had hoped for more."

"I can see that you love your daughter."

His whole demeanor softened. "She is my little girl and in many ways all I have left of my Esme. I want the best for her."

"Do you want your daughter to be happy?" Best she proceed carefully.

His eyes narrowed in thought, "Why would you ask me such a question? It is clear that I do."

"With all due respect, King Katar, wanting the best for your daughter and her being happy will not necessarily go hand in hand."

His eyes narrowed. "I am her father, I know what is best for Esral, she will be happy in the long run."

Tanya paused for a few seconds, using the time to gather her thoughts. She had one shot to convince the king. "Being forced to mate with someone she doesn't even know will not make her happy. I have talked at length with Esral, she does not want this union."

Katar clenched his teeth. "Is there something I should know about this Xavier?"

"Xavier is a good male."

"Well then?" he seemed to relax somewhat.

"Esral would like to date, she wants to choose her own male." She shrugged. "Who knows, she might end up choosing Xavier in the end. It needs to be her decision though."

He scowled. "Unacceptable. It is the way of our people. No highborn gets to choose. Esme and I found happiness, she will do the same."

"Are you sure?"

"Yes." Katar nodded his head, his eyes solemn.

"Are all the highborn matings at your court successful?"

Katar squared his shoulders, he raised his hand. His whole demeanor shouted yes, then, he sank back into the chair, a bewildered expression on his face. "Not all, but Esral will find success. Xavier will have to love her, how could he not?"

"Let's say for argument's sake that he does grow to love Esral, what if she doesn't feel the same for him? They would be miserable."

The king worked his jaw for a few seconds, his eyes took on a faraway lo

ok. "You said he was a good male."

"He is a good male, but love is a strange thing. We don't always love the right person or the good person. Heck, sometimes, even against our best judgement, we even end up falling in love with two people." She blew out a puff of air. "We don't have an on and off switch inside of us, as much as we may want one sometimes . . . the point is, just because he is good doesn't mean Esral will love him. Just because your daughter holds all of those amazing attributes doesn't mean Xavier will love her."

He shook his head. "My daughter is not defective. She must mate with this Xavier come the new moon. There is no other way."

"You are right, your daughter is not defective. Even if she were to stay unmated for the time being, it would not make her defective. Please allow her to choose her own mate."

His eyes widened in horror. "To mate with a commoner?"

"If that is who she ends up loving, then yes a commoner. You said it yourself, she is a princess and would remain a princess regardless of who she decides on."

"What if she ends up rutting with a male before she is even mated? What if she takes several to her bed?" He looked like he might have a heart attack, Katar's breath came out in pants and his face turned red.

"Do you really believe that of your daughter? Esral does not strike me as a female that would fall into bed with male after male. She has more sense than that."

"You make a good point, but it doesn't change the fact that my daughter will be seen as defective."

Tanya took a deep breath, feeling a little frustrated. "Do you believe that your daughter is defective?"

Katar's fists clenched and his face grew red. "Certainly not and it is for that reason that I insist that she mate with the prince."

"Let's say for argument's sake that the mating doesn't happen . . ." His face reddened up a whole lot more and she became a bit worried that he might die from that heart attack at any second. Was that even possible with older non humans? Tanya hoped not. "Would your daughter be defective?"

His jaw worked and he looked at a point somewhere behind her on the headboard not saying anything for the longest time. If there was one thing that she'd learned in a home where arguments and disagreements were a regular occurrence, it was how to get the upper hand in moments like this. Silence could be used as a tool to draw an answer from an opponent. Especially when the answer wasn't something they wanted to admit.

"Yes." His eyes shone and he blinked several times before catching her gaze.

Not what she'd hoped to hear. "Will *you* believe that your daughter is defective if she isn't mated come the new moon?"

He shook his head slowly, looking utterly defeated. "Yes," he whispered.

"It's just you and I between these four walls, Katar. I'm not asking if your daughter will be perceived as defective by the elven people, I'm asking if you will truly feel that your beautiful, intelligent, resourceful daughter will suddenly wake up defective if she herself chooses not to mate with someone she doesn't love?"

His shoulders sagged. "It doesn't matter what I think."

"You are the king. You make the rules. Moreover, you are Esral's father. Your opinion matters the most. Don't force this on her, please."

He remained silent.

"Go and talk with her. She told me that you have dragged

your feet in choosing a mate for her because you knew she disliked all the highborn elven males. The path you chose for her, offered the best success rate for her happiness even though it was the most unorthodox." The old male's face was set in thought.

Her hopes plummeted as he shook his head. "This would change everything. If Esral is not made to stick to her arranged mating. If I ensure that she is not labelled as defective, what of all the other highborn females? All the other arranged matings? This would change everything."

"Would that be so bad, King Katar? Why can't they also be allowed to choose? To have a real shot at happiness?" Tanya reached out to the old king, placing a hand on his. "Change can be a good thing."

"We can't have the commoners and the highborn mixing. It wouldn't be right."

"Why not? From the sounds of things, they mix plenty behind closed doors anyway."

The old man chuckled. "You are right on that count." He sighed. "I will think on it. I wish it were less complicated. What you are asking would change age old traditions."

"Will you talk with Esral?"

Katar nodded and smiled. "I will talk with her, but I can't promise any more than that. I can't just do whatever I would like. I need to keep my people in mind with each and every decision."

It would've been nice to hear him agree to everything she had said, but at the same time this type of major decision would affect a whole species. Katar would not be doing his duty as king if he didn't put his own emotions aside and think about the repercussions it would have on his people. Tanya respected that.

"Thank you for agreeing to see me and for hearing me out."

"No . . . thank you for caring for my daughter. This took courage." He patted her hand.

------·(✱)·------

Zane had not slept well. If he and Brant didn't manage to convince Tanya that they could make this work, she would leave them. He sighed. This was not the time for such thoughts. Zane watched as the elven king made his way over to them.

The crisp morning air caused the old elf's grey hair to blow about his face. Katar removed a leather tie from a silk sack at his back and used it to secure the strand at the nape of his neck. "When is the next new moon?"

By the look on Brant's face, Zane could tell that the question had also caught him off guard. "That wouldn't be for about another four weeks," Brant answered.

"That long?" Katar adjusted the tie on his robe.

Brant raised his eyebrows at Zane making a questioning look. Zane shrugged.

The old man sighed loudly. "If nothing else, it will give me the time I need to convince my people . . ." he said, clearly talking to himself. Snapping out of it, he lifted his eyes up to face Brant and Zane. "Please put a temporary hold on the mating between Esral and the prince. I do not want her dating until I have made a final decision on her future though."

Brant nodded and smiled at Katar. "Your daughter must be very persuasive for you to have changed your mind like that."

"Let's be clear, I may have changed my mind but it will need to be taken up with my council and the elven folk in general. Although I could force my people to bend to my will, I prefer not to operate in that fashion. Understand also that your brother and my daughter may still end up mating. There is much to be discussed and major decisions to be made that will affect the entire elven species. Though I do not approve or understand the need, I still hope that she will have her opportunity to date." The old male made a face like the thought was distasteful to him.

"I will convey your wishes to Xavier. I take it that Esral knows of your decision?"

Katar nodded. "She looked happier than I have seen her in a long while. I just hope I can convince my people to alter certain age old traditions or that radiant smile will be wiped from her face."

"I have to say, Katar, you surprise me. I have always seen you as being highly traditional. This is pleasing, but still unexpected," Brant said.

"I'm glad that I'm not too old to still surprise others. I was very lucky to have been given Esme. There are many of my people who have only found misery in their arranged matings. It is something I hope to change. I have to say that your female reminds me in many ways of my Esme."

What the fuck?

"She is a good judge of character. Has a way of putting things that encourages pause for thought. I am glad that I spoke with her. She helped me to see things differently. You are lucky to have her." Katar nodded his head, his eyes moving from Brant back to Zane.

"Extremely lucky." Brant smiled at Katar for a beat before turning narrowed eyes on Zane. Giving a quick shake of the head, Zane narrowed his eyes back.

"Since our female came into our life, everything has changed." Zane said shaking his head again at the truth in his words. A smile formed at the thought of his feisty human.

"Make sure that you work together with her in a solid partnership. Your relationship would work better and will be much more rewarding in the long run." He looked at them each in turn. "Without Esme, I am convinced that my kingdom would've failed a long time ago. In such a short time without her, I have almost ruined everything. I have taken to asking myself what my late mate would have advised. Things are going better as a result." He smiled. "Take the advice of an old man, do not make the mistake of pushing Tanya to the side, she could be a great asset."

They shook hands with Katar as was customary. Zane could see that Brant was lost in thought, not really paying attention as the old king got into the waiting vehicle. They watched in silence as the string of luxury cars pulled away and disappeared down the drive in a cloud of dust.

"What the fuck just happened?" Brant's eyebrows were knit in confusion.

"I think our female just defied us and spoke to Katar behind our back."

Brant grinned. "The little minx."

Zane grinned back. "I think we need to have a little talk with her."

Brant snorted and shook his head. "We need to have a long talk with her. Since she is fully healthy, I will put her over my knee and spank her."

"Now that is something I would like to see. The good news is that the doctor will be here this afternoon as a precaution even though we already know that the news should be good."

Brant growled low. "Thank God our female is better. I

hated seeing her bed ridden like that."

"You and I need to come to an understanding of sorts." Zane locked eyes with the other male.

Brant raised his eyebrows. "I'm not conceding."

"I don't expect you to."

Brant's eyes narrowed. "Are you conceding?"

"No, I'm not fucking conceding." He took a deep breath. "I have a better idea."

Brant eyed him wearily. "Let's go somewhere more private to discuss this further."

Zane nodded once, suddenly feeling nervous in the pit of his stomach.

Chapter SEVEN

Doctor Pollard removed the tight band from around her arm. "Your blood pressure is normal. That's the last of the tests I needed to perform. All is looking good at this stage Miss Milan."

Tanya breathed out in a huff. She hadn't even realized that she'd been holding it in.

"Now for the monitor to check the baby's heartbeat. He placed a device on the skin on her stomach. Almost immediately, a strong thumping noise reverberated around the room. Her mouth was pulled into an immediate smile.

"Excellent. I have to say, Miss Milan, you are a very lucky lady indeed. This baby is nothing short of a miracle." He fiddled with the stethoscope at his chest. "I'm happy to report that you're going to be just fine. I still want you to make an appointment with an obstetrician for the coming week though."

Physically fine, maybe.

It really bugged her that Zane and Brant weren't here. She hadn't seen either of them the whole day. Then again, maybe it was for the best. She'd received a clean bill of health. Both her and the baby were doing great. It was time to leave. Zane and Brant would only complicate things. It still stung though. They might not be together, but the males were still fathers to the baby. She let out a sigh, trying to smile back at the doctor while he packed up his things and said his goodbyes.

Tanya had already asked Xavier to drive her to Becky's place as soon as she could get herself ready. She'd never actually unpacked, so it wouldn't take long. After a nice hot shower, she pulled on a pair of jeans and a t-shirt. She brushed her still wet hair and then put the brush into her bag. With a last look around the room, she opened the door and walked straight into Zane's broad chest.

"Great, Cenwein, we're so glad you packed." Brant stepped in next to Zane. The two males side by side took up the whole hall.

"Yeah, um Xavier agreed . . ." she stammered.

"No need for Xavier," Zane's voice rumbled. "We're perfectly capable of helping you move out." Brant and Zane exchanged a knowing look.

"Yes, we are." Brant took the bag from her hand. They ushered her between them and she took up step with them.

As much as their acceptance of the situation was the right thing, it still hurt like a bitch. She'd kind of hoped that they would try and talk her into staying. Somewhere deep inside she'd actually prayed that they'd be able to convince her. Both males could be persuasive. Only that wasn't happening. They were actually going to see her back to Sweetwater.

It didn't take long for the anger to hit.

Bastards.

Tanya dug in her heels and the males moved ahead of her before turning to face her. "Where were the two of you?" She folded her arms across her chest. "Do you care so little about my wellbeing that you completely ignored my appointment with the doctor?" She made a sound of disgust. "Forget about me. Do you care so little about your unborn child? You should have taken the time. I know you're all busy running the covens and doing whatever the hell it is that kings do, but you should have"—she shook her head, putting her hands on her hips—"made the freaking time."

"Are you done?" Zane raised his brows.

"What do you mean? I have every right to be upset." She stomped her foot.

"No, you don't." Brant took a small step towards her. "We could scent that all was well with the baby and could hear his strong heartbeat. We knew you were well. I'm sorry, Cenwein. The doctor was merely a formality." His eyes moved across her face and a look of tenderness crossed his. "We sometimes forget that you are human. That you don't have our enhanced senses. We would have reassured you if we had known that you were worried."

Zane stepped in closer. "Besides, we met with the doctor. Had a long chat with the male just to be sure."

She felt her eyes narrow at them. "Oh, did you now?"

Zane nodded and a predatory gleam flared in his dark eyes. "He gave you a clean bill of health."

"Yup. It's why I'm out of that blasted bed and—"

"No, sweetness . . . you misunderstand. He gave you a clean bill of health to stay in bed, only you won't be alone this time."

She felt her brow knit. "How many times do I need to say the same thing?" Her heart gave a little happy leap. The traitorous organ proceeded to beat a little faster. Dammit, she loved hearing him say those words. It didn't change anything though. "This won't work for reasons you already spelled out in meticulous detail right before you nearly killed each other."

"This isn't the place to discuss such matters," Zane said.

"There is nothing to discuss," she reached for her bag.

"Would you like to do the honors?" Brant glanced Zane's way.

"I would love to," Zane growled. He reached for her almost quicker than her eyes could track. One minute she was standing and the next she was up against Zane's solid chest, his brawny arms surrounding her. She squirmed in his embrace. "Put me down." But Zane was already moving at a pace that scared her. She circled her arms around him and dug her fingers into his flesh. They were going up the winding stairs of the North Tower. Why the North Tower? She knew that neither of them stayed in this part of the castle.

Before she knew it, they entered a room and Zane deposited her onto a bed. A wide, extra big, extra-large expanse of a bed. It was a double king size bed to be exact.

Her heart raced.

Her cheeks heated.

Glancing up, she caught the scorching gazes of both Zane and Brant. The large males stood side by side. Zane folded his arms across his massive chest. Brant raised his brows.

"What's going on?" It came out a little stuttered, which pretty much summed up how she felt inside. If they thought that they could buy a new bed—even if it was ultra-accommodating and so very soft—and think that she would fall right into it with them . . . they had another thing coming.

"The doctor gave you the all clear. We are ready to mate you now," Zane rumbled.

"In a few minutes the new moon will be upon us." Brant threw her a half smile that could melt the heart and panties off even the most seasoned spinster.

"Hang on just a minute . . ." She slid off the bed and onto

shaky legs. "Has one of you conceded? What happened to the whole we're both too dominant thing?"

The males exchanged knowing glances that made her want to stomp on their feet. It was the knowledge that they wouldn't feel it even if she did that stopped her.

"Yeah, Cenwein, we concede." Brant winked which irritated her. There was no way in hell that either of these two had actually conceded. No. Freaking. Way.

"Which one of you?" It was her turn to fold her arms across her chest. She was sure to tilt her chin in such a way that she knew they would see that she meant business.

"Both of us." Zane smiled looking every bit the predator he was.

Tanya shook her head, sure that she hadn't heard him properly. "What . . . ? You can't both concede it defeats the whole purpose."

"We can and we have," Brant chimed in.

Sucking in a deep breath, she prepared to argue how stupid that was.

"We both concede. We concede to you, Ysnaar." Zane's voice had lowered to a deep rumble.

"Me?" She blinked a couple of times trying to make sense of what they were saying.

"Yeah, you. Now about that spanking." Brant grinned at her.

"What spanking?" she asked, her voice a little shaky. Unfortunately, the idea excited her.

"You went behind our backs and spoke with Katar. That deserves a spanking." Brant's eyes turned feral.

Before she could respond, Zane piped in. "About the terms of winning our little bet." He lifted his eyebrows, focussing all of his attention on her.

"Wait a minute." Tanya pointed at Zane when he took a step towards her. He took another step. "Stop!"

He grit his teeth but didn't advance any further. "The doctor gave the all clear and we will be careful. We have been told to take it slow, easy. Brant and I will take turns fucking you so slowly . . . with exquisite care. You are going to beg for release." He licked his lips as his eyes slid over every inch of her body. She had to work hard to keep from trembling. A raging need unfurled inside her with a speed that scared her.

Her pussy flooded with moisture. Her clit throbbed wanting some of that slow exquisite attention. Lord help her, but she had to bite down on her lip for a few seconds to stop herself from screaming, Yes!

After clearing her throat, she finally felt like she had gained sufficient control to be able to talk. "No," a breathless whisper. "That wouldn't be a good idea. Conceding to me won't help. One of these days you'll push me to the side and kill each other anyway. How the hell will I stop you? I'm just a puny freaking human."

"You're *our* puny human. We love you, Cenwein." Brant's eyes were filled with such tenderness as he spoke. He closed the distance between them, taking her hand in his. She was too dumbstruck to stop him. "It means that you have us firmly wrapped around your little pinkie finger."

Zane took her other hand. "You may be a bit puny, but you're also the strongest female we know. We love you, that's why we are able to concede everything to you."

"If Zane and I are ever at a deadlock, you will have the final vote. No need for any death battles. Look at how you handled Katar."

Could it work? "I don't know. Katar was different."

They both squeezed her hands. "You are right, Katar was

different. You don't have a hold over the male like you do over us, yet you managed just fine. Please." Brant's eyes flitted across her face staying on her mouth for the longest time before moving back to her eyes. "You love us." He bobbed his eyes up and down.

"You went behind my back. How do you think it made me feel when the two of you were ready to kill each other? Knowing that I might lose one of you." She bit her lip trying to stop it from quivering.

"We were wrong. It won't happen again." Brant's gaze was unwavering.

"When you were in the hospital"—Zane cleared his throat and swallowed hard—"fighting for your life, we realized how you must have felt at the thought of losing one of us. It made us see things differently. It made us realize that we would do anything to make you happy . . . do anything for you, sweetness. We agreed then and there that we would find a way to make this work. To stop acting like colossal idiots."

"Although, he was the bigger idiot." Brant gestured towards Zane while grinning broadly.

"Bigger everything." Zane glanced down at the noticeable bulge in his pants. He bobbed his eyebrows at Tanya and grinned, a feral gleam in his dark eyes.

Tanya laughed. "I don't know . . . I need to be able to trust you."

Brant's expression changed. "I do still need to come clean about one last thing."

The air seized in her lungs.

He ran a hand through his hair and glanced at Zane for a few beats before locking his eyes with hers. "You were Zane's first choice at the choosing ceremony. He decided to choose another because he could sense that I was going to choose you as well."

"You chose me? Really?"

"Don't sound so surprised." Zane's eyes darkened up a whole lot more.

Tanya fiddled with the fabric on her t-shirt. "It's just . . . there were some really gorgeous girls there and well . . ."

"No comparison, Tanya." The way he said her name sent shivers rushing up and down her spine. "None of them came even close to you. Let's get something straight, I chose you but I didn't want to cause a war between the covens."

"Zane did the honorable thing. I would've fought for you even if it meant war and untold bloodshed. The same thing happened to our fathers. It was the reason for the original Great War between the species. Our fathers chose the same female," Brant paused. "My mother. They fought for her and my father won. If the same thing had happened again, we would've been easy pickings for the other species. Thankfully one of us had the best interest of our people in mind. I never did thank you, and it's long overdue. You did the right thing more than once while I acted like a jerk." Brant looked at Zane, he hooked his thumbs into his jeans pockets.

Zane cleared his throat, running his hand through his hair. "Yeah . . . no problem. A female like Tanya will do strange things to a male's mind."

Her heart melted big time.

"Things have changed since that fateful day. We had to work together to try and win you back. We're . . . almost friends." Zane's eyes twinkled and his lips twitched.

"Almost . . . what the . . . I spent hours at that damned computer. Hours of strategizing to find the best solution for us to get our female back. I let you drink from my vein, damn you." Brant's face was comical.

Zane snorted. "Back to my earlier remark . . . I refuse to start stroking your dick."

"Fuck you." Brant turned to Zane, chest first, his fists clenched at his sides. "I don't need you, my female will stroke my"—then he broke out in a grin—"you're such a God damned bastard."

Zane smiled back. "Takes one to know one."

"You said it."

They were bantering with one another like . . . best buddies. She felt her mouth drop open.

"Now about that bet," Brant said.

"And about that spanking." They turned to face her.

"No one is spanking me. Also"—she swallowed hard, feeling so incredibly hot and bothered. Her jeans felt tight, her bra felt even tighter—"um . . . we need to establish some house rules. Firstly, we all have to sleep together."

"We bought the bed didn't we?" Brant pulled his shirt over his head and her mouth dried as she caught sight of his ribbed abs. She also noticed a tattoo on his chest that had not been there before. Large cursive letters.

"Oh my word, what is that?" She had to bite her lip to stop from crying. The word 'Cenwein' stared back at her in dark, ink, letters.

Brant threw her a grin that had his dimples out in full force. "This is a token to show you and all others that I am taken. I belong to you, Cenwein. Now and forever."

"It hurt like a bitch." Zane growled as he removed his shirt. "The needle had to be silver so that the wounds would stay long enough to cause the ink to be permanent." He pulled his muscles and his pecks bounced. The word 'Ysnaar' was in the same cursive ink. "It was all worth it though Ysnaar." His eyes darkened as they tracked the length of her body.

Tanya was speechless.

"Now back to the whole sleeping together arrangement. Only if you sleep between us at all times." Zane's rumbling voice caused her body to tighten and pucker. "As much as Brant would love for me to spoon with him . . . I refuse."

Brant snorted, shaking his head in disbelief. "So fucking full of it," his words sounded humorous rather than angry.

Licking her lips, she swallowed hard. "Um . . ." Her mind had gone completely blank, all she could think about was that vampire sandwich. "We're exclusive. No drinking or rutting with any other females."

Zane rolled his eyes.

Brant chuckled. "I like my balls, thank you very much. For the last time, Cenwein, we don't want anyone else."

"Maybe not right now, but what about when I'm as big as a whale?"

"More of you to love." Brant grinned, his eyes dropping to her chest.

"I read that pregnant women are horny and capable of achieving multiple orgasms. The endorphins will be good for the baby. Sex later on in the pregnancy can be good for inducing labor. You will give birth to a very happy baby, Ysnaar, if we have anything to say about it." Zane toed off his boots. She couldn't help but to notice that his muscles had muscles. His biceps were ridiculously big. He tore off his leather pants, she'd forgotten how enormous he was. *Everywhere.*

"Yeah." Brant also pulled off his jeans and his dick jutted forward. Just as impressive. "You will not be overdue in this pregnancy. We will ensure of that. Your breasts are larger, Cenwein." He growled the last part and licked his lips. "I can't wait to see your beautiful body, please remove your clothes before I am forced to tear them off you." If her panties weren't wet already, by now they would be soaked.

"No more killing each other?"

Both males shook their heads, their eyes solemn.

"No more fighting."

They both laughed, exchanging looks that said she was out of her mind.

Brant shrugged. "We'll argue."

Zane threw her a half smile. "We'll fight. Not very often but we will fight. We may even bleed, but we won't kill each other." He folded his arms over his chest. "Take off your clothes. The new moon is calling. Are you ready to accept us as your mates?"

In answer, she pulled her shirt over her head. "One last thing... I'm not sure what you guys had in mind, but I'm not sure about the whole you know... anal sex thing."

"I happen to really love that sweet pussy of yours, Ysnaar." Zane's eyes had heated. His voice had dropped to a husky growl.

"I agree with Zane but don't be so quick to discard different kinds of sex, it can be very enjoyable." Brant said as his eyes dipped to her ass.

Zane's eyebrows shot up, but he didn't say anything.

Brant narrowed his, which smoldered with a mixture of desire and longing like none she'd ever seen before. "It is something we might try some other time. When and if you are ready."

Her cheeks heated. Her breathing turned a little choppy. "How are we going to do this then?"

"I'm a little wired. It's been a long time..." Brant looked concerned. She'd even go so far as to say that he looked afraid.

"You go first then," Zane said. "It'll only get worse if you watch me rut with our female before you have found release."

"I'm over my anger issues . . . well mostly," Brant said.

Zane chuckled. "Yeah, but your need for our female will grow if you watch me fuck her. Admit it . . . you'd enjoy watching us."

"Fuck you." Brant growled flashing a fang but instead of arguing he reached for Tanya, tearing at the front of her jeans.

"Hey . . ." She said craning her neck to try and look into his eyes. "You said that you wanted to make love to me and you promised to stop ruining my clothes."

Brant closed his eyes, taking a deep breath, his hands settled on her hips. "Know that regardless of how we rut, whether I take you hard or really gently, we will always be making love. Being with you will always be special. As to your clothes . . . you drive me crazy."

"That's so sweet in a weird way." She gave him a quick kiss before looking over her shoulder at Zane. "Stop your shit."

Zane shrugged. "We are going to be ruling together, rutting together, sharing a fucking bed for blood's sake. You need to loosen up Brant. We both know how enjoyable this could be."

"I'm really sick of hearing how great sex could be. Please will you both stop arguing and just show me already."

"The lady has spoken, and I believe you have the final say." Brant picked her up, sat on the bed and flipped her over onto her stomach over his lap in a move that left her breathless. "If you think I forgot about that spanking though, you're dead wrong." He slapped her ass before she could respond. Hard enough for it to sting just a little. Tanya sucked in a breath, letting out a squeal when he smacked her a second time. Moisture pooled at her cleft. Her heart raced in excitement. First, he gently rubbed the spot with his hand, then he soothed the slight burn with his tongue until her skin tingled.

She moaned.

Zane groaned. "Our female has an exquisite ass."

"Let's get a better look at it," Brant sounded strained. There was a tearing sound and air hit her wet pussy. Another tear and her bra was pulled free. "I know I promised to make slow, sweet love to you, but I really need you right now, Cenwein."

Her clit throbbed and her channel felt empty. "I need you too."

There was silence, so she turned to Brant whose eyes were firmly on Zane. His jaw was tense and that fearful look was back.

"I am here," was all Zane said.

Brant nodded, he lifted Tanya placing her on her back on the bed. "I won't hurt you. Cenwein, you need to know that both you and the baby mean everything to me."

"I know." She felt her eyes prick. She trusted Brant even though he didn't trust himself. Tanya knew that he would control his bloodlust.

His eyes were glowing as he pushed her thighs open and leaned in closing his mouth over her clit. Her back bowed at the sudden onslaught. His tongue circled her tight bud several times before laving across the bundle of nerves in a way that had her moaning and clutching at his shoulders. The build happened quickly. On the verge of release, he pulled back breathing hard onto her clit in hot breaths that felt exquisite, yet he still left her wanting more. She squirmed trying to move towards his mouth, but his hands tightened on her thighs holding her in place. Brant gazed at her pussy like it was the most delicious thing he had ever seen. Licking his lips as he moved closer to tongue her pussy. He speared her opening over and over using languid strokes.

A groan sounded and her eyes darted to Zane. He palmed his dick, moving from base to tip on slow easy strokes. The sight was one of the most erotic things she had ever seen. "Does our female taste as good as we imagined? Her scent is driving me crazy," Zane said, his voice a husky rumble.

Brant made a sound of utter rapture as he tore away from her slick folds. "You should taste her yourself." Then Brant was moving away as Zane moved closer.

"Oh, sweetness." His hands trembled for the barest second as he took a hold of her thighs.

Holy hell.

She couldn't quite believe this was happening. Zane lowered his head to her pussy, slipping his tongue into her opening. He moaned and the vibrations had her skin tightening, her hands fisting on the sheets. She threw her head back as Zane picked up speed, his tongue doing wicked things.

A hot mouth closed over her nipple, the zing of pleasure shot straight to her clit.

"You are so beautiful," Brant whispered as he made his way to her other breast. The air seemed stuck in her lungs. Her whole body tingled. So close to orgasm it hurt. Even though she was dying to be taken over the edge, she wanted this moment to last. Squeezing her eyes shut, she moaned even louder as Zane moved from her channel to her clit.

He was so freaking good with his tongue it was scary. She opened her mouth to cry out with her pending orgasm but Brant captured her lips with his. Tanya tasted herself on him.

"That's it, sweetness," a low growl against her very sensitive pussy. "Come for me," Zane commanded and she did. Brant swallowed her scream, his tongue swirling with hers as he kneaded her breasts with his big hands.

The orgasm that tore through her body was off the charts

good. Way better than anything she'd imagined.

"Our female will be ready for you now." She heard Zane say in the far recesses of her fog induced brain. Strong arms lifted her.

She opened her eye as Brant positioned her in a sitting position on his lap. "You need to take control. I don't fully . . . trust myself." His eyes were still glowing. Brant put his forehead to hers for a few seconds. "I love you," he whispered as the tip of his cock breached her pussy.

She would have liked to have said it back, but he thrust into her in one swift motion that left her breathless. The move rendered her pretty much boneless. Brant tightened his hands on her hips. "Are you okay?"

Tanya nodded, not trusting her voice. It felt so freaking amazing. After a few beats, she grew restless.

"It's up to you, Cenwein. I would be too rough." He swallowed hard, his jaw working as she lifted. Brant growled when she dropped back down. It didn't take her long to establish a rhythm that had her crying out with every stroke.

Tanya could feel her pending orgasm with every thrust. Her nipples rubbed against his chest. She'd chosen an angle that hit every sweet spot. She was going to cum soon and really hard and without any clitoral stimulation. Throwing her head back, she moaned and her whole body tingled with anticipation. She couldn't wait to feel his fangs breach her skin. To feel untold pleasure as they bonded.

Brant cursed, withdrawing from her. Tanya made a sound of frustration at the loss.

Mouth a thin white line, he looked up at Zane. "I'm too close . . . too on edge." His cheeks reddened. "I feel like a fucking teen vamp."

Zane chuckled. "I know what you mean. I've almost cum

twice just watching you rut with our delectable female." To prove his point, using the tip of his finger, he wiped a bead of pre-cum off of the end of his dick. "I have an idea." Zane threw them a half smile that had her stomach doing flip flops. She had a feeling she was going to enjoy Zane's ideas.

"Turn our female around . . ." Brant did as he asked, flipping her around like she weighed nothing. Her legs were still on either side of Brant's thighs. "That's it . . . only a bit wider . . . oh yeah." Zane's eyes narrowed as they moved from her face to her breasts stopping for the longest time on her dripping pussy. "You have the most fucking stunning body I have ever had the fortune to lay my eyes on." By now she didn't feel the least bit self-conscious. If anything, they were both a major boost to her confidence. Brant lifted her slightly, thrusting back into her in one solid thrust. He hissed, his hands tightened on her hips.

"I'm going to lick your clit, Ysnaar. I want you to stay perfectly still." He threw Brant a tight grin. "I don't enjoy cock."

She wanted to laugh at the comment, but felt herself wondering how it would work if she didn't move? Great for her but not so much for . . . the thought died as Zane crouched between their spread thighs and sucked on her ultra-sensitive nub.

"Oh God," she groaned.

"I have been called that before," Zane rumbled against her clit.

"Don't you mean gods?" Brant's voice was strained.

"Gods!" She screamed as Zane sucked on her clit a second time. Stretched to capacity by Brant's thick cock, with Zane's sinful mouth on her clit, was just too freaking much. She felt the first flutter of her pending orgasm and Brant moaned.

"Feels so fucking good," he growled.

The flutters turned to all out spasms as she came all over his dick. Brant groaned loudly. Just as Zane pulled away, Brant thrust into her and his hands tightened on her hips as his movements turned jerky. As she was coming down, he sank his fangs into her bringing on another wave of unbelievable pleasure. A few more hard pulls had her head thrown back against him and her back bowing. There was a loud growling sound that brought goose bumps to every inch of her body. It took a few seconds to realize that it was Brant making the noise. He pulled away and roared what sounded like a victorious battle cry.

"I told you that you'd be able to control it," Zane said.

The bloodlust.

"We'll see. We both have to drink from each other before it really counts."

"One step at a time." Zane grinned. His face turning feral. "I would like to rut with my female now."

Brant's eyes turned hard. "I would like to still touch her while you—"

"Aside from mating our female before sun up, my only other goal is to please Tanya." Zane took a deep breath. "I get the feeling that she likes us both to touch her at the same time. Isn't that right, Ysnaar?"

Still panting from the exertion of coming so damn hard, she felt her cheeks heat. "Yeah," she whispered looking up at Zane from under her lashes. Her eyes darted to Brant. "I would like that." She would only ever get what she really wanted if she asked . . . or at least admitted to wanting it.

"Little minx," Brant growled.

Zane spread his long frame out on the bed. All six and a half delicious feet. "Take me, Ysnaar. I'm all yours." He put his hands behind his head. "Brant will touch you while I get the pleasure of being inside your tight pussy."

God, she loved it when he talked dirty like this. Taking her bottom lip between her teeth, she straddled him while running her hand over his chiselled abs and hard chest. Running her hand over the tattoo.

Tanya maneuvered into position, she slid her fingers around his thick cock placing him at her opening. "Are you ready for me?" she teased.

Zane's dark eyes lightened a few shades as they began to glow. "Fuck yeah and if you don't hurry up I'm going to—" He grunted as she took him in one smooth motion. So slick and ready that he was in right up to the hilt in less than a second. His lips thinned as they pursed together. His biceps bulged as his hands fisted at his sides. "I've missed you, sweetness," he said, his voice so deep it had her blood heating.

Placing her hands on his hard chest, she rocked against him until she found a position that had her panting. Big hands cupped her breasts from behind. Brant squeezed them, when he rolled her nipples she moaned. *So freaking good.* Slip, slide, she maintained the rhythm keeping her eyes locked on Zane's intense gaze.

"Stop hogging our female's tits," Zane growled. "I will enjoy watching them bounce while you play with her clit."

A rush of excitement flooded her. Brant gave a growl of irritation but slid his hands down her sides circling around her hips. "I love your big mammary glands, but I also enjoy touching your pussy." Tanya wanted to giggle but he slid a finger between her folds settling on a soft but insistent pressure on her nub. It caused her nipples to tighten up and her blood to pump faster. She made an animalistic keening sound from deep in her throat.

"You like that, Cenwein," Brant whispered, his breath hot on her neck. She whimpered in response. "Then you're going to love this." Using his free hand, he squeezed her ass and Zane's cock automatically penetrated her deeper. She was making the most ridiculous noises at this stage, but didn't give a damn.

Zane's eyes heated, dropping to her chest. Tanya could feel how her breasts jiggled and shook every time she dropped onto his cock. It was heady to know how she was affecting the big bad vampire.

"That's it, Ysnaar." He grit his teeth. "So . . . good," he growled.

Brant's hand moved from her ass to her back end. It was difficult to tell exactly what he was doing there, but it felt like he was using one of his fingers to push against her ass without actually breaching the very sensitive area. Between Zane's big cock and Brant's hands on her . . . she felt like she was being touched . . . everywhere and all at once.

"Let go, Cenwein." Brant urged her on, but the words were unnecessary because her pussy was already clenching with her release. Brant's hands slid to her waist as Zane moved to a sitting position, immediately zoning in on her neck. Brant held her hips, helping her to maintain the rhythm by lifting her up and down. Zane thrust from below as he sank his teeth into her neck. Every nerve ending exploded, the air froze in her lungs.

Brant was saying something, but she couldn't make out what it was. She felt a nudge at the back of her head as she was pushed towards Zane's neck. "Drink, Tanya," Brant urged. Once she caught sight of Zane's pulse, she couldn't have stopped even if she tried. Her fangs sharpened even before she closed the small space that separated them. Even the motion of breaching his skin with her teeth felt good. By the low rumble that vibrated through her, she could tell that Zane enjoyed it too. When his blood hit her tongue, her fading orgasm flared back up from a spark to a raging inferno. Every cell in her body sprang to life, every nerve ending fired at full force. Everything in her seemed to tighten and heat.

Zane sucked hard, his cock throbbed inside her and his hands closed around her upper arms as he jerked against her. He growled against her neck before releasing her on a roar as he continued to thrust into her hard. It was only when he finally stopped moving, his chest heaving, that she worked up enough self-control to retract her little fangs. Zane let his face fall between her breasts, his breath coming out in rugged pants. He kissed her softly in the vicinity of her heart and looked up, a smile lit his face. "We are mated."

Tanya smiled back, she leaned down and kissed him. As she pulled back, Zane lifted his eyes past her shoulder. "You ready?"

"Do you need to take a nap first, Cenwein?"

Zane still had his cock buried inside her, it hardened back up. She shook her head. "I don't want to wait." She turned, locking eyes with his beautiful chocolate gaze. She wished that he didn't look so nervous. Zane lifted her off his cock and she bit her lip to stop herself from whimpering at the loss. Brant closed his hands around her waist and pulled her against his hard chest, nuzzling into her neck from behind. Tension radiated off him.

"I trust you," she whispered.

"I'm honored."

Tanya turned, wrapping her arms around his neck.

"I'll be gentle." He laid her down with the utmost care. Caging her with his big body. His eyes flitted across her face before settling on her lips. He kissed her softly. His touch intense and passionate, igniting a need in her. His tongue rolled against hers in languid strokes that caused her toes to curl. Brant pulled back, holding her eyes for a few beats. When he moved down her body, she used her hands to cup his face. "I've had enough orgasms. I'm wet and ready. I want you to make love to me. Make me yours, Brant."

"Enough orgasms," he chuckled. "I hope you're game for one more."

She couldn't help but to smile as he moved back over her, settling his weight over her core. He put his hands on either side of her head. Using a finger, he brushed a few wayward strands from her face before slanting his mouth across hers. Ever so slowly, he nudged into her, pausing for a few beats before sliding home inch by excruciating inch. Once balls deep, he paused still continuing to kiss her with ardor. Tanya pulled her legs up linking her ankles on his back. Slow and deep, he made love to her like a man possessed. His kiss mimicked their coupling. Fevered, yet tender.

She would've thought that after all that had just passed, she would struggle to come again so soon yet her nipples tightened against his chest. The angle he used hit her in just the right spot while her clit was stimulated each time that he ground against her. Pelvis to pelvis. Tanya moaned against his mouth, her nails digging into his back. She cracked open her eyes, Zane fisted his cock in steady pumps. He watched them rut. His eyes, desire filled and glowing. He groaned picking up speed, his muscles bulging and his hips rocking in time to his hand. Digging her fingers deeper into the corded muscles on Brant's back, she felt the first flutter of her release.

With relentless focus, Brant wrung an orgasm from her that made her body go slack right before everything in her tensed.

This time she was the first to drink. Her fangs closing roughly on his smooth neck in a desperate need to taste him, to feel him. To be one with him. Brant held back for a few beats. Then on a savage growl that had goose bumps breaking out on her quivering flesh, he bit her sucking long and deep. His eyes wide and glowing fiercely. She mewled as the same feeling of rapture poured through her, igniting every part of her. Tanya let go while Brant took another savage pull. She moaned, at this point the pleasure was so intense that it was borderline painful. Brant's neck muscles roped as his eyes turned feral, but he pulled away. His long fangs gleamed, her blood on his lips. He snarled and buried his head into the bedding to the right of her head. There was a ripping and a tearing noise as he tore a chunk out of her brand new double king size bed.

"Hey." She swatted Brant lovingly on the arm.

He shook his head at her.

"Let me guess, you almost killed me?"

"You have no idea, Cenwein." His mouth pulled up into a lop-sided grin that made her want a repeat.

Holy hell, she was becoming one of these horny vampires.

"It's done. How do you feel?" Brant asked.

She rolled her eyes, putting a hand over her face. "Horny. Still thirsty," she laughed.

"You might notice a couple of subtle changes."

"Like what?"

Brant shrugged. "Glowing skin, tighter ass . . ." He smiled at her, "I don't know . . . just younger, fresher, healthier with way more energy, stamina"—he bobbed his eyebrows and she giggled—"higher sex drive . . . um . . . stronger. Your senses will improve."

Tanya gasped. "Am I a vampire?"

Brant shook his head. "No, not exactly."

"You have bonded with us and therefore have a small amount of our species' traits." Zane said, his eyes straying to the bed on the opposite side of where Brant was lying. "It will be amplified if you continue to drink from us."

Zane turned away quickly, looking distinctly sheepish. She looked down at the patch he had just been looking at. Her beautiful new bed was covered in spurts of semen. "Really? Seriously Zane?"

His eyes locked with hers. "I couldn't help it. Hearing you make those little noises. Watching you come." He cursed. "Just thinking about it makes me want you again."

"I am feeling really horny."

"You should rest." Zane squeezed his growing erection, trying to get it to subside. He failed dismally. "Too much rutting wouldn't be good for the baby."

"What was that about endorphins being *good* for the baby? Please do that thing with your hands again." She turned back to Brant.

"There's an even better thing I'd like to try." Brant threw her a half smile, his eyes smoldering.

Her heart raced and she groaned. "An even better thing?"

"There are many things we could try if you're game, Cenwein." Brant narrowed smoky eyes at her.

"I'm game if you are?" She locked eyes with Zane.

He grinned wickedly. "I'm all in, sweetness . . . literally." His eyes were glowing softly, his cock stood proudly from his magnificent body.

"First you need to clean up this mess." She pointed at the sticky semen on her new bed.

"I'll change the bedding once we're done with round two. We'd just ruin the new sheets anyway."

Her clit throbbed. Her pussy clenched. Moisture trickled down her thigh.

"On your hands and knees sweetness." Zane growled.

Tanya had to suppress an excited squeal as she did what he said. Both her males groaned loudly.

After a few beats, she turned to look at them over her shoulder feeling her face pull into a look of confusion. Both males stood side by side, arms folded across their chests. Eyes filled with such lust that she felt a shiver race through her.

"Best fucking view I ever saw," Zane growled.

"I'm so glad you gave us a second chance, Cenwein. We won't blow it."

"I really hope you do blow it." Palming his dick, Zane chuckled and advanced. Tanya's giggle died on her lips as Zane got closer. His expression turned tender, "I love you, sweetness." He cupped her chin and kissed her.

"So very much," Brant whispered and the bed dipped as he moved closer as well, his heat at her back.

When Zane finally broke the kiss, she had to wait a few seconds for her vocal cords to function. "I love you too . . . now take me already. I'm all yours. . . ." She looked from one male to the other.

———·C*)·———

Later, after several bouts of wild, sweaty sex . . . not too wild . . . it wasn't lost on her how careful her males were with her the whole time. They had fallen asleep within minutes of changing the bedding. Tanya lay between Brant and Zane, completely sated, completely exhausted. Brant had his arm slung over her with his head tucked into her shoulder. It amazed her how much an arm could weigh. Although that was nothing compared to Zane's meaty thigh hooked across her own legs. Zane's head was on her chest.

It was impossible to move, uncomfortable as hell, yet she couldn't suppress the smile on her face. She was sure that it tracked from ear to ear. Tanya had never been happier. She finally had her vampire freaking sandwich.

Chapter EIGHT

TWO DAYS LATER.

Stephany rounded the corner looking forward to closing her door to her suite for the night. Lance had pestered her nonstop since her return. The more she told him to shove off the more determined he became. The only place that seemed even the least bit sacred was her room.

Groans, moans, grunts, growls.

Well, all except for the annoying noises coming from the royal suite. She couldn't believe that they were still at it. Holed up in that room ever since the new moon. One marathon sex bout after another. Surely enough was enough.

Stephany sighed when she caught the little elf princess' wide eyes at the foot of the stairs that led to the threesome in question. "Esral, what are you doing here?"

"Um, I had hoped to visit with Tanya, but"—she bit her lower lip raising her eyes in the direction of the sounds which were rapidly increasing in tempo—" . . . um."

Tanya groaned. Loudly. Esral's eyes widened. "Are you sure she's okay? I mean, it sounds as if they're killing her." A high pitched keen was followed by a vicious snarl. "Or, at the very least really hurting her." The princess was breathing rapidly and looked as if she planned on rushing up the long staircase to save Tanya.

Stephany had to suppress a giggle. "I assure you that they are not hurting her. Far from it," she mumbled the last under her breath.

Tanya screamed, the sound followed by a roar that might leave cracks in the walls. Esral's large eyes opened even further if that was even possible. "By all that is green, I knew that intimacy could be good, but"—she bit on her lip again—"Tanya was screaming in pleasure wasn't she?"

Stephany nodded. "It is rude of us to listen. There's a reason they call it intimacy."

The princess' cheeks heated and she looked like she felt guilty for the outburst.

"I'm sorry, Esral, I didn't mean to snap at you. I know that you are curious, which is normal."

Another moan sounded, this time barely audible.

"Again?" Esral looked confused.

"It'll happen several times before anyone in this wing gets any sleep and within a few hours it'll start up again. Crazy." She tucked some hair behind her ear.

Esral sighed. "Crazy in love."

"Sex and love are two different things."

"It's love in their case and it's what I want. I can't wait to be with someone that completes me"—her eyes narrowed—"and that makes me scream with pleasure. I'm so happy my father has granted me permission to date." She giggled. "I'm going back to my room now."

"Where's Xavier?"

"I gave him the slip. Vampires are not the best trackers." Esral giggled again, giving a little wave as she skipped down the hallway.

The shrieking started up again. Loud and in time with a clunking headboard. It wouldn't be long now. Stephany would cover her ears, but she knew it wouldn't help. *A growl.* Silence for a few beats. *A shrill scream.* "Zane.... oh, God.... Brant..." Stephany squeezed her eyes shut trying to block out the sounds of untold pleasure.

She put a hand to her chest realizing how hard she was breathing, more like panting.

A roar sounded, it eventually turned into a deep grunt.

Her clit throbbed. Her breasts felt heavy.

Her body's reaction wasn't to the three upstairs, but rather to the memories that the noises evoked in her. What exactly had the alpha done to her? For years her libido had lain dormant. Buried somewhere deep inside her. Stephany hadn't even felt the urge to touch herself in the longest time. She couldn't remember the last time that she'd felt the burning need to cum. Ever since she returned from the wolf's clutches, she'd felt like her veins were on fire. What the hell had he done? What poison? What form of potent witchcraft was this? All she knew was that she wasn't the same.

The scent of her own arousal surrounded her. Stephany rushed to her suite so that she could shower. For the third time today. It was becoming an irritation.

The problem was, she didn't think these animalistic urges were going to go away any time soon. She ran a hand through her hair. By blood, she would find a way to control them. She just had to. The alternate was too terrible to contemplate.

Acknowledgements

To my amazing ARC Team. Thank you so much for your dedication. I appreciate you guys more then you will ever know.

I need to say special thanks to a couple of ladies. Firstly to Aisha (Ash P Reads Facebook Page- www.facebook.com/AshPReads) my wonderful beta reader, Bridgett Goodin for your enthusiasm and kind words, Judy Forehand Lewis (and her sweet, little doggiekins, Christina) for all you do for us indie authors—you always manage to write an amazing, heartfelt review and go the extra mile without fail—and last but not least, Lola Nettles—you were my first fan and have always been there for me. Thank you so very much to you all!

Author's Note

Thank-you for reading my vampire novel. At long last Tanya got her vampire sandwich.

I would love to hear from you so please feel free to drop me a line—
charlene.hartnady@gmail.com

Find me on Facebook—
www.facebook.com/authorhartnady

I live on an acre in the country with my gorgeous husband and three sons and an array of pets including a ball python. In my spare time you can usually find me typing frantically on the computer completely lost in worlds of my making. I believe that it is the small things that truly matter like that feeling you get when you start a new book or a particularly beautiful sunset.

Liked it?

If you enjoyed this book please review it so that others can find it. Even if just a line or two, every review is greatly appreciated.

Books by this Author

The Chosen Series:
Book 1 ~ Chosen by the Vampire Kings
Book 2 ~ Stolen by the Alpha Wolf
Book 3 ~ Unlikely Mates
Book 4 ~ Awakened by the Vampire Prince
Book 5 ~ Mated to the Vampire Kings (Short Novel)
Book 6 ~ Wolf Whisperer

The Program Series (Vampire Novels):
Book 1 ~ A Mate for York
Book 2 ~ A Mate for Gideon
Book 3 ~ A Mate for Lazarus
Book 4 ~ A Mate for Griffin

Demon Chaser Series (No cliffhangers):
Book 1 ~ Omega
Book 2 ~ Alpha
Book 3 ~ Hybrid
Demon Chaser Boxed Set Book 1–3

Tall. Dark. Deadly. Sizzling paranormal stories filled to the brim with hot alpha males and the strong, feisty women that manage to tame them.

Demon Chasers . . . Protectors of humanity. Sworn to uphold the peace. Oath bound to keep the existence of demons a secret.

OMEGA
Demon Chaser Cole rescues Katy from the claws of the Alpha of a resident demon wolf pack. Hunted by Bain and his pack, Cole must try and find out why the werewolves are willing to risk a long standing agreement with the Demon Chasers in order to have her. Bain is a cruel SOB who's had run-ins with the Demon Control Agency before so whatever the reason, it's sure to be depraved.

The Chaser suspects that Katy is not as innocent as she seems. Cole had better unravel this mystery fast because the shifters are closing in and more importantly, the longer he's with Katy the more impossible he finds it to resist her.

ALPHA

Gray, a newly appointed Alpha and half blood demon wolf, can only turn during a full moon. With only three days before the next cycle, time is running out to convince the highest ranking female wolf to become his mate. Success will see him become a full blood. Failure will spell his death. It is only a matter of time before the challenges start coming in.

Ashlyn, a hard ass Demon Chaser just happens to be human and the pack's newest resident. She's there on Demon Control Agency business. Her attraction for the new Alpha can't be allowed to stand in her way, after all, Gray is already taken. More importantly, she has a serial killer to catch, and then she needs to get the heck out of wolfville.

For both their sakes . . .

HYBRID

Ever since the experiments a few months ago, Brice has something inside of her. Something bad. It wants her to do violent, horrific things. She must fight it . . . has to try and stay in control.

The thing inside her calms the moment she meets Garrett. Her relief is fleeting because Garrett is a Demon Chaser, he works for the very agency trying to exterminate her.

Garrett must turn the hybrid in. She's a vicious, dangerous creature that deserves to be put to death. Why then is she in such control? Why is he feeling things for her that he really shouldn't? Surely his premonition about her must be true?

Sign up for my Latest Release Newsletter to hear all about releases and giveaways http://mad.ly/signups/96708/join

Printed in Great Britain
by Amazon